Ken Scott is one of th
crime fiction. Educated
or Cambridge, Oxfo
Comprehensive in the
school at fifteen without a qualification. (Thank goodness
for Editors, *Ken*) This is his second novel, a sequel to the
highly acclaimed, JACK OF HEARTS.

Scotty (his nickname from school) lives in Spain with his
long-suffering wife, Hayley and children, Emily and
Callum, who put up with so much. (Their words not mine.)

Visit his website. www.ken-scott.com

Also by Ken Scott

JACK OF HEARTS

and published by Libros International

A MILLION WOULD BE NICE

Ken Scott

Libros International

ISBN 978- 1- 905988- 00-6

Published by Libros International

www.librosinternational.com

Acknowledgements

So many… where do I start?
Firstly, to Newcastle for a great life grounding; to Steve
Fairs for allowing us to use his ugly mug on the cover; to
Alison Menzies who started my literary career; to Kelly
Walsh for the cover design (do her talents have no
bounds?); to my brother-in-law, Graeme Purvis, who
helped with the criminal technicalities; and to the team at
Libros International.

But above all, to my editor, Carol Cole. Her educated mind,
knowledge and professionalism allows mere mortals such
as myself, who have a little imagination and the ability to
spin a yarn, to be published. Thanks Carol, here's to your
pension fund!

THIS ONE'S FOR MEGAN BIRCH WHOSE FORTITUDE AT SUCH A TENDER AGE HAS BEEN AN INSPIRATION TO US ALL

Prologue

The little boy couldn't understand it. He wanted to love his mother, hug her, hold her, and kiss her like he had seen his friends do with their mothers. He wanted her to be like the other mothers in the small terraced street where they lived. A little peck on the cheek as he left his back gate for a day's adventure in the long summer holidays. Charlie Gilbert's mum did that, kissed him gently, and then waved with a big beaming smile until Charlie and the rest of the gang had disappeared out of sight. But she wasn't like that. She couldn't be. Her smile, for example, - well, it wasn't exactly a smile - more a grimace. In fact, come to think of it, he couldn't remember her ever smiling. He had caught a slight smirk every now and again, generally when she was beating him. Didn't care what she used: a cane stick, a leather strap, a slipper occasionally, and then, more frequently these days, the well-worn wooden rolling pin.

The other mothers in the street smiled. They smiled at him every day he passed, a strange, sympathetic smile. Even at ten years of age, he had noticed the other mothers in the street smiled at him differently to the way they did the other small boys. What was different about him? However, the smiles were infectious and he couldn't help smiling back.

He felt good raising a smile, something he just couldn't muster behind the darkened door of Number 13 Gladstone Terrace. The sunshine seemed to bring more smiles than the dark and gloomy grey days that were generally par for the course in the small village where he lived. The sunshine was what he lived for. Rain meant staying indoors, getting under Ma's feet and, occasionally, a beating for no particular reason. The sunshine or even a calm, still, overcast day meant Ma would kick him out every morning after his daily ration of porridge and a cup of sweet tea.

Christmas. Yes...he remembered now. Last Christmas she had smiled. He remembered it well. She had handed over the leather copy of the Bible at 6.30 a.m. on Christmas Day together with an orange and a few pennies which he would ultimately be forced to place in the collection box of the local church. Come to think of it, he couldn't even remember eating the orange. But she had smiled; smiled as she placed the gift into his sleepy, limp hands. Called it a gift from our Lord.

So, he had been left with the Bible. He didn't know why. He had a collection of six now and, as he read them through, he realised they were all exactly the same. He expected them to be different, couldn't fathom out why someone would give six copies of the same book, even if it were the greatest book ever written, (according to Ma, that is).

He could just about recite the Bible word for word, starting with the first book of the Old Testament. The Old Testament, that was Ma's favourite, and he could recite it almost perfectly. Ma certainly could as she stood to the side of him with the cane stick, administering a stroke across his backside when he slipped up. The tools of her beating came out every time he stepped out of line. Be it an occasion when his face was too dirty or a problem with an unfastened button, or perhaps his hair had moved somewhat from the style she'd set earlier in the day with a touch of lard and some hot water. And woe betide him if he ever came in muddy after a day's adventure with his two best pals who lived along the street. Climbing trees was outlawed, as, on the one occasion he dared to climb the old yew tree in the meadow just outside the village, he'd slipped and a particularly sharp branch had pierced his shirt. Ma had noticed it immediately as he ran up the stairs seeking the sanctuary of his sparsely furnished room. He tried to push the door shut but, with her immense strength and the fact that *the key to the lock was always in her flowered apron pocket, it was a hopeless task. She threw him violently onto his bed, about-turned and locked the door behind her. It wasn't over. The young boy knew that Ma had gone downstairs to select her instrument of torture.*

She returned after about forty minutes. Why did she take so long? Why did she torture him mentally as well as physically? He wouldn't have minded if she had returned straightaway, inflicted the beating and got it over with, but no, she always seemed to labour that part, always seemed to sit downstairs quietly contemplating.

Contemplating with her good book. And a grimace. That grimace, as her head appeared around the doorframe; that grimace that signalled the beating was about to begin. And begin it did, but not before Ma had recited several passages from the Bible. She had selected them carefully, for each passage seemed to coincide with the crime he'd committed, and, as she beat him, she reminded him it was God's will. God was always the punisher.

And yet Father Macdonald each Sunday from his pulpit in St Mark's Church spouted on about what a nice man this God figure was, as was his son, Jesus. Jesus, whom God sent to save us, - he too was a special man; a kind man; a man who could perform miracles; a man who helped the poor and fought against evil. Why then when his mother carried out this ritual evil punishment was it God's work? Religion - the small boy couldn't understand it. The little boy had one religion... the religion of fear.

The small boy would never know and he would never question God's will or his wishes or his work. On the one occasion he had questioned God's will and why God's work seemed to be so evil, his mother had returned another forty minutes later with a different instrument of torture, a wooden ladle and he had received twice the usual beating for his question.

Ma's face was different, different to the other ladies in the street. She didn't seem to have the lines that spreadeagled out

9

from the corner of the other ladies' eyes. The lines that were more visible as the ladies laughed. There were no lines extending out from Ma's eyes, just the lines or rather bitter, twisted cracks from the corners of her mouth. Hard lines, which had gradually appeared on her face from the years of grimacing and frowning and scowling.

"Run along to the shop," she'd said, "get me a loaf of bread and some soap." She handed him a few pennies and, without hesitation, he had jumped up and walked out into the street. "Run along quickly, I can't wait all day," she had screeched, as the door closed. A simple instruction, a 200-yard walk to the bottom of the street, to the general dealer's, Mr Cooper. Only the young boy never made it.

The clouds up above seemed to gather, darkening the cobbled street and blotting out the huge, shimmering globe that the little boy loved so much. He shivered, took stock of how cold it had become and marvelled at the power of this mysterious star fifty-three million miles away.

There was a clap of thunder in the distance as he took a short cut down the back alley of Bedouin Street. A sign perhaps? A sign from God, the small boy thought to himself.

He broke into a trot, then a gentle jog, and then, as a flash of lightning lit up the gloomy grey street, a full sprint. No rain. Strange, he thought. Perhaps if he ran that little bit harder he could complete his errand before the rain started to fall. Surely Ma wouldn't beat him for getting wet? After all, she had sent him.

Two of the street gang appeared at the bottom of the back lane. By the look on their faces the young boy knew they meant trouble. Without even thinking, he made a quick about-turn and ran back up the alley. He was a tantalising twenty yards from the top of the lane when another three members of the gang appeared. They were smiling. Taunting the younger boy. He looked over his shoulder and, to his horror, the other two members of the gang were advancing towards him. They marched slowly, like a division of soldiers marching in on a massacre.

He looked again to the top of the alley, - the other three boys had started their procession too. Within seconds, but what seemed like hours to the small boy, they had cornered him. He looked all around for an escape route. It was hopeless, - an eight-foot wall that he'd surely never manage to scale was his only chance. And even if he managed to climb it without the boys dragging him down, where would that leave him? Never mind, he'd give it a try.

Without thinking or even realising what he was doing, he charged the biggest boy who was loitering by the alley gate. Fearing a punch or an elbow to the face, the boy instinctively put his hands up to his head for protection. A fat, meaty thigh was exposed and the small boy leapt up onto it. He positioned his small foot perfectly into the thigh knocking the older boy noisily into the gate. He screamed out in pain as the heel of the small boy hammered into his femur. And the small boy jumped and reached for the top of the wall, grinning as both hands hit the spot. Several hands clawed and grabbed at his legs, but he grunted with one last effort and laughed as he swung both legs onto the top of the wall. He stood upright, slightly wobbly, and nervous of the view down below. He looked down at the gang and waved two fingers in their direction. "Fuck you lot o' big bullies. Fuck the lot of you."

His smile disappeared as he noticed one of the gang propped up against the gate, the fingers of his hands interlocked as the rest of the gang lined up for a run. Big Jack Donaldson started first. The small boy looked down in fear, they had obviously performed this exercise before. Without even waiting to see what happened next, he dropped down to his knees on the top of the wall and lowered himself into the backyard. He looked around. No escape. He ran screaming to the back door of the occupant. He didn't know who lived here, didn't care, anyone would do. He pummelled and screamed on the door. "Help me! Help me! Help me!" his voice grew louder with each shout.

Three of the boys now stood on top of the wall, a fourth hung over the wall, his hands lowered into the back lane helping the final member of the gang up onto the wall. The gang looked nervous. Jack Donaldson peered into the window of the house. He smiled. "There's no fucker in, Smudger. You're in the shit."

One by one, the gang on top of the wall started smiling. Nowhere to run, nowhere to hide. With a nauseating feeling rising from the pit of his stomach, the small boy realised Jack was right.

He cowered up against the back door of the terraced house as, one by one, the gang lowered themselves into the yard. He had dug himself into a far deeper pit than he would have done if he had just stayed in the back lane. At least there was a chance that somebody might have come to his rescue. Now, in this dark, forbidding, high walled cell there was no chance.

"Give us your money," Big Jack demanded.

Trembling now, the small boy recoiled as he tried to lie his way out of the situation. "I haven't got any."

"Then where were you going?" another member of the gang asked.

"I...I...I..."

"You were going to Cooper's shop, I reckon. Running a little errand for mumsy wumsy. You're a good boy, Smudger, even though you're a bastard. You do everything for that mum of yours, don't you."

The small boy didn't know the meaning of the word 'bastard' but was aware that others had used it before.

Another lad in the gang chipped in, "My dad reckons she interferes with you." And the others laughed and the small boy screwed up his brow in confusion.

The small boy knew the boys had figured everything out and he knew he couldn't prevent the five members of the gang claiming the prize they were looking for. He was crying now. Not crying because of the beating he was about to be given, but crying because he knew what his mother's reaction would be when he returned to the house empty-handed. Two beatings in a day, that's what it would amount to. And the small boy was right.

The Bedouin boys, despite finding his money and claiming

their meagre rewards without any resistance whatsoever, decided to teach the small boy a lesson for the lies he had told and the taunts he'd showered down on them from the top of the wall. "It's God's work," they goaded him, mimicking his mother's voice as the boots rained down on him from above. Battered and bloody, he had limped along the street and made his way home, more terrified of what he was about to receive.

His mother had accused him of fighting, said the money had rolled out of his pockets during the fracas and hadn't given him the chance to tell his side of the story. "But please, Ma, please I...." A rough, calloused hand along the side of the face stinging his already swollen eye. And the beating. Far worse than he could ever remember and for the first time with her bare fists.

And then, some hours later, his Mother had returned, naked as the day she was born, and slipped under the sheets beside him. "It's God's will," she had whispered in his ear as she caressed him gently.

* * * *

It was a week later when Social Services arrived at his house. A kindly woman approaching retirement age, he thought, took him into the kitchen and made him a cup of tea. He was aware of raised voices in the living room, an argument, and the noise of a plate breaking. His mother was losing it and, as he ran through to the room, he was aware that a large gentleman in a black suit was examining his mother's knuckles. They still bore the signs of the punishment she'd inflicted on him several days earlier.

The man turned around to face the small boy. "Your mother's been beating you, hasn't she," he said.

The boy stood rooted to the spot. Bizarrely, even at this young age, he knew he was about to be removed from his mother and the only home he had ever known. He should have cared. After all, people kept telling him there's no one like your old mum. He should have cried, should have pleaded that it was the boys from Bedouin Street, but he didn't. He kept quiet and hung his head. Not in shame, but in resignation. Surely, where they were about to take him couldn't be any worse.

And years later, when the night shift social worker had crept into his room, it had been worse. Worse then anything he could ever have imagined, and he wished he could have turned back the clock to that ill-fated day at Number 13 Gladstone Terrace.

CHAPTER ONE

Prostitute! A word Vicky Mackenzie associated with the low life elements of society, with dirty needles, popping pills, snorting coke, and alcoholics. Pimps in charge of their bitches, violence, and perversion. Cheap and nasty. A contaminated polluted word.

Vicky was fast approaching forty, too fast for her liking, and for the first time in her life without a man to support her, without a man to love her and to satisfy her.

It had all happened by accident that night in an unfamiliar hotel, but she didn't regret it. In a way, she had felt wanted and valued for the first time in a long while. She had been through the mill in the last few months. She needed some company, she needed some friendship; she needed someone to tell her she looked good and dressed well; she needed someone to tell her they loved her. She needed a man.

Who could have blamed her for what happened that first night? She had gone through more lately than some women went through in a lifetime. It had all been so innocuous. She was feeling low after the death of her husband. Okay, she hadn't really loved him, - never had, - but he was a good sort and he had cared for her, paid her attention, told her every day how glamorous she looked, but, most important of all, he had paid the bills. Some would argue then that she was a prostitute. Would she have cooked for him; would she have kept the house clean and tidy and as meticulous as he liked it to be; would she have accepted his physical advances if the money hadn't hit her personal bank account on the first day of every month? They had had sex three times in the month before his death. Vicky reckoned that that worked out at over £800 a time. How many men paid a prostitute £800 a time?

She figured a high-class hotel would be a good place to meet a new man. She chose the most opulent and fashionable establishment on Newcastle's Quayside. The Maracasa stood opposite the new Millennium Bridge. It was **the** place to be seen. It was full of the fashionable set, the beautiful people, groups of young men and women set for a good night out, for some fast action. But a different sort also frequented the several bars and quieter corners and select eating areas of the huge hotel. Wealthy residents, top executives, and businessmen from out of town. Some just wanted a quiet evening, something to eat and an early night with a bedtime read of the agenda for tomorrow's high-powered meeting. Others wanted an early night, but were inevitably drawn in to the infectious heady atmosphere of the surroundings, eventually retiring to bed several hours after their intended time.

And then there were the chancers.

Vicky could spot them a mile away. The chancers had left behind their wives and girlfriends and were unknown and unrecognised in this strange, vibrant, northern city. They liked what they saw, their eyes taking in the pretty girls who stood and chatted with their friends. Wandering eyes, - it didn't matter, - any pretty girl would do; a one-night stand in an alien hotel in a strange town. No one would know, no one would tell. They were willing to take a chance tonight.

Her long blond hair had been tied up for a change, a sort of dinner dance look. The low cut, but elegant and classy black dress clung to her slim curves accentuating every inch of her lightly tanned figure.

Vicky had been in the bar for about fifteen minutes when she spotted him. She had just made the decision to leave. She was nervous, felt as if hundreds of eyes were penetrating her. People were wondering why she had been on her own for so long.

He gazed across at her through the crowded atmosphere of the bar and, in an instant, she knew he was the one. She figured he was in his mid forties, maybe a company director or a national sales manager....he had that look. He wore an expensive-looking steel grey suit and an open-necked white shirt. He could turn a young girl's head: at least six foot in height, lightly tanned and well-groomed with dark, short cropped hair, mixed with an odd dash of silver. Not unlike a George Clooney meets Richard Gere look, Vicky thought to herself. She caught a glimpse of a tasteful gold necklace beneath his shirt. He smiled at her and she returned the look, a playful twinkle in her eyes. Her heart skipped a beat as he climbed from the bar stool and walked over towards her. He extended a hand. "Joe Saxton - I couldn't help noticing you've been on your own for a while. Has he stood you up?"

"Yeah, something like that," Vicky answered.

"He must be crazy." Vicky cringed at the old pickup line, but nevertheless took an instant liking to the man standing before her.

"I'm from out of town and eating on my own tonight. I'd be honoured if you'd join me."

Out of town, Vicky thought. You don't say! "I'm not so sure that would be a good idea," Vicky lied, "I was just leaving."

Two or three minutes of gentle persuasion and a few laughs secured the dinner date. Vicky suggested a small tapas bar adjacent to the hotel and Joe readily agreed. He took charge of proceedings and ordered several dishes from the Spanish side of the menu. Vicky was impressed with his pronunciation and how quickly he established a good rapport with the Spanish waiter.

"Muy bien. Gracias." The waiter collected the menus and walked away.

"Fluent in Spanish, very clever," smiled Vicky.

"Not exactly fluent but I get by. Restaurant Spanish I call it. I wouldn't be much good in a garage or a supermarket, but I can manage in a bar or restaurant."

By the time the waiter came back with the tapas, Vicky had

made the decision to sleep with him. The only problem was raising the issue. She was a little out of practice, and the recent rejection by her late husband's colleague had dented her confidence somewhat. She'd reassured herself that the rejection had been because her husband was his boss and nothing to do with her. But she needn't have worried. As the waiter cleared the table, her date for the evening slowly emptied the last of the wine equally into the two glasses. "Are you ready for a drink in the residents' lounge?" he asked.

"I'm not a resident."

"You can be if you want to."

Vicky smiled and drained her glass. "Okay, ready when you are."

They walked across to the hotel and Joe Saxton pawed clumsily for her hand. He found it. It felt good and, as they headed for the quiet lounge area, Vicky looked straight ahead at the elevator. "Let's not bother with that drink, Joe."

Joe smiled, walked over, and pressed *call*.

CHAPTER TWO

Donavan Smith cursed when he read the office instructions. Another company training schedule and another trip out of town. How much training could they give him, for Christ's sake? It was the way the industry had gone and Donavan Smith wanted out. He had done well out of city trading, but, as he approached forty, he now realised that it was a young man's game. Not a young man's game, a young person's game. Yes, the ladies were now on the trading floor. Donavan cursed under his breath. The politically correct brigade had seen to that. You couldn't turn around now without bumping into some glammed up career girl or some dyke trying to get one over on the men.

Donavan wished he could turn the clock back a hundred years when the floor was the domain of gentleman with high class accents and old school ties: Etonians, Harrovians, Lords and Earls. Not now. Cockney barrow boys and failed stockbrokers stood on the floor - wide boys who could think on their feet. The floor oozed with sexual tension now and many a good deal had been lost by some wet behind the ears rookie trying to climb up the pecking order.

Not Donavan. Not Donavan Smith. He never even noticed the girls once the floor opened. He concentrated on the job in hand. He was the best. His managers reminded him of this at least once a week and he took on board their comments every year as he renegotiated his contract.

When the floor closed, now that was different. When the floor closed, Donavan Smith began to play. He worked hard and he was damn sure he was going to play hard. He made a point of telling anyone who would listen.

When the closing bell rang, the young traders spilled into the pubs and restaurants surrounding the London Stock Exchange. It was during this initial wind down that Donavan would make his pick up. He had the kind of looks the ladies went for, he knew that. Blond hair neatly tied up into an almost invisible ponytail when he worked the floor, and, after hours, it hung loose just below the collar. The atmosphere and sweat of the working day darkened his hair a little and complemented his deep blue eyes. His features were pleasant on the eye and his character lines had all appeared in the right places over the years. He had a dimple in his chin and bore an uncanny resemblance to Michael Douglas in his younger years. And he had a reputation.

He was fun to be with, a big spender. Donavan's date for the night was guaranteed an evening she would be happy to tell the girls about the next day in the changing room. Dinner for two at one of Donavan's favourite restaurants would start the evening off. Something light, not too filling, and never too much to drink: it would interfere with the sort of evening Donavan had in mind. Then onto a fashionable nightspot or a lap-dancing club.

Donavan liked the lap-dancing clubs. It set out his stall, so to speak. He always took his first-time dates to the lap-dancing and enjoyed watching their discomfort as the girls gyrated, barely inches from their faces. Then to his favourite hotel just across from Green Park. A slow, romantic walk up Constitution Hill and across the road to St James's Street, where he had an arrangement with the manager of the hotel. He settled the four-figure bill at the end of each month, and he had kept every one, far better than any notches on his bedpost. They represented his track record stretching back over ten years. He studied them occasionally, trying to recall the details of the night he had spent with a girl whose name he had written alongside each payment.

A half bottle of champagne in the residents' lounge would

round the evening off nicely and just about persuade the girl to do the honourable thing. Not that they needed much persuasion. The restrooms in the City were awash with the gossip and exaggerations of Donavan's legendary equipment and sexual prowess. And the girls were only too eager to find out if the rumours were true. Then, on the trading floor the next day, he would take great satisfaction in totally ignoring his conquest. Perhaps casual glances at lunchtime; then, a meeting again in the pub a few days later; and perhaps another visit to the hotel near Green Park. Perhaps. Perhaps he would fancy a change.

Donavan had lived life in the fast lane since his late teens, but a change was coming over him. Sure, he still enjoyed work, and, of course, the thought of the thrill of the chase and an evening of unconditional, passionate sex ahead of him. But now, his whole working day was beginning to bore him a little and, just lately, he had cursed himself for losing an occasional big deal. That had never happened in the past. But he was stuck in a rut. He needed every penny of his recently negotiated £180,000 salary. And the bonus each year. Oh, how he needed the bonus.

He teased the young married men during the week the bonuses were announced. Donavan Smith was always up near the top of the list. "Hey saddo," he would shout at them waving his bonus salary statement. "What's the difference between a bonus and a penis?" They would shake their heads at him, but he would always deliver the punch-line they had heard so often. "Your wife's got no objection to blowing your bonus!"

Most years his bonus simply repaid the bank overdraft he had run up over the previous twelve months. Donavan's bank manager was an understanding type, acutely aware of the huge five-, occasionally six-, figure sum deposited into his personal account each May. He would continue to run his client's large overdraft and gladly charge him the fees and interest in the meantime. Donavan never checked the fees and commissions, just the bottom line.

He was proud of the assets and possessions he had built up over the years, many of which he had funded directly from a particularly big bonus year. The penthouse in Belsize Park, the holiday home in Cannes and the apartment just off Jardin du Luxembourg deep in the heart of the Parisian Latin Quarter. Plus his pride and joy: his bright yellow Dodge Viper SRT Ferrari. Not that it came out of the garage too often: he viewed it more as an investment and a means to an end when he wanted to impress a lady who hadn't succumbed to his gentle persuasion at the first time of asking. Yeah, that normally worked, a trip to the country in a gleaming yellow Ferrari, or, if she preferred, a lavish weekend in Cannes.

CHAPTER THREE

Vicky looked at her watch. It read 4.30 a.m She had used Joe Saxton to satisfy her needs but now she was tired of him. He had been a poor, selfish lover, and only when she had taken charge at the third attempt had she achieved orgasm. He lay fast asleep in the huge bed next to her and she hated him. She hated him for what he stood for and for what he had done. She wondered about his wife and their next lovemaking session. Would he think about Vicky Mackenzie? Would he regret his actions and would his lovemaking with his wife ever be the same again? She had done things that his wife would not even talk about let alone try, and he had enjoyed every minute of their brief sexual encounter.

She got up quietly and headed for the bathroom. The taxi arrived just after five and she made her way down to the front lobby. She passed the night watchman and he gave a knowing grin as he doffed his hat in her direction. She expected to feel cheap, a dirty stop out on a one-night stand or even worse. She didn't. She breezed towards the revolving doors with her head held high.

The taxi made quick progress through the deserted streets. Newcastle was eerily quiet and it fascinated her. An early morning worker crossed quickly in front of the taxi and she wondered about his job and his family. She wondered what sort of job dragged this poor man from his bed at such an unearthly hour and she figured somehow that it wouldn't be well paid. At least he has a job, she thought to herself. She would need to face up to that reality sooner or later. Whilst her husband hadn't exactly left her destitute, there had been no life insurance cover and the bank had stripped him of his death in service benefit and his pension rights that he had worked thirty years for.

She had consulted a lawyer, but her late husband had somehow been caught up in a robbery that had relieved his employer of half a million pounds. The lawyer advised Vicky that the bank had every right to withhold benefits. She remembered the fateful day when she had discovered the truth. She had sat in a meeting with a highflying director, Lord Harris. She had felt numb, unable to speak. She had expected to be notified of exactly how much they would be paying her; maybe a small speech telling her what a grand man he had been, devoting his life to the bank.

There had been no speech. The director had apologised but said there would be nothing. The robbery had been hushed up; it was clear that it had been an inside job. Her husband had been one of the prime suspects. Lord Harris made it clear that, if she pursued the case, he would place the information in the public domain. She pictured the headlines; the local news coverage; and she imagined the looks and the gossip.

She couldn't handle it. She let it drop and settled the lawyer's bill.

Now back to reality. She would need a job and a very well paid job at her current rate of spending.

The taxi crunched onto the long, red gravel drive, and came to a stop as daylight began to make an unhurried appearance. She opened her handbag to search for her purse and her jaw fell open in astonishment. She stared at a bundle of ten and twenty pound notes. Realisation set in. "He thinks I'm a whore!"

"Seventeen pounds please," the taxi driver requested from the confines of his secure glass cab.

"Sorry."

"Seventeen quid darling…for the fare home"

"Oh yes sorry… okay," she struggled for the words. She handed him a twenty and walked away without waiting for the change. The taxi driver shouted his appreciation but she didn't hear him. She fumbled with her key and let herself into the house.

A prostitute... he thinks I'm a prostitute. She was not a prostitute, her mind convinced her so, but the mind could persuade a person of anything.

She sat with a hot cup of coffee and any thoughts of sleep and rest had long gone. She felt a strange energy; she felt alive again. Vicky Mackenzie peered through the steam of the coffee as it drifted upwards and smiled. A strange smile, a contented smile. She had a feeling of independence and thoughts of a new career.

* * * *

Vicky Mackenzie returned to the same hotel several nights over the coming weeks. She plied her trade and prided herself on what a natural she was. It all seemed so easy.

She became more patient in seeking out her prey, often waiting for an hour before making eye contact with her quarry. She started looking and searching for the richest looking loner in the hotel and thought nothing of casting someone aside if she thought he didn't meet her very special requirements. He had to be handsome, younger than fifty, well dressed and slim. Above all, he had to be rich - cash rich. Vicky Mackenzie wouldn't jump into bed with anyone, and if she didn't like what she saw then she simply went home. Vicky Mackenzie wasn't a prostitute. She was a high-class escort. Yeah, she liked that name... an escort.

The men couldn't help themselves: a few drinks, then dinner and a quantity of wine or champagne. Vicky's subtle flirting would start, - an occasional accidental brush of the thigh or a hand on the shoulder. Vicky would groom herself in front of them, hoping they would pick up on her obvious body language. The hints and innuendoes would start, and, of course, Vicky would encourage them, laughing at each suggestion. Then it was just a matter of time before the suggestion was blatant. Vicky had her little act planned to perfection.

The first time she had used it, it had gone like clockwork. A computer sales director from Bristol on a two-day fact finding mission had eventually popped the question. "Stay the night with me."

Vicky's act rose to a new level. Her eyes nearly popped out of her head. "I beg your pardon, what did you say?"

He leaned across and confidently kissed her on the lips. She responded for a few seconds then pulled away, uncomfortable with their prominent position in the middle of the lounge.

"You heard... stay with me tonight."

Vicky took a long drink from her cocktail glass. "I'm sorry I can't."

"Why not? Don't you want to?"

"Of course I do, but I just can't."

The man took her hand as a fake tear welled up in Vicky's eye. "Your husband," he said with a look of disappointment.

Vicky glared across at him with a look of disgust. "No, of course not. Do you think I'd be sitting here with you if I had a husband back at home? What sort of girl do you think I am, for Christ's sake?"

He apologised. "I'm sorry, I just thought —"

"Well, you thought wrong," Vicky interrupted, "he's been dead for some time now. This is my first time with another man." Vicky felt comfortable with the lie. After all, she'd only stretched the truth out a little.

"God, I'm so sorry, I...I didn't realise."

The next five minutes were spent describing what a fine man and an important, respected pillar of society John Mackenzie had been. She went on to declare that she could never imagine sleeping with another man. "Until now that is."

The sales director's eyes sparked into life once again. He proceeded carefully and took the sympathetic approach. He took her hands gently and cast his mind back to his teenage dating years and the ploys and words he had used to get his girlfriends into bed. "Please then... stay with me tonight." His hands tightened. "Please."

"I can't, I'm sorry."

"But what's the problem?"

She turned away for a second and he begged her again to answer his question. "Money," she replied.

"Sorry?"

"I need the money since he died without a pension kicking in. I do three shifts at the local casinos, freelance. I'm quite good at it and I can make nearly £200 a night with tips."

He looked at her cautiously.

"I need the money, it's as simple as that."

He sat back and smiled, confident of a result. Vicky sat back and smiled, even more confident of a result.

"Wait there." He jumped up from his seat and went out into reception. A little while later he returned with a cheeky grin. He placed a small white envelope on her lap.

"What's that?"

"Your shift money. Take it."

"I don't understand."

"Your shift money - you need it and I've just covered whatever you'll make this evening."

As his smile widened, Vicky acted surprised.

"Tell me you'll spend the evening with me."

Vicky hesitated. "It's not right. I feel as if you've just bought me, … I can't."

He played his trump card. "So you'd rather spend a night working a casino than a night with me."

"No, of course not, I…." She stopped and shook her head. It wasn't hard, it came naturally to her, and she was rightly proud of her performance, both downstairs, and, later on, upstairs.

That was her first intentional foray into the world of prostitution and she had enjoyed every minute of it, from the prowl to the capture and, eventually, the kill.

Her performances improved with practice and the monetary rewards increased. Before long, she attracted the unwanted attentions of the hotel management, but she simply moved onto another hotel for a few weeks.

She learned to judge well. She knew exactly the kind of figure to hit her punter with and she altered her fictitious profession accordingly. The croupier was the line of work she used most often, but her occupation changed regularly, as she fantasised and dreamt up new lines of work.

Her biggest hit to date was an Arab sheikh. She had told him that she was a successful nightclub singer working on the cruise ships docked in the Tyne. She had mentioned the figure of a thousand pounds per night and balked at the amount as soon as she had said it. She thought he would see right through her. The sheikh sat back calmly and reached into a neat, leather gentleman's handbag on the chair next to him. He glanced quickly around the room and discreetly took out a huge sheaf of fifty-pound notes. He carefully counted out twenty and handed the bundle across to Vicky. She tried hard to disguise her astonishment and once again fell into the "Oh no, I couldn't" routine. When the sheikh eventually convinced her she could, she quickly deposited her prize into her handbag.

Within a few months, she was earning five thousand pounds a month. She was becoming very selective and, some nights, she enjoyed the company of her newfound friends but didn't quite like them enough to have sex with them. Some of the businessmen she liked a lot, and she gave them the number of the new mobile she had recently purchased. She kept the special mobile switched off and accessed the messages each evening. She only called back when the time and the caller suited her. Some of her clients promised to call her when they were next in town. She didn't quite know how she would manage to charge them a second time, but it was a challenge that she would deal with at the time.

Vicky began to tire of her new profession after about nine months. At first, it had seemed so easy. No emotional ties; no strings attached sex; nice evenings out with rich businessmen and payment on top. What better way could there be to earn a living, she had asked herself. Then it had dawned on her. She wanted to fall in love. She wanted a man to love her, not for her body or how good she was in bed, but she wanted someone to love her for who she really was. She remembered a client in the early months. He had been a little different. She had felt at the time that he genuinely believed her story about the croupier job. He had asked her several times about the blackjack games and the roulette table and whether it was weighted in favour of the casino. Fortunately, Vicky and her late husband had frequented the casinos regularly and she had bluffed her way through. She remembered the terrific sexual encounter that night and what an attentive adventurous lover he had been. As she stood up and prepared to leave the following morning, he took hold of her hands and spoke to her. His eyes welled up with tears. "This is a crazy thing to say, but I think I'm in love with you."

The word was alien to her. Her late husband had stopped using it several weeks after they were married and she had never used the word since her early twenties. She had only really loved one man and he had been cruelly taken away from her in a motorcycle crash in the prime of his life.

"What did you say?" she asked.

"I think I've fallen in love with you," he repeated, staring up at her from the bed.

She looked down at him. She wanted to respond but something stopped her. She wasn't ready. Let him down gently, she thought to herself. She was nervous… afraid, jumpy. She became aware of a fleeting facial twitch. The gremlins from way back took over her head. She laughed at him. "You don't get it, do you," she frowned, "I'm a whore - a prostitute - a lady of the night and you've just paid two hundred pounds to fuck me. There's no croupier, no job, no shift, no casino."

The colour drained from his face as realisation set in and the sequence of events from the previous evening began to fall into place. "You're a…"

"A whore," Vicky repeated.

"But it was so special."

She smiled again. "Yeah, I suppose I'm quite good in bed, that's why I get paid for it."

She walked into the bathroom, laughing out loud. She caught her gaze in the mirror. She smiled. Even without any make-up and only two hours' sleep, she still looked good. Her features were fine and delicate with high cheekbones and a cute upturned nose - the type men liked. With her two dimples either side of her 'come to bed' impish smile, it worked every time.

She stared back into her deep, olive green eyes, marvelling at how much they still shone after so little sleep. Her long, strawberry blonde hair, even in its current bedraggled condition, oozed life, and she prided herself on not once having turned to an artificial colouring bottle.

She turned on the shower, jumped in, and washed the stranger from her. Refreshed and cleansed, she stepped out and grabbed a towel. She liked hotel towels: they were large and fluffy and always hung over a heated towel rail. She rubbed herself vigorously and stepped back through into the bedroom. Her lover hadn't moved but the colour had returned to his cheeks. In fact, his face was an intense red, an angry red and it was deepening by the minute.

"What's up?" Vicky asked, as if she didn't know.

"I want you out of my room now."

All of a sudden, the alarm bells activated in Vicky's head and a slow sickening feeling began to well up inside her. She remembered the feeling from way back. "What... right now?" was all she could think to say.

He leaped from the bed and threw open the door. "Right this very minute," he screamed.

"But you'll let me put some clothes on.... right?" She stood there, naked, apart from a pair of pants she'd managed to climb into in the bathroom. She instinctively covered her cold breasts, now wary of her client's gaze.

"Now!" he repeated.

Her untidy heap of clothes lay on a bedroom chair. She took a slow, deliberate step towards them. Within an instant, he had beat her to the target, scooping up the clothes and casting them out into the long, dimly-lit corridor. He stood triumphant, a hand on the door handle.

Did she detect a wry smile? She looked at him in disbelief, yet strangely admiring him in his moment of victory.

She walked towards the open door. "It could have been so different," he whispered as she passed him, and, momentarily, she believed him.

She walked out into the corridor and gazed both ways. Empty. She reached down for her bra as her handbag sailed past her head. It thudded against the corridor wall.

"I've taken the two hundred out," the figure silhouetted in the doorway remarked. "I reckon there's some sort of law you've broken to get it. Fraud, deception, whatever. Call the police if you like. I'll be glad to answer their questions."

She looked up at him from the floor of the hotel corridor and wished she could turn back the clock. Twenty minutes would do; just twenty minutes ago she'd climbed from the bed satisfied, fulfilled and strangely content and at ease with the world.

She heard a noise off to her right. Her worst nightmare. An elderly couple were leaving their room, heading for breakfast. It took them a few moments to carry out the routine formalities a younger couple would have completed quickly. They checked the door and double-checked the location of the key. The old lady took her husband's arm and pointed him in the direction of the lift. Vicky had nowhere to hide. The door slammed shut causing them to look up. Their two mouths dropped open at the sight that met them.

Vicky scooped her clothes up quickly, and clumsily pulled on her skirt. Her mind cast back to a school time proverb. More haste less speed, and she tried to slow down. It was no good. She gave up trying to cover herself. The old couple passed as she began to button her blouse. The old lady stole a glance, trying to avoid eye contact. Vicky stared at her. "He gets angry if I don't swallow."

The old couple hurried past. "C'mon lady, you must have spit now and again?" Vicky attempted to pull on her high stiletto heels.Unable to keep her balance, she slumped to the floor. She sat quietly for a few minutes and a tear rolled onto her cheek.

CHAPTER FOUR

Donavan smiled to himself as he remembered one or two of his conquests. He recalled the challenges thrown down by his younger colleagues. The stunning Jenny McArthur, fresh out of university with a first class honours degree, determined to hit the high ground on the trading floor. And she was good. For once in his career, Donavan had taken his eye off the ball. He couldn't keep his eyes off her and marvelled at her tenacity, her arrogance occasionally, mixed with an abundance of confidence, and her ability to make quick decisions under pressure. The gossip on the trading floor and in the bars at night was rampant. Rumour had it that she would go far. Rumour had it that she was frigid, or worse, not interested in the opposite sex. Rumour had it that she was interested in the same sex. Two or three of his male colleagues had tried and failed to seduce her. What other explanation could there be? The man who managed to bed her would be the toast of the trading pits.

It started with the customary meal for two at Gianni's, an Italian restaurant on Queen's Gate in Knightsbridge. The manager fussed around and welcomed Donavan as if he was the top VIP in town. He showed the couple to Donavan's usual table by the window, positioning the napkins on the happy couple's laps.

Donavan started working on his victim immediately. The conversation was work-related and Donavan desperately tried to steer her onto something more appealing. She didn't seem interested and Donavan began to get a little agitated. "Look Jenny, no offence, but can we talk about something else? I've had a real pisser of a day and I'd like to forget about work until tomorrow morning."

Jenny was taken aback. "Oh sorry, Don, I... I didn't realise, it's just that I'm so lucky to get this break, and I don't want to waste it."

Donavan nodded his head and took a large mouthful of sparkling water. He tipped the champagne bottle and filled Jenny's glass.

"You're the best on the floor and the guy with experience, I could learn so much from you."

Donavan nodded his head and smiled. "Sure Jenny, I know you could, but let's just slow it down a bit, take it easy, relax."

He reached across and took her hand, made eye contact with her. He was prepared to stay silent forever. It was a game: who speaks first, loses. He didn't have long to wait.

"Tell me what you think, Don. Please. I need to know what you think. I respect your opinion. Any tips, Don?"

He sat back and sighed. "You're destined for the top, I know that, but it's still a man's world out there. Be careful, some guys will stab you in the back as quick as look at you."

Jenny broke his grip and made for her glass. "I'm not sure I know what you mean."

"Politics and ambition, Jenny. It's how the floor works. You'll get a bigger bonus next year than some of the guys who have been on the floor ten years. They'll be jealous and won't like it. You'll be head hunted fast and offered salaries that you could only dream of. You'll make enemies. I've seen it all before, and the next thing you'll know is that you're frozen out. The traders will gang up on you, try to trip you up." He took another mouthful of water and paused. "You need friends on the floor. Friends and respect, it's as simple as that. No friends and no respect and you'll die on your arse."

"I thought those days were long gone."

Donavan smiled again. "You're in your honeymoon period, Jenny, but it gets tougher from now on."

"But you said I'm good, destined for the top."

She opened her mouth to speak again, Donavan held up a

hand. "Enough.... we're talking work again."

"Yes, but —"

"Enough, I won't talk about work again tonight."

Jenny gulped at her champagne in frustration. "Perhaps another time."

Donavan grinned. "It would be my pleasure."

They left the restaurant and walked up Kensington Gore. Donavan suggested a late night drink. Jenny agreed. As they approached the lap-dancing club Jenny began to object. "I've never been anywhere like this before. I don't think I'll like it."

Donavan laughed at her. "You're kidding me, right? It's just a place for a quiet drink, expensive, no riff-raff, and music you can hold a conversation to. You don't need to look... it's not as if they'll dance at our table. If you can't handle this, you definitely can't handle the floor."

Jenny reluctantly agreed and they walked past the two huge black bouncers either side of the door.

A stunning, six-foot blonde girl showed them to a quiet table, situated in a private cubicle, deep within the heart of the club. She took the drinks order and Donavan slipped two fifty-pound notes into her hand. "Keep the change," he whispered.

He took Jenny's jacket. "Just ordering the drinks," he smiled.

The girl returned shortly afterwards with a large ice bucket containing a bottle of pink champagne. She pressed a button within the cubicle and a green velvet curtain swept around, cutting the trio off from the prying eyes of the masses. Donavan placed another large denomination note into the girl's hand and she sprang into an all too familiar routine.

Even in the dark recesses of the cubicle, Donavan could sense the uncomfortable, deep red embarrassment etched across Jenny's face. He felt himself getting hard, not from the ever-revealing flesh on the table in front of him, but from Jenny's hopeless position with nowhere to run.

But run she did. She lasted the duration of the first dance, then made her excuses and left. Donavan made no attempt to go after her and ordered the girl to continue with her performance. He smiled as he took in the full routine, second by delicious second. He smiled, a contented smile. He had enjoyed the evening.

* * * *

Jenny tried to apologise to him the following morning on the trading floor. Donavan ignored her. She persisted. "Look, Don, what do you want me to say? I'm sorry, I walked out on you, but it wasn't you I was walking out on. It was that club and those…" She struggled for the word, "Whores."

Donavan glanced at her, his face a picture of concentration. "Lunchtime."

"Sorry?"

"I'm working, - we'll talk at lunchtime."

A faint, hesitant smile crept across Jenny's face. "Sure, yeah, thanks, errr the Queen's Arms, one o'clock?"

Donavan nodded and his eyes returned to the huge diamond-vision trading screen.

Donavan arrived just after 1.30 p.m. Jenny was sitting at a table on her own, looking nervous, but very grateful that he had made an appearance. He ordered two bottles of Stella and carried them across. She looked up as he approached the table. "Busy?"

Donavan placed the bottle beside her. "You could say that. I'm trying to get tidied up. I'm heading to Paris for a few days."

Jenny's eyes lit up. "I love Paris. Just a little break, is it?"

Donavan took a mouthful of ice-cold beer. He shuddered as it caught the back of his throat. Every time alcohol hit the spot it was a get back at his mother, the woman he'd loathed so much; the woman who had dominated his life until her premature death on Donavan's twenty-first birthday. Yeah… she'd even ruined that joyous day too. He'd called her from his party just as it was getting in full swing. She wouldn't come, said she didn't feel well, pains in her chest, and anyway she didn't approve of the fact that it was being held in an establishment that served alcohol.

Right up until her death, she preached the doctrine of the Temperance Society. Drink is the curse of the community, she would say. Drink numbs every sense of shame, leaves the drinker in a fool's paradise. She studied in detail the writings of The Temperance Society supporters, George Sims and Angus Reach. Quotations from Theobald Matthew and the artist, George Cruikshank, hung in homemade frames in the kitchen of her two-up, two-down council house, the house from which Donavan had managed to escape at ten years of age.

And yet, he hadn't escaped. Still she'd managed to dominate him. Bizarrely, the courts had granted her visitation rights twice a month. And during those visits, occasionally there was a meeting behind closed doors, with just Donavan and his mother; encounters that Donavan, at the time, thought were normal. He cringed as he remembered them as vividly as if they were yesterday and took another mouthful as he answered Jenny's question. "Sort of. I'm on a fact-finding mission to the Paris Stock Exchange, trying to get a handle on how it works. See if it can improve my performance."

Donavan described the streets and cafes and monuments surrounding the Paris Stock Exchange and how the Opera House and the Louvre were all located in the same beautiful area of Paris. "And my apartment is just a two minute taxi ride away."

"You have a place in Paris?"

"Yeah, nothing flash, but it's real handy for everywhere."

Jenny sighed and repeated, "I just love Paris."

Donavan sprung the trap. "Then come with me."

"What?"

"I'll clear it with your boss. A business trip to improve your European knowledge of the markets and to brush up on your French for when you're dealing with the Paris traders."

Jenny's mind cruised into overdrive attempting to find one valid excuse why she couldn't go. Donavan described a likely itinerary. She could think of none.

Donavan smiled as he realised he had won, but, just to make

sure, he hammered in the final nail. "And I'll forget about last night."

Jenny couldn't refuse. She'd already walked out on the most respected and influential trader on the London Stock Exchange and here he was giving her a second chance. And what a second chance it was, a trip to Paris, for God's sake. She'd be crazy to refuse.

Donavan looked across the table and laughed. "Don't worry, the apartment has two bedrooms if that's what you're thinking."

Jenny blushed. "No, no, I wasn't thinking that, I was just thinking about clothes. What will I need?"

"Nothing extravagant, just a business suit, something for the Opera and something to mess about in during the day."

Jenny beamed like a schoolgirl on her birthday. "We're going to the Opera?"

Donavan shrugged his shoulders. "Why not, I think you'll enjoy it."

* * * *

Donavan finished packing his suitcase barely ten minutes before the taxi arrived. He carefully concealed a small packet under the cap of his expensive deodorant and pushed it deep into his toilet bag.

He walked out into the sunshine, dressed in a pair of old faded jeans, an expensive beige designer jacket and a loose white cotton shirt. Donavan liked the look: sort of Mickey Rourke meets David Beckham.

Jenny beamed as she waved from the back of the taxi. "I can't believe we're really going," she exclaimed from the back seat, as Donavan climbed in beside her. "You're looking rather trendy today, Don, a bit different from the old pinstripes, if I may say so."

Donavan removed his sunglasses. "And you're not looking so bad yourself." Jenny blushed slightly as she turned her head to the front of the cab.

Thirty minutes later, Donavan settled the taxi fare at Heathrow, careful to make a point of giving the cab driver a ridiculously large tip. A tip, of course, that he made sure Jenny noticed.

"Thank you, sir," the taxi driver said as he removed the fifty-pound note from Donavan's hand.

Donavan made his way quickly into the terminal, as Jenny struggled on behind with her huge suitcase. He walked over to the BA special priority check-in desk, and they walked through to departures a few minutes later.

Donavan flashed his BA Gold Card at a very attractive young lady on the doorway of the VIP lounge and signed Jenny in as a guest. He could tell by her demeanour this was her first visit to the Gold Card lounge and, by the look on her face, she was suitably impressed. "Just help yourself to whatever you fancy." He pointed to a well-stocked cooler cabinet, containing a wide array of fine wines and champagnes. Jenny pretended to study the labels and chose a small bottle of Chablis. Donavan went for a Laurent and Perrier Reserve. She looked around for the checkout, but couldn't see one.

"We don't have to pay?" Jenny asked, as they ambled over to the executive seating area.

Donavan laughed. "Your first time in a place like this, isn't it."

Jenny nodded. "It's as obvious as that, is it?"

Donavan unscrewed the top on her bottle and poured a large glass. "It's the only way to fly. You'll be a fully fledged member in a year or two."

He took a sip from his champagne and looked over the top of his glass. "As long as you play the right hand. Be keen, fly to Frankfurt and Madrid, check out the foreign markets and make a point of telling your boss you've done so. Your credibility has already gone up just because you're coming on this trip to Paris with me. The big boys think I've taken you under my wing. They think I'm schooling you to take my place. Kind of like an apprentice."

Jenny took a sip from the glass and looked around the lounge again. "I'm so grateful, Don, and don't get me wrong here, but why are you helping me this way? What do you get out of it, Don?"

Donavan smoothed an eyebrow down with his finger and laughed as he spoke. "I'll think of something, Jenny, I'll think of something."

Jenny nodded and Donavan congratulated himself at how uncomfortable she just looked. It was a points game, Donavan thought, a simple points game. Most of the girls succumbed after six points. One point equalled a nice drink out. A meal or dinner racked up three or four more. The lap-dancing club was at least a two and a weekend in Paris was a full five. A drive out in the Ferrari came somewhere in between and Donavan figured before too long Jenny would be edging towards the ten mark. No girl had managed to make it past the ten. Then he thought back. Well… one or two had, but then again, there was always his favourite little packet to fall back on.

* * * *

After collecting their luggage, Donavan took Jenny's hand and followed the *Sortie* signs at Charles de Gaulle Airport, down a series of long corridors and moving pavements. Her hand felt good in his and she did not attempt to remove it. Donavan grinned inwardly. One more point, he thought to himself.

The size of the Parisian airport annoyed him, but before long, he had managed to navigate his way out into the taxi rank. He quickly hailed a Paris cab and jumped into the back as Jenny followed his lead.

"Boulevard St Michele, Monsieur. Latin Quarter." The French taxi driver nodded his understanding.

Donavan pointed out the various tourist landmarks along the way and Jenny sat in silence, suitably impressed … he hoped.

A good hour passed before they reached their destination. Donavan settled the taxi fare and guided her into a small courtyard through a huge old wooden door, adorned with a least fifty shiny brass letterboxes and black iron door fixings from a different era. The interior walls of the courtyard were covered with a mass of climbing white jasmine and striking emerald green ivy. The sight took her breath away and Donavan looked on. "Beautiful isn't it?"

Jenny nodded. "And the smell, Donavan, it's absolutely amazing."

Donavan smiled. "C'mon, I'll show you to your room."

He led her to the first floor apartment and into a bedroom that overlooked the courtyard. "I thought you'd like this room."

Jenny walked over to the window and took in the view. "I don't know what to say, Don. It's just out of this world."

"Yeah, I like it here. I try to come at least four or five times a year."

The smell of the jasmine filled the room. Donavan stood behind Jenny and, closing his eyes, he edged a little closer. His nose lifted into the air and he took in the hypnotic fragrance of nature at its finest and a woman's natural appreciative aroma. His hand ventured down to his groin and he pushed hard against his growing erection. Easy boy, he thought, easy... Not long to wait now.

* * * *

Donavan reckoned the night at the opera added another two points to Jenny's already over heavy total. The midnight meal on a glorious illuminated Champs Elysee was worthy of at least two more.

Jenny finished her last mouthful of Parisian pâtisseries and he decided the time was right. "Enjoy the night?" he asked.

Jenny swallowed quickly, eager to offer her appreciation. "Don, it was just fabulous. I can't thank you enough."

You can, he thought. *You certainly can.*

She leaned across the table and kissed him politely on the cheek. "And tomorrow, the Paris Stock Exchange. I'm just so excited."

Donavan shook his head and smiled.

"What is it? What's up?" she enquired innocently.

"You don't get it, do you?"

"Get what, - what is it?"

Donavan leaned across the table and took her hands in his. He became aware of an uncomfortable resistance. "There's no Paris Stock Exchange tomorrow."

Jenny sat back, breaking his grip completely. "I don't understand, what do you mean? It's a business trip, - we have to go, - my boss, Frankfurt, the European markets..."

Donavan shook his head and thought about reaching for her hands again. He thought better of it. "I'm sorry. I've lied to you and your boss."

Jenny sat open mouthed as he delivered his final assault, proud of the false sincerity in his voice. As he said it he almost believed it himself, but cringed as he heard the words fall out of his mouth. "I'm in love with you... I ... I want to spend the evening with you and tomorrow and the day after and the day after that."

He waited a while and continued. "In fact I may want to spend the rest of my life with you." Donavan sat back and waited. Waited for a reaction. Silence is golden... usually, and then a beaming smile and a kiss as the young naïve girl succumbs to the sort of shit statement she doesn't hear too often.

The silence continued longer than Donavan was comfortable with. Jenny pawed nervously at the glass. Donovan watched her pulsing throat as she gulped the ridiculously expensive liquid. His trousers tightened.

"I'm sorry." Donavan looked at her in disbelief. "I'm sorry, Donavan, it's a business trip, nothing more, nothing less. I'm sorry if I've given you the wrong impression... I have a boyfriend back home, I —"

Donavan held up his hand. "Don't... just don't say anything. I understand. It's stupid of me to think that someone as young and attractive and as special as you would be interested in someone like me."

Jenny reached for his hand. "No, Don, please, you're really lovely, you're extraordinary. I've really become attracted to you. It's just… that… I'm in love with somebody else." She looked at him and smiled. Donavan despised the smile. "Perhaps if it had been a few years earlier, it may just have worked."

She's lying, he thought, the fucking bitch is patronising me. Who does she think she is?

Donovan looked over towards the assembled group of waiters. He clicked his fingers in the air. A slightly built French man took note and walked quickly towards their table. "Champagne please. The best in the house."

The waiter raised an eyebrow, took out his pad and scribbled down some figures. He discreetly allowed Donavan to view the price. Donavan nodded. "That will be fine, thank you."

Jenny sat back, a look of bewilderment etched across her face, and shook her head. "What are we celebrating, Don, for Christ's sake?"

Donovan rubbed his chin and looked out into the Paris night sky, his eyes focused on hers again. He raised his wine glass; Jenny raised hers in some sort of bizarre anticipation. "To Paris… to Paris and to honesty." Jenny's face flushed. "And to beauty."

He held up his glass towards her and she smiled. A timid smile. An anxious look. "*One man among a thousand have I found; but a woman among all those have I not.*"

Jenny smiled again. "That's nice, Don, where's that from?"

"The Bible. Ecclesiastes, from the Old Testament."

"I'm impressed, Don, I didn't know you were into that sort of thing."

Donavan laughed out loud. "I'm not. My mother drummed it into me as a kid. A staunch non-drinking Methodist."

"You really are very special, Don."

"Let's just enjoy the rest of the evening," said Donavan.

Jenny nodded. "I really must nip to the little girls' room, far too much to drink already."

She rose to her feet and Donavan smirked as she wobbled a little. She disappeared into the darkness of the restaurant. The waiter arrived with the ice bucket and produced two elegant, heavy crystal champagne flutes. He proceeded to fill them and, as he walked away, Donavan stole a careful look around the restaurant. He felt in his pocket and located the small packet. He took another quick look round before he carefully tipped the contents of the packet into Jenny's glass.

Rohypnol, ten times more potent than Valium. The powder gave the champagne a bluish tint at first, but had all but disappeared as Jenny returned. He raised his glass high and looked into her eyes with a look she hadn't seen before. "To you."

* * * *

Donavan and Jenny left the restaurant a little after two in the morning. He had seen the familiar signs half an hour prior to that and decided it was time to leave. Jenny had objected at first, wanted to see more of Paris, claimed it was too early to go to bed, didn't feel the need to go to sleep. Then she apologised, repeatedly.

Sleep wasn't what Donavan Smith had in mind. He held a supportive arm round her waist for the short walk to his apartment. She didn't resist, she would remember nothing about the walk home that evening, nor did she realise what lay ahead. By the time she woke the next morning, she would know nothing, but she would feel as if she had the mother of all hangovers.

What a marvellous drug, Donavan thought, as he planned the depraved acts he would perform on her. He almost forgot… he too would need to be helped during the evening ahead, helped by another little miracle drug of the advanced modern world. He located the brightly coloured pill in the breast pocket of his jacket, cleverly unwrapped it with one hand, and brought his hand up to his mouth. "For you, darling."

Jenny mumbled an unrecognisable reply; Donavan Smith didn't bother to answer.

By the time she reached the apartment, she was ready. Her eyes had glazed over and she had difficulty moving in a straight line. Donavan took hold of her firmly in the doorway. He looked directly into her eyes. He smiled as her eyes looked straight through him. He moved his head towards her and kissed her long elegant neck. Her hands fell to her side and she sought his body for support. He moved his mouth upwards and traced his tongue along her perfectly formed lips. He grinned as her mouth lolled open. "You'll do anything I say, is that clear?"

Jenny searched for some words but found none. Her head nodded in slow motion. He spun the drugged girl around and pushed her roughly into the apartment. As she fought subconsciously to put one foot in front of the other, Donavan caught the back of her ankle with his right foot. A gentle sideways kick was all it took and her trailing right leg crossed her left calf. She tumbled forward without the presence of mind or instinct to prevent it happening. Her head crashed into the corner of a small coffee table. Donavan winced at the sickening sound and the squeal of the half-comatose girl. A trickle of blood oozed from the side of her head, as she lay motionless on the floor. "Perfect," he whispered to himself, "absolutely perfect."

He bent over and whispered in her ear. "*Neither was the man created for the woman; but the woman for the man. First Corinthians, 11: 9.*"

CHAPTER FIVE

Jenny awoke the next morning as the first rays of the Paris sun penetrated deep into the darkened bedroom. She was aware that she was naked. She never slept like that, always a T-shirt and a pair of pants even in the hottest of holiday destinations.

Something wasn't right. She shivered, so cold, yet the bedroom was so warm. Her hand instinctively moved to the side of her face. She reeled as her fingers touched the four-inch split below her eye. She moved her hand to the side of her head fully aware that the shape she felt was totally foreign to her. She realized she could only see out of one eye.

She moved gingerly from the bed and moaned out loud as the pain in her head increased. It felt as if her brain had decided to relocate in that split second of a movement. She fought the urge to lie down again and moved slowly towards the en suite bathroom. Her mouth fell open as she focused on the sight of her reflection. Her left eye was completely closed and discoloured a bluey black colour. Her cheek was so swollen it was if a surgeon had stitched half a tennis ball in there the night before. The headache spread right across her brow and deep into her temples. She noticed that her good eye was also a bright reddish purple that would no doubt get worse as the day went on.

But worse, much worse, was the pain she was feeling internally. Her hand slid down her stomach. Her vagina ached and burnt with a sensation she had never felt before, not even after she had lost her virginity on the eve of her seventeenth birthday. This was an excruciating pain, her worst nightmare, and the worst bit about it was that she didn't know what had caused it. Her hands moved down until she located the delicate folds of her vaginal entrance. She carefully eased a finger inside. She caught her breath at the effect it had. Then she broke down.

Her mind was in turmoil, the tears flowed down her cheeks, and she sunk onto the cold tiles of the bathroom floor. She could remember nothing. The salty tears tore into her wounded face as if to add insult to injury. She sobbed uncontrollably for several minutes then pulled herself to her feet.

What had happened? Had she been attacked? She vaguely remembered the opera and having something to eat afterwards but that was it. After that, nothing.

And then a split-second flashback. A face. An evil face, grinning and leering at her. She fought to control the involuntary spasms in the pit of her stomach. The acidic bile and remains of last night's meal stung the back of her throat as she clenched her hand over her mouth. She barely made the toilet bowl in time, as the foul-smelling liquid spewed out from between her fingers. The sweat dripped from the end of her nose and she took hold of the tight muscles at the base of her stomach, massaging hard, as if the action would alleviate the cramps deep within. Another spasm and eventually her stomach emptied. She sat for a few moments with her head resting on the cold white ceramic, grateful for the cool temperature.

Then she rose to her feet, her headache a hundred times worse now. She opened the shower cubicle door and turned on the shower to an almost unbearable temperature. She stood under the powerful hot stream and cried out loud as the water cascaded all over her violated young body.

Donavan Smith stood in the doorway of the bathroom enjoying the sight unfolding before him. Jenny stood with her eyes closed, displaying her beautiful body for his personal pleasure. And what a body it was. He had experienced and enjoyed every inch of it over the course of a few hours the evening before. Not that Jenny knew anything about it; she wouldn't; she couldn't. Donavan's experience of the after-effects of Rohypnol was long-standing.

Both hands on her breasts now, rubbing hard. Overdoing it a bit, Donavan thought, as she scrubbed furiously, her nipples stiffening, responding to her touch. And Donavan wanted her again. Her hands journeyed downwards to her navel and her lightly tanned flat stomach. And on down, both hands now between her legs, pawing gently at the soft downy pubic hair and then inside. Donavan groaned quietly. Then he grinned as he noticed her pained, contorted expression.

The door swung open and Jenny stood naked before him. When she saw him, she made a grab for a towel from the heated rail and tried desperately to cover her modesty. "Get the fuck out," she screamed.

Donavan did not attempt to move. "So that's all the thanks I get after last night."

"What do you mean?" she asked, not really wanting to know the answer to her worst nightmare.

"You mean you don't remember?" Donavan sidled over to the toilet seat, closed the lid, and sat down.

Jenny reached for a hand towel, slightly regretting her initial outburst. "Too much wine, I suppose."

Donavan laughed out loud. "Yeah, something like that, and champagne, two bottles between us. Then three or four liqueurs, not that I was counting."

Jenny walked back through into the bedroom. Donavan strolled slowly after her. "Yeah, you were in some state. You tripped on the way in and caught your head on the side of the table. You were out cold. I spent twenty minutes with ice cubes and towels mopping up the blood and trying to get the swelling down."

Jenny sat on the bed, towelling her hair nervously. Donavan ambled over to the dressing table and sat down on the elegant French period seat. He leaned forward and rested his chin on his hands. He chose his moment perfectly. "But, my god, it didn't affect your performance. I've never had a night like that in twenty years. Where did you learn to fuck like that?"

Jenny fell back on the bed, her hands covering her face. "Oh God, we didn't."

"Oh we certainly did, young lady. You begged me for it time and time again. I tried to tell you that you'd had too much to drink but you pleaded for it. It was just as well I had a Viagra pill with me." Donavan stood up and left the room smiling. He left Jenny alone with the worst thoughts she could fill her head with. He returned a few minutes later with two large mugs.

The smell of hot coffee filled the room and Jenny gratefully accepted his offering.

"In fact, Jenny, I'd be amazed if you weren't a little tender down below this morning."

Jenny lifted the hot mug to her face in a bid to hide her embarrassment. "I didn't know what I was doing. You did something to me... I ... I wouldn't have slept with you, not in a million years." Then there was a pause as it dawned on her. "You drugged me. You raped me."

Donavan stood up and walked through to the lounge. Just before he disappeared from view, he stopped and turned. "Rape, eh? Well come and see if it looks like rape."

Jenny didn't understand. "What do you mean?"

He didn't answer and Jenny jumped from the bed to follow him. As she entered the lounge Donavan had turned on the television and started messing about with the connections to a laptop computer.

"It'll look better on this, more pixels I believe they call them, a clearer picture than on the old laptop."

Jenny stood open mouthed as the familiar surroundings of the lounge appeared on the screen. "Oh no. Oh no," she screamed out in panic, "surely to God you didn't?" She lunged at the small laptop and its connections but Donavan was too quick for her. His old black belt judo skills came into play as he swung his heavy thigh into her knees. His trailing right arm pushed down heavily on her shoulder blades and she turned a full somersault before she hit the floor. She scrambled around in desperation eager to regain her footing, but Donavan's fourteen-stone weight crashed down on top of her before she made it. "You bastard, you raped me, you drugged me. It was the champagne; it didn't taste right."

Donavan laughed at the pathetic wretch of a girl squirming beneath him. He smiled as he felt the blood returning into his penis. He pressed into Jenny's hips and watched the fear and discomfort flood into her eyes. "Rape? We'll just take a look, shall we? See if we can present any evidence to the police."

Donavan's powerful arms flipped Jenny over onto her stomach and this time she knew it was pointless resisting. "They'll tell you you're wasting your time, you ungrateful little whore."

He took a handful of Jenny's hair and pulled her head up. The blurred, bleak picture of the empty lounge filled the television screen. Donavan fingered the remote control and the picture started moving ever so slightly. The camera focused in and out and, eventually, a crisp, clear picture came into view.

Donavan grew harder as he moved down onto Jenny's buttocks with his two thighs resting either side of her body. He leaned forward and whispered into her ear, "Watch carefully, my little porn queen. Watch very carefully."

Jenny watched in disgust as the camera focused on a well-toned male torso. Donavan beamed as his shape came into view and his grin broadened as the camera zoomed in on his erect penis. "Quite impressive, isn't it, my little sex babe."

Donavan giggled like a little schoolboy as Jenny's head came into the frame. She looked into the camera clearly unable to focus and, as Jenny watched, the thing she noticed were her own eyes. Her own eyes, yet eyes she had never seen in a mirror before.

A tear fell to the floor as she watched herself start performing oral sex on him. Donavan's aroused state hit new heights. A few minutes later, the camera wavered a little and the picture was lost.

"Don't worry, angel, it comes back on."

"I'm not watching anymore, you sick pervert."

Donavan tightened his grip on her hair and whispered into her ear again. "You'll watch every single frame, you bitch, even if we have to stay here for a year."

Donavan focused on her screwed-up, damaged eyes and moaned with approval as they opened and glowered at the television. "That's better. Keep watching - you'll like this bit."

The camera steadied. It had been set on some sort of tripod. Jenny's naked profile looked up into the camera. She knelt on all fours. Donavan was positioned behind, thrusting powerfully into her, leering into the camera, holding a remote control, high above his head. The camera zoomed in on Jenny's head as it jerked backwards and forwards, coinciding with Donavan's movement. It was a contented face, a willing face.

"No, Jenny, I don't think that's rape, do you? Consenting sex between two adults, I think that's what they call it."

Jenny's tears dripped onto the cold wooden floor and Donavan Smith could control himself no longer. He stood up, unbuckled his trousers, and threw them to the floor. He tore viciously at the towel around Jenny's body. She made a half-hearted attempt to resist but knew it was useless. Donavan lowered his powerful body onto her and thrust her legs apart. She screamed like a banshee as he entered her and Donavan prayed that the soundproofing he had installed a few years earlier was up to the job. He cried out loud as he came. Then he climbed from her and calmly walked through to the bedroom cackling like a hyena.

Jenny lay naked in the middle of the floor, crying as she'd never cried before.

CHAPTER SIX

Province of Cadiz Spain

Bob Heggie thought it couldn't get much better than this. He sat on the small terrace of his renovated farmhouse watching the sun go down over the distant Cadiz mountains. The property stood outside the village of Niebla on the River Tinto. He figured he had covered every square mile of Andalusia before settling on his very own three thousand square metres of paradise.

Niebla was an old settlement dating back to the eighth century, known locally as La Roja, the Red One. Many of the old buildings had been constructed using mud from the nearby river, giving the buildings a deep reddish glow.

He watched as the deep crimson globe seemed to hover on top of the distant hill. Slowly but surely it disappeared, minute by glorious minute. He pictured the sun heating an arid African region, herds of wildebeest grateful for the coolness that would soon return to their parched dusty plain. He closed his eyes and visualised the Jalon Valley in the south of Spain. Surely the best place on earth to appreciate a sunset. They visited the Jalon Valley at least two or three times a year and sat in their favourite eatery, *The Fox Venta Figueral*, two kilometres south of the tiny mountain village of Tarbena, with awesome, unbroken views sweeping down the valley. The owners had converted a three hundred year old goat farm into a Spanish *Hostal* or inn, retaining somehow the ambience and atmosphere of long, long ago.

Hannah breezed through from the house and stood in front of

him with a cool glass of *aqua con gas*. One beautiful image replaced by another. "Thought you could use one of these."

Bob took the glass from her hand and ran his hand up her thigh, his way of saying thank you.

"Sure you don't want a beer?"

Bob shook his head. He was only too aware of how much alcohol clouded his judgement, dulled his thoughts, and, since his chosen relocation to Spain, fully appreciative of how well sun and beer went together He had drastically cut down on his intake. Back in the UK, he had had at least three or four beers every day and, at the weekend, doubled or even trebled his consumption. And then there was the wine and, occasionally, the whisky. Mmmm, the whisky, he thought to himself: the Jameson and the Glenfiddich, the Talisker and the Bushmills.

He'd been off the golden liquid for nearly a year now, but he knew that if someone put a malt whisky in front of him he'd find it difficult to resist. That's why he didn't keep it in the house anymore.

And he was feeling fitter and slimmer from his newfound lifestyle. Bob had had his forty-forth birthday earlier that month and prided himself that he could pass for a man ten years younger. At least that's what Hannah kept saying, but perhaps she was a little biased?

Nevertheless, he kept to good wholesome foods and worked out in the basement gym for at least forty-five minutes every day. After three or four months of perseverance and exercise made bearable by continuous doses of loud rock music from his iPod, he actually began to enjoy his daily sessions. Now he couldn't do without them, a sort of addiction. And he could see and feel the results, and Hannah told him so every day.

The sun helped too, made him feel good as it rose from its enforced slumber and woke him with its rays tugging gently at his thin duvet. Always an early riser, Bob would sit with a large mug of Earl Grey Tea and watch the early morning shadows gradually materialising in his garden.

The pace of life was a million miles away from the one he had left back in England. His old regime of the working day used to start at 6.30 a.m. with a seven-minute shower and a ten-minute breakfast. Then a short walk with the dogs and a mad dash, always a mad dash, to the train station. Twelve hours later he would return home, have some dinner, an hour's TV, a few hours' shuteye, then start all over again.

God, how he'd hated it, and he thanked his lucky stars for the plan that had allowed him to leave it all behind. A plan that had been totally out of character for Robert Heggie.

Never in a million years did he think he would have had the cunning, the resolve, and the strength of temperament to relieve his employer of half a million pounds. And the interrogation: he had survived it; in fact, he had actually enjoyed it; a battle of wits, one on one, or, rather, two on one most of the time with the odds stacked against him. But he'd come through in the end. He'd won.

He took a long drink and smiled at Hannah as she picked up the latest Ben Elton novel and settled down for an hour with a book. She went through two or three books a week, mostly crime thrillers with an occasional horror, Stephen King or Trevor Dalton. She'd enthused about the latest Dalton book, 'The Possession Legacy', and, although it wasn't his cup of tea, Hannah had persuaded him to read it. He had been surprised how easy it had been to read. Within a few pages, Bob had found himself actually wandering round the little Welsh hotel that was the focal point in Dalton's book. And the book had actually inspired him. It had encouraged him to invest in an iBook, a small laptop word processor, and to begin writing his own crime thriller. Only this novel wasn't exactly fiction and, of course, it could never be published.

CHAPTER SEVEN

Jenny hadn't been seen for three days now and, even though he hated to admit it, Donavan was a little concerned. The girls that he abused didn't usually stick around the office very long afterwards. On average, a few weeks and then a letter of resignation. A few weeks in the company of the man who had performed unknown depravity on them were just about all they could bear.

Donavan enjoyed those final weeks even more than the actual acts that had preceded them. He would humiliate them every chance he could get and he would enjoy watching their discomfort as they purposely tried to avoid him. But they couldn't avoid him.

His well-planned climax was to send still photos of the acts they had performed directly to their personal e-mail box.

He liked the oral shots best of all. Yeah, those generally worked the best. Nothing like an oral shot to make them pick up the resignation pen and start writing.

Samantha Thompson had lasted the longest, - nearly a month. She'd accidentally opened the first two photos he had sent and Donavan had been fortunate enough to witness the horror on her face each time. He'd keyed in his password, the name of the street of his apartment in Paris, then made himself comfortable and pressed the *send* button.

He watched her working at her laptop across the expanse of the modern open-plan office. A calm face, then a quick flick of the eyes to the bottom of the screen as the computer notified her of the new e-mail. Didn't even look to see who the sender was. It didn't matter anyway. Donavan had keyed it from his home-based e-mail with a name nobody would recognise. Samantha had just taken a mouthful of coffee as the frame appeared on screen. The look of horror on her face as the coffee cup fell to the floor would live with Donavan a long time. He'd viewed the very same image at the same time. Samantha kneeling on all fours, her face a picture of orgasmic contentment, as Donavan thrust into her from behind. Of course, Donavan's face was cleverly just out of shot, always was. And she opened the second image, the standard porn facial shot and Donavan's semen all over her. He couldn't believe that the silly cow could be so stupid again. She deserved everything she got and, sure as night follows day, her resignation letter would be on her boss's desk the following day.

Donavan got wind of her resignation before eleven the next day.

It wasn't the company's policy to make an employee work a standard month's notice. A member of staff could cause unknown damage in a month and even persuade several big clients to jump ship to a rival. Samantha began to clear her desk in the early afternoon. Donavan looked through several still shots of her performance and decided on a particularly humiliating position with an overlarge sex toy. It would be Samantha's farewell present.

He located Kieran Adamson's e-mail address and pressed *send*. Kieran hadn't been with the firm very long, he was eager and had a big mouth. How fortunate for Donavan that he sat at the same workstation as Samantha.

Donavan watched the familiar flick of the eyes, then an expression of delight as Kieran took in the contents of the attachment. "Jesus, lads, someone's sending me porn through on e-mail. Take a look at this talented little filly."

Des and Trevor, two young traders, wandered over to view Kieran's screen. As Samantha looked across at Kieran, the early warning system triggered in her head.

"Shit guys, how on earth does she fit that in there?" bellowed Kieran.

"Yeah, and look at her face, she's really enjoying it." The three young traders started to laugh in unison.

Trevor looked at Samantha and his jaw dropped open. Kieran shook his head and the telephone dropped from Des's hand and clattered onto the heavy oak desk. "Sam…fucking hell, it's …it's you."

Without even viewing the image on screen, Samantha knew exactly what had been sent and who had sent it. She quickly snatched her handbag from the desk and ran across the room, her face a contorted picture of broken emotion. Tears ran down the face of a girl kicked so hard she would never recover. The e-mail would fly round the City like wild fire to colleagues and competitors alike, her dreams and career aspirations shattered beyond repair.

Des walked slowly past Donavan's desk. "You sent it, Don, didn't you? You dated her last month."

Donavan grinned, but didn't answer.

"Jesus, Don, you're a right bastard."

* * * *

Donavan had been asked about Jenny by several of the staff, particularly the younger guys who had wanted to be copied in on all the gory details. Of course Donavan had told them nothing; he didn't have to: a smile and a grin, or an odd wink here and there told a story more graphic than any description ever could.

Donavan revelled in it, but deep down he couldn't understand why Jenny hadn't even called her boss to explain her unauthorised absence.

"You didn't shag her to death, did you, Don?" asked her boss as he passed Donavan's desk. Donavan didn't reply. He tried her mobile phone yet again.

"Hi, this is Jenny. I'm sorry I'm not able to take…" Donavan pressed the red button on the phone.

"Shit, where the hell is she?"

* * * *

Jenny's mind was at peace at last. The half bottle of Bacardi and the hazy thoughts that Donavan Smith could hurt her no more were enough. She lay in the bath, the water a little on the cool side now. She had lost track of how long she had been there.

She reached out for the transparent liquid and prepared to wash down yet another pill. Twenty more stared up at her from a neat line on the side of the bath. She couldn't remember how many she had taken, but figured it must be at least a dozen. She'd taken the first four or five quite quickly, but now the time between each one seemed to be getting a little longer. She'd chewed the last one like a Smartie. Funny, she thought to herself, they had no taste. You'd have thought they would have tasted of something? But the Bacardi, now that did taste of something. Didn't even know if she liked it, but it was certainly doing the trick.

She reached out for another pill and placed it onto her tongue allowing it to melt a little before slugging another mouthful of the harsh white rum. She wondered how many it would take. She'd read somewhere in a magazine that around twenty-five is enough to shut down a major organ. Kidney failure or the liver, wasn't sure which one, or was it a heart attack? She didn't care. She wouldn't know anything about it.

She was certain she'd picked the best way to go. She'd thought about opening the arteries on her wrist with a kitchen knife, but shivered at the thought of the blade slicing through her skin. Jumping from a high-rise building, - how could anyone do that? I mean, it's not as if you can change your mind halfway down.

A half smile crept across her face. Why would anyone want to change their mind? Changing her mind wasn't an option; she didn't want to change her mind; why was she even thinking about it?

She looked at the pattern on the tiles around the bath. They were out of focus now. She held up her hand that contained the glass and struggled to count her fingers. Then the glass slipped from her hand and splashed down into the water. She made no attempt to retrieve it.

She couldn't drive out the graphic images of the sickening video Donavan had forced her to watch. For three days she had tried. And at night, as she slept, she felt sure that at last she would find some peace, some relief from her torture.

No. The nights were worse. Nightmare after nightmare, her mind exaggerating the horrors she had encountered. And trying to get away, running through the Paris streets... naked as the day she was born. Around every corner, the wicked image of Donavan Smith leering, grinning and laughing at her futile attempts to escape. And then capture, dragged through the streets by her hair, closer and closer to that place. His lair.

People looked on. She cried and screamed for help. Why didn't they stop him? It was clear what he was about to do. Why didn't anyone stop him?

She lifted three pills into her mouth and scooped up a handful of bathwater to lubricate her throat.

She had heard the rumours about the mind games he had played with other girls, now long gone from the office. Samantha and an e-mail, total humiliation and a resignation. She couldn't face that, wouldn't give him the satisfaction of his final perversion.

She heard the faint ring tone of the her mobile phone far away in some deep recess of the flat and wondered who could be calling. Her sister perhaps? Or a friend, wondering how the weekend had gone? Should have switched it off. Why didn't she? Who would she want to speak to? Who could help her now? Was it her father? Why hadn't she called him? Why had he let this happen to her, his little girl, his little girl that he swore would never get hurt? Well, she was hurt and he had let her down. She hoped it wouldn't be him that would find her. No, she didn't want that. Especially naked, - not her father who hadn't seen her naked since she was eight years old.

But the suicide note, - that was for him. A few scribbled lines telling him how much she'd loved him, how she'd looked up to him all these years although he probably didn't know it. Yeah, they'd had their differences and, if she were totally honest, she'd put him through hell at times. His little baby.

A few lines tucked away in a bedroom drawer, blaming the job, blaming the pressures of life, but not mentioning the real reason why she was ending her life at such a young age. She couldn't put her father through that sort of mental torture. His little girl raped, violated, abused. No, she couldn't.

What was it he used to say? Don't get mad, get even. Yeah, get even, that was it. And she wanted to get even, wanted to get out of the bath now, wanted to turn the clock back, but she couldn't. Her brain fired a command to her hand. Put it on the side of the bath and lift, push yourself out of here, and put your fingers down your throat. Do it.

But her body wasn't responding. It was shutting down, just like she'd read in the magazine.

It was too late to change her mind. She gave up and slid down, submerged her head under the water. She opened her mouth and the lukewarm bathwater with just a hint of Bacardi flowed into her lungs. Her eyes closed and her final thoughts before she drifted into unconsciousness were of Donavan Smith.

Donavan Smith had won.

CHAPTER EIGHT

Donavan Smith hadn't been this far north before. Why the hell did his company have to send him up to Newcastle for a pissing two-day training seminar? What a waste of time, what a waste of money. What the hell did Newcastle have to offer? Flat caps and whippets, coal and fifty thousand idiots watching a football team that hadn't won anything for fifty years.

The taxi pulled up alongside the Malmaison Hotel on the quayside. The driver muttered something that Donavan struggled to understand, but he registered the seven-pound fare on the meter in front of the car. He handed him a ten-pound note. "Keep the change, buddy, but give me a receipt for twenty."

"Cheers, mate," the taxi driver answered, as he scribbled out a phoney bill. The company never questioned Donavan's expenses. It was a sort of perk, a privilege for the most respected senior trader they had.

A concierge, dressed in a vivid blue jacket that looked ridiculously over big, opened the door for Donavan and touched his hat as he walked through. That's right, thought Donavan, know your place.

He stopped and turned back round to face the doorman. "Where's the action happen in this godforsaken city?"

"How do you mean, sir?"

Donavan sighed. "The action, the nightlife, you know the pubs and clubs, the pretty girls."

The doorman smiled. "Right here, sir, right here on the famous quayside."

Donavan gave him a look of confusion. "Well, it can't be that famous, I've never heard of it."

"Are you from London, sir?"

"Yeah, but what the hell's that got to do with it?"

The man's tone changed a little and Donavan struggled to understand the broad Northumbrian accent. "I'm not surprised you've never heard of it. You Londoners' heads are stuck so far up your arses."

Donavan raised his eyebrows, convinced he had heard the doorman curse. "What did you say?"

The doorman flicked back into Queen's English mode and slowed his speech down. "I said, sir, many a Londoner's changed their mind about Newcastle after a quayside night out."

Donavan frowned. "I hope you're right."

The doorman doffed his hat again and Donavan walked over to reception to check-in.

Within half an hour, he had showered and changed and made his way back downstairs. He walked towards the concierge.

"Other way, sir," he instructed, pointing back across reception. "Take the rear entrance, that takes you straight out to the quayside. Try the Pitcher and Piano first, a real nice bar, and then back here around nine, tennish if you like. Our bar busies up then."

"Cheers," replied Donavan, "I will."

He walked into the Pitcher and Piano and was pleasantly surprised. He'd expected a sort of dingy, old-fashioned dockside hostelry, with perhaps a little sawdust on the floor. Instead, the bar was elegantly furnished with plush leather sofas and highly polished solid marble tables, and tastefully decorated throughout. Must have cost a fortune, he thought to himself. Even better, thought Donavan, as his eyes took in the full picture of the room and the clientele. He couldn't quite believe it. There were more ladies drinking in the bar than men. That just didn't happen in London.

Several all-female groups stood or sat around, drinking from overlarge wine glasses. And their clothes, Jesus, their clothes:

little short skirts and dresses, vest tops and thin blouses, and not a coat to be seen. Where were their jackets on this cool autumn evening? Everything they wore seemed to be at least an inch or two shorter than their southern counterparts.

Perhaps Newcastle might not be so bad, he thought to himself, as he sidled over to the long black granite counter.

He ordered a bottle of Budweiser and sat down on a highbacked plastic stool overlooking the River Tyne. The view of the river was spectacular and Donavan marvelled at the huge Tyne Bridge that he hadn't noticed from the train as it had crossed the old Victorian railway bridge a few hours earlier.

Never one to hang on a nice view too long, his gaze returned to the bar area once again and, in particular, to one elegant-looking blonde lady that Donavan noticed was looking at her watch a little too often.

He needed his fix again. The weekend in Paris and the satisfying debauchery-filled evening seemed a million years ago. Damn… where the hell had Jenny got to, why hadn't she turned into work? The still frames of her exploits had been selected and sat patiently in a coded folder on his laptop.

The final humiliation, the pièce-de-résistance. How he enjoyed that moment. His erection would burst into life as soon as he keyed the *send* button.

Never mind, plenty more fish in the sea, as his old grandfather used to say, and Donavan was confident that a nervous-looking lady over the other side of the room was just about to take the bait.

"Donavan Smith," he announced, his hand of friendship extended towards the stranger. "I couldn't help noticing your watch. You can't take your eyes off it."

She gave a hesitant half smile. "I'm waiting for someone. She's just a little late."

Donavan smiled at her, taking in and enjoying the close-up shot. A little older than he normally preferred, probably early thirties, but nevertheless easy on the eye with a finely toned figure that she carried well. "How about a drink while you wait?"

The lady lifted her full glass. "I'm fine, thanks, as you can see. She shouldn't be too long."

"Mind if I join you then. You can tell me a little bit about Newcastle. I've never been here before."

"If you insist… though she'll be here in a few minutes and you'll be looking for a new pickup."

Donavan grinned, pulled up a bar stool and made himself comfortable. There's no fuckin' 'she' he thought to himself. She was a poor actress. Unless Donavan was mistaken, and he very rarely was, this girl was looking for a date or even her next client. "I didn't catch your name."

"I didn't tell you it." She paused deliberately and took a sip from the glass. She fiddled with her hair and Donavan waited. One of her long slender fingers gently traced and smoothed an eyebrow and Donavan purred quietly with satisfaction.

The body language was good. He considered himself an expert, and this was definitely one of the female species grooming herself for her next mate. No crossed arms, no frowns or negativity; every signal this girl threw at Donavan Smith was encouraging.

Twenty minutes after Donavan took his seat, she left to make a phone call. She returned with a disappointed look on her face. "Yeah, I've been stood up. Stuck on a train at Darlington, she is. I'd better be going."

"I don't understand. If you've been stood up, why do you have to go?"

She drained the last of her drink "Work, that's why…money. I'm a croupier at Aspers' Casino. £200 a shift, they pay well. My colleague stuck at Darlington usually joins me for a few drinks before we start."

Donavan raised his eyebrows but remained silent and composed. She looked at her watch. "I've time for one more, but then I really will have to go."

Donavan caught the barman's attention, embarrassed at the lady's acting ability.

Twenty minutes later, she stood up to leave. "I really must go now." She looked a little uneasy. "It's a little embarrassing, but I really do need the money."

Donavan went through the formalities he had been through so many times before: the sob story, a woman scorned generally, but this time an exaggerated tale of a widow and a husband and a bank raid. Donavan knew a prostitute when he saw one and yet... and yet this lady of the night was a little different. Donavan sensed some truth in what she was telling him. He was curious and puzzled about how much of this woman was genuine.

Donavan found himself talking too. Normally he kept his private life exactly that and yet he found her very easy to talk too. For once, his brain wasn't forming the usual cunning sexual plan. "I still don't know your name."

"Vicky, Vicky Mackenzie."

Vicky Mackenzie found herself strangely attracted to her new client-to-be. He had agreed to replace her evening's wages, though he hadn't approached the question of spending the night with her, and the suggestion of sex hadn't even been touched upon. She supposed it would rear its ugly head within the hour.

He was certainly very attractive, if not a little over confident. This city trader from London seemed very interested in her past and she found herself blurting out the story of her ex-husband and the missing money and the bank's refusal to pay out the death in service benefit and pension.

"So that's why you need to work?" Donavan asked.

Vicky nodded her head. "Yeah, unfortunately. What I need is a little lottery win or a millionaire knight on a silver charger sweeping me off my feet."

Donavan laughed. "You and me both."

Vicky looked at him curiously. "Not you, surely? You've a great job in the City, a Ferrari and a house in the South of France."

"And an apartment in Paris."

Vicky choked on her wine. "An apartment in Paris as well? Good God, Donavan, you're absolutely bloody minted."

"Not exactly, Vicky. You see, I'm asset rich but cash poor and the oldest trader on the floor of the City… my days are numbered, two years at the most and then I'm out on my arse with a pension that won't even cover my petrol bill." He took a mouthful of beer from the bottle and smiled gently at her.

Then he shrugged. "Otherwise, I may just have been your knight."

Vicky tingled inwardly and tried to fight the thoughts and feelings coming into her head. She imagined Donavan Smith whisking her away from this lifestyle that she was beginning to tire of. She imagined spending her days flitting between Cannes and Paris, with an occasional weekend in Newcastle. There was something curious about the man, something mysterious, and she wanted to get into his head. He had secrets… yeah, he definitely had secrets, something he wasn't telling her. He had a dark side, she was sure of it.

"So, how did you know about this bank raid? Was it in the papers or did your husband tell you about it before he died?"

"Good God, no! He never told me anything, and the bank certainly didn't want to broadcast how easily they'd been duped. Apparently, some disgruntled employee staged the whole thing."

Donavan looked on intently, hanging on every word.

"Quite simple really. I'm amazed no one had ever thought of it before. A few weeks earlier, the bank next door had a raid for real. A young girl was gunned down, killed, shook the staff up big time. Several days later, maybe a week or two, an e-mail was sent to my husband's bank telling each member of staff that there would be an exercise staged. Everyone thought it was a good idea, a sort of mock bank raid to gauge the staff's reaction to the real thing. The e-mail informed them that actors would be used and that they should try to imagine themselves in a real time robbery."

Donavan whistled. "I think I know what's coming next."

Vicky nodded and took another mouthful of wine, eager to continue now that she was in full flow. "Yeah, I think you do. The employee was the actor; only he wasn't an actor, if you know what I mean. He walked into the branch and cleverly gained access to the secure area. So simple really. He just walked in and walked out with hundreds of thousands of pounds and nobody lifted a finger to stop him."

"Why should they," answered Donavan. "They thought it was just a training exercise. Brilliant...absolutely   brilliant."

"Exactly."

"And, of course, the money never came back."

Vicky took another large mouthful, acutely aware that her alcohol intake was way above her normal limit. "My husband deteriorated by the day, couldn't handle it. He was the man at the top, the buck stopped with him. He was even interviewed as a suspect."

"But it wasn't him?"

"Good Lord, no. He couldn't have dreamed up something that clever, let alone have the balls to carry it through. And, by all accounts, he didn't know about it, didn't even know about the exercise, had skipped over the e-mail." Vicky smiled and then felt guilty at the humour she was feeling at her late husbands expense. "He got caught up in the events, thought it was for real. He... "

Donavan raised his eyebrows over his bottle.

"He pissed himself. I had to take a clean suit in for him."

She regretted telling Donavan instantly and wondered whether her approval rating had gone down a notch or two with the stranger from London.

She needn't have worried. Donavan wanted more of this fascinating little episode and Vicky positively basked in her ability to command his attention.

"So who was it?"

Vicky hesitated and nervously pawed at her glass. She didn't know whether she wanted to continue with the next bit of the story.

"I'm... " she stopped in mid sentence, "...not sure really."

Donavan took her hand gently. "Look, if this is too hard for you, we can change the subject."

The touch of Donavan made her tingle all over. A shiver ran

the length of her spine and an overwhelming feeling of faith welled through her body. She trusted this man, wanted to share her great secret with him and wanted to unburden herself of the guilt and deceit she had harboured since finding her late husband's diaries. "No, it's okay, I want to tell you."

Donavan Smith seemed to sense the enormity of what was about to be disclosed and ordered two large gins. Vicky didn't object. The barman returned after a few minutes and Vicky picked up the glass and took in half the alcohol without stopping for breath. "I found a diary."

"A diary?"

"Three actually. Three diaries spanning the last three years of his life. Detailed diaries of every movement he had ever made within the last three years. Boring, mundane stuff mostly, work-related, targets and goals, his thoughts and dreams and an occasional mention of me."

Donavan sat on the edge of his seat, and Vicky enjoyed the way her dramatic account captivated him.

"Boring stuff, Don…that is until the last thirty or so pages."

"Go on."

"Look, I'm not sure if I can tell you this… I mean I hardly know you." Suddenly she was getting second thoughts.

Donavan took both hands in his and stared into her eyes. It was a hypnotic stare, a soothing stare, and Vicky's pupils dilated. He seemed to take an age to speak and whatever it was he was about to say, Vicky knew she would divulge every last detail of the diary this man wanted to hear.

Donavan sat spellbound as Vicky took him through her recollections of every page. She explained the suspicions and gossip flying round the bank and the investigations and interviews that followed. "No one was ever charged. My husband was killed following the man he thought was behind the whole thing."

Donavan sat fascinated, or at least that's what Vicky thought it was. There was more going on in his head. It was more than fascination. She almost expected him to take out a pad and pencil and begin taking notes.

"Your husband was killed?"

Vicky nodded slowly. "Shot…shot dead."

"Jesus Christ, Vicky, so why haven't they charged this guy? He shot your husband, for Christ's sake!"

Vicky paused again and took a substantial mouthful of gin. She waited until it had the desired calming effect and then continued. "Not quite as easy as that, Don. You see it was my husband's gun. He was following this guy that had ruined everything. He was following the guy that he was convinced had done it."

Donavan shook his head in disbelief.

"My husband had lost his job, lost his pride and his professional respect that he had taken thirty years to build up." Vicky surprised herself at how unemotional she felt painting the sad picture of her late husband's demise. "In the end I think he just lost it, couldn't handle it any more, needed to make this man pay for what he'd done."

"Where's this man now?"

"Bob Heggie…?"

"That's his name?"

"Yeah. No one really knows. He disappeared abroad after a few months. Nobody's heard from him since."

"This, er... Bob Heggie, Vic, your husband was convinced it was him?"

Vicky smiled; she liked being called Vic; it reminded her of someone she loved from way back… he started called her Vic after a few months. Now, here was this stranger using it after a few hours, only Vicky didn't feel he was a stranger any more.

"My husband was absolutely convinced. The diary portrays the events and his suspicions and Bob Heggie's exact movements before, during and after the raid. John… my late husband, deduced that he was the only person that could have done it. He timed the raid out exactly and this Bob Heggie character appears in exactly the right place at exactly the right time and mysteriously disappeared off the face of the planet for half an hour when all this shit took place."

Donavan leaned back onto the barstool. Vicky looked deep

into his eyes. "There's more."

Donavan leaned forward, as if realising Vicky's tones would be even quieter than they had gradually become. Almost a whisper now, Vicky continued, "The thing is, John reckoned he didn't even spend the money."

Donavan sat back and gasped. "Surely not, I mean what's the point of taking that sort of risk if you're not going to enjoy the spoils."

"I know… I know, only the diary says John followed him not once but twice to the lockers in Newcastle Central Station. It was as if he knew he was being followed, couldn't go through with it, bottled it on both occasions."

Vicky and Donavan sat in silence for at least two minutes. Donavan couldn't comprehend the enormity of what he'd just been told and Vicky Mackenzie felt as if a huge weight had been lifted from her shoulders. For the first time in months, she felt at ease with the world.

Donavan broke the silence. "Vicky."

"Yes."

"Any chance of seeing that diary?"

Vicky sat back confidently. "And why would I want to do that?"

"Because I have a retirement plan for both of us."

And, for once, Donavan Smith wasn't play-acting.

CHAPTER NINE

A mixture of lukewarm water, Bacardi, stomach acids and putrefied sleeping pills spewed up through the bathwater creating a torrent of foul brown liquid Jenny couldn't control or direct. At the same time, her lungs seemed to scream out in ecstasy as the oxygen, denied to them for so long, was gulped in. She sat bolt upright, jerking and shivering, yet at the same time praising and thanking a God she didn't believe in for sparing her life. But she was tired - so, so, tired.

She hauled herself from the bath, her legs giving way as soon as she touched the slippery floor. She crawled through to the kitchen on her hands and knees, the sweat dripping from her chin, her body craving liquid relief. With all the strength left in her, she pulled open the fridge door and located a litre of ice-cold orange juice. Mouthful after mouthful, she gulped greedily at the freezing cold liquid until once again the familiar spasms started in the pit of her stomach.

She collapsed onto the cold tiles and looked up at the ceiling. Her back arched and her mouth opened accepting the inevitable. She gagged as the citrus mixture burned the back of her throat. Onto her side now, the vomit exploded across the shiny surface forming a stinking orange oil slick, her hair wrapped around her face trailing in the polluted pool. The slightly uneven angle of the floor surface turned the foul liquid lagoon back towards where she lay. She watched on helplessly as it slowly flowed towards her naked form.

Colder now than she'd ever been before, she lay on the cold tiled surface surrounded by the stinking, freezing liquid. She focused on the scribbled suicide note sitting on top of the bathroom chair. She shivered violently, as helpless as a newborn, and her mind thought only of revenge. She pictured her favourite image of the man who had never failed her. *Get even*.

CHAPTER TEN

The last thing Donavan Smith expected to see was Jenny McArthur sitting at her desk tapping away at a keyboard twenty minutes before her starting time of eight thirty.

A little hesitant, he approached her desk and she looked up as his image blocked the natural light from the large window overlooking the busy London street several storeys below.

"Jenny?"

"Don! How are you?"

"Errr… I should be asking you that. No one's heard from you for a week."

"Three days actually, Don. I called in last Thursday, My young sister had a bit of an accident, had to head north. Anyway, all's well that ends well. She's okay now and I'm making up for lost time. Loads to do, I'm afraid, no time to talk."

Jenny's gaze returned to her computer screen and Donavan Smith reluctantly walked towards the cloakroom, slowly unbuttoning his long leather overcoat. Not the normal reaction of his victims, he thought to himself: over confident and far too relaxed and composed… something wasn't quite right.

Donavan sat down at his computer, a little preoccupied with memories of the weekend and his terrific sexual encounter with Vicky Mackenzie. His head filled with the mixed-up thoughts of where his life was going. He keyed in his password and a virus warning flashed across his screen.

He had never seen that before; couldn't understand it; the firm's computers were protected by some sort of firewall. His eyes flicked across the desk at Jenny. She didn't look up. There was no emotion, no change in the expression etched across her face.

Donavan attempted to bypass the warning and get into the backup that would allow him to access his previous week's work and a summary of his up to date position and pending trades. *Access denied* flashed across the screen followed by a further instruction to close his computer down immediately.

"Fuck it," he cursed out loud, annoyed at his limited knowledge of how to bypass a computer virus.

Just then his boss, Mick Grybowski, called to him from his office. "Don, what's up with your computer? The system's showing a problem."

Donavan stood up and walked over to the doorway. "I don't know, Mick. It's just telling me to close down, some sort of virus."

"We've a firewall installed, Don; it can't be a virus. Unless you've manually loaded anything on, that is, which as you know is strictly forbidden for that very reason."

Donavan thought about the shots of Jenny, but knew they were clean and free from any bugs. Samantha's images, together with a few others, were long gone. "Nothing, Mick… I've loaded nothing onto it. I was away most of last week in Newcastle, remember."

"Yeah, okay… I'll call Pete Minto in I.T. He'll sort it out, I'm sure. He'll bring a spare laptop down too. You can work from that." Grybowski picked up the telephone and punched in the number of the I.T. Department.

Donavan wandered back through and sat at his desk, unsure of what to do next. He realised how much he actually depended on the little plastic case that no longer sat in front of him. He couldn't quite figure out why, but he had a nasty feeling about this, something just wasn't quite right. The only foreign files on the computer were the images of Jenny but they were clean and yet… and yet his laptop had sat exposed for three days last week. A horrifying thought crept into his mind, but he quickly pushed it aside.

Donavan bluffed and blagged his way through the morning trading session, annoyed with his performance and bitterly disappointed with his results. It was happening a little too often these days; a little problem; a disagreement with a colleague; or too many sugars in his coffee. The little things never used to bother him, never affected his performance. Now... now it was different. "Shit," he cursed out loud, perhaps they were right, perhaps it was a young man's game.

Someone screamed at him from across the trading floor. "Don! Don! C'mon, think, get with it, man!"

But Donavan Smith wasn't on the trading floor, Donavan Smith was back in Newcastle with Vicky Mackenzie, Donavan Smith was thinking about *that* diary and the money and Bob Heggie and a retirement plan. Donavan Smith was even thinking about settling down and retiring with Vicky Mackenzie.

"Don, for fuck's sake... get with it."

Donavan looked across at his irate colleague. He slipped his middle finger in between his lips, pulled it free and thrust the glistening digit upwards in the direction of his astonished workmate.

Fuck you too, he mouthed back at Donavan.

Perhaps it really was time to go, he thought to himself.

For the rest of the week, Donavan religiously telephoned Pete Minto two or three times a day, begging for his laptop. On Friday afternoon, Pete promised him it would be on his desk by Monday morning.

* * * *

On Monday morning, Donavan got off the tube two stops early. He'd lost the will to be the first trader in now. He used to enjoy that feeling. Collecting the pink paper from the old man on the corner and walking into the office as the cleaners left. Jenny had picked up that mantle now by all accounts.

Mick had arrived for an early start on Friday and was amazed that Jenny was already at her desk and onto her second cup of espresso.

"She'll go far that one," Mick had commented. "A real good grafter and good results too!"

"Not if I can help it," Donavan muttered under his breath. "I'll give her a week."

And this was the week. True to his word, Pete Minto would have sorted out the problems on his laptop over the weekend. And then Donavan Smith would have some fun.

Donavan pulled up his coat collar and cursed the polluted London drizzle that soaked him right through. He began to wonder whether getting off the train early had been such a good idea.

His walking pace slowed as he turned into Vauxhall Bridge Road. This was one of his favourite streets in London, even on a day such as this. He took his time and lingered. He picked up the FT from a streetseller hiding inside the tube station, his paper income protected from the elements.

He ambled further down Vauxhall Bridge Road, almost at the end now, and still he didn't want to rush into the office. He walked on further, crossed a couple of busy thoroughfares. He hesitated as he stood outside the entrance to the London Stock Exchange. The doorman recognised him and opened the door. He wanted to move, but found himself rooted to the spot. His shoes felt as if they were cemented to the damp pavement.

He looked up the street over his right shoulder. The *Costa Coffee* sign protruded out, inviting him in, begging him to put off the working day just a little longer. His feet turned forty-five degrees, no longer fixed in place. Something was wrong. Something was stopping Donavan Smith from taking those oh so familiar steps into work.

Donavan lifted a steaming hot latte to his lips and congratulated himself on his decision, as the coffee lingered on his tongue and played with his taste buds. He was kidding himself. What the fuck was stopping him from going to work? Was it Mick Grybowski? Yeah, he'd had a few digs lately. Just his way, Don thought; just his way to try and get that extra pound of flesh, a few extra points on the board. Yeah - Mick. That was it. Or was it? Had he reached the crossroads? The older traders had told him all about the crossroads syndrome. One day you had it: the desire, the passion and the ability; then twenty-four hours later…. nothing.

The crossroads they called it, - had Donavan Smith hit the crossroads?

Bollocks! He was as good as any man on the floor and wasn't ready to take the route into training or management for a fraction of the salary… yet.

Or was it Jenny?

He couldn't get his head around her behaviour. It wasn't normal, wasn't par for the course. She was acting as if nothing had happened.

He stood up, poured the last of the latte down his throat and shuddered at the instant kick the caffeine gave him. It was all he needed. He picked up the paper, smiled, and walked quickly into the street.

The doorman greeted him again and he entered through the huge bombproof plate glass door. He took the lift to the seventh floor. The doors opened and the caffeine kick faded. The lead was back into his legs and the cement had set again on the soles of his shoes.

Jenny looked up.   He caught her gaze.   She smiled. *She shouldn't be smiling*

He wanted to take a step, but couldn't. Just then, Mick Grybowski rescued him. "Don, can I have a word please?"

Never was Donavan Smith so pleased to be summoned into his boss's office. "My laptop, thank Christ for that," he said as he spied his personalised machine sitting in the middle of the desk. "Shit, I didn't think I would miss it so much. I mean, that spare machine's good but you kinda get attached…."

Donavan hadn't been interrupted, but he'd noticed the expression on his boss's face. It was an expression he'd never seen before: sort of an apologetic look, crossed with the sort of look his old headmaster used to give him after Donavan had beaten up the schoolyard weakling for the fourth time that week.

Donavan Smith was about to get the cane.

He reached across the desk for the computer. "Is it charged?"

What a stupid thing to say, he thought, as soon as he'd said it. His hand lay on top of the grey casing as he attempted to pull it towards himself. Mick's hand grabbed the other side, preventing him from doing so.

"I'm sorry, Don, that laptop's going nowhere."

Donavan paused. "Sorry, Mick? What do you mean?"

Mick's face tightened in a grimace. The fingers of his right hand toyed with his eyebrow and his left hand played nervously with his Mont Blanc silver fountain pen.

"Mick, what's up?"

Mick sighed. "What's up, Don? What's up? We've had your laptop for nearly a week now. Why don't you tell me what's up? The guys in I.T. had to go into every crevice, every nook and cranny looking for something that might have infected your bloody machine. Why don't you tell me what they found? Tell me what it was that you loaded. Go on, tell me."

Donavan Smith smiled. "Just a bit of harmless fun, Mick."

"Harmless fun, Don," Mick shouted, "harmless fun! Is that what you call it? I'll tell you what I call it, shall I? I call it filth; I call it something that a sick fucking pervert would play around with; I call it something that should be printed off and placed in the hands of the Old Bill."

Donavan squirmed in his seat. He could feel his colleagues outside taking notice, peering into the glass-fronted office, and he regretted leaving the office door a few inches ajar.

Mick was overreacting. Donavan always thought he was one of the boys: he liked a laugh, liked a joke at the expense of someone else, enjoyed a drink as much as the next man. Why was he getting hung up about three or four photos?

"Look, Mick, I don't know what you're getting so heated up about. The images were clean. They're on my laptop at home and that's fine. The problem's not with my—"

"I couldn't give a flying fuck about the virus, Don. That's not why you're here."

"Mick, it's just a little porn. We've all seen that sort of thing before."

Grybowski rose to his feet, his cheeks flushed with anger. He walked around to Donavan's side of the desk and closed the office door. His face had reddened further by the time he returned to his seat.

"You're sacked, Donavan."

Donavan sat bolt upright. "What… I don't understand."

He couldn't believe what he was hearing.

"What don't you understand, you're sacked … sacked, fired, dismissed, you're out of here by lunchtime. Clear your desk. Three months' salary has been paid into your bank, but you don't need to work the time. Don't come back. I don't want to ever see your sick face again."

It was Donavan Smith's turn to stand up and get angry. "You've lost your fucking head, Mick. You can't do this to me just because you've found a few porn images on my laptop. I mean, how do you even know it was me that loaded them on?"

Grybowski stood up again and the two men stood nose to nose. "Because you've just admitted it, you daft twat. A bit of harmless fun you said. Now get out."

Donavan hated that word, 'twat'. It was a word that annoyed him. His older cousin, who had lived along the street from him, discovered it at an early age and used it in her armoury when she wanted to wind him up. It inevitably led to Donavan lashing out, but, being three years younger than her, he generally ended up the loser, with an even more severe beating from his mother.

"Don't call me that, Mick, … please don't call me that." Donavan felt an anger building like he had never felt before. He was acutely aware that every worker on the floor couldn't keep their eyes off the proceedings developing inside Michael Grybowski's lavish office.

Donavan reached across and gently took a hold of his tie. "What's up, Mick, can't you get it up anymore? Are you jealous of me? Is that it, a bit jealous of my manhood, is that it?"

Mick Grybowski fell back into his seat, but Donavan still held on to his tie.

"You mean… you're in those… pictures… you?"

Donavan grinned. "Yeah, I'm a bit of a natural, should have been a porn star."

Grybowski's decibel level dropped and the words barely slipped from his lips. "You sick twat."

Donavan's right arm had already started the involuntary movement. He had no control, it was a natural reflex. His fist clenched as his arm propelled forward and he connected perfectly with the bridge of Mick Grybowski's nose. He felt the bone tissue collapse as his fist followed through and Grybowski squealed as the force of the punch knocked him from the chair. Donavan looked across at a thick streak of blood covering the glass panel. His focus changed and he now looked through at his shocked and startled colleagues, who stood rooted to the spot, mouths open, unable to believe the events they had just witnessed. All, that is, except one.

Jenny McArthur stared straight through the blood-spattered glass. Their eyes fixed on one another. She was smiling, she was grinning, almost laughing, and she was laughing at Donavan Smith's expense. He suddenly realised that Mick Grybowski hadn't been talking about a few porno images. Something else had been uploaded, something he knew nothing about.

The office door crashed open and big Jimmy Mulligan pushed Donavan into the far corner. "For Christ's sake, Don, what have you done?"

Almost on cue, the broken form of Mick Grybowski pulled himself back onto his chair. "I'll see you never work in the City again, you fucking paedophile."

Donavan froze as the word registered. No, not that word, he wasn't into that.

Grybowski picked up the phone. "Security please! Up here immediately, there's a pervert that needs to leave the building."

Jimmy Mulligan spoke. "What did you say, Mick?"

Grybowski pointed a finger at Donavan. Donavan wanted to defend himself, but the words wouldn't come. "Our man here, Jimmy, is a child sex porn star. He admitted everything. I.T.

found the most depraved images imaginable on his laptop."

Donavan shook his head, but still the words wouldn't come.

"Quite proud of the fact too. Ask him."

Jimmy Mulligan looked directly at Donavan. "Tell me it's not true, Don."

But Donavan Smith hadn't heard. He looked back through the glass at Jenny McArthur. She nodded her head three times and Donavan immediately realised what it meant.

He still hadn't spoken by the time two burly security guards arrived.

"Take his pass key and ID away from him and escort him outside. Make sure he never sets foot in here again."

Donavan, flanked by the security guards, walked back through the office in the direction of the lift. He stopped at Jenny's desk, leaned over towards her and whispered quietly, "You. It was you. You've finished me."

Jenny smiled, a confident smile. Too confident, Donavan thought. "Finished, Don? No, not me."

She grinned at him and edged a little closer. "I haven't even started."

* * * *

Donavan got off the tube at Swiss Cottage. His head was full of bitterness and hatred as he walked towards Belsize Park. He crossed College Crescent and turned right into Buckland Crescent and lingered on the corner, wondering whether to call in at his local bar to drown his sorrows.

He looked at his watch. A little too early, he thought, and he pushed any idea of alcohol right out of his head. He needed to be focused.

He sighed in frustration. It was no use going back into work to plead his case; in fact, he wouldn't even be allowed in the building again. And yet, he was looking further ahead. He didn't want to go back. It was a kind of sign, and, for as long as Donavan could remember, he'd believed that things always happened for a reason. Perhaps this was his chance. His big chance to leave the industry he'd tired of. Yeah, that was it, he thought to himself, a chance. And he thought of Vicky and that diary, and half a million pounds, and how he could get his hands on it.

Smiling now, he turned and walked towards the large apartment block with spectacular views over the city. His gaze rose upwards and he smiled as he focused on his penthouse at the top of the building. He'd cheer himself up in a little while: a nice cup of tea, and perhaps one of his special screenings on the 72-inch plasma TV that almost covered his wall. And the Dolby sound, - oh how he adored the Dolby surround sound system. In fact, he was getting hard just thinking about it. Jenny probably. *Passion in Paris* he had written on the memory card. He laughed out loud. Yeah... Jenny and Paris.

And there were others, many others. Samantha was another of his favourites and Carol and Leanne. And Kay... yes, perhaps he would watch Kay; after all, he would never set eyes on Kay again. She hadn't run away abroad or to another part of the country. It was her own fault. She had had to go, should have kept her mouth shut.

"Early finish, Mr Smith?" the uniformed security guard asked as Donavan entered the hallway of number 19 Belsize Square.

"Yeah, Fred, something like that."

He took the lift to the sixth level and walked out onto the marbled landing. He checked his breast pocket for his keys.

"Shit. Where the hell did I put them?" he mumbled to himself, as he tried another pocket. He took his coat off and checked every pocket. He cursed again, wondering why the hell manufacturers designed coats with six or seven pockets. After checking all of the pockets at least three times, he pressed the *call* button on the lift and went back down to ground level.

"Lost my fucking keys, Fred, give me the spare, will you? I'll get some more cut tomorrow."

The doorman fingered a key on the silver chain hanging from his trousers and opened a metal cabinet on the wall. He handed Donavan the spare key. Donavan thanked him and wandered back over to the lift.

He thought back to his movements of the day. Where on earth could he have lost them? Had they been pickpocketed on the tube?

Then he remembered dragging his coat along the floor as he was unceremoniously escorted from his office. Must have fallen out onto the floor, he thought. Yeah, that's when I lost them.

CHAPTER ELEVEN

Vicky Mackenzie was a little surprised to take the phone call from Donavan Smith. Sure, she knew the evening had gone well, and he was the first man she had really felt comfortable with since the death of her husband. She'd poured her heart out to him and disclosed things she'd never dreamed she would. And he'd been so attentive and interested in everything she'd had to say. And the diary. Boy, had he been interested in that. She really did need to get her late husband's diary out again, needed to go over it, see if there was anything she'd missed.

She'd thought about Donavan ever since and wondered if he'd call. Wondered if he'd only been interested in the one thing she'd given him later that evening. They'd made love so many times she'd lost count. Anything went, and she couldn't quite remember a night when her lovemaking had been so satisfying.

Of course, he had said he would call, but then they all did, especially the out-of-towners. But it just never happened. They normally scuttled back to their frumpy, prim and proper, frigid, middle-class wives, never to be heard of again. Why else would they by banging away at a total stranger?

But Donavan was different. She was sure of it, and when she'd heard his familiar tone again on her mobile phone, she'd shaken like a love struck teenager. He'd taken a few days off work and wanted to spend some time in Newcastle, some time with her. She couldn't quite believe it.

"I'll book into the Malmaison again."

"You will not, Don, you'll stay with me." And, just for a split second, she regretted the impulsive words that came from her lips. Just for a second, and then the moment passed.

She drove her new, bright yellow Audi TT into Newcastle Central Station. She looked at her watch. *Shit, twenty minutes early*; nothing like playing it cool. She wandered through to the concourse and checked the arrivals board. The 18.22 from King's Cross was bang on time.

She looked around and walked over to the Station Bistro. Station Bistro, that's a laugh, she thought to herself. They could have thought of something a little more original. Never mind, it'll be fine for a quick caffeine fix. Or perhaps something a little stronger, she thought, as she stood at the counter.

"Can I help you, madam?"

"Errr, yeah, a black cof.... sorry, a straight brandy please, plenty of ice."

"Coming up, madam. Take a seat and I'll bring it to the table."

Oh well, she thought, at least that's a little continental.

The young waiter brought the brandy over and Vicky looked at her watch. Ten minutes to go. Her heart fluttered as she downed the brandy in one. Immediately she regretted it as the harshness of the poor quality brandy clawed at the back of her throat making her gasp. The ice cubes eased the burning sensation and she gulped in mouthful after mouthful of stale air mixed with the tobacco smoke that lingered on the concourse. Desperate nicotine addicts lighting up as soon as they stepped off their non-smoking trains.

She coughed gently, cursing the smokers and wished the whole damn city would become a non-smoking zone. They'd done it in New York, why not Newcastle?

The alcohol kicked in, giving her the artificial courage she required, and, a few minutes later, she dropped a tic-tac onto her tongue and made her way over the bridge to Platform Eleven.

She stood at the very end of the platform and gazed southwards across the old Victorian railway bridge. The station tannoy kicked in and announced the imminent arrival of the 15.17 from King's Cross, expected arrival time 18.22.

The train rumbled at a snail's pace into the station, and Vicky walked towards the footbridge as the driver applied the brakes and a piercing, screeching noise filled the whole station.

She stood at the bottom of the footbridge, sure she would recognise the man she'd last seen only a week ago. She didn't have a picture of him, and the wine had flowed freely on the one and only night she'd seen him, but she was still fairly sure. Or was she? She began to doubt herself as scores of passengers rushed past her onto the bridge.

She needn't have worried.

"Hi, Vicky, how are you?" Donavan Smith stood directly in front of her and for a split second she was back in the school playground on her first date. She felt the blood rush into her cheeks.

"Donavan, lovely to see you again."

He smiled at her. "You too. I guess I've missed you a little bit."

Vicky laughed.

He leaned forward and kissed her gently on the lips. She responded and instinctively wrapped her arms around him. Only when she felt that everyone was staring at her did she gently push him away.

"Shit, Don, we're behaving like teenagers. Let's get home."

"Yeah, good idea."

Vicky powered the Audi out of the station and joined the Newcastle rush hour.

"God, I hate this traffic, Don. You should have got a later train, given this lot a chance to get home."

"Traffic," he laughed, "you can't even spell it. You want to live in London; then you'd really know what traffic was."

"No thanks, Don, I'm quite happy here."

"Really? You like it up here in Newcastle? Wouldn't you rather be somewhere else, the south of France or the Canary

Islands, somewhere like that?"

Vicky signalled and turned left onto the Newcastle Central Motorway. She pressed the accelerator pedal hard to the floor and felt good as the g force pushed her back into the seat. "Wouldn't we all, Don, wouldn't we all? But there's fat chance of that. It's a pipedream, nothing more than that."

Donavan Smith didn't answer.

Vicky gazed across at him, taking her eyes from the road for a split second. She was puzzled. Donavan Smith was staring straight ahead into the dark Newcastle night as if mesmerised by the taillights of the cars in front. And he was smiling. "What is it, Don, what you are laughing at?"

"I'm not laughing, Vicky. I'm thinking. I'm thinking of a way that you and I can fulfill our dreams."

Fifteen minutes later, the yellow Audi pulled into the drive of Number 12 Western Way.

"Wow, Vicky, this is impressive! It must be worth a   fortune. Any mortgage on it?"

"Jesus, Don, there's nothing like being forward. But no, there isn't a mortgage on it. It was paid off when John passed away, some sort of protection insurance he'd arranged through the bank."

" It must be worth £600,000, at least."

Vicky turned towards him as she pulled on the handbrake and took the keys from the ignition. "Not a bad guess, a little bit more actually," she replied. "Come on, get your bag and I'll show you around."

Donavan leant over and grabbed his leather jacket and an overnight bag from the back of the car. "I can't wait."

And Vicky couldn't wait either. She couldn't wait to show her new man around her house. She couldn't wait to sit down with him, just the two of them and share an intimate meal that she'd cooked earlier on in the day. And she couldn't wait to show him the bedroom he would be sharing with her later that evening.

Before Donavan had a chance to put down his bag, Vicky grabbed his hand and led him towards the staircase. "I'll show you your room," she said, with a grin on her face.

Donavan didn't answer and she started climbing the stairs. She was all too aware that Donavan's eyes would be focused on the slender shape of her backside and she'd deliberately chosen the tightest Levi's she possessed for that very reason. They reached the top of the stairs and, still hand in hand, Vicky led him along the long passageway to the bedroom she once shared with her late husband. As she entered the room, she felt a momentary pang of guilt. But the moment soon passed.

"You're sleeping here, Don, will that be okay?"

Donavan turned her around and pulled her towards him. She could smell his breath, his aftershave, his natural musky body aroma and she wanted him. "Just as long as you're going to be here with me."

Vicky stepped forward and slipped her two hands around the small of his back. "Just you try and stop me."

Donavan reached round behind his back and placed her hands on his backside. She instinctively pulled him towards her and felt his hardness press into her groin. "Mmm, Donavan, you are pleased to see me, aren't you."

Donavan didn't answer. Instead, he pushed Vicky onto the bed. She lay back and with the ball of each foot, she kicked off her shoes. Then she undid the top button of her Levi's, put a hand either side of the thick denim material and pulled down hard. Donavan stepped forward, grabbed roughly at the bottom of her Levi's, and tugged hard. She shivered as Donavan hauled them from her. As Donavan removed his own trousers, Vicky slipped a thumb either side of her pants and slowly pulled them down over her thighs.

* * * *

Donavan sat at the rich mahogany dining table as Vicky carried several dishes through. "It's nothing much, Don, a beef in red wine casserole and a few vegetables."

"It smells fabulous, whatever it is. I must have worked up a bit of an appetite." Donavan looked up at Vicky and her complexion took on a red glow.

She disappeared again and returned a few seconds later with a bottle of red wine and two glasses. "And this should complement the food as they say on those wretched celebrity chef programmes."

Donavan fingered the bottle. "Châteauneuf du Pape, good choice, it's one of my favourites."

Vicky smiled and Donavan poured two full glasses of wine. He wondered how many glasses it would take before he could pop the question.

He made small talk for just over an hour. He was used to it; a bit of an expert; the usual shit, he thought to himself. How's your family? Where do they live? How long have you lived here? He listened as Vicky answered him and went into far more detail than he really wanted to hear. Then, as he drained the last of the bottle into her glass, he figured the time was about right.

He timed it to perfection. She raised the glass to her lips and as the delicate crystal touched her lips, she studied Donavan over the top of the glass. He stared deep into her eyes and he held the look. He held the look for what seemed like an age.

Vicky finally broke the silence. "What, Don? What is it? Why are you looking at me like that?"

Donavan took a sip of wine and lowered the glass. He reached across the table and took her hands. "I really don't know, Vicky," he paused, figuring it would add drama to his next sentence. "The thing is... I haven't felt this way about a girl for a long, long time."

Vicky broke the gaze and the blood flowed into her cheeks again.

"The thing is, Vicky, I think I'm falling in love with you."

He cringed as the words left his lips. How many times have I said that? he thought to himself. Must be dozens. But it was the first time he'd used the words for this purpose. Normally it was used on a girl to get her into bed. Normally a younger girl, eighteen or nineteen, a girl who'd maybe only slept with one or two lovers in the past, or even better, none at all. He remembered the virgins, remembered their names, the clothes they wore. And he remembered the look on their faces at the very moment he relieved them of their innocence. A mixture of fear, bewilderment and, of course, a little pain.

Vicky laughed and brought him back to the present. "You can't be serious, Don: I mean, we've only been together a matter of hours."

Donavan nodded his head. "I know, it's crazy. I feel like a lovestruck teenager, Vicky, but I can't help how I feel."

By the look in her eyes, Donavan knew she'd been reeled in. He prepared to land his catch. "Tell me how you're feeling, Vicky, tell me you're feeling the same. I can see it in your eyes. Tell me this is a little more than a naughty weekend."

He gripped her hands forcefully and watched as her eyes filled up with tears. They were tears of emotion; she was well and truly thrashing about in the landing net, and Donavan was enjoying every glorious second.

"Of course it is, Don, that first night was so very special, you were just so... so different."

Oh, I'm different, Donavan thought to himself. So different.

Vicky couldn't believe what she was hearing. This man that had awoken feelings in her that she hadn't felt for twenty years, and he was confessing his undying love for her. Her heart was beating faster than she could ever recall and chemicals that she couldn't even remember the name of were flying around her body, stimulating her nerve endings and bringing a colour into her cheeks that would tell her new lover just how flustered he was making her feel.

And he did make her feel flustered, and embarrassed and confused, but, above all, he made her feel wonderful. At that very moment, she realised that she had never loved John Mackenzie and cursed the loveless charade of a marriage that had lasted for nearly fifteen years. Why couldn't she have met Donavan Smith earlier?

Donavan spoke. "The thing is, Vic, I've got something else to tell you."

Vicky looked into his eyes.

"I walked out on my job this week."

"You what?"

"Yeah… packed the job in."

Vicky sat open-mouthed and knew that Donavan wanted to continue.

"I couldn't concentrate. You might think this is corny, but I couldn't stop thinking about you, about how many miles there are between us, and how I just couldn't bear to be apart from you. Management and my colleagues begged me to reconsider. Promised me a pay rise." He laughed. "A ridiculous pay rise. My manager, Mick Grybowski, took me for a three-hour lunch at one of London's finest. He plied me with the best champagne and promised me just about everything. Two directors joined us a little later; one had flown in from Dusseldorf specially."

"Wow, Don, they must think a lot of you."

Donavan took a small sip of wine and continued. "So there I was half pissed, figures and money and promises flying round my head and….."

"Go on, Don, go on."

"…and all I could think about was you."

The glass fell from Vicky's hand and a streak of red wine splashed across Donavan's white shirt. Vicky leapt to her feet. "Shit, Don, I'm so sorry, I'm—"

Donavan took her arms and moved round the table. He kissed her. She responded and yet more chemicals stimulated her senses. Different chemicals this time.

His tongue probed inside her lips and her own tongue thrust forward. She lowered her hand to his groin and found his hardness. She squeezed hard and moaned. He broke the kiss and his hand took her wrist. He panted gently. "Wait, Vicky. There's more I need to tell you."

Vicky looked down and felt the wetness on her own blouse. Now it was Donavan's turn to apologise. "Jesus Christ, how stupid of me, now we've got two ruined shirts."

Vicky began unbuttoning her blouse. "No worries, Don, I'll take it off, throw it in some cold water. Take yours off too."

Donavan ripped at his shirt without even bothering to unfasten a single button.

She smiled at him. Surely he couldn't resist the tiny, white, silk bra she was about to reveal, she thought. She wanted him so badly now. He had aroused an animal-like instinct in her. She'd never felt like this before. She wanted to be thrown onto the carpet or across the table. She wanted him inside her quick and hard. She didn't want an orgasm. No, this was different. This was pure sex in its most basic form, and she wanted him to use her for his own selfish purpose. He would know what she wanted, she felt sure.

And he did.

She gazed into Donavan's eyes. They looked sinister now, different from a few minutes ago, glazed over, and he wasn't smiling anymore.

* * * *

Vicky Mackenzie now knew what it must feel like to be raped. She fell forward into his arms and they held each other tightly for several minutes. A mixture of emotions flowed through her. She couldn't understand why she hadn't stopped him, why she hadn't protested. A shiver ran down her spine. She had wanted to resist him, but couldn't. Was it love or was it fear. She didn't know.

It was as if she had been in a trance. It was if she had floated above the scene and looked down on herself.

She looked into his eyes again; they were calm, relaxed, satisfied, and even gentle. He smiled and she returned his smile.

"You okay?"

Vicky nodded.

"Look I'm sorry, Vicky, I don't know what…"

Vicky pressed a finger to his lips. "It's okay, it's okay."

She relaxed in his arms and any tension she had in her body left her.

"You'd do anything for me, wouldn't you?" he asked her.

She thought about the question and wanted to say no, wanted to tell him certain things were off limits.

She remained silent. Donavan placed his arms on her shoulders and gently prised her from him. "Let's skip dessert and go through to the lounge. We still need to talk."

Vicky took his hand and led him from the room. The chill hit her as soon as she entered the large hallway and she remembered that they were naked from the waist up.

"Just go through," she pointed to the lounge, "I'll nip upstairs and get a couple of robes."

She returned a few minutes later with a large, fluffy white robe tied around her. She was naked underneath. She walked into the lounge and threw an identical robe in the direction of Donavan. "Put that on, it'll be a little more comfortable."

Donavan smiled and reached for the robe. After putting it on, he sat down in front of the real flame-effect, black lead stove, and Vicky dimmed the lights giving a deep, orange glow to the whole of the room.

"Come and sit with me," Donavan patted the floor beside him. "We still haven't had that talk."

"I'll be there in a second. I'll just sort some drinks out."

The ice in the crystal glasses tinkled gently as she carried two large Baileys across the room.

Donavan reached out, took a glass with one hand, and held out the other in front of him. Vicky took his hand and lowered herself to the floor. She lay back and her head sought comfort in the thick towelling material. His strong arms wrapped around her waist.

"So what do you want to talk about?"

The heady smell of the Irish liqueur seemed to fill the room as Donavan took a mouthful from his glass and spoke, "I want to talk about you and me, Vicky."

Vicky's heart skipped a beat as he said the words; they sounded so good, so comfortable, so reassuring.

"I want to talk about our retirement plan."

Vicky sat bolt upright. "What?"

He laughed. "I thought you might say that, but I'm serious,

deadly serious. I want to spend the rest of my life with you and I need to put plans in place in order that we can do that."

"But, Don, I—"

"Let me finish. The thing is, I think you feel the same way. In fact, I'm sure of it. But, as you know, we're both kind of on the dole right now, both unemployed so to speak."

Vicky nodded in agreement, knowing that she could never spend another night with a different man. Her temporary career as a high-class call girl had come to an abrupt end.

"And I know there was no casino and you were no croupier. So, I'm wondering how you're going to get an income in future."

Vicky wanted to defend herself, but remained silent. She wondered how much this man really knew.

"And I'm wondering how I'm going to get an income in future too."

"We'll manage, Donavan, we'll get by somehow."

Donavan shook his head. "Don't be silly, what we are we going to do? Sell all our assets and move into a council flat?"

"But we have loads of assets between us. You've got that flat in Paris and the place in the South of France. We could sell them, and live off the interest."

Donavan shook his head. "You don't understand, Vicky. I don't want to sell the apartment in Paris or the property in the South of France. I want us to be able to go to Paris whenever we want. I want us to spend June, July and August on the French Riviera, Cannes, Monaco, St Tropez, Nice. Maybe have a small boat anchored in the harbour. I don't want to have to worry about jobs and careers and where the next penny's coming from."

Vicky sighed. "And keep this house in Newcastle as well, I suppose."

"Exactly."

Vicky stood up, a little annoyed at the impossibility of his vision, but, nevertheless, daydreaming about what he'd just said.

"Exactly. I love Newcastle. I have done from the minute I set foot in the city. The people are great, so much friendlier than the London set. It has an atmosphere I've never experienced before. In fact, the way I'm feeling at the moment, I wouldn't care if I never set foot in the Smoke again."

"But you've got a penthouse there."

"Yes, I have, and the first thing I'm going to do when I get back on Monday is to pay a visit to the estate agent's."

"You're selling it?"

"Damn right I am, and, if it's okay with you, I plan to spend the next few weeks up here."

Vicky found herself agreeing without hesitation.

"And the money should tide me over for at least 18 months."

"Tide us over you mean. You can move in with me."

Donovan looked at Vicky and smiled. "So you *do* feel the same."

Vicky moved over and kissed him. The moment seemed to last forever, and, as they parted, she couldn't take her eyes off him. His face glowed in the orange light of the fire as the shadows danced across his face. Her heart ached and she imagined she was on a movie set with the cameras rolling in the background. It was a fairytale. She had missed out on love for far too long. But this was the real thing, and she would do anything for the man sitting in front of her.

* * * *

They sat at the breakfast table the next day, still dressed in the identical white robes they had worn the night before. It was time, Donavan thought.

"Have you ever thought what happens when the money runs out?"

Vicky looked at him across the table, a puzzled look etched across her face. "I'm not sure what you mean, Don."

Donavan forked a cube of melon into his mouth, chewed it gently, and swallowed. "You remember last night, what I was saying about the money from my house sale in London."

"Yeah, I think I remember."

"Well, it won't last for ever, Vicky, and I wasn't kidding about spending three months in France and visiting Paris whenever we like. I've been used to that sort of lifestyle and just because I'm now technically retired doesn't mean I want to give it up."

Vicky sat in silence.

"I've been thinking. Perhaps you should show me those diaries."

He assessed her reaction while he picked up a piece of toast and reached across the table with his knife. He sliced off a corner of the butter and began to spread it. And he waited.

"And why would you want to see them, Donavan?"

"I've been thinking about them. I've been thinking about them for a long time, ever since you told me about them. The way I figure it out, the money belongs to you. After all, it was you who lost your husband; you who lost the pension; lost his death in service benefit; and all because of this Bob Heggie character now living the life of Riley out in Spain."

"We hardly know he's living the life of Riley, Don."

"He must be. He's got away with half a million pounds. Your money, Vicky, the money I think you're entitled to."

He waited for her to look up. She didn't, but instead played around with a fork, toying with a cube of melon.

"Our money, Vicky; the money that could just see us hang on to the apartment in Paris and the property in the South of France, - the money that could see us spending three months there every year."

Vicky laughed. "Yeah, it's as easy as that, Don. Get the key, go to Locker Number 28 and pick up half a million pounds. Thanks, Bob Heggie, thanks very much, and then we live happily ever after in the South of France."

Donavan Smith was angry. His eyebrows narrowed together and he glared across the table at Vicky. He raised his voice a decibel or two and wiped the smile from Vicky's face with his next sentence. "Don't patronise me. Do you think I'm that stupid?"

He enjoyed the look that Vicky gave him. The look of fear.

"I'm sorry, Don, I didn't mean—"

"Just do as I ask and go and get the diaries. It's not much to ask, is it? Only last night, I pledged the entire equity from my property to support us for the next year."

He rubbed his brow as he looked down at the table. He slowly raised his head, dragging his fingers through his hair. "At the same time, I'm trying to plan where the next year's income is going to come from and the year after that and the year after that. Okay, it might be a long shot, but the one thing I don't want is to be laughed at."

"I'm sorry, Don I wasn't laughing at you, I was just laughing at the ridiculous thought that the money is still in the locker. I mean it can't be, it's impossible, he must have got it to Spain somehow."

Donavan dragged a finger across his eyebrow and smiled. "Then we'll just have to go and get it, won't we."

Vicky sat in silence and Donavan grinned as he noticed the faintest movement of her head nodding in agreement.

"Now, go and get those diaries like I asked. I've got some business to take care of in London next week and I can think of nothing better to read on the train."

Vicky stood up and walked from the room.

CHAPTER TWELVE

Donavan had spent every minute of the three-hour train journey going through the diaries of the late John Mackenzie. He had paid particular attention to the first two years' diaries and satisfied himself that he hadn't missed anything. He had flicked through the last year's entries and then meticulously studied the last few months of John Mackenzie's life. It made fascinating reading, it made interesting reading, and it was putting ideas into Donavan Smith's head. How could Vicky Mackenzie tuck these into a drawer and forget about them? Didn't she realise what they were saying, for fuck's sake. Deprived of her rightful widow's pension by the bank her husband had devoted his life to and all because of this bastard, Bob Heggie.

Bob Heggie, who was now in some far flung corner of Spain, enjoying the fruits of his ill-gotten gains. Enjoying the fruits of his labour. And, in a way, Donavan Smith admired him. According to Mackenzie's diaries, this man had been a nobody, someone who Mackenzie had held absolute power over during the years they had worked together. He'd been on the brink of dismissal and Mackenzie wanted him out. His diary had mentioned a fleeting concern at his wife's changing personality when Bob Heggie was around. She seemed to flirt with this man, preen herself, and act in a suggestive manner, but always when Mackenzie was present, as if she was doing it on purpose, just to annoy him. And annoy him it did, and the man had to go. And he had noticed that she seemed to be frequenting the branch more and more lately, and always made a beeline for Heggie's office. And then there was Vicky's confession.

Yeah, he would be out on his arse before the end of the year, Mackenzie had vowed. But that wasn't the real reason he was getting rid of his right-hand man. He was getting rid of him simply because he had the power to do so. It felt good. He could influence and affect people's lives at the drop of a hat, and he had done that. He had done that ever since his position allowed him to do so.

A sort of Harold Shipman of the banking world, thought Donavan Smith, as he remembered the serial killer doctor. The bespectacled doctor had killed hundreds, maybe even thousands, during his professional life stretching back decades. No one would ever know the real numbers. And, although the doctor had benefited from some his late patients' wills, the detectives and psychiatrists working on the case claimed the real reason for the killings was simply to exercise his power. A warped and perverted fascination with playing God.

Donavan took the escalator up from the platform at King's Cross. He cursed the crowds and dreaded the thought of the underground as he walked across the concourse towards the ticket machine. He stopped for a second and thought of the peasants and dirty people he would be mixing with, forced up against their perspiring, worthless little bodies. But a cab would take longer this time of day and would be ten times the price. He stopped and paused, and, although it didn't make any sense, he turned and walked towards the exit.

He studied the diary long and hard as the cab took over an hour to make the short journey through Camden Town, Hampstead and eventually on to Belsize Park. The cabdriver attempted to make polite conversation several times, but Donavan just ignored him. Normally he would give a polite one-word rebuff, but today there wasn't even that, so engrossed was he in the last of the diaries.

He was now convinced, as had been Mackenzie, that the mastermind behind this clever scam had indeed been the sad figure working in the office adjacent to Mackenzie's. All the signs pointed to him. He had a motive, in fact, he had two. Money and revenge.

He needed the money, of that there was no doubt. On top of a looming, expensive divorce, Bob Heggie had been addicted to the turf. Mackenzie had suspected that his bookie had been applying a little pressure. The week after the raid he'd brazenly pursued his addiction at a big race meeting down south, and had deposited large cheques in his account on his return.

And revenge. Why not? After giving twenty years to his employer, he knew that his days were numbered. His relationship with Mackenzie wasn't the best in the world either, with his boss blaming him for everything. What better way to get back at him than to ridicule his flagship branch, the branch that Mackenzie ran with a rod of iron? If an employee took a piss, Mackenzie knew what time he took it and how long it lasted.

The last few weeks of Mackenzie's life had indeed been tormented. Half a million pounds taken from under his nose after a mock training exercise had been staged. Mackenzie had walked in during the raid, thought it was for real, and then had breathed a sigh of relief as the staff explained that the robber was in fact an actor hired by head office. A training exercise in which lessons would be learned and new procedures implemented in the entire network of Martins Bank PLC.

Mackenzie had waited for the money to be returned, and, then, the full horror unfolded as he had realized that the entire bank had been duped: board directors, higher management, including Mackenzie, right down to the juniors and tellers working within the enclosed secure area where the raid had taken place.

In the last thirty or so pages of the diary, he related his suspicions and the interviews; Bob Heggie disappearing conveniently at each crucial moment, before, during and after the raid. Detailed accounts. Mackenzie was on a mission in the final few pages: a mission to prove Heggie's guilt and to save face. It was his only way to recover from this almighty embarrassment and to be reinstated into the position he loved, with maybe even a promotion or a special award.

But then nothing. A blank in the diary on the day he was shot dead.

Donavan let out a long sigh and the cab pulled to a stop.

"Thirty-five quid, boss."

"What?" Donavan looked up and couldn't believe how quickly the journey had been completed, so engrossed was he in the pages of Mackenzie's diary. He was thinking, thinking long and hard, thinking of a way he just might be able to work this to his advantage. Half a million pounds in a locker, or at least under the control of Bob Heggie, possibly in Spain. Either way, surely someone with his cunning and intelligence should be able to work out a way to take this money away from this loser, Bob Heggie, a glorified fucking bank clerk. What right did he have to pull off a scam like that and keep the money?

Blackmail was the obvious route, yeah, blackmail. With the help of Vicky, it just could work.

"Sorry it's taken so long, boss. This decongestion shit hasn't made any bloody difference. I swear it takes longer and longer every day."

"Yeah, right," Donavan mumbled as he handed him two twenties.

"Erm, don't think I can find any change, guv."

Donavan smiled. *They never have any fucking change* ."You'd better drive to a cash point then, hadn't you? I'll be upstairs, Flat Number Six."

The taxi driver opened the glove compartment and pulled out a fiver. "I forgot. I generally keep a little float in here."

Donavan took the money and climbed out of the cab. The doorman spotted him through the plate glass fronted door and pressed the release catch to let him in.

"Afternoon, Mr Smith, have a nice trip?"

"Yes, Fred. Really nice, I'm beginning to like it up there in Newcastle, might be spending a little more time up there."

Fred shrugged his shoulders. "Never been that far north.

York's the furthest I've been."

"You should try it, Fred, it's really not that bad. And the girls, some of the prettiest I've ever seen."

Fred frowned. "Oh yeah, Mr Smith, I nearly forgot, A young girl called in asking for you on Saturday, a really pretty little thing. Said she had a present for you, huge it was. She could hardly get her hands around the bloody box."

"What?" A cold shiver ran the length of his spine. "You didn't let her in, did you?"

"Oh no, sir."

Donavan breathed a sigh of relief.

"Didn't need to, she had a key of her own, said you'd given it to her. She stayed about thirty minutes, came down smiling, minus the big box."

Fred grinned and Donavan felt like punching him.

"I like surprises, Mr Smith. I bet you're really excited now."

Donavan took the stairs three at a time, ignoring the doorman and the lift. He stood outside the door to his apartment, pushed in the key, turned it and the door swung open. A feeling of impending dread hit him as he spied the large gift-wrapped box sitting on the floor. Ignoring it, he ran into the apartment moving quickly between each room.

Everything appeared untouched. Everything sat in its own little place just as he had left it prior to his trip up north.

He returned to the hallway and walked over to the box. He stared at it for what seemed like an eternity. He dropped down onto his knees and took in a deep breath. He sympathised with what must go through the head of a bomb disposal expert in the Bogside or Iraq or Lebanon, but quickly discarded these thoughts. He reached down and took a hold of the waxed silver ribbon, he tugged gently and the bow separated. As he pulled the ribbon towards him, the tawdry purple wrapping paper fell to the floor. He carefully lifted the box lid and jumped back as a pink, helium filled balloon in the shape of a heart floated slowly to the ceiling. It bobbed from the ceiling four times before it eventually settled and, bit by bit, gradually turned to reveal its message,

At that precise moment, Donavan Smith knew exactly who the sender was. She'd found the keys that day in the office, the day he'd been fired. Instantly, he shelved his audacious plans to blackmail Bob Heggie out of half a million pounds and began formulating new plans to get rid of Jenny McArthur.

A simple phone call to 118 212 gave Donavan Jenny's address in Plaistow.

* * * *

He watched her movements carefully over the next few days from his car across the street. She left the basement flat at the same time every morning and arrived back at the same time each evening. She was so predictable; *didn't the bitch have a social life?* Although Donavan didn't have the luxury of a key to Jenny's flat, gaining access proved unproblematic. An elbow to a pane of glass on the rear door allowed him to get his arm around to a large brass key hanging from an old-fashioned Chubb lock. He listened for a few seconds, straining to locate the warning tones from a burglar alarm about to blast out its high-pitched shrill.

Nothing.

He turned the key and pushed firmly on the door with his gloved hand. It stuck at the bottom a little, but eventually gave way. He would play her at her own game. See how she liked it. He carried the box into the hallway and placed it in exactly the same position as she had left his: centre of the hallway, four feet from the door. She would literally fall over it as she came through the door.

Then he went for a wander round her flat. He walked into the lounge. A cream, leather three-piece sat strategically positioned in front of a small plasma television. Donavan looked around the room and selected his weapon of choice. He picked up a heavy marble-based trophy sitting within a shelved alcove. He looked over to the television and hurled the trophy at the middle of the screen. The marble connected with the glass shattering it with a dull bang. Shards of glass spilled onto the floor.

Donavan walked over, bent down and picked up a long, thick splinter of glass. He took off his fleece and wrapped it around the fat end of the glass. He walked over to the three-piece and began to carve the initial "D" in every cushion and on every arm. When he had finished, he reached inside and pulled out every last bit of stuffing he could find and scattered it around the room. He walked through to the kitchen, and then through to a small utility room that housed Jenny's washing machine and tumble-drier. He grinned as he spotted a shelf laden with used paint pots and an aerosol can of matt black spray paint. He picked up a large tin of white gloss and dropped the aerosol into his pocket. As he left the kitchen, he turned towards the sink, shoved a dishcloth into the overflow, pushed the plug in and turned on the cold-water tap.

The lid eased off the paint tin with the help of a kitchen knife. He walked over to the open-plan dining area and, for a second, admired the elegant antique table, obviously a family heirloom handed down from the family, and not the sort of thing that could be purchased on Oxford Street. He admired it again. That is, until he started pouring the white paint into the centre. And he poured and poured, until the whole tabletop was covered and the paint started dripping over the side on to the natural teak wood flooring. He smiled as it cascaded over like a huge milk waterfall. It hypnotised him, and he stood there for several minutes until he realised he had one task left to complete.

Taking the aerosol from his pocket, he sprayed a series of thick black words on every available wall in the flat. *Bitch. Slut. Whore.*

A little later, he left through the broken back door.

* * * *

Jenny cursed the London rush hour as the Hammersmith &

City Line train stopped at Liverpool Street Station. Where do all these people come from, she thought, as yet another stranger barged into her as she held onto the overhead rail above her head. Two more stops and she'd be at Whitechapel where her car was parked and, with a little luck, just a twenty-minute drive home. Even the twenty-minute drive extended to thirty minutes some evenings and on Fridays, the very night where she longed to get home, the twenty minutes sometimes turned into forty.

She'd come to the conclusion that she hated London. Okay, she'd liked it to begin with, but then the novelty had worn off. She hated the rush around culture of London and the unfriendly natives. Everyone seemed to be looking after number one and, what with the recent London tube train bombings, everybody seemed to be suspicious of everyone else. Lakshanthi, a friend of Sri Lankan origin, had actually stopped travelling by tube as she found it so uncomfortable.

The train slowed down as it approached Whitechapel. She looked across at a young Muslim carrying a backpack, and cursed herself for what she was thinking.

She made her way out into the dark, wet night and turned right towards Mile End Road. Half a mile up and she turned left into Frimley Way.

Cambridge, that's where I'll go, she thought as she turned the key in the lock of her car. She liked the city when she visited it last week and her company had a satellite office there, servicing a few select clients. Yeah, Cambridge, why not? A new life, a new start, far away from Donavan Smith. She'd ask for a transfer just as soon as she had finished her remaining tasks.

She crossed the Blackwall Tunnel and turned right into New Plaistow Road. Five minutes later, she pulled into Tweedmouth Road, shifted into neutral and parked up. The rain fell harder as she crossed the road and made for the sanctuary of her flat. She would miss the only home she had known since she came to London. She had some happy memories, and everything had been fine until….. Okay, it wasn't the nicest area of London but, as soon as she closed the door, she felt safe and comfortable.

The key slipped into the lock and she gave the door a gentle kick. She would put the property up for sale tomorrow.

The first thing she noticed was the damp carpet as she stepped into the darkened hallway. She flicked on the light and looked down at the floor. *Shit.* The carpet seemed to be floating on an inch of water and her ears picked up the faraway sound of a running tap. She looked straight ahead and recoiled in terror as she spotted the black balloon floating at eye level

.

THE FEAR OF DEATH IS WORSE THAN DEATH ITSELF.

She wanted to run, to scream and to slam the door on the horror inside. The message hit her like a jackhammer to the heart. Her legs were like lead pipes, stiff and cold, so cold.

She turned back towards the door but stopped. The tap wasn't running anymore. She hesitated. Was he inside? She reached into her handbag for her pepper spray. She'd purchased it a few days after returning from Paris. The girl in the shop said it was easy enough to use, just point and shoot. She didn't want to run from Donavan Smith anymore; why should she? If she could only make the kitchen and take one of the carving knives from the magnetic strip screwed to the wall above the cooker. Self-defence, the police would say. After all, how much evidence would they need? He'd broken into her flat. That was as clear as day, and with the threat written on the balloon, what more proof would they need? If she could only make the kitchen. It wasn't a problem if she bumped into him on the way. The pepper spray would sort him out. At least two or three minutes the shop assistant had said, two or three minutes when Donavan Smith would be blind. Blind and incapable.

She brushed past the balloon and walked into the lounge, her pepper canister held out in front of her like a New York cop stalking the bad guy. She recoiled in horror as she walked into the lounge. It was a sight that sickened her to the pit of her stomach. Everything she had worked for over the years, deliberately destroyed by the man who had violated her. She looked at the antique dining table left to her only recently by her favourite aunt after she died. She lowered the pepper spray as she walked over. She took out a paper tissue and wiped the paint from the worn brass plaque. The gloss paint bled into the maker's name, Samuel Hill of Wordsley. Jenny had promised herself she would research the table and its origin, just out of curiosity. Her aunt had told her, on the last visit before her death, that it was Victorian and had been left to her by her grandfather. *Please take care of it* were the last words she'd uttered as she left the room never to see her again. She fell asleep peacefully that evening never to awaken again.

A tear rolled from Jenny's cheek and fell onto the pepper spray, a sign from her aunt perhaps, as if to remind her of the danger she faced. She lifted the spray again and pointed it towards the kitchen. Her gaze fixed on the word *whore* painted on the door and the pepper spray shook in her hands.

Just another few feet, she thought to herself, as she pushed the door open with her foot. She stole a quick look behind her then took a step forward. The knives glistened in the rays of a street light from outside and she walked closer. She reached out for the black, wooden handle of the largest knife on the rack - a six-inch blade. She wondered if she would have the nerve to plunge it into Donavan Smith, once, maybe twice, or even three or four times if necessary. Could she do it?

All of a sudden she felt very afraid, petrified. She'd reached her target, her protection and she expected to feel relief. But she didn't. She felt fear.

She walked back through to the lounge and into her bedroom. Items of underwear were strewn across the room and more graffiti taunted her, screamed out to her from every wall.

A slight calm came over her as she realised she'd checked every room. Every room and Donavan Smith was nowhere to be seen. She dropped the pepper spray into her bag and walked back into the hallway to be faced with the balloon. She jabbed the knife upwards and it let out a gentle hiss as the helium escaped from the wound. She watched as it floated down to the floor. She laid the knife on the telephone table by the door and picked up the handset.

It had gone too far. It was time to call in the good guys. She had tried to play Donavan Smith at his own game, but realised it wasn't in her nature. She located the number nine on the handset and wondered what to say she pressed the button twice. A burglary; she would report a burglary to start with, see what sort of coppers they were, whether she was comfortable with them. She looked down at the phone again and her thumb hovered over the shiny silver button in the right-hand bottom corner. She pressed it and placed the unit to her ear. The line was dead.

She was aware of an expensive musky aftershave filling the hallway, a familiar aftershave she'd smelled before. The hall door crashed open and a leather-clad hand pushed into her face. She tried to keep her feet, but Donavan Smith's heavy weight had caught her off balance and taken her by surprise. She cursed her lapse of concentration as he crashed down on top of her and her eyes fixed on the kitchen knife lying by the telephone. Donavan followed her gaze. He held his hands tight around her wrists.

"Oh I see, my little angel, that was meant for me."

He let out a sick laugh as she struggled for breath. She fought for air, his deadweight upon her and his full hand covering her nose and mouth.

He eased his face forward, just inches from hers. "How could you, angel? After all we've been through."

He eased the glove from her face. "Don't bother screaming, your upstairs neighbours aren't in." He cackled again, a hideous, demented laugh. "You see, darling, I've been watching you and your neighbours for a few days now, timing your movements, when you leave and what time you get home."

He looked at his watch. "And if my timings are right, I've got about an hour to play with you before your teacher friends arrive back home."

"How do you know they're teachers, you sick bastard."

"Jenny, Jenny, Jenny, give me some credit. They stick out like sore thumbs, probably met at college, never fucked anyone but each other. They just look like two teachers."

He grinned at her. "Am I right?"

She nodded. "They'll be home any second, generally call in to see me."

Donavan Smith shook his head. "No, they won't. My guess is they'll stay behind for a couple of hours, mark their books up, grab a quick beer in the local and come back around eight. You see I've been following them to Tooting Comprehensive in Fulham and, even if they aren't marking their books tonight, they'll encounter a slight delay with a couple of flat tyres." He smiled as he removed the glove from his right hand.

"So what do you want with me? Are you going to rape me again, is that what you want?"

The smile disappeared from Donavan's face, and he moved his knees up onto her shoulders.

"No, Jenny, sadly I can't. Oh, how I'd love to. In fact I'm getting quite hard just thinking about it."

He pressed forward with his hips and Jenny felt his hardness pressing into her breastbone. "You see, the semen inside you would give the Old Bill a bit of a clue."

An unimaginable thought entered Jenny's head.

"It's the first place they look when a young lady is found dead."

She choked back the phlegm in the back of her throat. "You're going to kill me?"

"No, Jenny." He grinned at her. "You're going to commit suicide."

He reached into his jacket and pulled out an envelope. "You've even written your little suicide note to Daddy. I found it in your drawer."

She recognised her personalised envelope and wondered why she hadn't destroyed the letter some weeks back.

"Made it so easy for me, you have."

He cast a glance over to the knife sitting on the table. "And your fingerprints. All over your own little kitchen knife. My guess is that the cops won't even bother looking up your sweet little pussy. Your dad will verify your own handwriting, and fingerprints are foolproof. The coroner will take all of two minutes to figure this one out before he delivers his suicide verdict."

Jenny made a last gasp attempt to break free, but he held her tight. He pulled her up by the hair and leaned over, whispering in her ear, " *I looked, and behold a pale horse: and his name that sat on him was death, and Hell followed with him. Revelation*, Jenny, *Revelation 6:8*."

He stretched, just managing to reach the blade of the knife with the fingertips of his gloved hand. He held up the fingers of his bare hand in front of her face and moved them down her body. She cringed as she felt his hand working its way up her dress and into the thin fabric of her panties.

One last chance, she thought, and, as she watched his eyes focus on a faraway place, she forced her right shoulder up with every ounce of strength left in her body. Every muscle ached, every sinew strained as she broke free and connected with a clenched fist underneath Donavan Smith's chin. His head snapped back and she heard the sickening crack as his jawbone shattered. Instinctively, he threw himself backwards and Jenny looked around for the knife. Donavan lay dazed against the hallway door. She spied the knife still gripped firmly in his left hand.

He felt at his chin and anger welled up in his eyes as he felt pieces of his jawbone moving under the skin. He grimaced in pain as he focused on Jenny and he raised himself to his knees.

Before she could even think, Donavan Smith rushed her and headbutted her in the chest. Every ounce of air squeezed from her lungs and she gasped for breath as she lay defeated on the floor. He crawled over to her and lifted up her wrist. She lay, unable to move, unable to fight, as he drew the blade quickly across her delicate white skin. She felt no pain, only a slight discomfort as the blade rasped across her wrist bone. Then she was conscious of warm liquid seeping down her arm. She looked onto the hallway floor as a thick, crimson pool formed bit by bit, like an oil slick from a stricken tanker.

Donavan lifted her other hand and smiled as he performed the operation again. Slowly this time, and this time she felt the pain as the cold blade sliced slowly through the skin and the rubbery sinew of the artery. And she felt helplessness, helplessness like she'd never felt before. Yet, she also felt a deep inner peace knowing that he could hurt her no more.

CHAPTER THIRTEEN

Samantha Thompson's mind was in turmoil. The visitor that had called on her last week had brought back memories that she'd managed to push into a distant corner of her mind. And that's where she wanted them to stay. She'd broken away from the torment of London and all that Donavan Smith stood for. If the truth be told, she'd felt quite proud of herself. She had managed to sever all links with the City and her friends there and, of course, most of the ex-colleagues and the contacts and associates from other companies and firms who were likely to be posted up on Donavan Smith's e-mail address list.

Anonymity. That's what she had in Cambridge. The ability to walk into a bar or restaurant without looking around, wondering who was sniggering, and who was pointing that accusing finger, the finger that said she'd asked for everything she'd got. But she hadn't.

She remembered little about the evening in question: a pleasant meal and a few drinks with a real gentleman, a true charmer. Then a walk back to Donavan Smith's apartment because he'd said all the taxis were booked. She cursed herself for believing him, although she remembered she was in no fit state to argue. And yet she didn't think she'd had that much to drink. The next morning, though, she woke up in a strange bed with a severe headache and a dry palate.

She remembered the feelings from a distant holiday as a child. Waking slowly…unable to locate her familiar soft toys and furnishings. Starched sheets and a throw instead of the soft patterned eiderdown. No posters, no pictures of the latest boy band or pop idol, just the bland, pastel-coloured walls of a seaside bed and breakfast. And, then, relief as the sun streamed through the thin curtains and the warmth penetrated her tiny body, and her mother was there for her, seconds after her eyes had fluttered open. How do mothers do that, she asked herself.

But, that morning, Mummy was nowhere to be seen. She'd walked through to the lounge, painfully aware that something or someone had violated her. Donavan Smith sat in a huge, leather armchair with a white, towelling bathrobe draped loosely around his body and a bare leg swinging over the arm. A large TV screen lit the darkened room as Donavan turned to face her.

"Pretty good performance you put on last night," he announced, as her gaze fell on the screen and her eyes focused in on what he was watching.

And it didn't end there. Just when she thought it couldn't get any worse, he'd embarked on a campaign that tormented her mentally, far worse in fact than the physical side ever had.

Six weeks she'd lasted. By then, he'd broken her. She ran away. He'd won.

Or had he? New friends, a new job, and, as each day dawned, the mental images of that night faded ever so slightly. Until, that is, she opened the door to the stranger.

What Jenny McArthur had asked her to do that evening, when she had arrived unannounced, brought the terrible memories flooding back. She'd quite naturally refused, despite the protests and continued persuasion of the unfamiliar person.

Now, on page fourteen of the London Evening Standard, Jenny McArthur's face jumped out at Samantha tearing at her heartstrings.

She'd so wanted to help; wanted to help crucify Donavan Smith. And she had been so close to agreeing to help.

But now it was too late. The headline reached inside her ribcage and clawed at her heart.

Shock suicide of young City Trader.

It frightened her and, yet, it puzzled her. It puzzled her because Jenny was far from suicidal the evening Samantha had seen her. In fact, if anything, she was in the most positive, determined frame of mind she could possibly be. She had the evidence, in the form of his sordid recordings captured on memory cards, which would be enough to convict Donavan Smith. Jenny had endured the same torture as she had. Abused while under the influence of a date rape drug, all captured on film for Donavan Smith's warped and perverted pleasure.

And Samantha knew just what sort of pleasure he had taken, wallowing in her degradation as the still images from the film had found their way onto the computers of all and sundry. And the very moment she'd booted up her computer and opened up the first attachment, he had sat watching her from across the room.

His grin, an evil twisted grin. She would never forget it. And back home that evening, no doubt he would watch an uninterrupted performance. A show that featured at least six past employees of Bass and Richards, the most respected City traders in London.

Jenny had managed to gain access to his flat. She'd located and stolen the memory cards. Jenny had asked Samantha if she would testify in court and if she could identify any of the other girls on film.

Samantha had refused. She couldn't bear to watch the films of the poor girls made to perform the most degrading sexual acts imaginable, performing their nauseating exploits whilst staring hypnotically into an abyss.

Jenny had taken the rejection well, said she understood. She had left the memory cards with her and asked Samantha to reconsider. "Think about the others," she'd said, "and think about every other girl frequenting the pubs and clubs of the city. How many more lives will he ruin?"

And now Samantha Thompson sat with the cards spread out on the table, each individually dated with a girl's name and a nauseating title. She looked at the title for her own personal performance and the memories and graphic images returned all too easily.

The bright screen of her laptop reflected a green, bluish tint

to her face and she fingered the cards. She had a decision to
make.

CHAPTER FOURTEEN

Donavan Smith rubbed at his jawbone. It had been four weeks since he'd been wired up at the hospital. He had told them that it was a sporting injury, a punch from an opposing forward in a scrum. Truth is, he'd never even played rugby, born on the wrong side of the tracks.

Now, at last, he'd had the wires removed and he longed for some solid food. He was sick to death of soup and sweet tea. He carried a freezing cold six-pack of Stella Artois with his left hand and a twelve-inch Sicilian pizza with his other.

He opened the door to his apartment. He'd looked forward to this evening ever since the surgeon had handed him the diet sheet: soup, Guinness, milk, and more soup. Tomato, chicken, lentil, and vegetable soups, - he couldn't care less if he didn't see another tin of soup as long as he lived.

Tonight, he would sit in his favourite armchair and enjoy solid food while watching one of his favourite movies. He figured tonight was just about the right time. The headline in the middle of the Evening Standard had warmed the cockles of his heart, given him a feeling of invincibility, and justified his actions. She was dead.

Jenny McArthur could cause no trouble where she lay now in the cold, damp clay of her grave. No more interfering, no more balloons. She had messed with the wrong guy.

He wandered through to the lounge, snapped the seal on a new bottle of Remy Martin, and poured himself a large glass. One or two, he thought, a perfect start to a perfect evening. It was one of his weaknesses in life, the greatest cognac of all time, one to be enjoyed slowly. He took in a small mouthful and allowed it to float to the back of his throat. His mouth opened slightly and he drew in a little air to oxygenate the alcohol, giving an even greater tasting sensation. And he remembered the words of Mme Dominique Heriard Dubreuil, "Taste is at the heart of everything we do."

Relaxation came almost at once, a prelude to what he was about to enjoy. He set down the glass and pushed a button on the remote control. The plasma screen flickered into life, he keyed another button and the word *comp* flashed in blue at the bottom right of the screen. His laptop was already connected to the TV. All that remained was to insert a memory card and savour the action.

There would be only one choice of movie tonight: a sort of celebration in honour of the coroner and the boys in the pressroom of the London Evening Standard. Tonight he would watch the suitably renamed *Jenny Mac and the last tango in Paris*. And it was her last tango, the last sexual encounter of her all too short life.

Donavan Smith stood up, took another mouthful of cognac, and grinned. And what an encounter it had been, he thought, as he walked through to the bedroom. He opened the top drawer to his bedside cabinet and pushed gently on the top right-hand corner. The bottom-left corner of the false-bottomed drawer rose an eighth of an inch and he slid his index finger underneath. He lifted the bottom to reveal….nothing!

Donavan froze.

The thirteen memory cards had vanished. He pulled the drawer violently from its runners and shook the contents to the floor. A watch, some coins, a few credit cards, and a gold necklace fell to the floor. He hoped, prayed that the cards had slipped down the back of the drawer underneath and he yanked that one from its moorings. Socks and underwear spilled onto the floor. But, even as he rummaged through the items, he knew deep down what had happened to the cards.

He breathed a deep sigh and sank back against the bed. After a few minutes, he composed himself and walked back through to the lounge. The green glow from the plasma screen greeted and taunted him from the darkened room and he cursed as he realised there wouldn't be any movie show tonight.

He walked through to the kitchen, picking his cognac up en route, and, sitting down at the pine kitchen table, he gulped down three large glasses, one after the other. By the time he'd reached the bottom of the bottle, the strong alcohol had seeped into his system. It didn't make him feel any better.

She'd entered his flat illegally, stolen the memory cards thus managing to get her hands on the graphic moving images of her own personal hell. That sordid evening in Paris had probably been the last thoughts in her mind as life oozed away from her at the hands of Donavan Smith.

But why the others? The video card was clearly marked with her name, a quick flick through and she would have found it easily enough. Why?

Spite, that's why. The spiteful little bitch wanted to deprive Donavan of his pleasure. No, it didn't make sense. There had to be another reason. He had to get the cards back.

Donavan tossed and turned all night. Sleep just wouldn't come. He turned towards the faint green glow of the LCD alarm clock. It read 4.10 a.m. He couldn't remember seeing any digits between twelve and two but was sure he'd registered every minute either side. He sat bolt upright and then stretched, his eyes gradually growing accustomed to the dark.

With no chance of getting back to sleep, he decided to get up. Within a few minutes, he was fully dressed and enjoying the harsh but pleasant taste of strong Arabic coffee. The hot liquid did little to take away the foul taste in his mouth. He regretted the last few glasses of Remy and wished he could turn the clock back. His head ached.

But now was as good a time as any.

He took his car keys from the hook above the fridge and slipped them into his pocket. As he walked down the stairs from his apartment and through the front door, he wondered when he'd ever been on the street this early before. He wouldn't take the Ferrari this morning; it was almost like inviting the police to stop him. No, the black BMW 3 Series was far less conspicuous.

He keyed the ignition and punched his destination into the satellite navigation system. It was still pitch-black and he wouldn't find his way to the street in Plaistow without it.

The streets were eerily quiet at that time of the morning and he enjoyed the experience of being able to work his way through the gearbox. Finding fifth gear in the everyday London traffic just didn't happen that often.

He would break in exactly the same way as he had when he'd murdered Jenny McArthur, an elbow through the rear door. He wished he had some sticky backed paper to deaden the noise of the glass breaking, but somehow he didn't think he'd be able to get his hands on any at this time of the morning.

The navigation system announced his arrival at his destination and he turned off the key in the ignition. He sat for a few moments, watching, listening, thinking. The street was quiet.

An electric milk float powered silently down the street and he cursed the driver for prolonging his task. He looked across the road to Jenny's flat and gazed upwards to the windows above. A lone light shone, three levels above. He gathered his thoughts. An insomniac surely? Perhaps a postman or a night worker returning from his stint at the factory? *Who the fuck gets out of bed at this time of the morning?*

The milk float disappeared from his rear-view mirror and he opened the door of the car. The cold, early morning air rushed in and an icy shiver ran the length of his spine.

He climbed from the car and pulled on the same leather gloves that had held the knife to Jenny's wrists, the same leather gloves that had held her down as the blood seeped from her young body.

He remembered her face, helpless, desperate, every minute growing paler and paler, and then realisation, and, finally, surrender in her eyes. He'd enjoyed the moment at the time, but now, as he made his way across the road, he wasn't so sure.

The pane of glass hadn't even been replaced. Instead, a six by six piece of plywood had been nailed crudely into place. Placing his elbow against the wood, he hit it with his hand. Then, a little harder, and he smiled as the nails began to ease. His fingers worked around the wood panel, which tumbled onto the floor.

He stopped and listened. He was fairly certain no one had heard, but he didn't want to take a chance. The last thing he wanted was to be caught breaking into Jenny McArthur's flat a few weeks after she'd been murdered.

He was no burglar; the police were clever enough to work that one out; so what was he doing in her flat?

He pushed these thoughts from his mind and reached around the back of the door for the handle. He stopped again and listened as the door swung open. Silence.

He turned on the Maglite and the beam penetrated the darkness of the kitchen. The creepy shadows played tricks with his mind and he half expected the torch to pick out the pale, lifeless, ghostly figure of his victim.

He stood rooted to the spot; an invisible force field preventing him from moving. He didn't want to go in there; he didn't want to take another step. He prayed for a noise from above, a reason to abort, a reason to run back to the safety of his car. But he knew he had to find the memory cards, he couldn't take the chance of anyone viewing them. They were his. They were personal to him, his property. He was the rightful owner and he wanted them back.

He broke the force field and moved slowly through the kitchen. The light picked out the knife rack and his heart skipped a beat as he spotted the space where the knife that had sliced through Jenny's wrists should have been. He was holding the knife now and cringed as he remembered the blade slicing through her flesh. Jenny, Somewhere in her flat, hiding, lurking in the shadows, holding that same knife high above her head ready to strike at her tormentor.

He became aware that he was trembling. Then the adrenalin kicked in and he took another slow step towards the lounge. More shadows and imagined shapes, and the light picked out the dining room table covered with the hardened gloss paint. He pointed the torch at the walls and, although an attempt had been made to remove the graffiti, he could still make out the exact letters of the insults he had painted.

The butchered leather three-piece sat in a wounded sorry state, begging to be carried off to the nearest council tip. He couldn't understand it. Why hadn't they cleaned up? Whoever *they* were.

Then he smiled. He didn't want them to clean up; didn't want them to move anything; that was the last thing he wanted. Everything appeared just as he had left it on that fateful night.

He turned around and his eyes scanned the room. He strained through the darkness following the beam of light. Where would she put them? Where would she hide them? Would she hide them? Yeah, probably, not the sort of thing you'd want your mother to find.

Something was missing; something or some things had gone. The room looked different. Barren.

Then it dawned on him. Photographs. The photographs and pictures that had adorned the walls had gone. The beam fell onto the white marble fireplace. Several small-framed photographs of family and friends had cluttered the top the night Jenny McArthur's life had been taken away from her. Now - nothing.

He rushed through to her bedroom and flicked the light on, not even bothering with the torch now. Everything of a personal nature had gone. The large glass clip frame that had hung above her bed with tiny two-inch square photographs in a carefully arranged mosaic had gone, as had the jewellery box, make-up, and perfume from her dressing table.

Donavan rushed over to the drawers and hauled each one from its runners. Empty.

He threw the small torch to the floor and sank down onto the bed, conscious of a trembling rage building up within. In a last dash of desperation, he ran through to the lounge. He pulled the door from a television cabinet, its hinges splintering from the cheap chipboard frame. He fell to his knees and looked into an empty shell. A race through to the kitchen and every drawer pulled out and every cupboard turned upside down. A few knives and forks, a couple of coffee cups. He picked up one of cups and threw it against the microwave perched on a steel bracket above the cooker. The glass door stood firm as the cup exploded into a thousand pieces. He picked up the microwave, held it above his head, and hurled it to the floor.

Then there was a noise from upstairs, a woman shouting at someone. He heard the word *police* and footsteps hurried across the floor.

A last look into the lounge, his eyes desperately trying to find some sort of nook or cranny he might have missed. Where were they? Where had they gone? Who had them now? Did that person know what they were? Had they even watched them? The questions gnawed away at Donavan and, for once, he couldn't find any answers.

He turned and walked back through to the kitchen, stepped over the broken microwave and reached for the handle of the door. He stopped. *They have to be here.* He could feel it. Something dragged him back into the lounge. *Where would she hide them?*

He walked over to the settee, lifted the cushions and threw them to the floor. He didn't know what he expected to see, an envelope perhaps, or a wallet or a purse with thirteen little cards tucked neatly inside. He dragged his hand across the dralon-covered base of the settee, feeling for a bump or a disturbance in the cloth, or maybe a tear in the material. Nothing. He looked around the room again, his eyes settling on the bookcase. The books were undisturbed. Not personal enough to be taken away by her parents or friends or whoever it was that had cleared the flat out. He searched through the titles looking for some word or some sign to give him a clue, a clue that said the book was false, no pages, just a little casket containing gold. He grabbed at the first book, a fiction novel by an author he hadn't heard of before. He opened the book and cursed as his fingers flicked quickly through the pages. He leafed through a dozen books before he gave up and turned his attention to the bedroom.

His feet sank into the plush, cream carpet as he entered the room. He looked around for something or somewhere to hide the treasure. He tried to place himself in the head of Jenny McArthur, tried to think where she would put something so important.

The two policemen positioned themselves at the front and back doors. They had heard the noise as each book hit the floor. The neighbour had explained that Jenny McArthur had taken her life some weeks back and that the flat should be empty. They had taken a decision to wait until the burglar came out.

P.C. Gerald O'Donnell, God as they called him back at the station, stood at the back door and prayed that the scumbag would walk through it. He also prayed that the same scumbag would resist a little, even throw a punch or two. He fancied a bit of action. The nightshift had been a bit quiet this week. Yeah, he liked a bit of resistance; nothing like it to get the adrenalin flowing. His partner, Jack Ashurst, took the front door, happy enough to have been allocated the door that was very rarely used as an escape route by the villains.

A figure appeared, silhouetted against the frosted glass of the undamaged panes of the kitchen door. God clenched his fist. He'd left his truncheon back in the squad car, but he didn't need it, never would. He'd made it through to the all Ireland Amateur Boxing Finals as a teenager and worked out on a heavy punchbag nearly every day. Just let the bastard throw a punch or even make a sudden movement. Yeah, that would do. He'd report back to the station that he'd thought he saw a knife. He'd work the bastard over good and proper; it was what real policing should be all about, what the public wanted.

The policeman moved quickly from out of the shadows and took Donavan Smith by surprise. He thrust his Maglite upwards instinctively into the face of the copper and, then, the last thing he remembered was a cold heavy fist connecting with his chin.

"You broke my fucking jaw, you monkey," were the first words Donavan Smith uttered when he came to. The two policemen held an arm each and dragged him towards the car.

"Lucky I didn't break your pissing neck, you scum of the earth," replied God. "People working fifty, sixty hours a week to have a nice home and you shitbags break in and take what you like. Well, not on my beat, you don't. You're nicked now and won't be doing this for a long time."

Donavan Smith held his teeth together as he spoke. "I'm not a burglar, I didn't steal anything."

The policemen levered him into position, ready to push him into the back of the car. God placed a hand onto his head as he ducked down. The policeman moved his hand round to the back of Donavan's head and when it was just a few inches away from the door arch, God slammed it forward. Donavan's head connected with metal and he cried out as the pain shot through his broken jawbone.

Donavan sneered at the copper, *"The heart of the sons of men is full of evil, and madness is in their heart while they live. Ecclesiastes 9:3."*

God laughed, much to the dismay of his colleague. "Oh dear, we seem to have encountered an unfortunate accident to a religious nut."

The tears welled up in Donavan's eyes and he felt a trickle of blood run down his brow. He felt a firm hand on his back and ended up sprawled on the back seat of the police car.

The two policemen got into the front of the car. God looked over the headrest of the seat to survey the damage. "You didn't steal anything….right, you didn't steal anything because the girl's family cleared out all of her possessions after she died. You were just a little unlucky in your choice of properties tonight, scumbag. No TV, no computer, jewellery or cash. All gone. Just your tough shit."

Donavan Smith thought of an escape route. "She was my girlfriend."

The policemen looked at each other and God spoke first, "You broke into your dead girlfriend's empty flat?"

"Jenny's flat," replied Donavan. "Jenny McArthur. I dated her for a while, took her to Paris not long before she died."

God's colleague leaned over the back seat. "Mustn't have been a very good trip. The poor cow topped herself."

Donavan placed a hand over his eyes and sniffed as the tears flowed. He didn't have to act, the pain in his jaw was excruciating. "I know. I blame myself. Should have seen it coming."

God spoke, "And just what were you doing, breaking into her flat?"

Donavan looked up and a tear rolled down his cheek. Both policemen tracked its path and Donavan sensed a change in attitude. "I don't know, just had to be there I suppose. It was the last little thing to cling to."

"A bit bloody stupid at five o'clock in the morning."

Donavan nodded. "I know. I'm sorry, I just couldn't sleep."

God leaned across to face Donavan. His breath stank of stale coffee. "Hang on, I'm not sure if I believe this shit."

"He's got the name right," his colleague stated. "That's the name the lady upstairs gave us."

God thought for a second. "Yeah, but he could have seen that on the door or on an old envelope in the house."

Donavan spoke again, this time praying his painful efforts would be enough. He was on the verge of passing out again. "Jenny McArthur, aged twenty-three, worked for Bass and Richards in the City, a trader, I worked there too. She was born in Scotland, educated at Loughborough University, graduated in 2002 with an honours degree."

He paused. The policemen remained silent in the front of the car. "Check it out. Check it out at the station when we get there. It'll give me a chance to phone my solicitor."

God keyed the ignition and pushed the car into gear. "Don't worry, we will."

They released Donavan Smith after a couple of hours. They'd agreed not to charge him and he'd agreed not to pursue any complaints about the way he'd been treated

He took a cab back to his car in Plaistow and, for a second, thought about going back into the flat. But then he pushed all thoughts of another break-in out of his head. He was sure the cards were still in the flat, but, if they were that well hidden, they could stay hidden. He turned the ignition and pushed the BMW into gear. He released the clutch and stamped down on the accelerator.

He glanced over to the flat as he sped past and, just for a fleeting second, swore he made out the shape of Jenny McArthur standing at the window. He'd taken a severe blow to the head; his mind was playing tricks on him again.

CHAPTER FIFTEEN

Vicky Mackenzie fussed around Donavan Smith like an old mother hen. He had rung her from Newcastle Central Station and asked her to pick him up. She'd jumped into her car and made the journey in record time.

During the drive home, Donavan had told her all about the mugging and how the two thugs had broken his jaw. "Caught me by surprise, they did, the bastards. Doctors had to wire my bloody teeth together, can you believe it? Soup and hot sweet tea for the next few weeks and nothing too energetic for my mouth."

He looked across at Vicky and grinned. Her cheeks flushed and, even in the darkness, he spotted it. He enjoyed her discomfort.

"Oh, Don, it seems so long since we last saw each other. It seems like months."

"Four weeks actually, Vicky. Like I say, I've had to take care of a few things."

Vicky's hand moved across to his thigh and she gave it a squeeze.

"And now I've taken care of things, we can put our plan into place."

Donavan talked for the rest of the journey and Vicky listened. A couple of times she tried to interject, but each time he'd held up a hand. "It's quite simple. First, we need to find out where this Bob Heggie character lives, then we make a phone call. We need to find out somehow whether he's taken the money out of that locker."

Vicky looked across at him. "That's easy enough, Don. I think a couple of the guys back at the bank still keep in touch. James Richfield, I think, still does. I guess I could nip into the branch next week."

"Good. That's a start."

Vicky indicated left as she approached the driveway to the house. "But what I can't figure out is how we're going to ask him."

The car came to a stop and Donavan reached over to the back seat for his holdall. "The way I see it, we need to put pressure on him about something. Something he cares dearly about. You see, I've read your husband's diaries over and over again and I don't think that Bob really cared about the money. It was a protest. A moment of madness, and, as soon as he started out on his little scam, he went past the point of no return."

They were talking across the roof of the Audi now. "In fact, I think the money might still be in that locker. He knew that other people knew about the money and it was too damn risky to attempt to recover it."

Vicky slammed the door and moved towards the house. "Go on."

"Your husband said Bob had made some big deposits in his bank account after the race meeting at Cheltenham."

"Yeah, he mentioned that to me as well."

"Well, I think he may have kept part of the money back, maybe got lucky at the races. Then there was his house sale and, maybe, some savings too."

"So you're saying he didn't need the money."

Donavan nodded his head. "I don't think he did. I mean living in Spain and the property prices out there, it's not as if he would need a fortune."

Vicky fumbled in her handbag and found her key. She opened the door and Donavan followed her in. She walked through to the kitchen and opened the fridge door. She reached inside and pulled out a bottle of Moet and Chandon. "I've been saving this till you came back. I figure we're sort of celebrating tonight."

Donavan smiled, took the bottle from her, and tore the gold seal from the bottle.

Vicky took two glasses from a glass cabinet above a well-stocked wine rack.

"So you think this Richfield guy still keeps in touch with Bob Heggie?" Donavan poured out the champagne and handed Vicky a glass.

"I'm not certain." She held her glass up and Donavan touched it with his. "But if anyone does, it's James."

"Tell me about Heggie's family. Does he have children?"

Vicky took a mouthful of champagne. "Yeah, two. A little girl and little boy, Elissa and Cameron, I think, they're called. Two nice kids. I met them in the bank one day. They were in with his wife, sorry his ex-wife. The kids live with her and her new husband. Bob only sees them a few times each year."

Donavan took a long drink and drained his glass. "Perfect," he replied. "Absolutely bloody perfect."

The following morning, Donavan woke early. The temptation to wake Vicky and make love was great, but last night's exertions had satisfied his urges....for the time being. He left Vicky sleeping and made his way down the long elegant staircase. As he sat in the kitchen sipping some tea, he made a few mental notes and scribbled a few questions on the back of a small notepad that sat by the telephone.

Twenty minutes later, Vicky appeared in the doorway. "I see you've made yourself at home, Don."

Donavan didn't answer, but drained the last of his tea. Vicky clicked on the kettle "Another cup?"

He nodded. He was deep in thought. He hadn't slept well. He hadn't slept with anyone for a long time, not the whole night anyway. He found it strange, it wasn't natural, preferred his own king-size bed all to himself. And the thoughts flying round his head: thoughts of Bob Heggie and Spain, the bank, Bob's children, his ex-wife and, of course, the money.

"You need to go to the bank today, make a lunch appointment with this James Richmond."

"You mean James Richfield?"

"That's him. You need to get Heggie's address in Spain or his telephone number."

The switch on the kettle clicked off and Vicky reached for a jar with *Tea* etched on it. "You're deadly serious about this, aren't you."

Donavan eased himself from the table and walked around to where Vicky stood at the kitchen sink. He took her by the hands. "You'll go to the bank today. We'll drive in together. Make sure you see Richfield, don't take no for an answer. Get as much information as you can. Tell Richfield that Heggie's been in touch with you, and tell him you've lost his details. Play it cool - casual, make out that it's Heggie who's been in touch."

"But, Don, why would Bob want to get in touch with me? They say he killed my husband, for Christ's sake."

"Like I said, play it cool. Make out Heggie wants to quash the rumours, maybe make a peace offering, you'll think of something. You can do it. We can pull this off."

Vicky shook her head. "Then what, Don? What next? Just supposing, just supposing we do manage to track Bob down, what next? Tell me what you're thinking, because at this very moment I haven't got a damn clue."

He guided Vicky across to the table and pushed gently as the back of her legs encountered the seat. He walked back over to the sink and took two mugs from a wooden mug tree on the kitchen windowsill. Then he poured the boiling water onto the tea bags. "Like I was saying last night, he doesn't want the money, doesn't need it. In fact, if I'm right, he would be damned happy to get rid of it once and for all. The money in that locker is enough evidence to put him away for twenty years."

He poured a little milk into the two mugs and removed the tea bags. He handed Vicky a mug. "And there's one other thing."

Vicky took a mouthful, waiting for him to continue.

"The diaries."

He stood up and walked over to the window. "He doesn't

know about the diaries. Doesn't know about your husband's suspicions, being followed, his exact movements being analysed. My guess is that he'll do anything to get his hands on those diaries. In fact, I can think of half a million reasons he'll want to get a hold of them."

Vicky laughed. "You're trading the diaries for the money. Why, that's —"

"That's right, blackmail. And no, I'm not doing it, **we're** doing it together."

Vicky sat shocked. The mug shook in her hands. She couldn't believe that she was actually thinking ahead to her meeting with James Richfield, let alone talking to Donavan Smith about a plan to rob, bribe, or blackmail Bob Heggie out of half a million pounds. Could she do it? Could *they* do it?

"You think it'll work, Don?"

"Why not? It's not exactly a difficult concept is it? Put yourself in Heggie's shoes. Two thousand miles away in the sun."

"With his young girlfriend."

"What?"

"His girlfriend, Hannah. She went with him. Only about twenty-five, a bit of a scandal. People talked more about that than they did about the damn robbery."

"But your husband never mentioned that in the diaries."

"He wouldn't have. It came out after he died."

"Okay, even better. Heggie enjoying himself in the sun with his young girlfriend. Life's great, not a care in the world."

"Except one."

"Exactly."

Donavan smiled at her and Vicky basked in his approval.

"Except one. One little doubt nagging away at him. What if someone or something gives the game away? What if somebody finds the money and traces it back to Mr Bank Clerk lording it up in Spain. And, all of a sudden, a total stranger makes contact with him, reveals the contents of the diary, perhaps even a couple of pages in the post."

He took a deep breath and a mouthful of tea. "That someone

threatens to hand it over to the police. Then maybe the police reopen the case and they charge him."

"And may even find him guilty."

"Yes. Twenty years for the robbery and another twenty on top for murder."

Vicky stood up and paced the length of the room. "What if it was all in my husband's imagination? What if there's no locker and no money?"

Donavan shrugged his shoulders. "It's a possibility. But there's only one way to find out."

"What I don't understand is why my husband didn't tell the police his suspicions."

"We don't know that he didn't. Maybe there wasn't enough evidence. But I'm willing to bet that Bob Heggie won't take the chance."

Vicky poured the last of her tea down the sink. Something was nagging at the back of her mind, telling her this wasn't going to work, but something else was telling her it was worth trying. "Better get dressed then. I want to look my best for Mr Richfield."

Vicky had telephoned James Richfield herself. At first, he seemed reluctant to meet her, didn't think it was such a good idea. But she'd persisted, perhaps even flirted a little. She was good at that and, eventually, he'd agreed. The appointment was at 1.30 p.m.

Donavan waited outside in the bank car park and Vicky breezed through the large double doors of the bank. She was nervous but tried not to let it show. It was only the second time she'd been in the bank since her husband had died. The first time she'd been sent packing without a penny, told how lucky she was that the bank had decided to let sleeping dogs lie or, more accurately, let the dead man be. They didn't think it was right to take it any further, as it wouldn't do any good. It wasn't as if they could press charges on a corpse after all.

Vicky was bitter as she climbed the stairs to the managers' offices on the first floor. She practiced her best smile as she pressed the entry buzzer. The intercom crackled and a voice asked what her business was.

"Vicky Mackenzie, I've a 1.30 appointment with Mr Richfield."

A few seconds later, James Richfield's face appeared at the glass window and he looked her up and down before opening the door.

He surprised her by giving her a gentle kiss on the cheek. "Nice to see you again, Vicky, really nice. Are you keeping okay?"

Without waiting for a reply, he beckoned her to follow him into his office. A few members of staff looked up, gave a nervous smile, others kept their heads buried in the papers on their desks.

It wasn't always like this, Vicky thought to herself. Yes, Mrs Mackenzie, no, Mrs Mackenzie, three bags full, Mrs Mackenzie.

Now, an embarrassment, a worthless bit of excrement scraped off somebody's shoe. Did they really believe that her husband had planned the whole thing? The stupid bastards.

Vicky glared at the young secretary sitting directly outside James Richfield's office. She walked through the door and James took his seat, motioning her to sit down. He repeated his earlier question. " So you're keeping okay then, Vicky?"

Vicky shrugged her shoulders, looked at him and gave him the most sincere look she could muster. She even felt her eyes filling up. "So so. How would you be feeling if your partner's employer had dumped you on your arse without a penny to show for thirty years' dedication to the bank?"

James looked embarrassed. "I'd heard the rumours, but I wasn't sure whether to believe them or not. So it's true, you didn't get a penny. They blamed Mr Mackenzie for what happened?"

"Not so much blamed him, James, made him a convenient scapegoat, albeit a dead one." Vicky wiped a pretend tear from her eye. "I didn't get a bean, James, not a sausage, but that's not why I'm here. I'm not the type to stay bitter. I just need to get on with my life."

James nodded, "I understand. That's the best way, Vicky, just get on with your life, fuck the bank - they're just not worth it."

The swearing took Vicky a little bit by surprise.

"So why are you here? I must confess, I didn't think we'd ever see you here again."

"Something really trivial, James. I don't know why I didn't just ask you on the phone. But I suppose I just wanted an excuse to bury my demons, so to speak."

"I understand, Vicky. It must have been really tough walking back through those doors, and must have brought back a lot of memories."

"Yeah, well, it wasn't too hard," she lied, "after all, it's not as if I have anything to be ashamed of."

Richfield didn't answer.

"The thing is, I need to get in touch with Bob Heggie."

The expression on James Richfield's face changed almost immediately.

"He's been in touch, James, left a message on my answer phone when I was away for a few days. He left a number where I can get hold of him, but the message cut out on the last few digits."

Richfield fiddled with his tie and loosened a button at the top of his shirt. Vicky sat and waited, determined not to speak. The bank manager's face flushed red and he stuttered his words. "Why, uh, would he want to get in touch with you, Vicky?"

"That's what I need to find out, James. I don't have a clue. He sounded okay, you know, on the voice tape. Perhaps he just wants to know how I'm doing."

She knew she didn't sound very convincing; she looked into the banker's eyes. They were cold. They weren't going to tell.

"And how do you know that I've kept in contact with him, Vicky?"

"I don't, James, it's just that you and Bob were always good mates; thought you might talk to each other now and again."

The eyes mellowed a little bit and Vicky's hopes raised a fraction. " I haven't spoken to him since he left for Spain. I don't even have an address, Vicky. I'm sorry."

He got up from his chair and walked towards the window. "The thing is, I wasn't convinced that Bob was as innocent as he made out. Certain things just didn't add up. The banking hierarchy suspected it too. They interviewed me for hours after Bob finished. Even accused me of planning the heist with him. And do you know, the more I think about it, the more I think he could've just pulled it off."

Vicky sat back, fascinated by James's words. She'd never suspected Bob Heggie until Donavan Smith came on the scene. Even her husband's diaries hadn't really convinced her. He'd been bitter and angry and, at times, the diaries rambled on and on. But one thing of which she was certain was that John Mackenzie had been absolutely convinced that Bob Heggie had pulled off the scam. And Donavan Smith, he was sure too, and now she sat in front of somebody else, someone who had also worked with Bob Heggie, someone who socialised with Bob Heggie, and that someone seemed to be suggesting the same thing. It took her breath away. She sat speechless as James Richfield poured his heart out.

It was as if he'd been waiting to unburden himself. He went on to describe in detail the interviews and what they'd accused him of, and, each time he mentioned their aggressive tactics and threats, Vicky sympathised with him. It was ludicrous to think that Richfield was party to the scam. I mean he didn't even look the part. How on earth did they ever think James Richfield could have been behind the crime? Or Bob Heggie for that matter. How could Bob Heggie possibly be behind such a clever and daring plot?

For twenty minutes, James Richfield rambled on, apologising now and again for not being able to provide her with any information as to Bob's whereabouts. The more he went on, the more she believed she would never set eyes on Bob Heggie again. Richfield had been the first and last port of call. No one else in the bank knew where he lived, of that she was sure. The grand plan was falling apart, dead in the water, and she didn't relish the meeting with Donavan Smith.

She was growing tired of James Richfield's ramblings. "Look, James, it's okay. If you haven't got his address or phone number, it can't be helped. He probably didn't want me for anything special anyway."

She stood up, slinging her handbag onto her shoulder. James stood up too and they walked over to his office door. James went to depress the handle, but stopped and turned to face Vicky. He peered through the glass door and into the open plan office beyond. He lowered his voice to a whisper. " I shouldn't be telling you this, but I've an old e-mail address for him. He e-mailed me a month or two after he left. I sent him a couple of e-mails, but we both figured the bank was monitoring them. I'm not even sure if the e-mail address still works."

Vicky clung to the lifeline; something to take back to Donavan. She reached into her bag for a pen.

"You won't need that, Vicky; it's the easiest e-mail address ever. Bob Heggie at hotmail.es. The es is for España. Apparently, there aren't too many Spanish Bob Heggies."

"A fucking e-mail address, is that it?" Donavan Smith didn't appear too happy. "We're not going to get very far with that, are we? Dear Bob, send us the key to the locker or we'll come and get you. Oh, and by the way, can you tell us your address so we can find you."

Donavan took a deep breath. "Fuck, fuck and double fuck."

"It gets worse, Don. James Richfield isn't that convinced that the e-mail address still works."

"Great - bloody great."

They drove back to Vicky's house. Hardly a word was spoken. Vicky signalled left and pulled the car onto the red gravel drive. The car shuddered to a stop. Donavan turned to face her. "Supposing the e-mail does work, just supposing. What we need is some reason for Heggie to send us his address. It's easy enough for me to create another e-mail address so he won't suspect anything."

"You mean like one of those competitions. Send us some money and we'll send you a hundred thousand."

Donavan rubbed his brow and screwed up his face. "Yeah, that sort of thing, only something a little more believable."

CHAPTER SIXTEEN

It was six in the morning as Bob Heggie turned on his laptop and watched it booting up. The heat had woken him up yet again, but he didn't mind. It sure beat being woken by heavy rain hammering against the windowpane. He didn't miss the northern winters one little bit.

Tired of waiting for the computer, he wandered through to the kitchen and flicked the button on the kettle. He was still an Englishman and couldn't do without his morning cup of tea.

Hannah appeared in the doorway. She glided as she walked, almost as if on castors, silent like an elegant tiger stalking her prey. Nearly twenty years his junior, he couldn't help counting his lucky stars every single day of his life. She watched what she ate, hardly ever touched alcohol and jogged at least five kilometres each day, no matter how hot the weather was.

She smiled as she fixed on his eyes. Her long dark hair hung around her shoulders and she screwed her face up as the sun streamed through the bamboo blind in the kitchen. His eyes moved down and he picked out the glorious contours of her young lithe body silhouetted against the fabric of her oversized T-shirt. And all of a sudden, he wanted to be back in the bedroom.

"You've got an e-mail, darling."

"What?"

"An e-mail. Didn't you hear it coming through?"

Bob thought for a second. Must be from Elissa or Cameron. They were the only people with the e-mail address. Them and a few banks and insurance companies, and their e-mails just didn't come in at this time of the morning.

Hannah pulled a high bar stool from the corner of the kitchen and sat at the island in the middle of the room. "What're our plans for today, Bob? What surprises do you have in store?"

Bob smiled. He was full of surprises these days. In their short time in Spain, he'd managed to purchase two near derelict properties and a four-acre olive grove.

The last three months had been spent in the four acres of the olive grove. Between Hannah and Bob, they'd worked their way through eleven books on olive farming, production, and sales. At the end of the farming season, Bob had forecast a near ten thousand euro profit. Hannah had reminded him that six hours each day in the fields didn't amount to a wonderful hourly rate. But neither of them cared.

Bob picked up his cup and sauntered through to the small study and sat down at the desk. He dragged the cursor over the e-mail icon and double clicked.

The e-mail message box told him he had one unread message from *i-revenue.co.uk*. Normally he didn't open e-mails from anybody he didn't know; he didn't have too much faith in the Spanish I.T. troubleshooters either, and therefore avoided anything and everything that might just contain a virus.

He'd never corresponded with the Inland Revenue since he'd left England, and they certainly wouldn't know his new Spanish e-mail address.

He took a long drink from his cup as the cursor hovered over the address bar. Hannah wandered through and placed a hand on his shoulder. His fingers instinctively reached for her hand.

"Who's it from?"

"Looks like it's from the Revenue."

Hannah laughed. "Not been paying your taxes, Bob?"

Bob pressed his thumbs into his temples and rubbed hard. "I can't understand it. I was on pay as you earn. The tax was taken off at source, before I received a penny."

"Could it be anything else then? Your redundancy? Capital Gains Tax on your house sale?"

Bob thought hard. He'd been proud of his negotiating skills

in those last few meetings with the top brass of the bank. How on earth he'd talked them into giving him a redundancy package, he would never know. Combined with the profit from the sale of his house and the incredible luck he'd had at the races, he and Hannah had been able to start their new life in Spain.

"I paid the tax on the redundancy and there was nothing to pay on the house. It was exempt. I can't understand why they want me or how the hell they even found me."

"Nobody in the bank with your e-mail?"

Bob thought for a second. "Yeah…Jimmy Richfield. The pay section could have called him." His finger still hovered.

"What is it, Bob, what's wrong?"

"Jimmy wouldn't have given them it. Not if —"

"What, Bob. Tell me."

He stood up to face her. "….not if he thought it was bad news. He would just plead ignorance."

Hannah looked down at the screen. "So you think it could be good news?"

"The only thing I can think of is that it's a rebate of some sort."

Donavan Smith squealed with delight as the return e-mail address flashed onto the screen of Vicky's PC.

Vicky looked up from her book. " What is it, Don, what's up?"

"I don't believe it. The silly bastard's only gone and fallen for it and sent an e-mail back."

Vicky jumped out of her chair as Donavan double-clicked on to the address bar.

"Don't count your chickens, Don. He may just be telling you to piss off."

He didn't answer. Instead, as he read more and more of the e-mail, his smile broadened. "Hook, line and sinker, his full address. All we need to do now is get on the phone to the Spanish telephone people and we'll have his telephone number as well."

"Unless he's ex-directory of course."

Donavan glared at Vicky. "Why do you have to be so damn negative all the time? Good God, I can't believe I've even included you in this sometimes."

He got up from the chair and stormed off into the kitchen. Vicky ran after him. "I'm sorry, Don. It's just, I mean, I'm just trying to be practical that's all."

He sat at the pine table studying the few lines of the address. "Cadiz Province - any idea where that is?"

Vicky thought hard, remembering her Spanish Civil War studies from college. She pictured the scenes and maps of the big battles and the atrocities carried out by General Franco and his enemies.

"Yeah, I think I know where that is. It's on the West Coast, Portugal way."

Donavan nodded his head, looking back down at the e-mail. "Round about Seville way, is that right?"

Vicky nodded, eager to get back on his right side. "I think you're right, Don. If I remember right, there's an airport at Seville too."

Donavan turned to face her, placing a hand firmly on her buttock. "Then, my dear, I suggest you get your pretty little arse moving over to this computer. Check on the flight details to Seville, what days they leave, which regional airports they fly from, and let's plan a little trip to Spain."

Vicky smiled, but she couldn't disguise her concern and Donavan caught the look. "What is it now?"

She hesitated. "It's just…"

"You're wondering what we'll be doing there."

Vicky looked across the table at him. Then her eyes stared over his shoulders, at a picture, anything to avoid his stare.

Donavan Smith eased from the table, stood tall, looking out of the window. "It's what the Army call a recce, a reconnaissance mission. We're going to take a look at the area, see what's there, what the terrain's like. Come to think of it, what do he and his beloved Hannah look like?"

"But I don't understand, Don. I thought we were just going

to send him the diaries."

He sat back down. "Yeah, but we have to plan it well. We have to have a plan B."

Vicky raised her eyebrows. "I'm not sure what you mean."

"Listen carefully, Vicky." He held up a hand. "And, for Christ's sake, don't interrupt me until I say you can."

Vicky shook her head like an obedient lapdog. "I won't."

"Okay. Let's suppose the money really is in Locker Number 28 at Newcastle Central Station, and let's suppose Bob gets the copy of the diaries and they scare the shit out of him."

Vicky looked across at him, but she looked everywhere except his eyes.

He continued, "So far, so good. He pops the key into an envelope and everybody's happy. But then again, let's suppose the money is with him in Spain. If it is, and if he decides to part with it, we have a problem. We'll have to collect it. There's no way he would jump on an aeroplane with half a million pounds in a suitcase and hand it over to us, is there."

"I suppose not," replied Vicky.

"That's why we need to go over and see where he lives. We need to see if he lives in a quiet area, a detached house or a semi with neighbours. Does he live in a rural area or in the heart of a village? We have to be prepared for all these sorts of things. Where's he going to make the drop, where's safe, where isn't?"

He stood up again and began walking slowly around the kitchen table. "But supposing he's made of sterner stuff. What if the diaries don't worry him one little bit? I mean, he survived all of the Old Bill's questions at the time. What if Bob doesn't even read the bloody diaries; what if he reads them and decides that they are the biggest heap of shit he's ever read? And it's not as if new evidence has surfaced. And what if he's determined to hang onto that money?"

He looked directly into Vicky's eyes. A cold, hard stare. "Yeah, I think he'll be pretty damned determined to keep hold of the loot. After all, according to your husband's diaries, he worked pretty damned hard to get it."

Vicky shrugged her shoulders.

"You see, Vicky, it's fairly obvious. We need a plan B."

Vicky opened her mouth as if to speak, but his hand rose as he spoke again, "And what if...."

"What if he's spent it?" Vicky asked.

Donavan paused. "Exactly, Vicky, what if he's spent it? A nice boat in the harbour, a nice house bought and paid for with half a million pounds in stolen money. Laundered cleanly, of course. He's worked in a bank, so he'd know exactly how to do it."

He walked over to the kitchen window and gazed out into the garden, eyes not focused on anything in particular. A deep sigh and a smile, as he turned back to face Vicky. He began a slow and deliberate walk around the table. "I have a feeling that the money is still there. I don't think our little bank clerk even had the balls to take it out of the locker. I figure it's still sitting there gathering dust just waiting, waiting to be spent."

Vicky spoke again. She figured she hadn't been shouted down the last time, so, maybe, it was okay. "So, what is plan B?"

"A good question, Vicky, and, to be honest, I don't know, but I've got a few ideas floating around in my head. He's got kids, right?"

Vicky nodded.

"Do you know them? Do you know his wife, or rather his ex-wife?"

"Yes, but —"

The hand came up yet again and Vicky stopped in mid-sentence. A look of horror flashed across her face.

"Yes. I'm afraid you're thinking what I'm thinking. A nasty word, isn't it."

"What word?"

"Kidnap!"

"Oh no, Don. Oh no. I won't be any part of this. I don't mind sending some threats just to see if Bob Heggie buckles, and, who knows, we could end up half a million pounds the richer, but I certainly won't be part of any kidnap plot."

Donavan strolled over to Vicky, stood close to her, a little too close for comfort. His eyes were cold, determined and hostile, very, very hostile. She hadn't seen a look like that before.

He knelt down, his eyes level with hers now. She was conscious of a tremor in her legs, and she couldn't stand up and walk away, even if she wanted to.

"Vicky," he whispered, his lips inches away from hers. "*I suffer not a woman to teach, nor to usurp authority over the man, but to be in silence. First Timothy 2:12.*"

He leaned forward and brushed her lips with his. "You've got to ask yourself if you trust me? If you love me, and, more importantly, whether you want this relationship to last longer than the next ten minutes. Because from where I'm sitting, it doesn't look as if that's what you want."

He leaned back and Vicky lurched forward. "I do, Don, I do, oh yes, I do."

A smile flicked across his face, then disappeared again. He stood up to his full height, cutting out the sunlight flooding through the kitchen window. She reached out for him and he caught her hands as they thrust forward, pushing them away.

"I'm not sure you do, Vicky. Your mind is full of doubt and you're lacking any trust. I think I should just go now, back to the Smoke and forget the whole thing."

"No, Don, I do trust you, honestly I do. I'll do anything. Please don't go."

Donavan moved away and Vicky found herself clawing pathetically at his trousers.

He walked over to the doorway and she rushed across, blocking his path. She felt as if the relationship was hanging by a thread. Once he walked through the doorway, there would be no going back.

"I do trust you, Don, I do. Please."

She couldn't stop herself. She realised what a pathetic, quivering wreck she must look, but she didn't want this man to leave. She now realised she would do anything to stay with him, anything to keep him. She'd been so long without love, so long without a lover like this. She remembered how they'd been so good together, how he'd been so attentive and caring, and how she'd succumbed to every demand he'd thrown at her. She cringed at some of the perversions he'd demanded, but not once had she refused.

"Anything, Don."

Donavan stopped and she thought his eyes warmed up slightly, if that were possible. "Okay, listen to me."

She found herself nodding.

"First, we're going to book that trip to Spain, that little recce."

She breathed a sigh of relief. He wasn't going.

"Say, a couple of weeks from now? Then, later this afternoon, you're going to play the little Sherlock Holmes. You're going to find out where Heggie's ex-wife lives, get her telephone number and you're going to call her."

"Debra."

"Sorry?"

"She's called Debra. We've been out for coffee several times, even had dinner together, me and John with Bob and Debra."

Donavan grinned. "Excellent. Fucking hunky-dory. Shouldn't be too hard to arrange another little date then, should it."

Vicky shook her head. "Shouldn't be too hard. She got married again a few weeks ago. The new husband's called Stephen, though I've never met him."

Donavan walked over to her and took her gently by the hair. "And you're going to trust me from now on, aren't you."

Before she could answer, Donavan leaned forward and kissed her. She felt frozen to the spot, helpless, stranded like a kitten in a sack, as the cold water rushed into the darkness. She couldn't move. His tongue probed gently between her lips and her knees weakened. His tongue traced a sensuous trail along her lips, she felt a pressure pushing down on her shoulders and she fell to her knees.

* * * *

150

Vicky dialled the old number in her diary. Debra answered the phone. They talked. She came over as very caring and seemed genuinely sorry for what had happed to John Mackenzie. Of course, she didn't realise that Bob Heggie, her ex-husband, had even been implicated as chief suspect in the raid, let alone mentioned as the possible murderer.

Yeah, the bank had done a bloody good job in disclosing just enough information to suit themselves and the City. Donavan sat beside her with the telephone on loudspeaker and smiled broadly as the conversation progressed. Although a little nervous at first, Vicky became more confident as each minute passed. Debra apologised several times for not keeping in touch and Vicky pushed the conversation along gently, patiently waiting for the right moment to suggest a get-together. "The thing is, Debbie, I'm really happy at the moment. I've met this terrific fella."

Donavan squeezed her thigh and slid his hand slowly up her skirt, teasing her by tracing a finger along the thin material of her pants. She took a deep breath and gripped his wrist firmly. "I wish you could meet him. He's so good looking and has some real hidden talents too."

Debra laughed. "You don't say, Vicky. Better keep him away from me then, you know what my track record is like! What's his name? Where's he from?"

"Don Smith and you won't know him, he's a trader in London."

"So you don't see him too often then?"

"On the contrary, Debbie, he's up most weekends."

"I bet he is, you little harlot."

The two girls shrieked with laughter and Vicky seized the moment. "The thing is, Debbie, I feel the time's right to mend a few bridges. The truth is, I've missed John's old social circle: his old colleagues, Jim Moody, James Richfield, you and Bob when you were together, and I don't think I even know the name of your new husband."

She paused for a second. "And I would just love to meet him."

"Brilliant, Vicky, and I would just love to meet this Don fellow, and hear about his hidden charms."

The two girls laughed again.

"Let's do dinner then. When's this man of yours next up from London?"

Donavan jumped up and nodded his head frantically. Vicky looked up at him and raised her eyebrows as if asking a question. Donavan mouthed *next weekend* at her.

"How about next weekend?"

"Should be okay. I'll firm it up with Stephen, that's his name by the way. He's great, so easy-going and relaxed, totally different to Bob. I'll need to fix up a babysitter, but it shouldn't be too much of a problem. I'm sure the two guys will get along great."

"I'm sure they will," replied Vicky, "I'm sure they'll get on like a house on fire."

CHAPTER SEVENTEEN

Bob Heggie sat on his veranda, pawing nervously at the envelope in his hands. It was marked with a priority mail sticker and the address was typewritten with no details of a sender. The first one hadn't really bothered him but this was the fourth one in as many days.

He slid a finger under the seal and tore it open. He looked inside and a foul-tasting bile crawled up his throat. He took a quick mouthful of lukewarm tea, swallowed hard, and pulled out the contents of the envelope. Another photocopied A4 page of the late John Mackenzie's diary. No instruction, no clues, nothing.

A bead of perspiration fell onto the page as he read, and he wondered whether it was due to the early morning warmth, nervousness, or a little too much wine the night before. Probably a bit of everything, he thought, as he devoured the script quickly.

And the script worried him. The text had clearly been written by John Mackenzie. It was his handwriting, his exact thoughts and his suspicions a few days after the mock bank raid that had been staged in his bank. Mackenzie was describing how the money that had been taken during a fictitious bank raid hadn't been returned to the branch. He was worried.

The page in Bob's hand described Mackenzie's first concerns that perhaps the raid hadn't been a training exercise after all. Bob read the final line and a shiver ran the length of his spine.

Money still not turned up, Bob Heggie acting very strange.

Hannah had flown back to England just before the envelopes had started to arrive, to a friend's birthday party, and to visit relatives. In a way, he was kind of glad she wasn't here, best not to see him this way. Perhaps they'd stop by the time she got back. And yet, Bob knew that they wouldn't. Something told Bob that this would run and run, and it wouldn't stop running until there was an end result.

Vicky Mackenzie was the obvious sender of the diary pages, but he just couldn't see the purpose or the reason behind it. Okay, he'd rejected her all those months ago, but she hadn't seemed to take it personally and, Jesus Christ, it had been over a year ago. Had Mackenzie any family that Bob didn't know about, and if so, how the hell had they found out where he was? What did they want?

Not for the first time, Bob wished he could turn back the clock.

Then he thought again. Pulling off the bank scam had saved his life. It had allowed him to get out of the bank forever, and it had pulled him through his divorce when, at times, he figured suicide was the only option.

He sat overlooking the vineyards on the hills as the shadows from the sun danced around the garden in a slow motion waltz; and he thought of Hannah and he thought of his children, Elissa and Cameron, and how wonderful his life had been before the envelopes started arriving through the letterbox.

And he knew they wouldn't stop. They would keep on coming day after day, each new page of the diary revealing more and more from Mackenzie's twisted mind.

Bob walked through the warm naya, the page from the diary held loosely in his hand. He reached for the kettle, not particularly thirsty, but not knowing what else to do. He studied the page again. He opened the fridge door and reached inside for the milk. In the back of the fridge, an ice-cold, golden tin of San Miguel begged to be opened. Bob looked at his watch, 8.30 a.m. Too early.

Back on the veranda, the cool liquid stung the back of his throat, but, as soon as it reached its destination, Bob began to feel better. He drained the small tin with two quick gulps and stood up to find more. Deep in the basement of the underbuild, he opened the large fridge-freezer and smiled as a twelve-pack caught his eye. He held the transparent plastic seal and tore at a can with his other hand. As he walked up the stairs, he cracked the ring pull and took a large mouthful. He walked out into the bright sunlight and looked across the valley. He held up the shiny tin and focused on it. Then he looked back at the house where he'd spent the most idyllic and peaceful year of his life. He looked across at the olive groves and took in the pungent aroma of the almond blossom lingering in the valley bottom. *I won't give this up, I won't.*

The can flew through the air and tumbled down the mountainside, bouncing on rocks and clattering against the stony terrain of the hill.

The following morning, a further envelope arrived. Bob breathed in deeply as he opened it, but figured he wouldn't be as shocked as he had been on the previous days.

It was the same format, a further page detailing Bob's movements following the raid. Furthermore, Mackenzie had taken the opportunity to run a credit check on Bob by logging onto the bank's internal computer system and scrutinising his finances. Details of loans, overdrafts, and credit cards. It didn't look good. Mackenzie had penned a comment right at the end of the page about the purchase of Bob's Harley Davidson and just couldn't imagine where the money had come from to finance it. Mackenzie had found one thing the private detectives employed by the bank hadn't.

A motive.

* * * *

Bob stood in the arrivals lounge of Jerez airport, nervous and on edge. To make matters worse, Hannah's flight had been delayed forty minutes. He paced the marble floored complex and wandered through to a small cafeteria. He craved a beer, but ordered a double espresso. The concentrated shot of caffeine and sugar mix hit the spot and Bob rose to his feet eager to be united with Hannah. She'd only been away for six days but he wanted her back. He should have gone with her like she'd suggested. Then, at least they could have faced this together. He wondered whether it would be fair to burden Hannah with something like this, despite all they'd been through together. She'd asked about the raid and the money at the time. She had had her suspicions as well, and Bob had lied to her. She'd never mentioned it since.

"Jesus H, Bob, you look like shit. If this is what a week away does to you, I'm not leaving you alone again."

Bob smiled, took Hannah's suitcase with his one hand and her hand with his other. She leaned forward and embraced him. They kissed. Bob held her tight, didn't want to let go. He kissed her like she'd been away for years, and, although he was conscious of people beginning to stare, he didn't care. Hannah broke the kiss and took in a deep breath. "Wow, Bob, you've kind of missed me, I guess."

Bob nodded. "Yeah, you could say that. Let's get home. There's something I need to tell you."

CHAPTER EIGHTEEN

Donavan Smith took particular care getting ready that evening. Nothing too flash, but not too casual either. A black pair of Armani jeans and a thick cotton DKNY white shirt. Labels were important to him; his clothes were one of his extravagances in life. He stared into the full mirror; he looked good… felt good.

He walked downstairs. Vicky stood at the hallway mirror, applying the finishing touches to her make-up. Too much, Donavan thought to himself.

The taxi arrived a little after seven and sped quickly through the exclusive roads of the Darras Hall Estate, home to the rich and famous, successful businessmen, TV presenters and Newcastle United footballers.

Five minutes later, they passed Newcastle International Airport and Donavan couldn't help thinking of the trip to Spain the following week. He went over the plans in his mind, how he would find Bob Heggie, and what he would do when he got there. He thought about his strategy tonight, how he would be introduced to Bob Heggie's ex-wife and her new husband and how he needed to take things slowly, one step at a time.

They would be dining at Rockafellas on the Quayside. Terry Miller owned the restaurant, a down-to-earth Newcastle man who had won a bizarre 'fly on the wall' reality TV show. The show had attempted to turn the contestants into chefs, with the best one, or rather the most likeable one, taking the spoils. The prize had been enough money to start a restaurant.

Donavan hadn't seen the programme and wouldn't even

know Terry Miller if he stood in front of him. Vicky waxed lyrical about how addictive the show had been and couldn't wait to meet the main man.

The impressive sight of the illuminated Tyne Bridge came into view and Donavan asked the taxi driver to pull over.

Vicky looked across, slightly bemused.

"We're a bit early, let's have a quick drink."

"But, Don, we said we'd be there at…"

Don held up a hand and whispered in her ear, "I said, let's get a fucking drink."

He kissed her delicately on the cheek and then brushed his lips across her neck, feeling a slight tremor shudder through her. He loved the power he held over her. He knew exactly what she liked, knew exactly what she wanted to hear, and how she wanted to be controlled. "And, if you're a good girl tonight, there's more where that came from."

She smiled and Donavan leaned over with a twenty-pound note for the taxi driver. The meter read nineteen pounds fifty. "Keep the change, pal."

The taxi driver stole a cheap look in the rear-view mirror and Donavan couldn't help smirking as he left the car.

Donavan made his grand entrance into Rockafellas twelve minutes late. Vicky waved at a couple sitting by the window, and a waiter escorted them across. The handsome-looking couple stood politely as Vicky made the introductions. Stephen seemed a little nervous, even uncomfortable. About to partake in an evening's forced pleasantries with two strangers he'd never met before. Donavan would work on him first.

Debra wasn't exactly what he expected: tall, dark and elegant, she reminded him of Nigella Lawson.

"Pleased to meet you, Don," she extended a hand. "Been hearing all about you."

Donavan leaned forward and kissed her politely on the cheek. "Lovely to meet you." Then he turned to her husband. "And you too, Steve. Vicky tells me you've recently tied the knot."

As the couple turned to each other, Don cringed. Pathetic

little teenage grins flashed across their faces. Stephen reached for Debra's hand. "About three months now, Don," Stephen answered. "Happiest days of my life. We had a fantastic day, about forty friends and close family."

Debra interjected, "We had the whole day up at the Horton Grange Hotel, by the airport; couldn't fault them; a beautiful five course lunch and then we partied until the early hours."

She turned to Vicky. "Even Elissa and Cameron made it to midnight."

Donavan laughed, "I hope you didn't take them on honeymoon with you."

Stephen's smile evaporated, "Couldn't quite manage the old honeymoon, Don, what with the pressures of work and things."

"And the children," said Debra. "Babysitting, school, you know, the usual sort of thing."

"Yeah… I understand," said Donavan slowly, the gears in his brain setting in motion. "You really should try to get away a little later in the year."

"Perhaps," said Stephen, "maybe we can."

They sat down and ordered some drinks. Donavan sat opposite Debra. The small talk flowed for half an hour, and, occasionally, he caught her staring at him. Any other occasion and he would have tried it on with Debra. He found her extremely attractive and very intelligent in conversation, no matter that she had only been married for a few weeks. It would have made it all the sweeter.

He imagined what she would look like naked beneath the dress, wondered if she'd scream out on the point of orgasm or perhaps give just a more conservative moan.

He'd read somewhere that the average man fantasised about sex every ten minutes. He figured that was accurate, as he looked longingly at Debra's deep red lips, the expensive lip-gloss she'd applied that evening catching the light of the flickering candle on the table. Her soft tongue licked at a droplet of wine in the corner of her mouth. Vicky would come in useful later on that evening, but his thoughts would be elsewhere as her delicate mouth and expert tongue brought him to orgasm.

He pushed the thoughts aside now though. On this occasion, he would refrain from flirting with his new acquaintance. Donavan had his line of attack all mapped out.

Stephen was hard work, a little shy, but, during the course of the evening, Donavan drew him more and more into the conversation, making sure his wine glass never fell below half level. At the same time, Donavan kept a clear head. He ensured that for every half glass of wine he drank, he took a full glass of water.

As the desserts arrived, Stephen was slurring his speech slightly, and Donavan had managed to prise more than enough information from him, making mental notes that he would easily recall when he got back home.

Donavan looked across at Debra, caught her gaze, held it there for a second, and congratulated himself as she blushed slightly. "Tell me about your children, Debbie."

"Elissa and Cameron?" She looked across at Vicky. "She's told you all about them, I suppose?"

Donavan nodded. "I just adore kids. Unfortunately, I've never got round to marriage and children, that sort of thing, and, anyway, it's great when you can just hand them back again."

Stephen laughed loudly, "You can say that again."

Donavan caught a look of disapproval from Debra and figured that perhaps Stephen wasn't so committed to the cause as he made out.

Vicky turned to face him. "I didn't know you liked kids so much, Don."

Donavan smiled. "Oh yeah, every chance I get, I take my sister's two. That's why I don't get up here as often as I can."

Stephen drained his glass. "Looks like we've found the perfect babysitter, Debra."

Donavan raised his glass. He couldn't believe he'd achieved so much in such a short time. "I'll drink to that, Steve." He looked at Debra. She didn't seem as sure, but it was early days.

At the end of the evening, they shared a taxi with their newfound friends. Donavan made a point of sitting with Debra and Vicky in the back, while Stephen sat in the front supported by the door. It was only a short journey to Stephen's apartment on the Quayside and, as the car lurched around by the Guildhall, Donavan leaned heavily into Debra. As he apologised and righted himself, he removed her mobile phone from her open handbag and placed it on the seat next to him.

The taxi came to a stop and the driver opened the rear door. Debra gave Donavan a gentle kiss on the cheek and apologised for the condition of her husband, claiming he hadn't drunk this much for years.

Twenty minutes later, the taxi arrived at Darras Hall and Donavan jumped eagerly from the cab.

"I'm so tired, Don," Vicky sighed, as they walked through the door, "so tired."

Donavan thought back to the restaurant and his beautiful new friend sitting opposite him. "Yeah, me too, Vic. Let's go straight to bed."

* * * *

Donavan awoke early, went down to the kitchen, and took out a notebook from a kitchen drawer. He had made three pages of notes by the time Vicky walked into the kitchen. She looked at him and he noticed a wary glare.

"What's up, Vic?"

She didn't answer.

"I said, what's up?"

"You were a little rough last night." She flicked her hair and Donavan looked at the scratch marks on her neck. "And Jesus, Don, I swear there's half my hair left in the bed."

Donavan laughed. "You shouldn't be so good, my little sex queen. You do things with that little mouth of yours that take me to heaven and back."

Vicky smiled and Donavan Smith tried to figure out what was behind it. A nervous smile. Perhaps a little fear?

Around midday, the phone rang. Donavan listened as Vicky

took the call. It was Debra. After a few minutes, Vicky shouted through to the kitchen, "I don't suppose you found a mobile phone in the taxi, Don. Debbie seems to have lost hers last night. She called Rockafellas but it's not there."

Donavan walked through. "Oh Jesus, yeah, I did, I forgot to mention it. It was lying on the back seat; it must have fallen out of her bag in the taxi."

Vicky relayed the good news to Debra and Donavan walked through to the lounge with the mobile phone in his hand. "Tell her we'll drop it by later, on our way into town."

Vicky screwed her face up, a puzzled, confused look. "We'll drop it off later. It looks as if we're going into town."

She hung up.

"I need a few bits and pieces; thought we'd have some lunch out."

Vicky nodded and took his hand, all smiles again, having forgotten about her treatment last night and the silent tears afterwards as Donavan slept.

They're all the same, Donavan thought, as a smile crept across his face. Treat them like shit, like a slave. Push the boundaries to the limit, time after time, and, then, a little tenderness and a reward and the bad stuff is forgotten. Not unlike a game of golf: a bundle of bad shots, then that one clean strike as the ball soars two hundred and fifty yards up the middle of the fairway. The relationship between the player and his club is restored and the bad shots don't matter anymore.

Vicky pulled the Audi into the underground car park on the Quayside and Donavan jumped eagerly from the car.

"It was a real stroke of luck, Don, you noticing the phone on the seat last night. Jesus H Christ, I just don't know what I'd ever do if I lost my mobile. I mean half my life is in the damn thing."

Donavan looked across the top of the car as she stood up. "You really are amazing, aren't you. No wonder you have blond hair."

She dropped the keys into her handbag and looked up at him.

"What do you mean?" she asked.

Donavan smiled, a smug smile, a smile as if to say he was always one or two steps ahead of the game. "Two reasons why I lifted the phone from her bag. Firstly, it's full of useful numbers, - people at the bank, her Mum and a number for Bob Heggie in Spain, a Spanish mobile too."

Vicky stood in silence, her mouth hanging open, waiting for Donavan to speak.

"And secondly," he said, as he took her hand and led her into the bright sunlight. "I get to meet the delightful Cameron and Elissa."

* * * *

Donavan sat opposite Vicky at Costa Coffee in the departure lounge of Newcastle Airport. It was several weeks since he had been introduced to Debra and Stephen but he'd been reasonably pleased with his slow, but steady, progress.

Donavan hated airports and, on this particular occasion, it was alive with holidaymakers and he hated it even more. At least in Heathrow or Gatwick you got the celebrity set and the international business traveller dressed in expensive non-crease Italian designer suits. Not here, not in Newcastle airport. The airport was awash with the *holidaymaker*, all dressed in comfortable clothing as if a three-hour flight represented a day's train journey on some third world cattle truck. And they milled around with no real purpose, eager to buy a last minute duty free gift or trinket. The stupid bastards, didn't they realise that the airport company simply replaced the duty with a higher profit margin? And they sat around in the bars two or three hours before the flight eager to swill as much beer down their necks as possible, forgetting there would only be two toilets on the cramped aeroplane they were about to board.

And the football shirts; Jesus, what was that all about? I don't want to know that you come from Sunderland and support that wretched little football team, nor do I want to see your man boobs and your fat, bloated beer belly poking out from your skintight England shirt.

Donavan took a sip of his espresso and looked across the cup at Vicky. "So tell me the itinerary, Vic."

Vicky had taken to the secretarial role well. Donavan had delegated the task to her: she was to be the organiser, and he would be the fixer.

She beamed. "The flight lands at Seville 14.22 Spanish time and we pick up the hire car from Alamo situated near Gate 24. We have a Vauxhall Zafira, nothing too flash you said, don't want to be noticed."

She flicked a smile at Donavan and he nodded approvingly.

"And, from there, it's only a forty-five minute drive to Peurto Real. I chose one of the larger towns near to where Bob lives. I thought staying in the same village might be too risky. After all, he does know me."

Donavan leaned across and rubbed her shoulder. She took a mouthful of sparkling water and continued, "I've rented a small town house as opposed to a hotel, less conspicuous, and from there, Bob's village, Niebla, is about a twenty-minute drive. I've a map of the whole area together with a *callejero*, a street map of Niebla. Bob's house, *Casa Calemlio,* is clearly marked."

Donavan took the map and studied the thick red ring around the property and the contour lines surrounding it. "Perfect. We should get a great view of the house from this hill," he said, pointing at the map. "You've done a great job. You do have the photocopy of the diary, don't you?"

Vicky reached across and lifted the over heavy flight bag resting on the seat. "Safe and sound, Don, safe and sound."

Donavan Smith smiled, stretched in his seat, and then sat back. He was looking forward to a week in the sun.

CHAPTER NINETEEN

It was three days since the last envelope containing a page from John Mackenzie's diary had arrived through Bob's letterbox. The Spanish postman wasn't exactly predictable, arriving anytime between seven in the morning and midday. As Bob looked at his watch, it was 1.15 p.m., and he was fairly certain that Jose had delivered all he was going to deliver that day and was now safely ensconced in the local tapas bar with his amigos. Although he breathed a sigh of relief for that day, he somehow knew that another delivery was imminent.

And, earlier that day, he had confessed all to Hannah. He'd taken her through every stage of his life, from the moment Debra had walked in to tell him their marriage was over, right through to his little fantasy of robbing a bank. He sat her down on the terrace steps with a bottle of cool white Rioja and two glasses, and he talked. While he talked, she listened and never said a word.

"I'd suspected Debbie had been having an affair for a while. We hadn't slept together for a couple of months, and I couldn't remember the last time she'd told me she loved me."

He laughed. "We used to have a silly little pledge that we'd tell each other every day. It didn't matter whether we were apart, if I was away on business, or whatever. I'd call her on the phone. *Tell me,* she'd whisper. And I would and she'd whisper it back. Then she dropped the first bombshell. *I don't love you anymore,* she said on a dark, stormy night at Christmas time. I retreated into a shell, refused to believe what I'd heard."

He took a long mouthful of Rioja. "A few weeks later, she mentioned divorce. I refused, said we could continue for the sake of the children. We carried on for a few months, but it got worse. In the end, we weren't even talking and the kids were asking questions. I immersed myself in the children. I took them to every activity I could come up with. Ice skating, tennis, badminton, the pictures, Pizza Hut, anything. Anything and everything. Of course, Debbie didn't come. I suppose it gave her more time to be with Steve, although I didn't know about him at the time. But, day by day, I began to suspect there was someone else. She would come back to the house after the children had gone to bed, and I could smell the bastard on her. Sure, she'd had a shower after her sordid little encounter, but as she left him, she couldn't resist one last little hug."

Hannah looked on sympathetically as his eyes filled with tears.

"Then she admitted she'd met someone else. Claimed it had only just happened. I knew different. My best friend, Dave Valentine, reckoned it had been going on for a couple of years. He'd seen them once in Darlington when he was on business and didn't have the heart to tell me. They were in a hotel. I recalled the occasion exactly. Debbie claimed she'd been away to York on a girlie weekend. Like an idiot, I still wanted us to stay together, told her we could work it out, told her I understood, I was to blame, hadn't gave her the attention she deserved. I can change, I blurted out to her, crying like a two-year-old child."

A tear trickled down his cheek and he wiped at it with the back of his hand. "I didn't realise how cruel she could be. The letter arrived from the solicitor a few days later, and she even brought Steve round to meet the children the following week. They told me when I came in from work. Just accept it's over, was all she could say." He gave a long and deep sigh. "And, I guess, at that point, I did."

An uncomfortable silence ensued. A minute that seemed like a lifetime, and then he continued. "I don't know how I ever went back to work. I took a few weeks off, then ran out of excuses. I hated every day. Mackenzie seemed to sense my weakness and turned the screw tighter and tighter every damn day. Then it happened." He looked up. "The shooting."

"When the young girl was killed?"

Bob nodded. "Yeah, and I was shot."

He took a long mouthful of wine and described how he'd viewed the shooting from another angle, floating above the action as a sort of unwelcome onlooker. "I thought I was dead. I wanted to be dead. I prayed the bullet had hit my heart. The kids would get the life insurance, they'd get over me eventually, and, though I hated to admit it, another father figure would be there ready and waiting to take my place."

He paused and looked into Hannah's eyes. She inched a little closer to him.

"I changed from that day. I considered suicide for a few days. I remember driving down to the Quayside in Walker, on the outskirts of the city on the east side. It's a depressing place at the best of time, but, on a grey, misty evening, when you felt like I did, it seemed…."

He poured some more wine into his empty glass. "It seemed so easy. I sat with the engine revving, calling Debbie all the bitches and Mackenzie all the bastards under the sun. I inched towards the Quayside and the murky, black waters of the Tyne loomed up in front of me."

He laughed. "And then something crazy happened inside me. I started laughing, right there in the bloody car, like some escaped lunatic. Bollocks to them, I thought to myself, fuck the lot of them. I hammered the car into reverse, swung a one-eighty, and drove through the city at twice the speed limit, laughing all the way. How I didn't get caught I'll never know."

He revealed how the daydream was born on the mountaintops of the Lake District, how he dreamt up the scam, and how it seemed to be the only way out.

And he went on, explaining how the fantasy ran out of control and turned into reality. It had started with the phoney e-mail he sent from head office and then he described how the runaway train gathered speed and fooled everyone. It fooled the bank and the managers, and it fooled the director at the top, John Mackenzie. No one suspected anything; at least, that's what Bob thought, until the pages from Mackenzie's diary started to arrive.

"I had no intention of following it through, Hannah. I was ready to pull out at any time. I just needed my fix of excitement, something to pull me through the mess that my life had become."

Bob looked at the bottle; it was empty. Hannah caught his stare.

"Stay there, I'll get another one." She drained her glass and placed it on the step.

She returned a few minutes later with another bottle and poured herself a glass too. "I don't want you to stop. I need to hear this. I need to know the reason you lied to me."

Bob opened his mouth in an apologetic gesture. She held up a hand as if she knew what was coming. "Just go on. We'll sort us out afterwards."

Hannah filled up his glass and he took another long drink. Bob placed the glass on the old stone step, each one worn away in the middle from a hundred thousand footsteps. He moved the glass to the edge of the step trying to find a horizontal lie. He looked high above the house and marvelled at the beautiful blossom-covered slopes of the mountains. The sun flashed against something, the camera lens of a hill walker perhaps, or a watch face or piece of jewellery. He could just about make out the shape of two people enjoying a cool drink, perhaps, or was it three people? He couldn't really tell.

"I wanted to pull out, believe me, I did. I just wanted the stimulation, the thrill."

"But you didn't, did you?"

Bob lowered his head. "I couldn't."

Hannah rose to her feet. "What do you mean, you couldn't? For Christ's sake, Bob, you're a criminal. You could've got twenty years in jail."

Bob looked up and grinned at Hannah, then regretted it instantly. "Still could."

She frowned. "What?"

"I could still get twenty years. Maybe more. Elissa and Cameron would be adults by the time I got out."

"And….what about me?"

He took another drink. It didn't taste as good anymore. He nodded, "Yeah, you. You'd be in your forties, maybe fifties and…" He noticed the tears welling up in her eyes and her bottom lip quivering ever so slightly. He stopped and left the statement unfinished.

What would she do, for God's sake? She was a young woman, beautiful, stunning even, and intelligent and, at times, Bob wondered what on earth she saw in him.

"And the money, Bob, that's what we're living off? Dirty money?"

Bob shook his head. "No. That bit isn't a fraud. You remember the races at Cheltenham? When I won all that money? Over a hundred thousand."

Hannah cast her mind back to that glorious spring day that seemed like a lifetime away. "Do I remember? It was just brilliant."

"Yeah, well, together with a healthy little pay-off from the bank and the settlement from my divorce, I was able to buy the properties in Spain. I mortgaged them a little and we've worked hard building up a legitimate income. I never touched the money from the scam."

"So our money is clean?" Hannah asked.

"Clean as a whistle."

Hannah exhaled, a long, deliberate sigh. She reached across the table and took his hands. "Two more questions. How much and where is it?"

Bob took his final mouthful of wine. "Half a million pounds."

Her mouth fell open and she sat in stunned silence. Then she picked up her glass, stood up and walked away. She left him sitting in the hot afternoon sun.

Alone.

Again.

Perhaps he should just give himself up. It would be better for everyone. Better for Hannah anyhow. She could get on with her life. Perhaps meet someone else, get married and have a family. Bob Heggie on the run. Selfish.

And then there was the other option. Leave the children with a nice trust fund courtesy of the fat life insurance policy he'd taken out a few years ago. The bank accounts and property, all in joint names. It would simply revert to Hannah, the advisers had said. Everyone would benefit.

And he remembered his blackest day as he had sat on the banks of the Tyne.

CHAPTER TWENTY

Donavan and Vicky sat 250 metres above *Casa Calemlio* on the gentle, dusty slope of *Montana Espia*. If anyone should walk this way, they were simply two eccentric English birdwatchers enjoying a day out in the Cadiz hills and mountains.

No one would come this way. The more sensible hikers and climbers had long since gone, eager to escape the punishing afternoon sun, as it blazed down from a cloudless blue sky. The gentle undulations of the orange blossom-covered slopes stretched out before them, giving a perfect view of the house. Pale pink, wild geraniums surrounded them, and Donavan couldn't help feeling a little bit envious of his intended target, sitting on the steps of his finca way below them.

"What on earth are they doing?"

Donavan held up a hand as he studied the images coming through the powerful four-by-four screen attached to the binoculars set upon the matt black tripod. He liked the recently purchased technology. Steiner Senator 10X50's with a crisp, clear 400 + pixel screen, videoing the action for posterity. They were coated in grey plastic and the Senator line was quoted as *the top of the range.*

"Looks like they're getting pissed"

Vicky frowned.

"See for yourself. They're already on their second bottle of wine and it's not even four o'clock."

Vicky studied the image and frowned as Hannah walked

inside the house and disappeared from view. "She's gone inside."

Donavan refocused on the screen as a bead of perspiration fell from his nose onto the lens of the binoculars. "I think it's time to make that delivery, Vic. Let's make our way down the hill. This sun is unbearable."

Without waiting for her agreement, Donavan unscrewed the binoculars from the tripod and carefully removed the detachable screen. He packed everything into the leather carry case and set off down the hill. Vicky scuttled along behind him.

Bob lay on the sun lounger, shaded underneath the bougainvillea-covered pergola. It was his favourite spot in the garden. The wine had pushed him into a Spanish-style siesta.

"Wake up, wake up!" Hannah screamed, "they're here, they're here!"

He focused on the large, brown envelope Hannah was holding and wiped the sleep from his eyes. She handed him the package and he pulled out at least a hundred sheets of bright white A4 copy paper.

"It was left on the front doorstep, I noticed it an hour ago and I've read the whole lot, the full version of Mackenzie's diary."

Bob slipped the blindingly white paper back into the envelope.

"Aren't you going to read it?"

"What for? I know what's in there. Remember?"

Hannah smiled, "I suppose you do."

The smile warmed Bob. It was infectious. "So you're not mad with me?"

Hannah sat down beside him. "I've had a couple of hours to think. Mad…definitely, but only because you lied to me. I asked you, pleaded with you, to tell me the truth at the time, I suspected you all along."

"I was only trying to protect you."

"I suppose so, but you still lied and that's what I'm angry about. We shouldn't have any secrets between each other."

"We haven't now."

Hannah didn't answer him. Then she smiled. "But, also, I'm quite impressed that I've fallen in love with a desparado on the run."

Bob stood up, stretched and took a few paces to ease the stiffness.

"And you didn't answer my last question."

Bob took her hand and looked down at her. "I'm not with you."

She squeezed his hand gently. "The money, you dummy. Where's the money?"

Bob thought about a lie. Another one. He looked into her eyes staring up at him like a big soft, trusting, puppy dog. Maybe a boxer pup, with those eyes, especially at dinner time. He broke her grip, turned towards the garden and looked up at the hill again. The couple still stood in the same place. He turned back to face her. "In Locker Number 28 at Newcastle Central Station."

CHAPTER TWENTY-ONE

Bob didn't leave the house for the next few days. He was on edge. He was anxious, awaiting another delivery of some sort, but not knowing exactly what. Hannah seemed nervous too, not her usual bubbly self.

Bob sat on the sunlounger in his favourite shaded spot, and every now and again, scoured the hills with a pair of old Russian Army issue binoculars. They were out there, he was sure. But just who were *they*?

He focused on a couple of hikers taking the long, gentle traverse up *Montana Espicio*. The soft white stole of a cloud lingered high above the valley. Every now and again, the hikers disappeared from view, obscured by large orange trees or the natural rugged terrain of the mountain. He studied them for two hundred metres, but not once did they look in the direction of the binoculars. He lowered the field glasses as they disappeared from view. He placed them on the table beside him and wandered around to the front of the house. He focused on the step where the copy of the diary had been left a few days before. He walked to the front gate and looked up and down the dusty lane.

He was awaiting the next onslaught, the next offensive. *They* were attacking his head. Not knowing was round the next corner, and always expecting the worst. He didn't know who *they* were or what *they* wanted and he didn't have a clue what their next move would be. Why didn't they just pick the phone up and tell him? It was torture of the worst kind. They were professionals.

Bob remembered a bully at school, bottom of the class in most subjects, but top of the league in violence and intimidation. A broken home, a single parent, rumours abounded of abuse by a stepfather. And, one day, as Bob brushed past him on the school bus home, he'd knocked a can of lemonade from the bully's grip, the contents spilling onto the dirty bus floor. The bully had demanded the price of the can there and then, and Bob had agreed to bring the money in the following day. And he did. But the bully had demanded it the next day and the next day and Bob had been so frightened he'd complied with the demand for over a week, scraping pennies here and pennies there, even resorting to stealing a few coppers from his father's loose change. But then, one day, the money had run out and he couldn't beg, steal or borrow the price of the can. And he'd been terrified during the twenty-minute journey to school and reduced to a quivering wreck as the bully came across looking for payment. "Today," he said, "after school, you're getting it. I'm going to kick your head in."

And so the mental torture continued. It was the worst day of Bob's school life. The six and a half hours seemed like six and a half weeks, and, as Bob walked up the old tram track to catch the bus, the bully and his pals stood waiting. As the first punch connected, Bob sank to his knees, signalling a victory for the bully and praying he would see it that way too.

He was out of luck; the onslaught continued, nor did it stop when he curled up into a tight ball. More kicks now, more than one boot, as Bob realised the bully's pals had joined in the beating. It was a savage hiding and it hurt like crazy, but Bob began to realise that it wasn't as bad as the tortured day he had just endured.

Bob realised that his mind and his thoughts could inflict more internal damage to his head than any boot could and, as the kicking continued, he drew strength. He looked between his fingers as a size six Doc Marten boot moved quickly towards his face. It connected with his eyebrow and Bob winced as he heard a crack. Bob launched at the boot with both hands and held on tightly. The bully wobbled, slightly off balance and Bob sank his teeth into the soft flesh of his calf muscle. He bit harder than he had ever bitten anything in his life and he wouldn't let go. The scream echoed through the trees and, for a moment, the beating stopped.

"Get the fucker off me," he screamed to his pals and the kicking resumed once again. But Bob wasn't letting go. Blood gushed into his mouth as his teeth sliced through the warm flesh. A hand clawed at his mouth attempting to release his vice-like grip. So Bob let go of the bully's leg and clamped his teeth instead onto a bony finger. It belonged the bully's friend and, in an instant, he regretted assisting his wounded pal. There was a piercing shriek as Bob locked onto the digit like an excited pit bull terrier at a rabbit. The adrenalin was flowing; he was beginning to turn the tables. Within a split second, his teeth had cut through the flesh and he felt raw bone. Squealing like a pig that had had its throat cut, the boy begged for mercy. He pleaded with his friends to stop, realising the kicking wasn't slackening Bob's grip. Then the kicking stopped and the cowards backed off leaving the stranded friend at the mercy of Bob's jaws. As he struggled to release his finger, he gave a desperate final flick with his wrist. The finger snapped like a tinder dry twig. Another blood-curdling scream and, this time, Bob let go.

"Me finger, me finger, it's broken, the fuckin' nutcase." The boy fell to the ground, holding the broken digit high in the air as if it would help ease the pain. His pals looked on, bewildered at the damage the feeble specimen had caused. Bob rose to his knees, his hands stretched out in front of him like an animal ready to pounce. Blood ran from his mouth; he grinned, his teeth awash with the blood of his victims. An uninjured member of the assault squad moved forward ready to resume the onslaught, but something stopped him as Bob locked eyes on him.

"C'mon then," Bob commanded, "you too."

The youth never took another step. The four aggressors limped away, physically and mentally hurt. They never bothered Bob again. It was a lesson that Bob would live with forever.

Mental torture was far worse than any physical punishment. And here he was again, undergoing the same head games he had endured all those years ago. And, until the tormentors made their next move, there was nothing he could do about it.

* * * *

Vicky Mackenzie wrapped the small toy up in a gold-coloured gift box. Jasper was a small, cuddly plaything: a boxer dog, Cameron's favourite. He'd cried for three nights after Donavan Smith had removed it from the apartment early on a Sunday afternoon. It wasn't difficult; Donavan had just tucked it under his coat as Debra and the children talked to Vicky. It was a pure stroke of luck he had chosen the child's favourite toy.

* * * *

Bob was up unusually early. He just couldn't sleep. Something gnawed at him. He noticed the shiny box on his customary morning stroll through the pre-dawn darkness of the garden. It had been left in exactly the same spot as the pages of Mackenzie's diary. It hadn't been there late last night, unless, of course, he'd missed it in the dark. No. Bob was sure that the strong moonlight from the clear sky would have shone on the burnished box and he'd have noticed it.

A shiver sped up his spine; the tormentor had visited them during the hours of darkness. What could it be he thought, *this little gift*, as he struggled with the strong, gold ribbon wrapped around the box? The smell of his son from the toy hit him before he opened the thin cardboard box. Seeing the toy was a double whammy and, as his hand came in to contact with the soft fur, his legs buckled and he sank onto the cool stone steps. Tears welled up in his eyes and he peered out into the blackness of the mountain unable to focus on anything. He screamed out his son's name. The piercing cry awoke Hannah and, half way up the mountainside, as he viewed proceedings through his infrared binoculars, Donavan felt that his patience had been amply rewarded.

"Jesus Christ, Bob." Debra cried out in disbelief, "it's five-thirty in the morning. What the hell's wrong?"

"Cameron, just tell me Cameron's okay."

Debra tried to protest, but Bob wouldn't take no for an answer. He insisted she checked his bed and, eventually, in an attempt to get back to bed, Debra agreed to check the little boy's bedroom.

By the time she returned to the phone, Stephen had heard the commotion and was up too. "What's up?"

"It's Bob, he's hysterical. Bleating on about Cameron."

She lifted the receiver up. "He's fine, Bob, sleeping like a lamb, now let me get back to bed. Jesus, what the hell is up with you?"

Bob sat on the floor, Hannah's arms draped around his shoulders. He sighed, "A dream, Debra... just a bad dream, I think."

Debra pushed the *end* button and turned to Stephen. "Nightmares. He's having those bloody nightmares again. It happened when he used to drink too much, especially Stella Artois. I think he's hit the bottle again."

Stephen shook his head as he walked back along the hallway. "The wanker."

Debra killed the light and, just before she went back to bed, she checked on her son again.

CHAPTER TWENTY-TWO

Donavan had every right to feel smug as they sat on the 17.22 flight from Seville. Mission had certainly been accomplished. He felt like James Bond, with his own little Moneypenny sitting beside him.

The diaries had been delivered; he'd photographed the entire area; walked through every nook and cranny of the old village; and just about trodden every square centimetre of the terrain that overlooked Bob Heggie's pleasant Spanish home. He'd enjoyed the daily expeditions, especially those in the hills. He remembered the fragrance as he'd battled his way through the rosemary bushes, occasionally interspersed by a waft of lavender or thyme that grew in abundance all around the area. He'd filled two small notebooks with scribbles and diagrams of the area and he'd taken a red pen to the *Mapas Militar* of the area and marked out every feature of significance with an estimated driving and walking time between each point.

He chuckled to himself. He'd had some fun too. Quite dramatic, the effect a cuddly toy can have on a grown man. He remembered, as he focused the binoculars on full zoom, seeing Bob collapsing as he opened the box and the tears rolling down his face.

Vicky leaned across and whispered. "You seem rather pleased with yourself."

Donavan slid a hand across the seat and rested it gently on her thigh. "You could say that. I think we've both done a fantastic job."

Vicky smiled and Donavan moved his hand further up her

thigh. "In fact, I think it's time you had a little reward."

His hand slid under the material of her skirt and, as he moved further up, he felt the silky material of her pants.

She whispered again, "Donavan, not here, somebody will see."

He took no notice of her and eased a finger under the thin fabric. She tensed up, her face flushed. Both wrists gripped him now and, with all her strength, she removed his hand. "Jesus Christ, Don, what are you like? I said no. Don't you know what that means?"

As Donovan looked across at her, he thought of the girls who'd said no before and how he'd still had every single one of them. He glared at her. He knew the look made her uncomfortable. Then he smiled, leaned across the seat, and whispered in her ear, "Do you know that every single member of the animal kingdom rapes its mate? You don't see a lion asking permission of a lioness. No. He just sees what he likes and gets on with it. Sure, she might give a little bit of a growl and, maybe, take a token bite at him, but, once it's in there, she's happy, he's happy, everybody's happy."

"You don't half talk some shit sometimes, Donavan. We've evolved; we've set rules and laws; and we've moved on a little bit more from the animal kingdom and the beasts in the jungle."

She took a nervous drink from the glass positioned on the tray in front of her. She frowned, "At least, some of us have anyway."

Shortly after, Donavan caught the attention of a stewardess pushing the duty-free trolley down the aisle. He ordered two large tins of sweets and two replica models of the aeroplane they were flying in. He handed the stewardess his credit card and scribbled his signature on the receipt as she handed it to him with a smile that said she didn't want to be there.

Donavan leaned over Vicky and looked out of the window. "I think that's London down there. Shouldn't be too long before we land."

Vicky shook her head and pressed the play button on her

MP3 player. As James Blunt's melodious tones filled her ears, she closed her eyes.

The plane touched down at Newcastle International Airport five minutes early. Vicky hadn't uttered a word since Donavan's little speech about human nature. As they walked down the long corridor towards passport control, Vicky put the MP3 earphones back onto her head. Donovan grinned. He didn't mind. It would give him time to think about the next part of his plan.

As they walked out into the cold Newcastle night air, Donavan suddenly stopped. He turned round and signalled to Vicky to remove her earphones. She did as she was instructed.

"Phone Debbie and Steve tomorrow. Let's have a little get-together. Tell them we've picked up a couple of little presents for the children. I think it's about time we got to know Elissa and Cameron a little better."

Vicky didn't answer him, but Donavan knew she would comply with his instruction.

* * * *

The following weekend, Vicky and Donavan drove over to Newcastle's Quayside and pulled into the underground car park. Donavan sensed Vicky's discomfort as they climbed from the car. "Do you want to tell me what's wrong, darling?"

Vicky slammed the car door and looked at Donavan. She was shaking… a nervous tremble.

"What's wrong?" he repeated.

She turned around and walked towards the exit. He resisted the urge to follow, knowing she would stop. He placed both elbows on the roof of the car. Sure as night followed day, when Vicky reached the electronic black and yellow barriers, she turned round to face him. He smiled. She raised her voice, "I don't know what you're grinning at. I just can't get my head around this."

He walked slowly towards her, his well-polished brogues crunching on the gritty surface. He stopped just inches from her, his six-foot frame towering above her. He felt in control and he looked down at her. "Tell me what you can't get your head round."

Her eyes welled up with tears as she blurted out, "Kidnap! That's what I can't get a hold of. We're going to kidnap two bloody kids."

Donavan looked around the deserted car park, anger raging deep within him. Who the fuck did she think she was? He was doing this for her. Now, here she was shouting out his next move in a public car park. His hand reached out and he took her by the scruff of the neck. He spun her round quickly and slammed her face into the roof of a nearby car. A trickle of blood appeared at the corner of her mouth.

"No, please, Don, I'm sorry, I'm sorry."

His grip tightened and his mouth moved down, level with her head.

"I'm sorry, Don, please, I'm sorry."

Pathetic, he thought to himself, pathetic little creature. He pushed her face harder into the cold steel. She let out a muffled squeal.

Suddenly, there was a shout from across the way. "Oi! What's going on?"

Donavan looked behind and loosened his grip. A grey-haired, elderly man walked towards them. He wore an old leather jacket two sizes too big and his face hadn't seen a razor blade for several days.

"Fuck off, Grandad, it's just a lovers' tiff."

The old man continued towards them. "Then let her up. Pick on someone your own size, you big coward."

Donavan smiled. He admired the little guy's courage and didn't want to hurt him, not really. He released Vicky and she whimpered as she slid to the floor. As he walked over to the old man, he opened his coat and pulled out his wallet. "Look, Grandad," he said, handing him a twenty, "you look like you could use a drink. Just turn around and pretend you didn't see anything, there's a good man. This has nothing to do with you."

The old man held out his hand and took the twenty-pound note.

"You know how it is with women, treat 'em mean, and keep 'em keen."

The old man nodded and looked straight through Donavan, over in the direction of Vicky who lay crumpled on the floor. An adrenalin shiver ran the length of Donavan's spine.

"You promise to leave the lady alone?"

Donavan was puzzled. He took a step forward and grabbed the old man's lapel. "Look, you old cunt, why don't you just —"

The old man's fist containing the twenty-pound note crashed into the bridge of Donavan's nose and, as he fell to the floor, the little old man sprang on him like a wild dog at a bone.

Old Tom remembered his mistakes from the past. He remembered his failed marriage and the one and only time he'd raised his hand to his wonderful wife. Okay, he was drunk and he swore it would never happen again, but she wouldn't ever take that chance.

She'd walked out with the children two days later and Tom had lived with the guilt and regret for twenty-five years. Now, in an underground car park on Newcastle's Quayside, this six-foot brute was making the same mistake. Tom wouldn't let him, wouldn't let him hurt this delicate beauty lying crumpled on the floor. With all his strength, he launched another brittle-boned fist into Donavan's bleeding mouth.

Tom didn't realise that the damsel in distress was no longer lying in a heap on the cold stone floor. No. She'd managed to get herself back onto her feet and was rummaging around in the boot of the car. She located an L-shaped wheel brace and staggered over to the tangled limbs wrestling on the floor. She raised the brace above her head and brought it crashing down onto the old man's skull. Tom wondered for a split second at the strange grin on the abuser's face as he snarled at Tom, "*And there shall be weeping and gnashing of teeth. Matthew 24:51.*"

And then … blackness.

Vicky had restored her reputation with Donavan Smith. She'd performed the violent act out of desperation, a need to convince her lover that she would do anything to help him, anything to protect him, and she was ready to assist with any task he undertook to achieve his goal. After all, it was for both of them. *Their retirement plan,* as he'd described it. And, as she walked away out of the deserted car park, with Donavan Smith's arm wrapped tightly around her shoulders, she purred like a mother cat. She cast an eye back over her shoulder. The old man stirred. She cared nothing for him; she cared nothing for Bob Heggie either, the man who had effectively killed her husband and left her penniless, the man who had rejected her.

She was ready. She had changed and was ready for anything. Even kidnap.

CHAPTER TWENTY-THREE

In Stephen's apartment, Debra fussed around the couple. She had been completely taken in by the story of the attempted mugging that had happened several levels below, in the exclusive underground car park. "I just don't understand, Don, nothing like this has ever happened here before. Bloody scum of the earth."

Vicky played the part well. "Don sorted them out, Debbie, two of them at once. You should have seen them scarper."

Cameron and Elissa stood mesmerised in the corner, nervously excited by the unfolding story. Stephen stood with his arms around them.

"You really should let me call the police, Don. I mean they could still be waiting for you or even return with some back-up."

Donavan shook his head. "Look, folks, could we just calm this down. We're frightening the kids. Let's think of them. The last thing they need is two or three coppers turning up at the door. No one's been hurt and they got nothing, so no harm done."

"But you're both bleeding," Debra commented in exasperation. "And what if —"

Donavan held up both hands. "The children."

Donavan swore he saw a tear of emotion in Debbie's eyes.

"Oh Christ, Don, you're so caring. I can't believe you weren't blessed with kids of your own. You would have made a great father."

"Hey," shouted Vicky. "I'm not that old. It's not beyond the realms of possibility, you know."

Donavan cringed and forced a rather unconvincing smile. "Who knows what life might deal us. Who knows?"

Vicky reached for his hand and gave a little squeeze. He snaked an arm around her. "Anyway, let's forget this."

He nodded his head at Vicky, raised his eyebrows, and smiled. Vicky reached down for the carrier bag containing the children's presents. The children rushed forward to claim their prizes and Elissa even managed to give Vicky a token peck on the cheek. Cameron held back, still a little nervous.

Donavan got ready to play his ace card. He looked directly at Debra, already reasonably confident of success. "Debra, my two nieces were due to visit Newcastle this weekend: twins, lovely girls aged nine. I adore them so much."

He beamed with pride as he tried to imagine two fabricated little girls. He stole a glance at Cameron and Elissa and lingered on them just long enough for Debra and Stephen to notice. "Vicky and I were due to take them to see Chitty Chitty Bang Bang at the Sunderland Empire."

Vicky took over, just as they'd rehearsed. "Only Don's sister has been involved in a car accident, nothing serious, but it means she can't make it."

Don spoke again. "I'd offered to drive down, of course, but my sister thought it was too far there and back in the one day. She lives in Romford, just outside London."

Debra spoke, "Yeah, five or six hours each way, Don. She's probably right."

Donavan looked at Vicky and they smiled at each other. "The thing is, Debra, we've two spare *little people* tickets to get rid of."

The penny dropped with Cameron and Elissa as Donavan and Vicky looked towards them.

"Oh yes, Mum, can we go?" shouted Cameron. Elissa backed him up. "Emily Allan says it's fantastic. Mum, please can we go, please?"

Debra and Stephen looked at each other. Stephen smiled as he spoke first, "What a great idea, Debra, we could get a bite to eat ourselves. We haven't had a night out on our own for at least a month."

By now, the children had draped themselves around their mother, realising she held the casting vote. Donavan held back and didn't say another word, knowing that the maternal instinct of wanting to please her children would win the day.

"Please, Mum, please."

How can you refuse? Donavan thought.

"How can I refuse?" she replied.

The children cheered and danced around the kitchen and the four adults laughed at their antics.

Donavan sighed quietly and congratulated himself on a job well done. He looked forward to the next part of the operation, but not to a Saturday night at the theatre in the company of two spoilt brats.

* * * *

Though he hated to admit it, Donavan had actually enjoyed Chitty Chitty Bang Bang. It was just a shame he'd had to adopt the fun-loving uncle role all evening. And boy, how he'd worked hard at it.

From the moment they picked up the children with two large bags of pick 'n mix, he'd laughed and joked and bought just about everything the two little children had dreamed of. Programmes, a T-shirt each, ice creams at the interval, anything and everything. And Vicky had played along too. Cameron and Elissa had quite happily held her hand during the five-minute walk from the car park to the theatre. On the way back, Donavan had offered his hand to the little girl but she'd politely declined. Probably just a little shy, Donavan thought.

And now, as he drove the fourteen miles back to Newcastle through the darkened streets, the children snuggled up to Vicky in the back seat of the Audi. Donavan had even had the presence of mind to put a couple of soft pillows in the back seat for added comfort.

By the time he pulled into the underground car park, Elissa

and Cameron were fast asleep. He lifted the mobile phone and keyed in Debra and Stephen's number. "Hi, Steve, yeah, it's Don. They're fast asleep. Do you think you could come down and you and me can carry them straight to bed. The little fellow's a bit too heavy for Vicky."

A few minutes later, Stephen and Debra appeared at the car window. Stephen opened the door and reached inside for Cameron. Don carefully lifted Elissa from the car and she stirred for just a second before making herself comfortable in the soft leather of Donavan's jacket. Debra smiled and stroked her hair. "Jesus, Don, it's as if she's known you for a hundred years."

Stephen chipped in. "Yeah, Don, thanks. And you too, Vicky, they must have had a fabulous evening."

Vicky reached inside the car for the programmes and T-shirts. "Don't forget these, Debbie, just some little souvenirs."

Debra made another token gesture to hand over some money, once again offering to pay for the tickets. Donavan pushed her hand away. "It's our pleasure, Debra, we probably enjoyed it more than the kids."

He turned and walked towards the lift. Stephen followed carrying Cameron, with Debra and Vicky following on behind discussing the show.

Donavan eased Elissa into her bed as Debra pulled back the covers in the darkened room. Debra sat on the bed and removed the little girl's coat and shoes like only a mother can without waking her. "She can sleep in her clothes for one night, I suppose. It won't do any harm."

The light from the full moon shone across Debra's face and she looked up at Donavan. "Thanks, Don, I really appreciate this. Are you sure you really enjoyed yourselves?"

"Absolutely, it was great fun, honest."

She stood up, her face inches from his. She expected him to back out of the bedroom, but he stood still. He could smell her breath, her perfume, the natural pleasant odour of a woman he wanted.

A shaft of light streamed into the bedroom and Stephen stood silhouetted in the doorway. "Is she sleeping, Deb? The little man's flat out, never even opened his eyes."

She walked over to the doorway and kissed Stephen on the lips. "Like a log, darling. Now, come on, let's offer these nice people a drink before they go home."

Donavan contemplated the evening as he drove along Newcastle's Quayside. He turned the corner of the old Guildhall and Vicky pointed him in the direction of Forth Banks. It had just turned midnight and he was amazed at the throngs of people milling around.

"Jesus, Vicky, where are they all going?"

Vicky grinned, "Just keep your eyes on the road and not on the young girls. We want to get home in one piece."

It had been another good night, another successful evening; another piece of the jigsaw had been safely fitted in.

He made love to Vicky that evening. He was tender, caring, and attentive. He brought her to orgasm again and again. He insisted they made love in the dark and, as he eventually climaxed himself, he pictured the image of Debra, her face glowing in the moonlight of her daughter's bedroom.

The following morning, Vicky glowed too. She sat at the table clutching a steaming cup of black coffee. "That was such a good night last night, Don. I enjoyed it so much."

Donavan swallowed the warm liquid and looked across the table. "What was?"

She crunched a piece of toast, chewed it several times, and swallowed. "Everything, Don. Everything. It was such a great evening. The show, the kids, a couple of drinks with Steve and Debra and ..."

"What?"

She grinned. "The sex was pretty good too."

I'll wipe the smile off her face, he thought to himself. "Don't go getting too attached to those kids." He laughed out loud, as Vicky's expression changed; he was proud and quietly impressed at how quickly he could knock her down from her little pedestal. "It's a game, remember? You weren't supposed to be enjoying last night. You were supposed to be working."

She tried to interrupt. "But…"

"Plotting, planning and scheming. We're working our way into their sad little lives, building up trust, a little confidence."

"But the children, what about them? We're not plotting and scheming about them, are we?"

Donavan shook his head in disbelief. "Jesus Christ, Vic, of course we are. How else do you think we're going to get them to come away with us?"

Vicky shook her head this time, totally confused as to the direction Donavan's mind was heading.

"You remember a few weeks ago, when we first had dinner with Steve and Debbie? They mentioned they hadn't had a honeymoon."

Vicky sat, ashen-faced, a slight nod of the head indicating she had heard him.

"The problem with kidnapping a child is that, generally, you drag them kicking and screaming into the boot of a car. And then, once you get them to wherever it is you plan to keep them, the little bastard's natural instinct is to escape."

He lifted a segment of grapefruit with his fingers and dropped it into his mouth. He spoke immediately, not concerned that Vicky viewed the entire contents of his mouth. "So, then, you have to keep the little buggers locked up. Maybe even tied up. And then, after the hardest part of the operation - the pickup. Even if you manage to achieve the impossible, you still have a little problem of a locked-up little kid who can identify you and put you away for a long stretch."

Vicky was smiling again. Within the space of a minute Donavan had played with her emotions like a cat with a mouse. "So we're not going to kidnap them."

"We won't need to kidnap them. We just need to make Bob Heggie think that we have."

"Now I am puzzled."

Donavan stood up and walked slowly behind Vicky. "Mind games. That's what we need to play with Heggie. Hit him in the head; make him think that a real nasty piece of work is holding onto his kids. Make him think that they're locked up, and yet they won't be. They'll be having a holiday with you and me."

"I like the sound of that."

Donavan strolled across to the window. Vicky's gaze followed him as he walked past her. "Yeah. I think it's time Bob Heggie got a call."

* * * *

It had been twenty-three days since the toy dog had been left on the back step of Casa Calemlio. For the first time in a few days, Bob and Hannah hadn't discussed the huge cloud that hung over their very existence. But it was still there: the fear of the great unknown.

Bob tried to work out some logical explanation as to why the perpetrators would wait so long. It just didn't make sense. A few days perhaps? Maybe even a week or two? But not this long.

Perhaps he had been killed in a car accident, Bob thought, if indeed he was a he; maybe it was a she; or, perhaps, more than one. A team even?

An accident would possibly explain the lack of action. It just didn't make sense: the pages from the diary, the full manuscript, and then the cuddly toy. A shiver ran up his spine as he remembered that dreadful morning when he discovered his son's favourite sleeping partner on the back step. He'd rung the children nearly every day since and couldn't wait to see them again.

But he'd resisted the urge to climb aboard the daily Easyjet flight and see the children in the flesh once again. It had been too long, but he figured it might put them in greater danger. Debra had agreed to them spending a month with him in the summer holidays, which was a little over seven weeks away. He would wait till then.

Yeah, a car accident, or even just a natural death; a heart attack; a stroke; it was the only logical explanation he could think of. What he didn't realise was that Donavan Smith was using the time to good effect. Donavan Smith had become a frequent visitor to the Newcastle apartment. And Donavan Smith had been to more cinemas and Pizza Huts and playparks than he cared to remember.

Bob stepped out into the garden and began his morning ritual, walking through the fruit trees that filled his garden. Spring was slowly turning into summer and the blossom of the trees had begun to fall to the ground, leaving perfectly formed fruits in miniature. He marvelled as he fingered the beginnings of a tiny lemon, not much bigger than a pinhead. By the end of the summer, the fruit would have swollen to fifty or sixty times their present size and end up as a perfect accompaniment to a gin and tonic or as a plate decoration, or a squeeze here and there to bring out the flavour of prawns or a barbecued piece of *dorada.*

He turned around to face the tapping noise that had disturbed him. Hannah stood at the window, mouthing the word 'telephone' and holding her hand to her ear with her little finger outstretched and her thumb touching her earlobe. Unusually early, he thought, as he jogged gently towards the house.

"Who is it?" he asked, as he breezed past Hannah and made his way into the kitchen.

"Wouldn't say, said it was a surprise."

Jimmy Richfield, he thought, as he picked up the phone. It had been a while since he had telephoned and, with the big Cheltenham Horse Racing Festival just a week away, he probably had some *sure things* he wanted to crow about. "Hello."

"Hello, Mr Heggie, listen very carefully and don't interrupt."

"Who is this?"

"I said, don't interrupt. If you interrupt again, I'll hang up."

Bob stood rooted to the spot as the horror of realisation set in.

"You don't need to know who I am. I know all about you and that's the main thing. I know where you live; I know all about you and your girlfriend, Hannah, and I know even more about the delightful Elissa and Cameron. In fact, I know more about them than you do. I know where they live and where they go to school; I know what time they leave in the morning and what time they arrive back each evening; where they play; where they eat; where they shit."

Even if Bob wanted to speak, he couldn't. A mixture of emotions spread through his body: fear, rage, but, above all, a feeling of helplessness. The stranger continued. "Oh yes, and I know all about Locker Number 28."

The stranger fell silent; it was Bob's cue to speak. "I don't know what you're talking about. If you touch a hair on my kids' heads, I'll —"

"You'll do what, Mr Heggie, kill me? How can you? You don't know who I am, what I look like, or where I am. I'd say that was rather impossible, wouldn't you?"

Bob's bottom lip quivered, the handset trembled in his hand, and, for a second, he thought he would drop it.

"No, Bob, you won't do anything until I tell you. Unfortunately for you, I hold all the aces. When I shout jump, you ask how high, is that clear?"

An uncomfortable silence elapsed. Bob broke it. He took a deep breath and whispered into the mouthpiece, "What do you want?"

The stranger cackled on the other end of the phone. "That's better, Bobby, now we're playing the game."

Bob heard the unfamiliar person sigh.

"A million would be nice."

"What?"

"One million pounds. No police, no tracing the telephone calls, no tricks, no phone calls to Debra or her darling new husband, Stephen. He's the man she left you for, Bob, isn't he?"

Bob bit his lip and ignored the taunt. "A million? Are you off your head? Where would I get that sort of money?"

"Oh you'll get it, Bob, there's no doubt about that. Half a million each for your children. I think that's fair. I mean there's half a million in that locker for a start. It shouldn't be that hard to let go of that little lot. After all, it's not exactly yours, is it?"

Bob's mind was in turmoil. Who was this? Could it be a police trick? He tried to remain calm. "So, you're telling me you've kidnapped my kids, is that it?"

"No, Bobby, not yet, I only plan to do that if you don't follow my instructions. I mean, they're such nice kids, aren't they. Why would you want to put them through that ordeal?"

"So I pay you a million and you leave them alone. I don't come up with the money and you kidnap them and hold them to ransom until I do?"

"Well done, Bob, you seem to be getting to grips with this. Tell me, how's Jasper enjoying life away from Cameron? He's really missing him, you know, cries nearly every night."

Bob finally snapped and he screamed into the phone, "How do you know that, you fucking twisted bastard?"

Hannah came running through. "Bob, what's up?"

Bob sank to the floor, his knees unable to resist the pressure any longer. A tear escaped from the corner of his eye. He wanted to let go of the phone, but he needed to keep the link a little longer.

"Oh, I know, Mr Heggie, I know everything, and if you make that phone call to the police or Debra, I'll find out. Believe me, I'll find out, and then….. Well, I'm sure you can guess."

The line went dead.

"Bob, what is it?"

He looked up through a veil of tears and took in the distorted, blurred image of the girl he loved. "It's him, Hannah… it's him."

Vicky Mackenzie sat enthralled at Donavan's telephone performance. He smiled as he pressed the *end* button on the mobile phone, quietly pleased with his performance.

"What did he say, Don?"

"Not much, Vicky, just swore a bit. I was the one doing the talking."

"Yeah, Don, I heard. You were brilliant. What do we do now?"

Donavan stood up, took half a dozen paces then turned around and walked back. "We wait, Vicky. We wait a few days, and then we invite ourselves over to Debra's. Then, sweetie, you've a little work to do. I want you to find out whether Bob Heggie rings Debra after this phone call. Of course, I've told him not to, but I'm sure he will. He'll want to check on his precious babies and, when I ring him back and tell him I know, it'll drive him round the fucking twist."

* * * *

Donavan pulled into the multi-storey car park, located the telephone number, and handed Vicky the mobile.

He cut himself off from the small talk, ignoring the sickening opening pleasantries. Within a few minutes, Vicky took up her instructions. "So you see, Debra, we're in town already and, if you haven't planned a meal, we can share a takeaway."

Vicky sat in the car with her fingers crossed, she had the phone on loudspeaker, and Donavan listened intently.

"I'm sure it'll be okay, but I'll just check with Steve. I've a piece of beef lifted from the freezer, but it'll keep until tomorrow. Just a second."

Donavan and Vicky heard the receiver being placed down, then footsteps gradually fading across the polished oak floor. A couple of minutes later, the footsteps grew louder and Debra picked up the phone. "Steve said that'll be fine, Vicky, as long as you don't mind two kids hanging around you all night."

"Not at all, Debbie. In fact, I think that's why Don wants to come. He absolutely adores those children."

"Around eightish then."

"Okay, and we'll just bring one of those Chinese banquets from Stowell Street."

"Brilliant, see you then."

Vicky had been primed on exactly what it was she had to say. It worked like clockwork. "So Bob doesn't get to see them too often, Debra?"

"No, not really, but what the hell does he expect, living in Spain, for Christ's sake? I mean, it's hardly just the other side of town, is it?"

"But he calls now and again, right?"

"Yeah. A little too much lately, if you ask me. I think he's going through some bloody midlife crisis. He's called every day this week, just checking everything's okay, he claims. Bloody nuisance, if you ask me."

Donavan held a separate conversation with Stephen, but prided himself on his ability that allowed him to listen to two conversations, snatching the important bits from each exchange. He had been able to do that as a child: read a book, and listen to television at the same time. That is, until his mother had removed the TV set just after his eighth birthday. The *evil electronic box* she had called it after she'd heard the F word on some late-night talk show. Donavan's strict two-hour allowance of television each evening had been replaced by two hours' bible study. And his mother tested him at eight o'clock each evening just before he went to bed and woe betide him if he got it wrong. Her assortment of assault weapons included a rolling pin, a well worn leather belt, and her slipper or shoe. And always on the bare backside. She'd physically strip him before every beating and direct the blows at his bare arse. As he lay upstairs crying, she'd apologise to him and lie in bed beside him, caressing his cheek gently and telling him it was God's will. One night, she'd fractured his arm with the rolling pin as he tried to protect himself and, despite his screams and protests, insisted on applying the splints herself. And afterwards, as he lay sobbing, she comforted him by reading the entire Second Book of Chronicles, repeating again and again, *there is no man that sinneth not.*

After they'd dined, Donavan asked if he could read Elissa and Cameron their bedtime story. The children pleaded with their mother to allow him, and Debra led him into Elissa's room. The two children curled up in the three quarter bed, Cameron sucking his thumb, while Donavan went through an entire chapter of the latest Horrid Henry book. By the time he'd finished, Cameron was asleep, Elissa's eyes were half closed, and Donavan could feel his own eyes growing heavy with boredom. As he left her room, he slipped something into his pocket.

They left a little after midnight and Donavan forced a ten-pound note into Debra's hand, insisting she take them for some sweets the following day. Donavan thought at one point he may just be overdoing it a little.

CHAPTER TWENTY-FOUR

As Bob opened the envelope, he felt inside, already sensing that the contents would be bad news. He pulled out a gilt-edged piece of card with a sparkling blue sapphire attached. The birthstone of a child born on the fourth of September. It was the birthstone Bob had bought Elissa on her first birthday. She had treasured it ever since and it took pride of place in the centre of her dressing table. The stranger had violated Bob's family yet again.

Twenty minutes later, Bob received the call.

"You've been a naughty boy, Mr Heggie."

"You bastard, how did you get her birthstone?"

"You didn't hear me, Mr Heggie, I said you've been a naughty boy. You've been ringing the lovely Debbie, haven't you?"

"And you didn't hear me. How did you get my daughter's birthstone?"

"*Ye shall loathe yourself in your own sight for all your evils you have committed,*" a slight pause while the statement registered then, "*Ezekiel 20:43.*"

And the line went dead.

Bob shouted at the telephone in desperation, knowing his efforts were futile. "Hello, hello, are you there, you warped bastard?"

Vicky sat listening to the drama unfolding before her. "You're one cool customer, Don, not sure about that religious shit though."

"It's not shit. You should learn it, might do you some good. Do you know there's a quotation in the bible for every human action or emotion? Take any letter of the alphabet, R for example: regret, rebellion, redemption, rejection, respect, retribution, risk, revenge, it's all in there, a pearl of wisdom for every damn one. It's without doubt the greatest book ever written."

Vicky spoke, "Okay, clever clogs, let's take 'revenge'. I like revenge, kind of sums up where we're going, give me a quotation on revenge."

Without pausing for breath, Donavan Smith turned to face her, looked deep into her eyes and yet looked straight through her as if in a trance. *"Though shalt give life for life, eye for eye, tooth for tooth, hand for hand, foot for foot, burning for burning, wound for wound, stripe for stripe. Exodus 21, 23:25."*

Vicky's mouth gaped open. "Wow, Don, that's impressive, so you really are into this bible shit."

Donavan laughed. "Yeah, I'm into it alright, ever since I came to the conclusion at ten years of age that it was the biggest con in history."

"I'm not with you. What do you mean?"

"Over two thousand years since it was written, and still we follow the Ten Commandments like little lost sheep. We base our legal system on nonsense written by ancient fraudsters and charlatans. We believe and worship every damn line of the bloody thing; drum it into young kids; tell them there's a big man with a beard up in the clouds who can see everything they do and that they'll be punished if they step out of line. The ancient crusades, Moors and Christians, Northern Ireland, Protestant against Catholic, Palestine, Iraq, Iran, the Gulf War, Israel." He turned to face Vicky. "It prays on people's fears. Fear, Vicky, that's what religion's all about; fear that drives the Catholics to confession, fear that drives the terrorist to bomb, a fear that some person or something will punish them forever and a day."

He took both her hands in his. "And that's what's running

around Bob Heggie's little head right now. The fear of the unknown. Where will we strike? When will we strike? How will we strike?"

Vicky spoke, "And what about Bob Heggie? What's to be done with him? We punish him now, right? Punish him for making those phone calls to Debra."

Vicky looked excited. She had been hooked into the little game and was past caring about the risk factor, whether or not anyone got hurt. She was enjoying the thrill of the chase. The incident in the car park had convinced Donavan that she was ready to step over the line.

"Right. We punish him."

"And how do we do that, Don?"

Donavan turned around to face her as he wanted to take in her reaction. "By taking his children on a little holiday."

CHAPTER TWENTY-FIVE

Bob didn't know yet why he was sitting on a late afternoon flight back to Newcastle. He didn't know where he was going or who he was looking for. It was plain stupid. He wanted Hannah with him, but someone had to be back in Spain to take any phone calls. Despite her protests, she knew it had to be her and she had instructions to pass Bob's mobile phone number on to anyone who wanted it.

He made his way through passport control and warmed to the familiar Newcastle dialect once again. He listened to the airport officials, the baggage handlers and, as he passed the coffee shops, the assistants and customers in conversation with each other. He began to realise how much he still loved Newcastle.

He walked right through the airport concourse, past domestic arrivals and down the escalator to the Metro. Normally he'd take a taxi into town, but, today, he couldn't face the thought of a twenty-minute conversation about the weather or how badly Newcastle United were playing or of their striker crisis. He'd felt the change in climate as soon as he stepped from the plane, and he could see and feel it, so he didn't want some taxi driver giving him the forecast for the rest of the week or indeed for that very minute of the day. He could never understand why, on the TV reports, the forecaster told you what the weather was like at that very minute. What was the point of that, he thought. I can look out the window and see the bloody rain. I don't need some channel to spend ten million a year on Met Office predictions to tell me that.

And as for the football team, well, he really didn't want to talk about that either. He'd followed their lack of success by telephone, Internet and teletext, not to mention the couple of times he'd managed to fly back and take Cameron to a game, making sure the trip back home coincided with a Newcastle United fixture. How sad was that?

The train was already in the station as Bob walked onto the platform. The cold wind whipped along the exposed area and he gratefully took sanctuary in the warm carriage. The train went right into the heart of the city within twenty-five minutes and Bob looked up at the stations en route. Where was he heading? He didn't know. Perhaps Jesmond, where there were plenty of guest houses and hotels, or perhaps Newcastle city centre, near to the children. It was a little late to call over and see them tonight, but he would telephone first thing tomorrow morning.

He decided to get off at Haymarket and ambled around the city centre with no real purpose or final destination in mind. It had just turned seven and the evening revellers were beginning to drift into the pubs and nightspots of the city. Seems like a good idea, Bob thought to himself, and he thought of the old pub down by the Central Railway Station and a few old friends he thought might just be in there. He picked up the pace of his walk.

The Sour Grapes had been a favourite haunt of Bob's as he waited for his train home in the evenings. Old Tom, the local newspaper seller, had been a regular there. Too regular, Bob thought, and, as he walked through the door, he looked over to the old table he had sat at so many times. An old man crouched over a nearly empty pint glass. A grimy, large, off-white bandage peeked out from beneath a black and white tartan cap. He had aged a little, but there was no mistake: it was Old Tom.

Bob ordered two beers and casually sauntered over to the table. He pulled out the chair with his foot and placed the two glasses on the table. The old man looked up and his eyes sparkled as he recognised the familiar form standing before him.

"Bob…. how the hell are you? What are you doing here? Where are you going? What are you —?"

"Whoa!" Bob said, holding up a hand and taking in a mouthful of beer. "Jesus, Tom, you're sounding like the old missus, and, looking at the state of your head, it should be me asking the questions."

"Cheers," Tom said, raising his glass and ignoring Bob's question. "Lovely to see you, Bob. Are you here for a while?"

Bob shook his head, "I don't know. I've got a few small problems to clear up, maybe a week at the most."

"Well it's great to see you again, must be well over a year since you were last in here?"

Bob thought for a second, calculating the months in his head. "Yeah, Tom, all of that. So what's been happening, who have you been upsetting?" He raised his eyes in the direction of the bandage.

"You don't want to know. Some religious nut in a car park just about to beat his lady up, and, like an idiot, I got involved."

"And he won."

Tom wiped the froth of the beer from his top lip. "No. I was on top of him, caught him with one or two good shots when, all of a sudden his missus, the ungrateful cow, the one I had been trying to help, banjoed me with something hard."

Tom laughed, "Serves me right for getting involved."

Bob pictured the scene in his head and couldn't help smiling a little. "Well, it doesn't seem to have had much effect on you, you old bastard. You look just the same as when I left you all those months ago."

Tom grinned. "I've a thick skull, and you're wearing pretty well yourself, Bob. The sun seems to be doing you good, sort of an older looking Des O'Connor."

"Thanks mate, I'll treasure that one, you cheeky old bugger."

Bob and Tom sat for a good hour, catching up on old stories and tales from the past. As Tom returned from the bar with two more glasses, he leaned over and whispered to Bob, "So you've come back for the money then?"

Bob spluttered in his beer; he hadn't even thought about the money within the last hour, or the children, or the threats from the tormentor.

"It's still there, Bob, in locker twenty eight. All but a few hundred quid I've helped mesel' to over the last year."

Bob shook his head. "No… I mean, maybe… I hadn't even thought about it, Tom, to be honest."

Tom smiled, catching the lie immediately. "You're in trouble, Bob. Want to tell me about it?"

Bob sank back in his seat, shaking his head. "How did you know?"

Tom took another mouthful of beer and licked at his lips. "It's my sixth sense, I suppose: always know when someone spins me a yarn or a tale; always know when someone is hiding from something. And, judging by your eyes, you're in some big kinda shit."

Bob stood up. "I'll get a couple of whiskies, stay there."

Tom looked up at Bob as he fumbled in his pocket for some change. "I'm not going anywhere."

It was two in the morning, when Tom's conversation came to Bob again. He lay wide awake in the hotel bedroom in Jesmond, staring at the ceiling. He walked over to the old-fashioned sash window and opened it six inches. He drank in the Newcastle night air, it felt good, and he listened to the faraway sounds of the life he hadn't heard for so long: taxi doors slamming, a police siren wailing in the distance somewhere, alcohol-induced happy voices, the sound of stilettos on the pavement. He stood for five minutes before the cold air eventually persuaded him back to bed.

He had poured his heart out to Tom as they sat in the Grapes hour after hour, and he felt so much better for getting it off his chest. He'd told him everything, from the diary to the threats. A problem shared is a problem halved, he thought to himself; he could see the logic in that proverb now. And as he had left, Old Tom shook his hand warmly and he had felt the cold steel of a familiar shape pressing into his hand. And the smile Tom had given him, probably the same sort of smile Bob had given to Tom all those months back.

But it was something Tom had said at the beginning of the night that gnawed at him. Probably nothing, but what exactly had he meant when he'd said he'd been attacked by some religious nut? He'd ask him tomorrow.

The early morning sunlight tugged at Bob's eyelids and he reluctantly dragged himself from beneath the warm eiderdown. He had never had the use for one in Spain, even in winter: a sheet and a thin blanket generally kept the cold at bay. Not here. Not in Northern Europe. Not in England's most northerly city.

"Jeeeesus," he mumbled, as he darted over to the open window and closed it, "it's spring for heaven's sake. It shouldn't be this cold."

After breakfast, Bob ventured out into the street. It was a little after nine, and the last of the rush-hour traffic headed towards the city centre. It was only about a mile or so to the Quayside and he prepared for a leisurely walk. He pulled out the mobile phone from his pocket and located *Debra home*. Unsure of what story he was about to make up, his finger hovered over the button. He pressed it and figured that it would come to him as he spoke.

Debra sounded a little surprised at the early morning intrusion; she liked sleeping late at the weekends. "A bit early, Bob, we've only just got up. To what do I owe this pleasure?"

"I'm in Newcastle. I have a little business to attend to, but thought I might take the kids out somewhere?"

He cringed. The lie stood out like a sore thumb.

"Business? What business would that be?"

Bob stumbled, trying to think of something to say. "A distant uncle died, lived up on the moors near Otterburn. I need to see his solicitor."

"What uncle was that, Bob, didn't know you had one, you've never ever mentioned him."

Bob glanced around the street looking for a name of some

sort and spied the fascia board of The George Hotel.

"Uncle George, only ever seen him two or three times, but apparently he's left me a couple of thousand in his will."

"Good for you, Bob. I don't suppose I'm entitled to anything, am I?"

Bob couldn't help laughing; she'd bought into his lie. "I'll pretend I didn't hear that, Debra. What about the children, when can I see them?"

"Not today, Bob, we've got plans; football for Cameron at St. James's Park. Newcastle are playing Manchester City and Steve's got two tickets; and Elissa is horse riding this afternoon."

Bob's heart sank, he needed to see them, to take them somewhere, to the pictures, for a pizza, anywhere. He needed to touch them, needed to hold them. "How about tomorrow?"

"Not tomorrow either. Cameron's playing football in the morning and, in the afternoon, Elissa and I are on a pamper day at Linden Hall."

"Look, Debra, I really want to see them. Jesus, I'm only here a couple of times a year. Can I come over now? I'm only half an hour away." The tone of his voice had changed. He was losing his temper.

"It's not my fault you ran away to Spain, Bob. You can't just turn up unannounced. Why didn't you ring me last week?"

Now he was angry, he was desperate; he wanted to say it wasn't his fault she couldn't keep her knickers on; it wasn't his fault she'd walked out on the family home; it wasn't his fault she'd taken the children; and it wasn't his fault the judge had given custody to the mother. And he remembered how he had begged and pleaded for her to return home despite what she'd done. Think of the children, he'd said, they need a stable home, need a father and a mother living under the same roof. And she'd refused.

He tried to stay cool. "Debra, please, just half an hour. I'll call in at the deli and bring some bacon rolls with me. They can have some breakfast with me."

Debra seemed to mellow and she sighed deeply into the

telephone. "Oh, I suppose so, they'd like that. They haven't had breakfast yet, in fact they've only just got up. You can bring some for Steve and me, save me cooking."

"Thanks, Debra, thanks, I really appreciate it."

"Only half an hour though. I need to get organised this morning."

Bob pressed *end* and picked up the pace of his walk.

Elissa and Cameron answered the door together, fighting each other for the handle. They fell into Bob's arms. It felt good. He wanted to hold them forever, never let them go, and, for a second, he regretted his decision to move to Spain. Tears welled up in his eyes as the children hugged him even tighter.

"How long are you staying, Dad? Are we going to the match?" asked Cameron.

Before Bob could answer, Stephen appeared in the doorway of the large entrance hall. "Just me and you, Cameron. I'm afraid your Dad can't stay very long."

Yes I can, Bob wanted to answer, it's you two bastards that won't let me.

Bob managed to stretch the visit out to a good hour. He didn't beg or plead with Debra, the children did it for him. Debra sat on the arm of the big, leather reclining chair, her arm resting on Stephen's shoulder, just like she used to with Bob.

"Look, Bob, I really think it's time you got going. I've got loads to get through today."

Stephen nodded in agreement and seemed anxious for Bob to get going. "Yeah, sorry, Bob, but we really should be getting on."

Bob stood up and the two children rushed over to him.

"I want to go to the football with you, Dad!" cried Cameron.

"I'm sure you don't mean that," Stephen said, as he walked over to the little boy.

"I do, I do. You're not my dad; you won't ever be my daddy. I want to go to the football with my daddy; I want to live with my daddy; I don't want him to go." Cameron burst out crying and Debra rushed over to comfort him.

"That's not very nice, Cameron, after all Steve has

done for you."

"And I won't call him daddy, I won't call him that," he screamed.

Debra's bottom lip began to quiver and her face blushed bright red.

Bob stood rooted to the spot, stunned. "You're making them call him Dad?"

"Him's got a name, Bob, and, yes, I thought it would make us more of a family. Steve's good with the kids. He's stepped into your role just fine."

Bob couldn't believe what he was hearing. He stood openmouthed feeling a little guilty for deserting his children, but remembered then that it was Debra who had done the walking.

"Look, Bob, I think it's best if you go," said Stephen, as he walked over to comfort the little boy. He placed a hand on Cameron's shoulder and ruffled the top of his hair.

Elissa stood in the corner, taking in the proceedings as if she'd seen it all before. "He hits Cameron, Daddy."

Bob looked over, shell-shocked. "He does what?"

Stephen looked daggers at the child, then across at Bob. "Just a little discipline, Bob. Never hurt anybody."

"You hit my children?"

Debra chipped in, "You've no idea how hard it's been, Bob. Steve and I couldn't control them. We think it's for the best."

Stephen spoke, "Just a little tap now and again, Bob, didn't do me any harm, won't do them any harm."

Bob walked over to Stephen and saw him start to tremble. "THEM," he shouted. "You hit my daughter as well."

Stephen stuttered, seeing the anger and hatred in Bob's eyes.

Bob looked at Elissa. She slowly and deliberately nodded her head. Bob felt the rage building up inside. He wanted to pull back his fist and smash it into the face of the man who had stolen his wife, the man who was now beating his children. He turned and faced Debra.

She hurried the children from the room despite their protests. Elissa started crying as Debra steered her towards the door. "It's okay, just go to your rooms for a little bit. I need to talk to Daddy."

She eased the children through the door, closed it, and walked over to Stephen. He took her hand in his.

"Why, Debra, why? We never hit the kids, you and me, never had to, we agreed it was wrong."

"Yeah, Bob, well, things change."

"No, they don't, we agreed. One look from me was all it took to discipline them. Where's the sense in telling a child they've done wrong, then dishing out physical violence to them."

"But you're not here anymore, Bob, remember? It's a decision Steve and I took together. They changed when you went, started working Steve, tormenting him, seeing how far they could push him."

Bob was glad for all the wrong reasons. He wanted them to miss their father, wanted them to be hostile to the man who stood in front of him. They were his flesh and blood, they were part of him and, as young as they were, they realised that this man had broken up their happy family unit; he had ruined everything and driven their father from their lives.

Bob was pleased with them and he wished he could take them away. But he couldn't. It was hopeless. The judge had spoken: Bob's rights as a father had been ripped to shreds in the courtroom that dark January day. He had been warned not to contest custody, but he did. He knew he'd lose, knew he'd end up with a hefty solicitor's bill, and he knew he'd end up walking from the court with his tail between his legs. But he'd done it because he felt he had to; he owed it to the children, a final cry that he wouldn't let them go without a fight.

Bob stood lost in his thoughts. Stephen interrupted them. He'd grown in confidence at Bob's silence. "I'll show you out, Bob, we really should be getting on."

"I need to say goodbye to Elissa and Cameron"

Stephen frowned and looked across at Debra. Debra sniffed, "Bob, please, just go, you've upset them enough."

Stephen took Bob by the elbow, "C'mon, Bob, it's for the best, we'll see if you can't have them for a few hours before you go back to Spain."

Bob nodded meekly and walked towards the door. He didn't turn back. He didn't want to look at the woman who had betrayed him, not once, but twice. Stephen took him into the hallway and fumbled with the front door lock. He smiled as he opened the door. Bob walked past him and out into the salubrious decor of the community corridor that led to the lifts. Just inside the apartment, a pale blue, leather two-seater settee stood adjacent to the front door. A modern painting hung above in an elegant stainless steel frame. Bob looked at it. A series of vivid colours thrown at the canvas, acrylic paint, not oils. Bob could imagine the artist laughing as he or she slapped a three or four hundred pound price tag on it, then persuading a Jesmond restaurant owner to display it with twenty-five per cent commission added, of course. And Bob could just picture the scene as Debra set her eyes on the price tag, not the painting, the price tag. And the scene in the restaurant as the purchase was made.

Stephen spoke, but his words didn't flow. He croaked as he just about managed to spit out the sentence. It was meant to send Bob on his way. "A couple of hours, Bob, before you go. They'd like that."

Bob turned away from the painting and looked at Stephen, focusing on his eyes. He took a step forward. Stephen stepped back but found his way blocked by the hallway wall. Bob took another step forward and now their faces were only inches apart. Bob whispered through clenched teeth, his voice barely audible, "Let's get this clear, fuck-face. The judge's visitation directive just flew out the window. From now on, I come and see them anytime I want."

A bead of perspiration fell from Stephen's top lip as Bob edged closer. "What's more, they spend every holiday with me, and I'll telephone them anytime I want, be it six in the morning, six at night, or fucking midnight, if I so desire. Is that clear?"

Stephen didn't reply.

"And if, during any of those visits, or during any of those phone calls, I hear that you've laid a single hand on MY children, I'll be on a flight back within the hour and I'll break your fucking legs. Is that clear?" It was a kind of threatening language Bob had never used before; sure… he'd heard it used a few times by the undesirable characters that frequented the seedier pubs and night clubs of Newcastle. He figured he'd acted well and that Stephen had bought it one hundred per cent.

Stephen nodded his trembling head and Bob smiled. He slapped Stephen gently at the side of his face. "Good. I'm glad you understand. Now off you go and tell that whore of a wife of yours the same thing."

Stephen couldn't wait to scramble back through the doorway and the door slammed in Bob's face. Bob bent down on his knees and opened the letterbox. Prising the black wire brushes apart, he looked through. Stephen stood propped up against the far wall, face flushed, breathing heavily. Bob put his mouth to the open slit, "Remember, pal, I'll be checking on you every day."

Stephen pawed at the door handle to the lounge and, as it gave way, fell through the doorway, his legs spreadeagled like a newborn foal on ice.

Bob figured it was time to go. He took the lift to the ground floor and, as the door opened, a familiar face stared at him. Bob thought for a moment, he hadn't seen the face for a while, and then said out loud, "Vicky… Vicky Mackenzie. How are you?"

Vicky's face flushed and her mouth fell open." Bob. What are you doing here?"

"Oh, just a little business to take care of; an uncle died, had to see his solicitor. I'm back over to Spain in a few days."

Donavan stood rooted to the spot, a little excited, but also with a little trepidation. This was the main man. Bob Heggie stood in front of him holding a conversation with Vicky. He couldn't believe his luck.

Vicky introduced him. "Em, this is my boyfriend… err….Don. We're just on our way to visit a couple of friends."

Donavan nodded. He couldn't speak, couldn't take the chance that Bob might recognise his voice.

"Pleased to meet you," Bob replied, offering his hand.

Don shook it and nodded again, smiling slightly. He gave Vicky a little push in the back.

"We really should be going, Bob, we're running a little late."

Bob looked at his watch. "Yeah, me too, Vicky, really should be on my way. Nice meeting you, Don. Take care, bye."

Donavan Smith smiled and walked into the open lift. He pressed *door open*, kept his finger pressed on the button, and watched as Bob walked across the foyer and out into the street. As Bob disappeared from sight, he released the button and the shiny steel doors closed.

Vicky exhaled a deep breath. "Jesus H Christ, Don, that was a bit scary. Imagine meeting him here. What on earth's he doing in Newcastle?"

"Isn't it obvious, Vicky? He's keeping watch over his babies."

"Jesus, he didn't half frighten me."

The lift doors opened and across the hallway stood Debra, a half smile on her face.

Donavan whispered quietly. "He's getting too close. Time we took his babies away."

Donavan couldn't have planned it better. On the very day that he prepared to sell the concept of a holiday to Debra and Stephen, Bob Heggie had entered their world and rattled their cages.

"He's a total bastard, Don," said Stephen as he stood at the kitchen sink, preparing a pot of coffee.

Donavan looked at Debra. She didn't look so sure. "You must remember, Steve, he's their father. It must be hard for him."

"Don't defend him, Debra, he's no right to interfere. It was him who decided to move abroad. He shouldn't think he can just turn up unannounced."

Donavan stood back, enjoying the domestic drama unfolding before him. After several minutes, he spoke, "What you two need is a holiday."

Stephen looked across as he poured from a carton of milk. "I couldn't agree with you more, Don."

"Without the kids," said Donavan, with a sympathetic look.

Debra sank into a chair. "And just how the hell are we going to manage that, Don?"

Donavan looked over to Vicky, who, until that point, had been standing quietly. She explained to the warring couple about Donavan's villa in the south of France, and how she and Donavan had discussed taking the children to Euro-Disney. She explained about his place in Paris too, and even suggested a couple of dates.

Donavan chipped in. "You're only talking the price of two flights, Steve. It's not as if it'll break the bank."

Stephen smiled, nodded his head, and looked at Debra. She spoke, "I'm not so sure. I mean, the kids, will they —"

"C'mon, darling, it'll be great, just me and you. The kids will be fine with Vicky and Don. How can you even think about not letting them go?"

Right on cue, Elissa walked into the kitchen. "Go where, Mum?"

Debra had been outnumbered and outvoted, one lone voice in a crammed kitchen. Donavan figured it had taken about four minutes before she eventually gave in. He sat down beside her and keyed the photographs of the villa on the screen of his mobile phone.

Stephen settled it once and for all. "We're going, Debra, and that's final."

Donavan looked across at him. A deep hatred was building inside. He loathed the man. He stamped his authority only when he knew it wouldn't be challenged. Donavan wanted to hurt him.

Donavan and Vicky left the quayside apartment after an hour. All arrangements had been made, and dates finalised. Donavan was a little anxious, as Debra had only agreed to a long weekend. It might not be long enough for what he had in mind.

It was just after twelve as Bob entered The Sour Grapes. Thirty minutes later the door opened and Old Tom smiled and waved as he spotted Bob in the corner. A shake of his hand to signal the universal sign language for a glass of beer and Bob nodded and held up his thumb.

"Early start, Bob," said Tom as he sat down at the table.

"We need to talk, something you said yesterday."

Tom took a mouthful of beer and frowned. "Something I said?"

"You said you were attacked by a religious nutter. What did you mean by that?"

Tom placed his glass on the table and drew the sleeve of his dirty jacket along the top of his mouth. "Yeah, Bob, quoted something from the Bible he did, as I lay on the ground. At least I think it was the Bible, that's what it sounded like."

"What did he say?"

Tom took another mouthful. "Shit, Bob, I can't remember exactly."

"Think, Tom, think!"

Tom looked up to the ceiling and screwed his eyes tight shut. "It was from the Bible, I remember now. He quoted the name of the exact book it came from." Tom held up a hand. He needn't have bothered; Bob had no intention of interrupting. "Matthew 24, he said, something about there being weeping and gnashing of teeth. Yeah, that was it, Matthew 24."

A cold shiver ran the length of Bob's spine.

He leaned over gently and took Tom's hand. "You've a great memory, old fella. Now think again, and describe to me exactly what this couple looked like."

CHAPTER TWENTY-SIX

Donavan enjoyed the thirty-minute ride along from Nice International Airport. For once, he wasn't driving. He sat on the back seat of the French taxi as it threaded its way along the busy A8 that hugged the French Riviera coastline. It was a quick visit, not even time for an overnight stop. Donavan had taken the early morning flight from Newcastle and, after he completed his task, he would catch the early afternoon flight back again.

The taxi pulled into the elegant entrance of the exclusive urbanisation set back two hundred metres from the seafront. The elevated position offered spectacular views of the Mediterranean and, one kilometre along the coast, the harbour of Cannes. Donavan climbed from the taxi, took a long, deliberate stretch, and looked back at the view he never tired of. The jetties were crammed with the millionaires' elegant white bath toys. One day, thought Donavan, one day.

He pulled his briefcase out from the back seat of the taxi, handed over fifty euros and walked over to Villa Serres, named after a small market town in the heart of the French Alps. He inserted the large brass key into the lock and turned it towards the wall. The well-oiled barrels of the lock submitted easily and he pushed the gate open and walked through. He took a long, slow walk around the perimeter of the villa. The gardener and housekeeper he paid by direct debit every month had maintained their high standards of work. The large swimming pool looked inviting as the midday sun glistened off the surface, and Donavan felt a bead of perspiration on his brow. He regretted his decision not to spend more time there.

He made his way past the elegant entrance to the villa and fumbled in his briefcase for the electronic gadget that powered the garage doors, praying that the batteries that hadn't been used for so long were still up to the job. He smiled as the garage door creaked and groaned, but slowly revealed the prize within.

Donavan had studied the owners' manual of the Volkswagen Beetle in detail. He had also sought technical information from a VW mechanics' website. It was simple. The hydraulic brake fluid had to be above a certain level for the brakes to work. Drain the hydraulic reservoir and the brakes were useless.

He didn't particularly want Debra and Stephen dead, just a little accident to keep them out of the way for a bit. But then, if something a little more serious did happen, that was okay.

Stephen killed, now that would be nice, he detested the man. Then he could work on Debra. Yeah, he liked Debra, maybe just a few broken ribs or something minor. Stephen, he was expendable.

He removed the four screws to the hydraulic reservoir, situated just underneath the engine casing. He inserted the syringe and pulled the handle back, watching as the thick brown substance eased slowly into the glass chamber. The only brake fluid left in the car would be in the brake pipes. Donavan estimated the brakes could be applied no more than fifteen to twenty times before they failed completely. He replaced the screws and located the Beetle's fuse box. He shone the pencil torch inside and his eyes fixed on a fuse that read *dashboard-warning display*. He removed the fuse and dropped it in his pocket.

* * * *

Debra and Stephen were liked two excited children at the airport as they stood with Donavan and Vicky and the two children.

"This really is so good of you, Don, you don't know what this means to us."

"Don't be silly, we're going to have a great time too."

Donavan looked across at Cameron and Elissa, then reached across and stroked Cameron's hair. "Aren't we, kids."

The two children nodded. It was a great big adventure to them, flying to Paris and going to Disneyland with their two new adult friends. They were the only two adults they knew that actually treated them like grown-ups. Donovan had worked it out well and knew they wouldn't refuse the opportunity of a trip to Disneyland.

"Oh, by the way, I nearly forgot." Donavan reached inside his jacket pocket and pulled out the keys to the Volkswagen. He leaned over and handed Stephen the set of keys. "There's a left-hand drive car in the garage at the villa. You're welcome to use it while you're there."

"Bloody hell," Stephen replied, "are you sure?"

" I insist Steve, it keeps the engine ticking over, and it means it won't be seized up the next time I'm over there."

Stephen took the keys, smiling like a Cheshire cat. " I suppose you're right. Anything special?"

Donsvan smiled. "I think so. A beetle convertible, yellow with a black roof."

Debra grabbed Stephen by the arm, a huge grin across her face. "Jeez, Don, my favourite. Oh, Steve, can you imagine cruising along the coast in that?"

"Brilliant, Don, absolutely brilliant, you think of everything."

I certainly do, thought Donavan, I certainly do.

Before Donavan could soak up any more praise, the airport tannoy kicked in and announced that the 14.24 flight to Nice was boarding. The children hugged their mother warmly and showed some token affection for Stephen.

"Be good for Don and Vicky," was the last instruction Debra gave them before she took Stephen's hand and walked away towards the departure lounge. Just before she walked through the gates, Debra turned around and waved to the children. The children waved and waved until she disappeared from view.

Donavan turned and took both pairs of hands in his. "C'mon,

let's go, I'm sure your Mum and Steve will have a smashing time."

The following morning Stephen and Debra skipped out to the garage, eager to start their mini-break the right way.

"We'll drive along the coast road to Monaco," announced Debra, studying the map. "It should only take an hour. We can mooch around a bit and have lunch in Monte Carlo around one-ish."

"Sounds perfect, I can't wait to get the roof off this thing."

Stephen eased himself into the passenger seat and keyed the ignition. The engine started straightaway. "Got to hand it to Don. He thinks of everything. He's so kind; who else would just throw you the keys to something like this?"

Debra nodded, but didn't answer.

Stephen pushed the gear stick into reverse and carefully manoeuvred the car out from the garage and into the bright sunshine. A quick fumble with a few strange looking buttons and he located the electronic roof button. The cover groaned as it moved slowly across the car. A small hatch opened just above the engine compartment at the rear of the car and the canvas cover disappeared slowly and neatly into the space. "Clever stuff, Debs, jump in, let's go."

Debra didn't need to be told twice and ran around to the passenger side of the vehicle whilst fumbling in her bag for the Gucci sunglasses she'd bought in the duty-free lounge at Newcastle airport. "A hundred and ten pounds these cost, Steve, got to look the part, haven't I."

Stephen smiled, found first gear, and gently eased the nose of the vehicle into the busy street. He touched the brake pedal with his foot and held it there, waiting for a gap in the traffic. A silver Mercedes C class sped towards him. Beyond it, Stephen spied a fifty-metre gap in the traffic. He pushed his foot hard on the accelerator and eased off the clutch, the car lurched forward and he fumbled at the gear stick, searching for second gear. He cursed at the unfamiliarity of the controls on the left-hand drive car and his foot instinctively hovered over the brake pedal. The car jerked forward and Debra shot back in her seat.

"Don't worry," Stephen said before she could criticise, "I'll get used to it in a few minutes."

The town traffic was thick and, before he hit the open road of the A8, he had touched the brake pedal at least ten times. Debra relaxed, eased back in her seat, and began to enjoy the experience. The noise of the car and the wind was just about bearable at 110 kilometres per hour, but far more pleasant below hundred, and he touched the brake gently as the needle of the speedometer hovered on 95.

"That's better," Debra smiled. "This is incredible. I can't believe I've had to wait until I'm forty years old before I've experienced this."

Stephen returned her smile before remembering it was Donavan Smith who was providing this moment of satisfaction for his wife. Donavan Smith: handsome, confident, wealthy. And the way he looked at Debra sometimes, what did it mean?

He shook his head and pushed the thoughts from his mind. How could he think such things about his new friend: the friend who had insisted they use his villa and car for the weekend and wouldn't think of taking even a token payment to cover expenses? Stephen gripped the steering wheel a little tighter and convinced himself that he wished he'd met Donavan Smith years ago.

The needle on the speedometer touched a hundred again, and Debra gave Stephen a look that said slow down. He looked at the gentle, sweeping bend in the road up ahead and touched at the brake pedal again. He frowned and tensed up; something didn't feel right. Was it his imagination or did he have to apply a little more pressure to the pedal? Then he relaxed as the pads began to bite and the car held the road firmly as he leaned into the bend as if on a motorbike.

Stephen concentrated hard, keeping his eyes on the road. It was difficult. The spectacular views of the sparkling blue Mediterranean Sea drew him in like a magnet.

A little later, Debra gave him a nudge and pointed up ahead.

The red-framed road sign of Monte Carlo stood at the side of the road two hundred metres away. She gave a cry of delight as they crossed the imaginary line.

Stephen laughed. "You're like a big kid at Christmas."

"So what? Aren't you excited?"

Stephen looked across and smiled, "I suppose so, I can't wait to get parked up and have a wander round."

The traffic was heavy, and Stephen felt a little frustrated as he was now driving part of the circuit of the Monaco Grand Prix. All he wanted to do was hammer the accelerator to the floor. Instead, his foot hovered over the brake pedal.

Debra tugged at his arm as they went under the Mirabeau Hotel. "This is the hotel on the Monaco Grand Prix, isn't it?"

Stephen didn't answer. He cursed. *Damn, that brake pedal just isn't right.* He looked at the speedometer, now barely above ten kilometres per hour. He wasn't unduly concerned, he would take the car down through the gears and use the handbrake if necessary. He changed down into second. He'd get a garage to look at it over lunch. Momentarily, he forgot about the brake pedal as the spectacular view of Monaco Harbour burst into view with hundreds of floating white palaces crammed into the most expensive moorings in the world.

Debra sighed, "Jesus, Steve, what an amazing sight. Can we park next to the harbour and take a look at some of them?"

"We sure can. Who knows, we might even bump into someone famous. They've all got boats down here, you know."

The traffic opened up a little and the speedometer crept up to twenty. "Sean Connery has a yacht here, and David Beckham. Al Pacino has one valued at about ten million and Michael Douglas and Catherine Zeta-Jones have one too."

Debra didn't answer but, by the look on her face, Stephen figured he'd impressed her with his knowledge. He racked his brain to try and remember more names he had read in the Sunday Times article. "Most of the Hollywood set stay on their yachts for the Cannes Film Festival. They throw lavish on-board parties trying to outdo each other every night."

Down into first gear, Stephen left the main road and crawled into the neatly cobbled harbour parking section.

Debra frowned. "We won't get parked along here, it's packed to the gunnels."

Stephen looked up ahead as row upon row of BMWs, Mercedes, and Porsches crammed every single space adjacent to the harbour barrier. Just as he was about to give up, he spied the reverse lights of a gleaming red Audi convertible fifty metres ahead. The car reversed slowly and Steve had only one thought on his mind. He pushed down hard on the accelerator. "That space has my name on it!"

A gentleman in his late fifties sat in the driver's seat, the sun reflecting from his shining, over red, hairless scalp. A twenty-something blond with oversized designer sunglasses sat in the passenger seat. She frowned as she noticed the VW speeding towards them. The gentleman shook his head, found first gear and sped away.

"Slow down, Steve," cried Debra as the car lurched to the right, but Stephen smiled and congratulated himself on his judgement as the car slipped perfectly into the gap vacated by the Audi.

He took his foot from the accelerator pedal and pushed down on the brake pedal, intending to bring it to a dead stop a metre from the end of the quayside. The brake pedal barely moved, instinctively he stamped again, but it was locked solid, the brake pipes now completely drained of fluid. Again, he stamped down as he looked ahead at the fast approaching blue sea. He fumbled to his left for the handbrake and cursed as he found nothing and remembered he was in a left-hand drive. The car's front end ploughed through the old wooden barrier as if it were made of balsa wood. It hadn't been replaced for over twenty years and the mixture of salt and sun had baked it until it was brittle. It was his last chance now as he located the handbrake and jerked upwards. The four wheels locked in position and Stephen and Debra lurched forward in their seats. He looked across at her and smiled. It was a token smile, a smile that seemed to say trust me. The smile disappeared though as the four wheels gripped nothing but thin air. The front end of the VW dipped violently and the rear end continued its forward motion, the heavy engine positioned in the boot propelling the car over onto its roof.

The car hit the oily ocean flat on. The force of the impact crushed the windscreen and, with Stephen's six-foot frame, his head was positioned at the perfect angle to connect with the steel frame that held the glass in place. There was a sickening crunch as his skull shattered and his blood mixed with the diesel and salt.

Debra tasted the salt and the oil and the blood. She opened her eyes to a swirling, deep black and crimson mixture as the car began to sink downwards. She screamed in horror as she looked across at the lifeless body of her husband and regretted her action as the foul-tasting liquid spewed into her mouth. The car continued its slow, but steady, downward motion.

Survival instinct took over. No thoughts for Stephen now, no sympathy, no heroics. She grappled with the seat belt and a surge of energy came over her as she felt the buckle break free. Still the car drifted downwards to the seabed, and she paused for a split second before focusing on the bright sunlight ten metres above her. She felt for the windscreen and kicked against the lifeless body beside her. It gave her the momentum she needed and, even though her lungs screamed out for oxygen, she convinced herself she'd make it to the surface. With a final kick and push on the windscreen, her body broke free from the steel coffin and her head filled with thoughts of her children. However, Debra's heart sank and her mouth opened instinctively as her rapid progress was suddenly halted. A cool rush of the foul-tasting liquid again filled her mouth. Then, the upward motion of her progress was reversed as the car continued the journey towards its resting place.

Realisation of what had happened set in. The seatbelt had twisted and caught up around her ankle, dragging her downwards. A severe pain raked across her chest; her lungs were ready to explode. She arched and twisted her body and, with all the energy she could muster, propelled herself down into the car. She took hold of the belt and, with a calmness the origin of which she was unsure, yanked the belt from her ankle.

She kicked free for the second time as the car settled on the seabed. The shattered windscreen bent inwards and crumpled flat against the main shell of the car. Debra cried out as it trapped her lower leg against the steering wheel. The calmness had gone and she thrashed around like a dragonfly caught in a web. Instinctively, she swallowed again. The mixture of salt water and silt from the harbour bottom poured into her lungs, rasping at the back of her throat like a sheet of liquid sandpaper. She gagged. Desperation, this was her last chance of survival and her confidence in making the surface evaporated. She kicked furiously and thought she felt her leg move a little, the oily bloody liquid acting as a lubricant. The last oxygen in the VW escaped and rose in a huge air bubble towards the surface. The car settled another few inches and the steering wheel collapsed under the pressure. Debra's fibula and tibia snapped cleanly like two delicate twigs in a frozen forest.

She felt no pain, only peace.

CHAPTER TWENTY-SEVEN

Vicky Mackenzie in Paris and Bob Heggie in the Province of Cadiz took the phone call from the French police within thirty minutes of each other.

They located Bob first. They traced the plate of the stricken car back to the villa in Cannes and gained entry. Once inside, they found the passport of Stephen Blackett and Debra Heggie. For some reason, Debra hadn't got round to changing the passport to her new married name and, ironically enough, the next of kin was her ex-husband. The passport had noted his telephone number at Martins Bank, his previous employer. The French police had telephoned the bank and the call had been put through to James Richfield, one of the few people who had his contact number in Spain.

Bob had been enjoying a pleasant lunch with Hannah and, although the malicious phone calls were still at the back of his mind, he hadn't had contact from his tormentor for nearly a fortnight. Little did he know it was a two-week period in which Donavan Smith had grown ever closer to his children.

As Bob picked up the phone, he concentrated on the broken English of the French police sergeant and a terrible feeling materialised in the pit of his stomach. He looked at Hannah as the colour drained from his face.

"Bob, what is it? What's wrong?"

Bob continued with his telephone conversation. "You're sure it's her? And what about the children, where are they?"

Bob listened to the French policeman carefully. "Yes, I have two children. Where are they?"

"Bob, what is it? Tell me please." Hannah walked across the room and Bob reached for her hand.

"There were only two bodies in the car? Do you know where the children are - Cameron, Elissa - where are they?"

It was Hannah's turn to go weak at the knees. "Oh, Jesus Christ, Bob, what's happened?"

"Are you sure? How do you know?" Perspiration built up on the back of Bob's neck, a dank, cold perspiration, the kind caused by fear and anxiety.

"Can you give me a number and I'll call you back." Bob signalled to Hannah for a pen and, after she had handed him one, he scribbled the telephone number of the Monte Carlo Police Department on the back of an old newspaper. "Pierre Masselle, yeah, I've got it. I'll give you a call later."

Bob's voice was barely a whisper as he replaced the receiver. Hannah didn't need to ask again, she knew he was about to announce something terrible. "Debra's been killed."

Hannah collapsed into a chair. Bob sank to the floor, tears welling up in his eyes. "I shouldn't be feeling this way, Hannah. After all she did to me. But we were together on and off for twenty years, I loved her once; worshipped the ground she walked on."

A tear trickled down his cheek. Hannah slid to the floor to join him and kissed the tear as it fell.

"She gave life to my children."

And Hannah held him tight as he sobbed like a baby.

As the French police searched Villa Serres, they came across the mobile phone number of Vicky Mackenzie written on the kitchen noticeboard. Monsieur Masselle decided to call the number to establish who she was and what connection, if any, she had with Monsieur Blackett and Madame Heggie.

Vicky's mobile rang as she sat with Donavan and the children having lunch in Euro Disney. "A foreign number, Don." She looked at Cameron and Elissa as they munched on a huge pizza. "It's probably Mummy wanting to speak to you."

She frowned as an unfamiliar voice established who he was

and started asking questions; no niceties, not even polite, and certainly to the point.

"Yes, I know Debra Heggie, or rather that's what she used to be called. She's Mrs Blackett now."

She frowned again. "Can you speak a little slower please."

She covered the mouthpiece and whispered to Donavan, "I don't suppose you speak French, Don. I can only just make out what this fella is saying; claims he's a French policeman."

Donavan shook his head. Vicky looked at Elissa and couldn't understand why the happy, contented face had disappeared and, instead, a worried look had replaced it and the colour had drained from her cheeks.

"What's wrong, Elissa?" her brother asked.

Vicky was about to find out. "Yeah, she's my friend. I mean they're both my friends, they're on holiday. We're looking after their children. What's wrong?"

Vicky glanced across at Donavan. She didn't know what sort of expression to expect on his face: a look of surprise, even concern?

But Donavan Smith sat back in the uncomfortable, small chair, relaxed and at ease.

Vicky glowered at him as she noticed a half smile, a slight grin, as he took a mouthful of Coca Cola.

Then the French policeman dropped the bombshell.

"How do I know who you are? Is this some sort of sick joke?" The telephone slipped from Vicky's grip as her hands became wet and clammy. She quickly snatched at it in mid-air and, as she fumbled with it, just about caught the last sentence or two from the policeman. She pressed *end*.

"What is it?" Donavan asked calmly.

Elissa regurgitated the contents of her stomach into the empty pizza box in front of her.

Vicky sat in a momentary trance, unable to speak.

Donavan looked at Elissa, then at Cameron.

"I'm afraid there's been a car accident. Mummy's been hurt," Vicky blurted out eventually.

The first tear of what was to be many fell onto Elissa's cheek and her small brother ran over to comfort her. Within seconds, they were crying in unison and hugging each other, as they'd never done before.

Vicky stared deep into Donavan's cold eyes, which were like two ponds of stagnant green water tucked far away in an uncared-for inner-city park.

She looked for a denial. She found nothing. "You!" she whispered quietly.

Donavan stood up and took Elissa's arm. Cameron clung to her for all he was worth. "Into the toilet, Elissa, you too Cameron. Get yourself cleaned up. Everything'll be fine."

The two children held hands and walked away from Donavan Smith. Elissa stared back over her shoulder, giving him a strange look and, almost instantly, the tears subsided. The children disappeared into the toilet

Donavan walked slowly back to the table.

"Everything will be fine, won't it, Don?" Vicky stared at him impassively, drumming her fingers on the hard plastic table. "Everything's going to be fine then... and I guess it's you that's telling those kids their mother's lying on an ice-cold mortuary slab."

"She's been killed?" he asked.

Vicky's eyes welled up with tears as she spoke. "Both of them, Don; Steve as well, an accident in Monaco or Monte Carlo, I can't remember which one he said. They ended up in the harbour trapped in the car. They both drowned. In your car, Don, the Volkswagen Beetle. The car you flew over to sort out last month. As ever, the nice guy: went to recharge the battery and make sure that the villa was spick and span."

Donavan sat back and smiled.

"It was you, Don, wasn't it. You tampered with something on that car. You sent them to their deaths."

Donavan glanced over Vicky's shoulder in the direction of the toilets. "I didn't mean to, Vicky. I only meant for a little accident, something to keep them out of the way for a week or two; a little time so that we could put together the final part of the operation."

Vicky shook her head, a combination of rage and disbelief building up inside. "Jesus fucking Christ, Don, I don't believe it."

"I didn't mean to kill them, just a broken leg or two, that's all." He paused, took a long mouthful of Coke and wiped his mouth.

"But now they're dead." His eyes stole a quick sideways glance at her, then looked straight through her as if she wasn't there.

"Doesn't matter, dead is just as good. Probably better, actually." He laughed like a hyena struggling for breath. The sound ran the length of Vicky Mackenzie's spine. "Now we can take as long as we want."

After a few minutes, the children reappeared. Elissa calmly walked up to Vicky. "Mummy's dead, isn't she."

Cameron looked at his sister in horror.

The silence that followed gave the little girl her answer.

Donavan had insisted Vicky drive back to the apartment. It was a little cruel as she'd never driven a left-hand drive car before, let alone in the heart of Paris in the middle of the rush hour. She had protested, of course, but Donavan Smith gave her the look that she knew had to be obeyed. It's for the best, he had explained, it'll take your mind off things.

But it hadn't.

Vicky was thinking about murder and being an accomplice to murder and kidnap, and an accomplice to kidnap, and how they would all be found out sooner or later and inevitably end up in jail for at least twenty-five years. And she thought about even greater horrors that this beast sitting beside her was capable of committing. Her maternal instincts took over and she glanced in the mirror at the two siblings as they clung to each other in a grip that would need a crowbar to prise them apart. I won't let him hurt them, she vowed. I'll pick up the phone to the police and confess everything if he even suggests it.

She became aware that Donavan was staring at her. She felt

like he could read her every thought and quickly tried to act cool, calm and collected. "You're right, Don, I'm beginning to get the hang of this. It's not too bad. And yeah… it kind of takes your mind off things."

"Give me your phone, Vic, I need to make a call. My battery is out."

Without questioning him, Vicky handed her mobile across. It had her life in it. Every number and address she possessed. It contained a diary of every meeting she'd been to in the last eighteen months and, of course, every date with her partner in crime. She'd begun to type in her innermost thoughts and her concerns. She'd meant to back up everything to her laptop on many occasions, but, of course, had never got round to it.

"Take a left here," he pointed up ahead. "A little short cut I know."

Vicky obeyed and turned left along the north bank of the Seine. Donavan was right; it was quiet and there was barely enough room for two cars to pass each other safely. Vicky slowed down to twenty-five kilometres per hour and Donavan pressed the window button on his   passenger door. He kept his finger on the button until the window disappeared into the door.

"It's a little cold for that, Don, isn't it?"

Donavan said nothing and hung his arm out of the window. Vicky looked across and spotted her mobile phone in the palm of his hand. Donavan bit his bottom lip and, with a quick, skilful motion, hurled the phone into the air. The mobile phone flew in a huge arc across the roof of the car and Vicky caught sight of it a split second before it hit the surface of the river with barely a sound.

"Are you crazy? What the hell have you done that for?"

Donavan grinned, leaned across, and whispered in her ear, "Cutting us off from the outside world, of course. Now, no one can find us darling. Just you and me and our route to a million in the back seat. No one can even contact us. Not your mother or the French police, nor can our friend, Mr Heggie, when he eventually puts two and two together."

Vicky sat stunned and barely managed to keep the car in a straight line. "My whole life was in that phone, Don. All my friends' addresses and telephone numbers. I —"

Donavan gripped her thigh hard, so hard it hurt. "Like I said, darling, just you and me. You don't need friends anymore; you've got me."

He looked straight ahead into the rapidly approaching night sky. *"Be content with such things as ye have. Hebrew 13:5."*

The high-pitched tone of the telephone shattered the silence in the small lounge in the village of Niebla. Bob had hardly uttered a word in the previous hour and Hannah sat at his feet stroking him gently, not knowing what to say or what to do. Bob leapt to his feet and made a frantic dash for the phone. It had barely started its second ring as he grabbed at the handset. The cup of sweet tea beside it, which had stood for over an hour, crashed to the floor. " Shit! Shit! Shit! Hello, hello, Bob Heggie speaking, is that Monsieur Masselle?"

The French policeman confirmed who he was and continued, telling Bob that four frogmen had searched the harbour for nearly two hours and could find no evidence that any children had been in the car. There were no bodies, nor were there any toys or books or sweets, the sort of things you would expect to find in a car if two small children were travelling in the back seat. Monsieur Masselle sounded concerned and asked where the children were.

"I, err, don't know." Jesus, thought Bob, I should know, I'm their bloody father. Why didn't she tell me where they were staying? What if I wanted to call them? Christ, why didn't she ask if I wanted them? I would have flown across, given the damn chance. "Probably with their grandmother in Newcastle... that's England."

Hannah knelt in front of him, mopping up the cold tea.

"Their grandmother's number, yes, I have it. I'll call her and ring you back. What, you'll call me in thirty minutes? Yes, fine, okay."

Bob couldn't wait to put the phone down, but managed to remember to thank the policeman for all his efforts.

"Debra's mother," he shouted to Hannah. "Her telephone number, do you have it?"

Hannah shook her head. "Are you crazy, Bob, why the hell would I have her number?"

"Yeah, yeah, how stupid of me. I've got it somewhere."

Thank God, thought Bob, the kids are fine and then a pang of guilt crept over him for feeling so good as he pictured Debra's body in her waterlogged steel coffin. Or worse, a pale, almost white, bloated body on a cold slab with a ticket tied to her big toe. Huge oversized red eyes and discoloured pale blue lips.

He had to find that number though; he needed to know where Cameron and Elissa were. They'd need their father. He'd fly to Newcastle to see them, comfort them, and perhaps even bring them back to Spain for a few weeks. The school would understand.

He found Debra's mother's number in a five-year-old diary he'd fortunately kept. It was one of those diaries that everyone had, listing the most obscure numbers he could think of, numbers he would never ring but, curiously, didn't want to throw away. He was glad he hadn't thrown it away and tried to remember the last time he had spoken to her. Must be at least a year, he thought. Not a lot you can really say to the mother-in-law of a wife who has run off with another man. Of course, Sheila had rung Bob a few times to sympathise with him, to ask how he was keeping and, at one point, to almost apologise for her daughter's action.

He punched the number into the phone and, as he heard the familiar ring tone of an international call, it suddenly dawned on him that he may have to deliver the terrible news that every mother dreaded. Had the French police somehow traced her and got the British police to call on her?

Before he had time to think, Sheila McAnespie answered the phone. "Hi Sheila, it's Bob, Bob Heggie, remember?"

Sheila McAnespie broke down as soon as she heard the familiar tones of Bob's voice. In a way, Bob was relieved. Sheila explained the police had called within the hour to deliver the gruesome news. Between tears, she babbled on about retribution from the Lord and a punishment for breaking up the family home. "The Lord works in mysterious ways, Bob."

"Yeah, Sheila, I'm sure he does. How are the kids? Do they know yet? How are they taking it?"

"The children, Bob? I don't know. They're not with me; they're with some friends; don't even know their names or where they are."

Bob struggled to hang onto the handset and the cold perspiration began seeping from the pores on the back of his neck.

"Don't worry, Bob, I've got the lady's mobile number. I was going to call it just as you rang."

Bob's mouth was as dry as tinder and he barely managed to croak out the next sentence. "I'll do it, Sheila, it's my duty. It's best if it comes from me."

"Oh, Bob, thanks. I was dreading that phone call. Those poor little things, how do you deliver that type of news?" Sheila had stopped crying and she began to be practical, discussing funeral arrangements and offering Bob a place to stay. Bob supposed it was her way of coping and tried not to interrupt. He so wanted that number to call the children.

"This lady's name, Sheila, and her number, do you have it handy?"

"What, Bob? Yes, Bob, I'm sorry. I'll just get it for you."

Bob heard the receiver clatter against a hard surface and Sheila's footsteps disappearing into the distance on a hard wooden floor. He strained to pick the sound of them again, looking at his watch on more than one occasion.

"C'mon, c'mon, what's taking you so long?" he whispered into the mouthpiece.

After what seemed like an eternity, there was the sound of footsteps growing louder and he heard the receiver being lifted. A rustle of paper, another delay and, at last, Sheila McAnespie spoke. "Like I said, Bob, I have the number but not a name. I'm sure Debra mentioned her name but I can't recall it. Wait just a second, it's coming to me... begins with a 'V' I think. Veronica, she said.. yeah, that was it, Veronica, I think."

"Never mind, Sheila, just give me the number. I'll soon establish what her name is."

Bob scribbled the number down on the back of the newspaper next to the Monaco police number and wrote the letter 'V' next to it. It looked sort of familiar to him, but then he recalled several friends' mobile numbers that began with 0777. He exchanged a few niceties with Sheila McAnespie and told her what a special girl Debra had been. He almost told her he still loved Debra, but stopped short and wondered if there was still a faint flickering flame burning for Debra deep within him.

As soon as he replaced the handset, he snatched it up again and began hitting the numbers. Hannah had sat patiently throughout and Bob turned to her. "The children are with one of Debra's friends, Veronica somebody. I don't know her but Sheila had her mobile number. I'm calling her now."

Hannah nodded and forced a half smile. Bob keyed in the last three digits. He stood waiting for the ring tone; wherever the children were, he'd fly out to meet them as soon as possible. He couldn't tell them over the phone. It wouldn't be right. He needed to be there in person; he wanted to hold them and comfort them.

"Shit!" he shouted loudly, as he smashed the receiver down.

"What is it, Bob?"

Bob paced across the room. "Shit, shit, shit!"

"Isn't she answering?"

"The bloody phone isn't even switched on." Bob mimicked an American accent. *The Vodaphone you are trying to call is unobtainable. Please try again later.*

And he did. He called the number every few minutes and each time he heard the irritating American tones.

After at least a dozen attempts, he walked back to the phone. Before he could pick it up, it rang. His face lit up. "Probably her returning her missed calls."

"Or the French police," Hannah replied. "They're due to call."

It was neither the French police nor the unknown babysitter. Bob cringed as he heard the familiar tones of his tormentor. The colour drained from his face. Hannah looked on and realised immediately who was at the other end of the telephone line.

"Bobbeee... lovely to hear your voice again."

Bob didn't reply. He wanted to put the phone down, but something stopped him.

"Bobbeee... have you heard about the accident? Poor, poor Debra, the children will be so upset. And Stephen too. Such a nice man, the perfect replacement father, don't you think? Poor Debra, poor Stephen, poor Cameron and Elissa."

"How do you know, you sick bastard?"

"That's not important right now, Bobby. What's important is that I know and that I have your children."

Bob had dreaded this moment for many weeks but the words still hit him like a Chieftain Tank. He sank to his knees. "You've... wh...what?"

"I have Cameron and Elissa here with me right now. In fact, Bob, they've had a great time today. Best day little Cameron had ever had, he said. That is, until we had to tell him about the accident."

"No, you haven't, you lying bastard. They're with a friend of Debra's. You're lying."

The tormentor cackled and a familiar shiver ran the length of Bob's spine. "Oh, Bobby, you don't sound very convinced. Have you tried calling this so-called friend?"

Bob remained silent; he didn't want to tell the tormentor he hadn't located the children.

"Number unobtainable, I suppose?" he laughed again. "You see, Bobby, I can read you like a book. I guess you rang Debra's mother for the number. Only it won't connect, will it?" Another cackle.

"The French Police are onto you. They're calling back soon. I'm going to tell them everything."

The tone of Donavan Smith's voice changed. He didn't laugh any more. He growled at Bob and, though he hated to admit it, the voice sent the fear of God through Bob's bones. "You listen to me, Bobby, and no interruptions. If you interrupt, I'll hang up and take out my frustrations on your children."

A slight pause and Bob remained silent. "I have your children and you know it. You don't know where I am nor do the French police. Debra's mother doesn't know where the children are and the only two people that could tell you are dead. I know Bobby... I killed them."

Bob couldn't help himself. "It was an accident...the French Police —"

"No interruptions, do you understand? That was your last chance."

"Okay, I'm sorry," Bob whimpered like a whipped dog.

"I think you'll find that the brakes failed on the car, but it was certainly no accident. Now listen and listen well. I want one million pounds in used notes for the safe return of your children. Let's say half a million for each of them. If you can only raise half a million, and I know you can raise at least that, then you choose which one dies. The worst decision to have to make in the world, Bobby. Cameron or Elissa? The Japanese used to do it during the war, you know? They'd march into the Chinese villages and tell the parents that they would spare one child. The poor fuckers had to choose one or they would bayonet the lot of them to death. The parents were faced with a decision you couldn't even imagine. If they took too long to decide, the Nips would butcher the lot of them." He laughed again. "Cruel bastards, those Japs. I had an Uncle who was a POW out there. He wouldn't buy a box of matches if they were made in Japan."

Bob Heggie stood rooted to the spot. He couldn't have spoken, even if he had wanted to. A psychopath had his children and there was nothing he could do about it.

"Anyway, Bobbeeee...you don't want to have to make that decision, do you?"

Bob shook his head and somehow Donavan sensed it. "Good boy, Bobby. I'll be in touch in a few days. You have one week from now to come up with the money. Friday at noon in seven days time, that's when you'll hand over the money. I'll take good care of the children unless you involve any police. Do I make myself clear, Bobby?"

Bob nodded again.

"Good boy, Bobby. Good man. *Cursed be he that taketh reward to slay an innocent person.* That one's from the book of Deuteronomy, Bob. Thought I'd leave you with it."

Then the line went dead.

Five minutes later, Hannah answered the phone. It was Pierre Masselle. She spoke a few words in French that Bob didn't understand, then handed the receiver to him. "Hello, Monsieur. Yes, Bob Heggie speaking. Thank you for calling. No....yes....fine, everything's okay. I spoke to the children; they're with some friends on a little vacation. I'm flying out to meet them tomorrow. No, everything's fine. You've been very good, very professional. There's nothing else you can help me with. Just one thing before I go, Monsieur, how did the accident happen?"

The Frenchman's reply chilled him to the bone.

"Thank you, Monsieur. Goodbye." Bob held the receiver to his ear. He wanted to tell Pierre Masselle everything; he wanted to tell him about the murders and the kidnap, and all about this vile maniac tormenting him.

He'd never felt more alone as the line went dead.

CHAPTER TWENTY-EIGHT

Bob tossed and turned all night, barely sleeping for more than fifteen minutes at a time. The LCD on the clock radio read 4.24 when he sat bolt upright as if he'd just been hit with fifty thousand volts. "Vicky Mackenzie!"

Hannah stirred beside him. She hadn't slept either. She'd felt every turn and movement of the man she loved and so wanted to help. "What?"

"Vicky Mackenzie!"

By this time, Bob had the light on and was raking through the old diary he'd searched through that evening when he'd found Sheila McAnespie's number. "I thought the number was familiar."

Hannah sighed. "Bob, it's twenty-five past four, what are you doing?"

Bob sat back on the bed. Hannah groaned. "I recognise the number, the 07775 followed by 5060. It's Vicky Mackenzie's number, I'm sure of it." He thumbed through the diary, desperate to try and match the last two digits.

"And who's Vicky Mackenzie?"

He didn't look up, but smiled as the diary opened at the address page beginning with 'M.' "Marshall Tom, Mackintosh, MACKENZIE. Here it is. Vicky Mackenzie."

He leapt from the bed and ran through to the lounge. He came back with the newspaper he'd scribbled the number on earlier that day. He studied the newspaper and his eyes flicked back to the diary. He grinned at Hannah like the cat that just found the cream. "It's her!" he shouted. "It's her number."

By this time, Hannah had opened her eyes and, although she didn't know who Vicky Mackenzie was, she realised that Bob's discovery was significant.

He snatched at the phone and began punching in the numbers. "Vicky was John Mackenzie's wife."

Hannah frowned and shook her head.

"John Mackenzie, the manager of Martins, the poor bastard shot in Leazes Park."

Hannah sat up and nodded. "Yeah, I remember now."

"Vicky wanted an affair. Or rather, she wanted sex. She pestered me for weeks, lured me to her house on one occasion and stripped off right in front of me... I ran away like a frightened schoolboy."

He held up a hand to silence Hannah as he entered the last digit and waited for the phone to ring. "Shit!"

Hannah repeated the words he'd just heard. "*The Vodaphone you are calling is unobtainable?*"

He stood up and nodded. "I don't think that phone will ever work again. This sicko is onto us. He knows I'd have rung Debra's mother and got hold of the number, and he obviously doesn't want Vicky Mackenzie to give the game away. It all fits together now."

Bob went on to explain the meeting with old Tom, how Tom had been attacked and how his attacker had used the quotations from the bible. "Tom described the lady he'd been trying to help. It was Vicky Mackenzie, I'm sure of it, and he was attacked in the underground car park where Debra and Steve lived. Vicky and this bloke had been going to see Debra and Steve. That's how they got to see the children and that's how he took those things from their bedroom."

He paced the room like a tiger in a cage. Slow steps. His finger traced a line along his chin. "But I'm wondering if he realises I know the number."

"Wouldn't Vicky have told him?"

Bob shook his head. "I don't think so. I mean, Vicky never ever gave me her number. I never returned any calls, and she's hardly going to tell him she chased me, is she? My guess is that she wouldn't dream I'd recognise her number and neither would that sick, religious nut. I mean, how many mobile phone numbers do you know off by heart?"

"None, they're all keyed in under names anyway. The numbers don't even register."

"Exactly! This bastard's just made his first mistake."

Bob sat on the bed again. Hannah knelt behind him and slid her hands around his waist. "The phone's out of order for good, I'm sure of that, but not because they think I'd recognise the number. He just doesn't want anyone to know where they are."

Hannah kissed him gently on the side of the cheek. "I hate to bring you down to earth again, Bob, but this information doesn't exactly get you anywhere. I mean, supposing Vicky Mackenzie and her accomplice have the children, we don't know where they are, let alone how to get them back."

As if a light bulb appeared above Bob's head, his eyes registered excitement again. "I do know where they are."

"You do?"

On his feet again, striding the strides of a tiger, Bob smiled. "France!"

"France? "

"France!"

"Explain, Bob."

"You know when you take an international call, whether it's a mobile landline or whatever, the connection sound is very different for every country."

Hannah shrugged her shoulders. "I hadn't really noticed, Bob."

"It is. It's different. You can tell whether someone's calling from England and it's different in Spain because the mobile goes through Telefonica."

"Oh yeah, I know what you mean now. But I still don't get it. How do you know he's in France?"

Bob picked up the pace; Hannah wanted to scream at him to stand still. "The two phone calls from the French copper and our friend: they connected in exactly the same way, I'm sure they did. The calls came within minutes of each other, as if from the same phone. Exact connection time, exact tone, and exact echo. They're in France, I know they are."

Hannah opened the curtains, it was still dark, but she somehow guessed they wouldn't be going back to bed. "A big place, France, Bob, it ain't going to be easy."

"They've pulled off the perfect kidnap."

"They've what?"

"The perfect kidnap, Hannah! To everyone else, he's taken the kids on a little holiday, but he's blackmailing us to the tune of a million pounds."

"We need to call the police, Bob. If you know what Vicky looks like and you're sure they're in France, Interpol will find them."

Bob stayed quiet.

"And you've photos of the children, Bob, the police will find them in no time."

He looked over to Hannah, her figure accentuated by the darkness behind her, like a lost soul painted onto the natural photograph frame of the window, and her eyes begged him to listen.

"I'm sorry, Hannah, we can't take the chance."

"What chance, Bob? We wouldn't be taking a chance."

He walked over to her and took her hands in his. "We would… the bastard has murdered Debra and Steve."

Hannah fell against the window frame. By the time Bob had explained everything, she sat in a crumpled heap on the floor. "Where do we go from here then, Bob? I still think we should call the police. I mean we're dealing with a murderer. Who knows what he's capable of and what he's done in the past."

Bob kissed her full on the lips. "You're a genius!"

"What? I only said he…"

"A genius! That's what you are. His past, you said. He's bound to have a criminal record. I mean, you don't just start murdering and kidnapping as some sort of midlife crisis."

"Yeah Bob, I guess you're right. So, we go to the cops and…."

"No cops, Hannah. I know what the bastard looks like… I met him." And Bob went on to explain how he had met Vicky and her new boyfriend in Newcastle. Hannah's face drained of colour as she sat and listened intently, much like a small child listens to a ghost story.

Bob rose to his feet again. "Think, man! Think! Where can he be? Where would he take children on a holiday in France? Paris…The Riviera….Brittany?"

Hannah shrugged.

"No. Not Brittany, no airports, and it's too far to take two small children in the car. I don't think it's quite hot enough for a beach holiday in the south of France yet. My guess is a city break to Paris or Nice or Bordeaux."

"My guess would be Paris too."

"He said they'd had great time. Best day of Cameron's life, he said. Where on earth could…"

"DISNEYLAND!" Hannah squealed. "Paris Disneyland, it's obvious, Bob, Euro Disney. Where else would you take two kids of that age?"

Bob smiled. "You know, Hannah, I think you're right. Go and pack a bag."

"Why, where are we going?"

"Euro Disney, of course. We can be there by early afternoon if we get our skates on."

Hannah looked at Bob as if he'd taken a mad turn. "What for, Bob? If they were there, they'll not be there today. What on earth are we looking for?"

He was smiling now. "Photographs."

"Photographs?"

"Yeah, photographs, thousands of them. These theme parks take them all over the damn place and line them up at ten euros a shot as they leave, making sure they prise every little cent from the parents' pockets."

Suddenly Hannah clicked into Bob's mode of thinking. "And, of course, they never buy all of them. They'd need a bloody mortgage application form."

"Exactly. They must keep the unsold ones for at least a few

days. People buy two and three day passes for these parks."

Hannah tensed up. "Jeez, Bob, what if you-know-who has bought a two or three day pass?"

"I'd love to think he has, Hannah, but somehow I don't think he'd be that predictable."

"Imagine bumping into him. What would you do?"

Bob's face flushed and he trembled with rage. "Let's not go there. Just throw a few things in an overnight bag."

Hannah smiled and pulled an old leather holdall from the top of the wardrobe.

They hit the outskirts of Paris just after 3 p.m. "There's the sign for Euro Disney," Hannah pointed at a slip road sign two hundred metres ahead. "Twenty kilometres, that's where all the hotels are. We can book in for a night or two. You never know, they might just come back."

Bob sighed and shook his head. "I wouldn't count on it."

Half an hour later, they checked into the Holiday Inn Euro Disney and were on the shuttle bus to the theme park within twenty minutes. Bob held Hannah's hand. It shook with fear. He held it tight. He hadn't asked her if she even wanted to be part of this little adventure, but she'd never questioned him once. As the theme park loomed up ahead, Bob began to wonder if this menace might just come back for a second day. What dangers lay up ahead for Hannah and the children? The man was a murderer at least twice over and God knows what horrors he'd committed in the past.

Bob took his favourite photograph of Cameron and Elissa from the inside pocket of his jacket. It had been taken three months prior on Newcastle's Quayside during a brief visit back to Newcastle. He'd been back for three days, but, because of one thing and another, Debra had only allowed him two hours with them on a wet Saturday afternoon. They were huddled under an umbrella, their beautiful smiling faces pressed against each other, the Tyne Bridge just about visible in a grey misty background. The children were perfectly in focus and their smiles were infectious. Bob couldn't push away the feeling of dread that this might be the last photograph he would ever take of them.

"Come on, Bob, stop dreaming. We've work to do." Hannah pulled him to the entrance of the park and handed her credit card to the smiling French cashier. Bob slipped the photograph back into his pocket.

They walked quickly through the park, the only tourists not looking at the wondrous attractions on offer.

Bob turned to Hannah. "I haven't seen one photograph display yet. Where the hell are they?"

"I don't know. I suspect they put them out later in the day."

Bob pointed up ahead. "Information office, come on, let's try our luck and go straight for the jugular."

They walked into the brightly decorated office and a dour-faced, middle-aged female assistant greeted them in English. How does she know we're English, Bob thought. Nevertheless, he was glad of her grasp of the English language. He looked down at her breast pocket: a garish, oversized, plastic Disneyland Paris nametag read 'Nicole Saumarez'.

"I wonder if you could help me." Bob pulled the photograph of the children from his pocket. The assistant smiled as she focused on the photograph. *Good start,* Bob thought.

"My children were here yesterday with a couple of friends. They had a wonderful time, met all the characters, Mickey Mouse, Donald Duck, Goofy, and err… you know the other ones. They had such a good time they forgot to pick up the photographs taken during the day. They've gone home now and, as we are staying in Paris for a few days longer, we promised them we'd try and collect them."

The assistant lost her smile. Bob tried to appear casual. "Is that possible?"

She gave a Gaelic shrug. "Oui. It is possible. Where did they get photographed? And at what time approximately? We will try, Monsieur, and, of course, there will be a charge."

Bob's heart sank and he threw the assistant his best schoolboy smile. "I don't know, I'm afraid. They didn't say."

The assistant sighed. "Monsieur, we have dozens of attractions and over thirty characters the children can be photographed with. We have tens of thousands of photographs left over every single day of the year. It would be an impossible task to look through them all."

Hannah chipped in. "Could we do it then?"

"No, Madame, that is not possible. It's against regulations."

"But you have somewhere where all the photographs are kept?"

"Oui, such a place exists. We keep the photographs for one week, then they are incinerated. For obvious reasons, the public are not allowed access."

Bob had lost his casual, relaxed demeanour and now began to get agitated. "But surely someone could look for them if we paid for their time?"

"I am sorry, sir. It is not possible." The assistant looked over Bob's shoulder as a young couple came into the office. "Could I ask you to leave, Monsieur? There are other people waiting."

Hannah tugged at his jacket. "C'mon Bob, this isn't going to work."

"Shit! Shit! Shit!" Bob exclaimed as he stepped aside and the young man spoke to the assistant in a thick American accent.

"Look, Bob, it was a long shot anyway. You said in the car that they probably haven't even been here."

"No… they've been here. I can feel it."

Hannah shook her head and walked towards the door. Bob lingered in the office as he heard the conversation between the assistant and the Americans ending.

The assistant frowned as he approached the counter again. "Sir, I will have to —"

Bob held up his hands and leaned on the counter, his face inches from hers. He whispered gently, "I'm so sorry, Madame, but you see we really are quite desperate and would do anything, pay anything, to get the photographs." He tried to make eye contact.

"I have already said, Monsieur, that it is not poss —"

"My children had to rush home yesterday." He took a deep

inhalation of breath. "Their Mother died in an accident. That's why they couldn't collect the photographs."

The assistant recoiled in horror. "Monsieur, I am so sorry. Why that is terrible."

Bob wiped at the corner of his eye. "A car crash, I'm afraid. They are devastated. We thought if we could get these photographs, it may help a little."

"You were not with their mother in the car?"

"No. We're divorced."

"And they were here yesterday with their mother?"

Bob hesitated for a second. "Errr…yes."

The assistant picked up the telephone and began conversing with a colleague. Bob turned around. Hannah was standing outside; she peered through the glass door, flicked a sympathetic smile, and looked at her watch.

"Monsieur."

Bob turned back quickly.

"If you leave me the photograph of the children, we will try to help."

"Yes. Why certainly. Thank you so much." He handed the photograph across.

She smiled briefly. "The poor children."

"Thank you. Thank you very much."

"It may take many hours, Monsieur. Are you able to come back this evening?"

Bob nodded his head, thanked his new friend at least another six times, and ran outside to Hannah. Before she could speak, he'd blurted out the story and explained they had to return later that evening. He expected Hannah to smile or at least show a little bit of enthusiasm, but she remained stone-faced. "What is it? What's wrong?"

She took his hand. "I just hope you're not disappointed, Bob, that's all."

Bob counted thousands of children who resembled Cameron and Ellisa. Each sighting, generally from a distance or from behind, plunged another painful dagger of disappointment into his heart, and, as the afternoon turned into evening, he became more frustrated.

He looked at his watch. "It's gone eight. Do you think we should go back yet?"

"I'd leave it a bit longer, Bob. Let's get something to eat."

Bob examined his watch again, as if the three-second lapse in time would somehow turn into an hour. "I'm not hungry."

Hannah frowned. "Neither am I, let's go."

At eight fifteen, they opened the door to the information office and Nicole Saumarez greeted them with a sympathetic smile. "Monsieur, you are a little early." She picked up the telephone. "I will call them anyway."

Bob nodded his head in appreciation as Madame Saumarez punched four digits into the telephone handset. She listened carefully. "Oui…oui…oui."

It sounded positive, Bob's heart raced ahead, then she replaced the receiver. But now she had a frown that had sympathy written right across it. "I'm sorry, Monsieur, nothing."

His heart sank. He looked at Hannah. She had a look on her face that said, let's go. He turned back to Madame Saumarez and thanked her for her help.

"Monsieur, you misunderstand, they are still looking. They will be finished in one hour."

Bob looked at his watch. "The hour's up. Shall we go?"

Hannah took his hand and led him over to the office. "Just don't be too disappointed, Bob, that's all."

The French lady had the same look of disappointment and Hannah flicked him a look that said, told you so.

"I am sorry, Monsieur."

Bob frowned and Hannah sighed.

"They have just finished and called me a few minutes ago. Henri is coming over now."

Bob looked puzzled.

"I'm sorry, Monsieur, there was only one photograph, and it is not very good, I'm afraid."

Bob could have dragged her across the counter and planted a huge kiss on her luscious French lips. But, just then, a spotty-faced French youth walked into the office. He handed the colour photograph to Madame Suamarez who studied it for a moment. "It was taken on the train of Thunder Mountain. The little boy is covering his face, but the little girl is quite clear."

She handed the photograph across. Cameron and Elissa sat in a two-seater car as it hurtled around a darkened bend. The flash of the camera illuminated their faces that looked like startled rabbits caught in headlights. Behind them sat Vicky Mackenzie with a nervous smile on her face and, next to her, sat the crystal clear image of Donavan Smith.

It was weird: a moment of extreme elation, triumph, a kind of I told you so and yet a moment of where do we go from here.

Back at the Holiday Inn, Bob had logged on to the Internet via one of the laptops that sat in a row opposite the reception area of the hotel. Hannah drummed her fingers on the desk beside him. "Not quite the time to go surfing, Bob. We've got a bit of a deadline, remember?"

Bob looked up, smiled, and then turned back to the screen. "Newcastle."

"Sorry?" Hannah asked.

"Newcastle. We need to get back to Newcastle to see Kev the fixer."

"Kev the —"

"Kevin the fixer. He's a guy I grew up with in Newcastle. Ebor Street in Newcastle. Not the greatest area in the world, but we didn't know any better. It was easy to get into trouble, get involved with the wrong people and, whilst I avoided it, Kevin didn't. He got involved with some real shady types, villains. He's perfected his craft well. He holds down a steady job, but if anything needs doing, Kevin knows someone that'll do it."

Bob laughed. "For a fee, of course. If you need a gun, or someone's legs broken, Kevin knows the man to do it. It's rumoured he can get someone killed for a couple of grand."

"Jesus, Bob… and you know this guy?"

"Know him? He's one of my best mates. He drives around in a top of the range Jag and bases his office in the North Heaton Sports Club, a sort of gentleman's private drinking club, only there ain't too many gentlemen frequenting the establishment."

Hannah shrugged her shoulders. "And?"

"And we need to get to Newcastle to see him."

The Easyjet webpage appeared on the screen and Bob took his credit card from his wallet. "There's a flight leaving at 10.17 tomorrow morning. We could drive there, but it would take a good twelve hours from here and we'd be knackered."

Hannah stroked his shoulder gently. "I like the idea of the flight better, let's get showered and changed, I'll book a table in the restaurant and you can tell me exactly what this fixer is going to fix."

As the waiter handed out the menus and moved on to another table, Bob spoke. He outlined his plan, smiling throughout, giving off an infectious aura of confidence. "Kevin has a contact in the Northumbria Police. The first thing we need to do is establish who our friend is. Like you said, he must have some sort of criminal record. We need to establish who he is and we also need to find another half a million pounds."

Hannah laughed, a frightened nervous laugh. "Yeah, like that's an easy one. I'll call my bank manager, shall I? Ask him to increase the overdraft limit."

Bob placed his finger over his lips as the waiter returned to take their order. Suddenly Hannah didn't feel hungry. Bob started speaking as the waiter headed towards the kitchen. "I've just over fifty thousand in bank accounts and I've already been onto the banks trying to remortgage."

"And?"

Bob shook his head. "It's a non-starter. They figured they could advance about two hundred and, even then, it would be a month before the money hits my account."

Hannah wanted to speak. She wanted to come up with a solution, but right now, her mind was a blank. Bob beat her to it. "Kev the fixer is our only chance."

"He lends money too?"

"No. Well, he may do, but certainly not those sort of figures."

She raised her eyebrows, "I'm listening."

Bob stopped talking as the waiter brought an iced bottle of Chardonnay to the table. He uncorked the bottle, poured a little in a glass, and handed it to Bob. Bob took a quick mouthful and, before it even hit his taste buds, announced it was fine. The waiter looked a little put out as he filled the two glasses. He wiped the top of the bottle and walked away.

"Counterfeit."

"Counterfeit?"

"Yeah. I'm hoping Kevin can get his hands on some funny money, to top up the real stuff in locker twenty-eight. I don't want to think of the scenario if we can't get it."

Hannah spoke, "I'm confused now, Bob. I thought we were checking this guy out through your mate's police contact; then, if we find out who he is and that he has a criminal past, we turn it over to the police."

The waiter returned to take the order.

"Give us five minutes please, we haven't made our mind up yet."

The waiter nodded, "Oui, Monsieur…" and turning to Hannah "… Madame."

"We can't take that chance, Hannah. Remember, he's hidden somewhere in France. Even if he were in Paris, it's a big place to find someone in a few days."

"But Interpol. They're good, they'd manage it."

Bob shook his head, glanced at the menu and settled for the sirloin steak without even looking at anything else. "They keep lookouts at the airports and the ferry terminals, the border crossing points and places like that. Sure, if our little friend decided to take a trip, they might well find him, but I'm pretty damn sure he wouldn't take a trip with the children. He'd likely leave them with Vicky. I'm also fairly sure that if he got caught or in fact had any intimation that we'd involved the police, he would have some sort of contingency plan to punish us."

"So we make the drop, then try and incriminate him?"

Bob shrugged his shoulders. "I don't know yet… haven't figured that one out. I just need to know who he is and where he lives. If we find him afterwards, we might just employ the services of the fixer."

CHAPTER TWENTY-NINE

Bob sat in the North Heaton Sports Club. He'd been nursing a bottle of Budweiser for over an hour. This was his territory, his old haunt from fifteen years back, but it had changed now out of all recognition. Gone were the old guys who had sat in the corner, putting the world to rights, and there wasn't the usual crowd mooching around the pool table. There wasn't even a bloody pool table, Bob thought. Where were the bin men, the joiners and plasterers on job and finish, who worked so damn hard they finished an eight-hour shift in five hours? And it was hard work. They'd tell anyone who was prepared to listen that they deserved their five or six pints before returning home to their families saying they'd nipped in for a quick one on the way home. No postmen, who knocked off at lunchtime, and none of the benefit boys who always seemed to find the price of a pint. And none of the regulars Bob used to sit with: Billy Graham, Davey Val, Andy and Big GJ.

He looked around at the students and what appeared to be a car salesman checking out the latest brochure over a lemonade. But there was no Kevin Oxley.

Kevin was called KO, not because of his initials, but because of his favourite pastime of street fighting, or 'rolling around the floor' as he described it. Bob had asked him one day why he did it. He'd challenged three students in a takeaway. Unfortunately, he'd picked on three of the county rugby team who were at little bit useful themselves and he took quite a beating. "I love it, Bobby, fuckin' love it. It's an adrenalin thing. Even when I'm getting the shit kicked out of me on the floor, I just love it."

Bob looked at his watch. Three forty. KO should be in soon.

Four o'clock came and went and so did four thirty. As each minute passed, Bob became more and more despondent. Kevin Oxley was not coming into the North Heaton Sports Club. It wasn't his scene. At four forty-five, he went up to the barmaid. "What time does Kevin Oxley get in?"

"Kevin who, darling?"

Bob had his answer. He walked up Chillingham Road, a street of many memories, all of them forgotten as he desperately tried to work out what to do. Where would Kevin have gone? He couldn't imagine him stopping the routine of a lifetime. There were other clubs, other pubs, all in all about a dozen in the immediate vicinity.

He eventually found him in the 'Gaza', a local watering hole that had been so nicknamed because of the amount of fights that took place in its immediate vicinity. Knock Out sat with two or three shaven-headed individuals. Bob recognised one of them as a local hood who spent more time in jail than he did a free man.

Kevin jumped from his seat as soon as he looked up. "Bobby, Bobby." A grin wide as a mile and his huge arms open, inviting the gangster hug. Bob walked over and, before he could resist, Kevin wrapped his arms around him.

"It must be five years, Bobby?" Kevin asked.

"More like ten, Kev. How the hell are you?"

"Couldn't be better, Bob, and you? Where the fuck you been holidaying, you look like a fucking Paki man!"

Bob laughed, "Living in Spain, Kev. Have done for the last couple of years. Thing is though, I'm in need of a little help."

Kevin took Bob by the arm to a two-seater table in the corner of the room. "We can talk here, Bob. This is my office." He grinned. "When I sit here, everyone knows I'm on business. No fucker dares come near."

Kevin waved at the barmaid and she sauntered over. "What'll it be, Kev?" she asked.

"Two more Carlsbergs, darling." He looked at Bob. "That

okay, Bob? You do still drink?"

Bob nodded, "Yeah, Kev, that's fine."

The barmaid returned with the beers and, after exchanging pleasantries and a few old tales, the two long-time pals got down to serious negotiations.

"So you see, Kev, I need about half a million in dodgy notes."

Kevin shook his head and rubbed his chin. "Jesus, Bob, twenty, thirty thou' wouldn't be a problem, but half a fuckin' million?" He sighed. "Give me a week and I'll see what I can do."

It was Bob's turn to shake his head. Kevin Oxley noticed the look of despair immediately.

"How long, Bob?"

Bob took a long drink and placed his empty glass down. "I need it by Friday at the latest."

Kevin nearly dropped his glass. "Jeez, Bob, you're taking the piss, aren't you?"

"I'll get the drinks, Kev ... there's more."

Bob returned and placed the glasses on the table. He pulled out the photograph from the theme park and placed it in front of Kevin. Kevin's eyes sparkled. "Little Heggies, right?"

"Yeah, Cameron and Elissa. Any of your own?"

Kevin slurped at the froth of the beer and wiped the remnants from his top lip. "The same. A boy and a girl, a little younger than your two, I'd say." He smiled and raised his glass in Bob's direction. "I'd say we've both been quite lucky."

Bob wondered what story to weave for Kevin. What would it take to make him pull out all the stops? He'd known Kevin and his brothers since he was six years old. He'd trust him with his life. So he told Kevin everything over the next few hours, leaving out only his involvement in the bank raid. He was conservative about the ransom money, telling Kevin it was only half a million.

Kevin sat open-mouthed throughout. "Kidnap. Fucking kidnap. I'll have the bastard tortured, Bob, you see if I don't, and there won't be a fee either."

Kevin took his mobile from his pocket. Within twenty

minutes, a rather nervous member of the Northumbria police joined them and Kevin handed him a copy of the photograph. "There's five hundred quid in it for you if you get his name, and another pony if you can find out where he lives or works."

The man disappeared without finishing his drink.

"He doesn't like to be seen with me, Bob. I can't think why."

Kevin made a few more phone calls and, during the evening, two more undesirable-looking characters called at Kevin's 'office.'

A little after nine, Bob made his excuses and left. He took a taxi to the New Kent Hotel in Jesmond, where Hannah waited patiently. Bob would fill her in on the details of his meeting with 'The Fixer.'

CHAPTER THIRTY

The children were now severely annoying Donavan Smith. Vicky was doing her best to entertain them but, for some reason, Donavan had insisted they stay indoors.

"But, Don, it's a lovely morning. Can't I just take them out for an hour?"

Donavan eyed her suspiciously; she had been acting strangely the last few days and Donavan knew he had to make the trip to Newcastle alone. He had to trust her.

"When will we see Daddy?" Cameron asked, for what seemed like the hundredth time that day. And Donavan relented.

"Okay, take them out, get them out my sight for Christ's sake."

Vicky looked over at the children and pointed to their coats hanging over the back of the chair.

Donavan ushered the children out in the hallway, explaining he needed a private word with Vicky.

"Just wait downstairs in the courtyard. I'll only be a minute," Vicky shouted as they scurried away along the corridor.

Donavan led her through to the kitchen, out of earshot of the children. "I'm leaving for Newcastle this afternoon. I'll be away two days. I need to make the final arrangements for the pickup."

"Do you think he'll have the money, Don?"

Donavan looked a little nervous, the façade of supreme confidence that he displayed so well just slipping for a second.

"And how will you pick it up? That's when most of the

kidnappers get caught."

He snarled at her through gritted teeth. "And how the fuck would you know, Inspector Morse."

She trembled visibly and he prided himself on just how easily he could frighten her.

"I'm sorry, Don, it's just that —"

"Button it. Just fucking button it and listen. The pickup will be easy. No one will be there and no one will even know what time, day, or month I'll be picking the money up."

Vicky frowned. "I don't understand."

"You don't need to. You just need to promise me that you're still one hundred per cent behind me."

"Of course I am, Don, you can trust me."

He edged ever closer and a tiny bead of perspiration leaked onto Vicky Mackenzie's top lip. She wiped at it with her index finger. He leaned forward and kissed her gently on the lips. Her skin crawled as a shudder ran the length of her body.

"I'll be away two days. When I get back we'll pack up, get everything ready and fly into Teeside Airport Friday afternoon."

"Why Teeside?"

"Just a precaution, just in case he's a little bit wiser than we think he is."

Vicky nodded her understanding. "And then what?"

"By that time the money should be where I want it to be and we wait a few days, weeks, whatever, just to make sure things are okay. We won't release the kids until we have the money and we're one hundred per cent sure that the police aren't on to us."

Vicky knew she shouldn't ask the question, but she did anyway, "And what happens if he doesn't come up with the money?"

Donavan looked at her through demonic, green eyes and grinned. "Like I say, don't go getting too attached to those kids."

Donavan sat in the back of the taxi en route to Charles de

Gaulle. He pulled out his mobile and punched in the number of the airport. After half a dozen rings, an operator politely answered the call, deep in the heart of downtown Calcutta.

"I'd like to book some tickets please, Paris Charles De Gaulle to Teeside." He could barely make out what the operator was saying. "What, sorry, no. Could you speak a little slower. Jesus, why can't you speak English? That's Teeside, T-E-E-S-I-D-E. Jesus Christ, Teeside." He covered the mouthpiece and bellowed to the taxi driver, "Fucking foreigners."

The taxi driver smiled at him in the rear-view mirror as if he understood every word.

"That's right, Teeside, Friday the thirteenth, this month. At last," Donavan muttered, "I'm finally getting somewhere."

He stole a quick look at his watch. "Three tickets please, one adult and two children."

CHAPTER THIRTY-ONE

Vicky Mackenzie figured she had to act quickly. She'd already called the airlines and was annoyed that there were no flights back to Newcastle that day. Never mind, nothing she could do about it. The lunchtime flight tomorrow would give her plenty of time; Donavan's return flight would touch down six hours after her flight landed. There was no way he'd be around Newcastle airport that early.

And then what? What would she do when the flight landed at Newcastle? She didn't know…nowhere to run, nowhere to hide.

The Northumbria Police Central Division in Market Street seemed like a good place to start.

CHAPTER THIRTY-TWO

Bob pressed *end* on his mobile and breathed a sigh of relief. Kevin had come up with the counterfeit money at a cost of twenty-five thousand pounds. He'd actually apologised for the price.

Kevin called at the New Kent Hotel just after four to collect Bob's money. Bob sat at a table in the bar. A Nike gym bag containing twenty-five thousand pounds sat on the seat next to him. Kevin looked nervous, on edge. It was not the cool, calm 'Kev the Fix' Bob was used to.

"What's up, Kev? You don't look happy."

"I'm not. A pal of mine said the money wouldn't be great quality. He said it's too cheap. Good counterfeit money sells for about twenty per cent of its value."

"So what are you saying?"

Kevin pulled a Marlborough from a packet on the table, lit up, took a long drag, and blew the smoke from the side of his mouth. "I'm saying an experienced bank teller or a shopkeeper who handles real money all day will spot it a mile off."

Bob fished for a positive. "But ordinary Joe in the street won't?"

Kevin shrugged his shoulders. "I don't know, Bob. I really don't know. I'm picking the money up in an hour, we'll know sooner or later."

He took another pull on the cigarette. "You sure you want to go ahead with this?"

Bob nodded. "I haven't got any choice, Kev, I'm at the door

of the last chance saloon. This man expects to collect on Saturday and he's got my children. He's holding all the aces." Kevin took Bob by the arm and gripped him firmly. "I know you said no coppers, Bob, but I can have the drop watched. Three or four good guys can watch him, maybe follow him."

Bob shook his head. "I can't take the chance, Kev. He spots one of your boys and he won't make the pickup. He'll think they're cops."

Bob sighed heavily. "And I don't even want to think about the consequences."

"I suppose you're right, Bob. You got the money?"

Bob slid the bag under the table. "Yeah, it's all there."

Kevin stubbed the cigarette out in the ashtray. "Good, I'd better get going."

Bob followed Kevin as he walked towards the door. As he stepped through the door, he took his arm. Kevin turned around. "When you come back, Kev…. we'll talk."

Just as Kevin got in the car, as if on cue, Bob's mobile rang. *Number withheld* flashed across the top of the small display screen and Bob's heart seemed to stop for a moment. He pressed the green button on the phone.

"Bobbeee….it's me. Time to make the drop. It's all systems go, time to make me a millionaire."

"The children. How are the children? Where are they? How do —"

"Whoa, Bobbeeee… slow down, in fact just stop there and listen. The children are fine."

"How do I know they're okay?" asked Bob.

He held the telephone from his ear as a gross, cackling, high-pitched laugh burst into his eardrum.

Then a pause, and a whisper, "You don't, Bobbeeee!" Another five seconds of the strange, perverted laughter. "In fact, you know jackshit, Bobby. You don't know where they are, how they are or who they're with. You don't know who I am, what I look like or where I'm going after you make me rich."

Bob bit his lip, wanting to jump in and correct one or two inaccuracies. "But I need to know if they're okay before I hand over the money."

"No, you don't, Bob, you've been watching too many movies. I have the upper hand here. Anything goes wrong and the children meet with a little accident. I disappear into the sunset, and you torture yourself until you die, wishing you'd done something different."

Donavan Smith paused for a few seconds, enjoying the silence. "You don't get to talk to them and I don't need to send you a lock of hair. That only happens in the movies."

"But I —"

"You just need to listen, Bob. In fact, one more word from you and I'll hang up, maybe go back and see how the kids are doing. Forget about being a millionaire just yet."

"No, okay, I'm sorry."

"Listen, my friend. And listen real well. From now on, you only speak when I ask you a question. Is that clear?"

Bob cleared his throat and couldn't understand why it was so dry. "Yes."

"Good, Bobby… that's better. You see, you can do it if you really want to. Now, where are you right at this very moment?"

"Newcastle."

"I thought you might be, back on home territory, so to speak. Well, I must tell you that's real handy, because that's where you're going to make the drop. Where are you staying?"

"A hotel."

"Which one?"

"The New Kent Hotel in Jesmond."

"Good, Bobby, excellent. This is going to be real easy for you. Now, I'm going to ask you a few questions and I want you to think real hard about the answers, because, if you lie or give me the wrong answers, I hang up. Is that clear?"

"Yes I understand," Bob stuttered.

"Good. Have you got all the money together?"

"Yes."

"Excellent, Bobby, me and you can do business then. Okay.

Is half of the money sitting in a locker in Newcastle Central Station?"

"Yes."

"Locker 28 perhaps?"

"Yes."

The reply triggered Donavan Smith's unmistakable laugh once again. "You see, Bob, the diaries were telling the truth, weren't they."

"When do I get the diaries?"

The line went dead.

"Hello, hello, shit, shit, shit. Jesus H Christ, he's gone."

Never had Bob Heggie felt so many emotions coursing through his veins. His tormentor would phone back. He was sure of it. Bob had made a mistake, asking a question instead of listening.

Donavan wanted Bob to feel hopeless, vulnerable, wanted him to feel as if he'd been left high and dry, like a puppet at the complete beck and call of the puppeteer. And Donavan Smith was the master puppeteer.

Bob sat in the hotel bedroom with Hannah. He had explained everything to her leaving out none of the details. It was now gone seven. He hadn't heard from Kevin The Fixer, who was at least an hour late, and his tormentor hadn't rang back either. Bob paced the small room every few minutes.

At eight fifteen, Bob's mobile rang and he leapt over to the dressing table to get it. He looked at the display, *Number withheld.* He looked over to Hannah who lay on the bed. "It's him! It's him!" he smiled.

Then Bob's face fell as he heard the abrasive tones of Kevin Oxley. "I've got it, Bob. Is it okay to come up?"

Bob was pleased that Kevin had come up with the goods, but began to wonder whether the money would ever be put to the test. Kevin smiled as he came into the room. He nodded politely to Hannah, as Bob gave the briefest of introductions telling Kevin that she knew the full picture.

"It's better than I thought it would be, Bob," Kevin said, as he reached inside a cheap unbranded sports bag. "Twenties and fifties. He reckons it took over forty-eight hours to print it all."

Kevin tossed a bundle of twenties over to Bob. Bob took the elastic band from them and inspected a twenty-pound note for a few seconds.

"Jesus, Kev, they look real enough to me. I'd never know they were dodgy." He handed a fifty to Hannah. She held it up to the light, rubbed the note between her finger and thumb.

She shook her head. "Me neither," she replied.

Bob looked across at Kevin. "We've another little problem though."

He explained the abrupt end to the telephone conversation. "I could have kicked myself. Just listen, he said, and, of course, I had to jump in, didn't I."

"I'm sure he'll call back, Bob. You told him you'd pulled the money together, didn't you?"

Bob nodded. "Yeah, all of it."

"He's just playing with you, Bob. It's a standard kidnapping technique."

Bob grinned. "Is that part of your repertoire too?"

Kevin looked at Hannah and seemed a bit embarrassed. "Course not, Bob, it's just that I've read a few books, seen a couple of movies, y'know."

"Yeah right, Kevin, whatever."

"Well, we did kidnap somebody once. He'd burgled one of the lads' mother's. Only he didn't just rob her. He left a disgusting present on her bed. You know what I mean?"

"I think so, Kev."

"Poor Ma was devastated. Anyway, I put the word around a few of the pubs and clubs and we came up with a name. A real little shit he was. It was his party trick when he robbed. He always picked an older person's house, generally old dears on their own. He'd even battered a few of them because they'd caught him and tried to have a go. Anyway, we kidnapped him, took him to a little cottage in the country." Kevin smiled. "We tortured the bastard for three days and three nights. I'd never seen a grown man cry so much. I even felt sorry for him in the end."

He laughed. "Well, for about three seconds anyway."

Hannah and Bob sat open-mouthed as Kevin went into graphic detail.

"If we get your man, Bob, we can arrange a similar journey for him."

Bob walked to the door. "Fancy a quick beer?"

Bob wandered back up to the room just after eleven o'clock. Hannah had dozed off. She awoke as he closed the door.

Bob explained he still hadn't had the call. "I'm getting really worried now, Hannah. What if something has happened to him? What if…"

"Don't even go there, Bob. Come over here and try to get some sleep."

At three minutes past three in the morning, Bob awoke to the sound of a familiar mobile phone ring tone.

It was his man.

He jumped out of bed quickly and ran over to the dressing table. The mobile phone's tiny screen illuminated the whole room. "Bobbee…. sorry to wake you."

Bob was never so pleased to hear the tormentor's voice.

"This is your last chance. The children are really missing you, I think it's time to get rid of them. I'm sick of the sight of the little fuckers. Are you listening, Bobby?"

"Yeah, I'm listening."

"One word answers are fine, Bobby. Understand?"

"Yes."

"Good, Bobby. Remember the last time? No questions."

"Okay."

"Tomorrow morning you will receive an envelope by special delivery. It will arrive by courier; they have guaranteed delivery by lunchtime. Inside will be the key to Locker Number 26 in Newcastle Central Station. You got that, Bobby? Locker Number 26, just one down from the other one."

"Yes."

"In Locker Number 26 you will leave half a million pounds and the key to Locker Number 28. I've made a copy of key 26,

Bobby. You can keep your copy as a sort of souvenir." He laughed again. "You got that, Bobby?"

"Yes."

"Now, Bobby, here's the important bit, are you listening?"

"Yes."

"You don't know when I'm going to collect. It might be within an hour, it might be after a month. But one thing I'm going to do is check really carefully before I do. I'll check the fucking station for ten hours if I have to, just to make sure I'm the only one with an interest in those two lockers. Once I'm happy, I'll pick up the money. You got that, Bobby? Do I make myself clear?"

"Yes."

"Good, Bobby...good. Now, when I've made the collection, I'll jump on a train. I'll change trains several times and I'll be looking over my shoulder constantly. I don't want to see anyone following me, is that clear?"

"Yes." Bob couldn't hold back any longer. "The children, when do I get the children? Are they okay? When will I see them?"

An agonising silence followed. And yet, suddenly, Bob felt a little more confident. He recalled his conversation with Kevin that evening.

The tormentor continued, "I'll still be watching and not until I've counted every last penny do I pick up the phone and tell you where the children are. They'll be fine, Bobby, just as long as you don't go and do anything stupid."

"I won't, I haven't."

"Good, Bobby. Good. Then I'm sure everything will be just fine."

Without another word, the tormentor ended the call.

CHAPTER THIRTY-THREE

A day later, Vicky Mackenzie left the Latin Quarter apartment at ten o'clock on a warm muggy Parisian morning. A damp fog hung over the buildings. Visibility was poor. The children seemed excited, particularly Cameron; she couldn't help herself, she'd told them they were going home.

"Will Dad be there to meet us?" Cameron asked.

Vicky didn't answer. She was on edge. Cab or Metro, she thought to herself, as she eyed the heavy rush-hour traffic. She made her mind up as she spotted the Metro sign for St Michelle.

"C'mon kids, quickly, we've a plane to catch." She took Cameron's hand as she waited to cross the busy road. The traffic seemed to be flying in all directions.

Jesus, she thought to herself, how do I cross here? If she had been on her own, she'd have taken a little chance and sprinted through a gap, but not with Elissa and Cameron. They were her prime concern. She wouldn't let anything happen to the two small children she'd grown very attached to.

She took Cameron's hand. It was small and delicate and he was unconditionally trusting. She looked at his sister. Elissa caught the look and returned a nervous smile.

"Are we running away from Donavan?" she asked.

Vicky couldn't lie any longer. The little girl needed an answer. "Sort of, Elissa. We can—"

An all-too familiar voice came from behind them. "Going somewhere, my angel?"

She froze in horror as Donavan Smith appeared in front of

them. The look on her face gave away the lie she was about to tell. She stuttered nervously and, within seconds, was a bumbling, shivering wreck. The thumping of her heart strangled her vocal chords.

Elissa took the look in too and wondered why her new friend was so petrified of the man standing before them. Suddenly the young girl was very afraid.

"Just out on a little excursion, Don. The Louvre, we thought; the children wanted to see the Mona Lisa."

Donavan shook his head slowly and grinned. "With a suitcase and, no doubt, passports in your handbag."

He reached across and took her handbag from her shoulder. He pulled the three passports from within and held them up three inches from Vicky's face.

"They've been in there all along, Don… honestly."

Little Cameron spoke, "We're going to Newcastle, Don. Dad's going to meet us."

Donavan laughed, his stare fixed on Vicky. "Really, Cameron, you're going to Newcastle, are you?"

"Yeah, Don, the afternoon flight."

Donavan took the little boy's flight bag and slung it around his shoulder. He slipped the passports into his jacket pocket. "I'm afraid today's flight to Newcastle has been cancelled. We'll have to wait until tomorrow."

"But I want to see my dad," cried Cameron.

"Soon enough. Soon enough."

Donavan took a hold of the little boy's shoulder, forced him into an about-turn and herded Vicky and Elissa back up Boulevard St Michelle towards his apartment. He was uncomfortable at the little girl's penetrating eyes.

After they entered the apartment, Donavan turned the heavy, black lead key and several deadlocks clicked noisily into place. He took the key from the lock and slipped it into the breast pocket of his jacket.

He turned around to the children. One more night playing the nice man, then it would all be over. Whatever happened, he would never have to put up with the children again.

"Right, kids, let's get some pizza and watch a movie. Vicky can nip out and get it, I'll stay here and keep you company."

Elissa stood in the corner. She studied Vicky's face, then Donavan Smith's. She became aware of a heavy feeling in her chest, her whole body seemed to tingle. She remembered the same feeling as she watched a video or a DVD with a particularly nasty character, a ghost even. She spoke quietly. "Can't you get it, Don?"

"No, Elissa, it would be better if Vicky went."

And the little girl had her answer.

Elissa lay awake, fighting the sleep she craved. The voices were still active in the lounge. Television or real people, it didn't matter; Donavan Smith was still awake. She hadn't figured out her master plan. She just knew that either way they had to escape from Donavan Smith. She'd seen the fear in Vicky Mackenzie's eyes when he'd approached them on Boulevard St Michelle. And why was she running away from him? Why hadn't he gone for the pizzas? It was all coming together. Their mother had been killed in an accident and their father hadn't called them. It just didn't make sense.

And where was Daddy? He promised he'd always look after them. Even on that awful night when he told them he was moving abroad. Emigrating, he'd called it. She always imagined when someone emigrated you never saw them again. But Daddy had been as good as his word. Within a few weeks, they had spent an idyllic week at his new home with his new girlfriend, Hannah. Elissa had felt closer to her father than ever before. She remembered how lovely the weather had been and how they'd spent hour after hour splashing around in the lukewarm water of her dad's new pool.

And they'd fished in the small river at the bottom of his garden and they'd talked like never before. He was relaxed, at peace, and, for once, he didn't have that damn bank taking up all of his time. That was all she recalled from his days at the bank. Poor Dad. Away to work before they got up in the mornings and just about back in time for bath time. And she remembered how, as the three of them had sat on the riverbank sipping from ice-cold cans of Cola, he'd told them he'd never let anyone hurt them. She felt sure her father would turn up soon, because she had the most awful feeling that the man sitting watching television in the other room had plans to do just that. She fought hard against the sleep that was inevitable and slowly, but surely, she succumbed.

"Are you serious, Don? Go out at this time of night? Where to? What about the children? We can't just leave them alone."

Donavan stood up and reached for his jacket that hung on the back of the chair. He felt for the oversized key in the breast pocket of the jacket and slipped it into his trouser pocket. "I'm not asking, Vicky, I'm telling you. Get your bloody coat and don't argue. The children are fast asleep. I'll lock the door."

"But, Don, I —"

He raised his voice a decibel or two. "Get your coat, Vicky. I've been cooped up here all day. I just want a couple of coffees and some fresh air."

He stood above her while she sat. He glared at her. She felt his eyes penetrating the top of her head. A hypnotic stare. A stare that made her slowly rise to her feet. She felt feeble and weak as she asked, "Are you sure the kids will be okay? What if they wake up?"

He didn't answer her.

She didn't ask the question again. Donavan threw her coat to her and walked towards the door. He stepped through into the darkened passage and, as Vicky walked through the door, she pulled it hard towards her.

"Jesus Christ, Vicky, you've probably woken half the fucking block up. What are you playing at?"

"I'm sorry, Don, it was the wind, caught me by surprise."

He shook his head as he inserted the big black key and turned.

"Where are we going anyway?"

He walked away and she followed behind him. As he stepped out of the courtyard, he pointed down the street. "There's an all-night café by the river. We'll take a walk down there.

What was it that had woken Elissa up? A door closing? A window slamming? It was a door, she was sure it was a door. Then it came to her. It was the front door of Donavan Smith's apartment. She pressed the *illuminate* button on her watch. It was 12.17 and the room was pitch-black. She eased herself out of bed and looked out of the window. The courtyard was still, as she would expect it to be at this late hour. Small Hittorff-style lamp posts stood either end of the courtyard, emitting a faint, low voltage glow. It just about allowed her to make out the shape of two figures walking slowly out of the door at the far end of courtyard, the door that led into the street. Who on earth would be going out at this time of night? It couldn't be. Surely not.

And yet, the noise of the door banging that had woken her had definitely sounded like the door she'd heard closing for the last ten days. The figures she'd just seen were Donavan Smith and Vicky Mackenzie.

She looked over at the bed her brother slept in. He was fast asleep, a faint snore barely audible. She would need to look after him; he didn't understand.

"Wake up, Cameron. Wake up."

Cameron didn't stir.

"C'mon, Cameron," she raised her voice a little louder, pulling the soft eiderdown away from his small body.

He reacted to the cold immediately. "Stop it, stop it, I'm cold. Leave me alone." His eyes flicked open for a split second and he hauled the cover back on to his exposed little body. "Go away, it's still dark. Let me sleep."

"C'mon, Cameron, we're going home."

The little boy sat bolt upright. "What?"

"Going home. We're going to see Dad." She was already handing him his clothes as he swung his legs over the side of the bed.

"But it's dark still. What time is it?"

"Never mind that and don't ask questions. Just get

your clothes on."

He grinned slightly, a little puzzled, but nevertheless pulled his trousers over his underpants and began struggling with his favourite Newcastle United replica shirt. Elissa was already dressed and cautiously crept through the apartment. The television was still playing in the lounge. The sound was turned down to minimum. She walked slowly into the passageway and felt for the handle to the door of the bedroom that the two adults shared. She pushed it open slowly. Another gentle push, the door creaked one last time and she stepped into the room to find nothing but darkness. She contemplated walking over and feeling around the bed but, instead, flicked on the light switch. The room lit up and she breathed a sigh of relief as her eyes took in the tidy, undisturbed bed. She froze as she felt a gentle tug at her sweatshirt and she swung around slowly, her body rigid with fear.

"What are you doing in here?" a voice said.

"Shit, Cameron, why are you creeping up on me like that?"

"That's swearing. I'm telling Dad."

She bent down so that her eyes were level with her little brother's head. "Nothing would give me greater pleasure than if you told Dad that."

Cameron shook his head. "Sometimes I just don't understand you."

The little girl took his hand. "C'mon, let's get some things together. We're getting out of here."

Elissa ran round the apartment pushing extra clothing and some food into her flight bag. She spied Vicky's handbag in the corner of the lounge, found her purse, and took out just over two hundred euros.

Cameron stood in the corner, wiping the sleep from his eyes. "What are you doing?"

She looked up. "We need money."

"But where's Don and Vicky? Aren't they coming?"

Donavan drained the last of his second cup of espresso. Vicky sat with her first and barely a mouthful had passed her lips.

"C'mon. Drink your coffee; let's go for a walk."

"Yeah, Don, let's go back. I'm worried about the kids."

Donavan beckoned the waiter across. "L'addition, s'il-vous plaît."

The rather bored and tired looking Frenchman reached into a small leather pouch hanging around his midriff and pulled out two paper slips. Donavan handed him a ten-euro note. He lifted up the cup, handed it across the table to Vicky. "C'mon, drink up, it'll make you feel better."

Vicky reached across and drained the last of her cup. "Jesus, Don. That's awful! I thought the French were supposed to be good at making coffee."

He reached across for Vicky's hand and pulled her from her chair. "Mine tasted just fine."

He'd held her hand a couple of times during their brief relationship, but this time it felt different. In the past, she'd felt security, comfort and yes, love. Now it was different. Now she felt only fear and despair and an overwhelming hatred for the man she'd trusted with her life.

Her anguish deepened as they walked out of the restaurant and turned in the opposite direction to the apartment. "But, Don, the children."

He didn't answer. His grip tightened on her hand and he led her down towards the river. Notre Dame loomed over to the right, its ornate towers tastefully illuminated. The shadows of the gargoyles taunted her, high above the Parisian skyline, silhouetted against the full moon. She was Esmerelda trapped in the tower with her tormentor. They climbed down the steps towards the riverbank and she offered only token resistance. "Please, Don, the children."

Donavan smiled. It was a smile that seemed to say trust me. "It's a lovely night for a stroll, Vicky, isn't it."

They turned to the right and walked towards the Cathedral of Our Lady. It was quiet, they were the only souls on the riverbank; the other night owls frequented the cafés and bistros of the Left Bank. There was perhaps the odd lover or two further up river, but down at this end, there were only shadows and gloom.

"Let's sit here," Donavan said, almost politely. He pointed at an old seat directly beneath Le Pont Louis-Philippe. The bridge, built in the late 1860s to connect with Saint Louis Island, was very low and eerie.

Vicky sat down and shivered as the cold steel penetrated her thin cotton skirt. Donavan looked out over the water; the lights from the Cathedral glistened on the surface and danced like a million white seahorses. Vicky stared out too, in an almost trance-like state. She stared. She stared into the abyss.

She didn't like water. She never had since she'd been a small child, caught in an oversize wave at the seaside somewhere in Devon. It had rolled her over repeatedly; all she could taste was salt and sand. Only the quick actions of her father had spared her from drowning.

She remembered Donavan asking her if she could swim a few days ago. The question had been totally out of context. She regretted giving her answer.

"It's pretty here, isn't it?"

Vicky didn't reply.

"Where were you going with the children, Vicky?"

Vicky didn't answer.

"You were betraying me, weren't you?"

Vicky looked into his cold eyes. His face took on a strange, hazy look; she found it hard to focus. She looked across the water at Notre Dame and then up high, trying to pick out one of the magnificent stone sculptures. The figures blended into one vague mass of sandstone.

"Don, I.....I feel kind of strange."

Donavan patted her thigh. "Let's go for a little walk and I'll explain."

Vicky tried to get up. Her legs felt weak, like lumps of heavy lead pipe. Donavan took both arms, lifted her gently, and placed her right arm around his waist. She was conscious of the river flowing fast beside her and wondered why she wasn't on the inside. She'd feel far more comfortable next to the wall. She wanted to object, wanted to tell him, but couldn't muster the energy. "It must have been those two gin and tonics in the apartment."

Donavan steadied her as she took her first steps. "It wasn't the gin, Vicky."

"How do you mean?"

"It was the coffee."

Her legs were like rubber now and she concentrated on one step at a time. "Don't be daft, Don. Coffee doesn't have this effect." She was conscious of slurring her words now.

"Rohypnol does."

"Ro…what?"

His arm slid up around her shoulder, pushing her ever deeper into the shadows, the giant cathedral blocking out the light from the moon. And she wanted to resist, she wanted to tell him she wasn't walking any further.

"Rohypnol. It's a little like Valium only much, much stronger. I put it into your coffee over an hour ago when you went to the toilet. It's just starting to kick in now."

"But —"

"You betrayed me, Vicky. You were ready to run. You were going to turn me in."

She opened her mouth, ready to protest, ready to issue another denial but, before she could engage her brain, Donavan continued, "One million pounds in two lockers at Newcastle Central Station. It's there now. Our friend, Mr Heggie, has come up trumps. I have a key and I can pick the money up anytime I want. It was going to be our little retirement plan, remember? Our escape route to anywhere we wanted."

He stopped, turned around, and faced her. She looked at him and, yet, she looked straight through him.

"But you fucked up. You fucked up and decided you were going to turn me in."

"No, Don, I —"

"It was the perfect kidnap, Vicky."

He released her and took a few steps downriver. She shuffled towards the wall and leant against it, unsure whether she could

283

stand up without the support.

"Perfect. Most kidnaps end up with the kidnappers getting caught at the pickup, because even if a kidnap is successful, the bad guys get the loot and the kidnap victim is returned unharmed. But, as you know from the movies, Vicky, the aggrieved person always calls the cops. Every time, Vic. Every time."

He turned around and faced her. "But not this time, Vicky, not this time. You see, our friend, Bob Heggie, can't go to the cops; he'd have too much to explain. The money is stolen, and sure as God made little green apples, it would be traced back to that phoney bank raid. And then what? Then what, Vic?" He smiled, "Think about it."

She shook her head. "You're crazy. You've murdered people. How's that the perfect kidnapping?"

He ignored her. "And then there's the diaries. More explanations to the police. Our friend thinks he's getting them back."

He laughed. "He isn't. I'll hold onto them forever. Who knows, I might even use them a few years down the line. Extortion…blackmail. I don't know, haven't figured it out yet. But I will."

Vicky continued to look at Notre Dame, the point of her focus for the last five minutes. She could now barely make out the magnificent structure. It blurred into the background of the elegant period buildings and apartments of the Marais district on the Right Bank.

"Perfect. Everything's just perfect. Except for one little problem." He thrust a finger into her chest. She didn't feel it. Her body had now slipped into shutdown. Her chest registered the blow, but the brain didn't pick it up. Her eyelids grew heavier; all she wanted to do was sleep. Sleep forever.

"You!"

She struggled to focus on him. His voice dropped a decibel or two, almost to a whisper. He came close and she smelt him: stale aftershave and piquant coffee on his breath. She wondered why her sense of smell hadn't been affected by the drug he'd administered.

"And now, my dear, I must deal with the little problem." He prised her from the wall and she leaned into him. He walked, she struggled to keep up with him, but his powerful arm around her waist hauled her along. She was conscious of her two legs dragging behind her.

He didn't even have to push her into the freezing waters of the Seine. He just gave a little nudge and she lost her balance, turning a full somersault before disappearing head first into the blackness three metres below.

The icy waters countered the drug momentarily, and she struggled for a second or two. A slimy, thick, black sludge poured into her nose and entered her lungs. At that point she knew her efforts were futile…

She gave up.

She slipped slowly downwards, looking up at the shimmering, illuminated vision of Notre Dame. And, this time, she could make out the statues and she could see the expressions of the gargoyles thirty metres above her. They were laughing. They were laughing and grinning and sneering at Vicky Mackenzie.

And her final thoughts were of Cameron and Elissa.

"So where's Don and Vicky?"

The girl looked at her little brother, so trusting. She was his guardian now, she was his protector. Their mother was gone and their father hadn't been in contact. Elissa figured that's what had made her realise she had to get away. That and the cold, calculating personality of Donavan Smith. She had to get her brother out of here; they were both in danger, she could feel it.

"I don't know. It's not important they're not here anyway."

"But they wouldn't just leave us here."

"Well, they have!"

Elissa could feel herself getting frustrated. She wanted to get a hold of him and shake him. She couldn't. She knew that would only make her task more difficult. She knelt down to his eye level again. "Cameron. You trust me, right?"

"Yeah...I guess so."

"Donavan Smith isn't your friend. He's nasty and he's keeping us here against our will."

"How do you mean?" asked Cameron

"I must have told him a dozen times that I want to see Dad; I want to go back to Newcastle, but he keeps stalling. And the way he looks at Vicky, I've seen him."

"But we're going back tomorrow."

Elissa looked at her watch. "Today actually. And we're not flying to Newcastle we're going into Teeside."

"Where's Teeside?"

"Down south somewhere. It's a small town in Yorkshire, I think. But it just doesn't make sense. Why would we fly to Teeside?"

Elissa took her brother's tiny hands in hers. Her mini-speech had to be the best of her life if she was going to persuade him to run into the darkness of the Paris night with her. "I heard them talking a few nights back. Rather, not so much talking, but arguing. Donavan sounded really angry."

She paused and took in a deep breath. "Then I heard the word and everything fell into place."

Cameron looked across at his sister, suddenly interested. "And what word would that be?"

"We've been kidnapped."

He shook his head and stuttered a little as he spoke, "But that only happens at the movies, and people die and get killed and stuff like that."

Elissa smiled. It had worked. "Exactly. So do you want to stay here and take a chance or are you coming with me?"

Cameron reached for his favourite cuddly toy. "I'm coming with you."

As they walked towards the door of the apartment, hand in hand, the little boy stopped. "Wait. How are we going to get home? Don has everything."

Elissa looked at him, grinned, reached into her pocket and pulled out two passports and two airline tickets. "I took them from his jacket pocket earlier on."

The little boy grinned too. "You'll end up in jail, Elissa. Wait till I tell Dad."

As Elissa reached for the door handle, she instinctively knew it would be locked.

"Damn and bloody hell." She felt it was okay to swear given the circumstances. "We'll have to go out through the kitchen window."

Before the little boy could protest, she had dragged him through into the kitchen and they stood looking up at the window above the sink.

"I think we should go back to bed, Elissa."

Donavan reached for the keys in his pocket as he turned the corner into Rue de la Sorbonne. The pocket felt strange, as if something was missing. He inserted the key into the courtyard door. Then realisation set in. The pocket was empty. It was the pocket he'd carefully placed the three passports in; the passports he'd confiscated from Vicky some hours earlier. He patted the opposite pocket. The flight tickets had gone too.

He slammed the heavy door shut and sprinted across the courtyard. He took the stairs three at a time up to the first floor corridor. Fumbling with the heavy key, he remembered his mother's words: more haste less speed. Relax, he thought to himself, they can't go anywhere.

He hadn't convinced himself as he ran into their bedroom. The room was in darkness and he could vaguely make out the shape of two small bodies in the single beds. He listened hard. He held his breath and listened again. He listened for the sound of their tiny bodies breathing or perhaps a tiny snore. Nothing. He groped for the light switch and turned it on. The two shapes in the bed had been made up from the spare pillows Donavan Smith kept in the bottom of the wardrobe.

"The little bastards," he shouted out loud.

He ran round the apartment wondering if they were hiding somewhere. He ran to the front door. Had they slipped out when he was in the bedroom? Running along the corridor, he figured their little legs wouldn't carry them far. Out into the courtyard, he ran for the big, heavy door and cursed the residents who didn't lock it each time they ventured out. He leaped out into the deserted street. He could see two hundred metres of the deserted street in either direction. If they had slipped out when he was in the bedroom, they couldn't have run that far in a matter of seconds. They must still be in the apartment.

As he entered the kitchen, his heart skipped a beat. Surely not. He leaned over the sink and looked out through the open window. The courtyard floor was a mass of ivy leaves and broken branches.

He would find them. How hard could it be to locate two small kids in the deserted streets of Paris?

He hailed a taxi within two minutes. Just drive, he told the driver. And the driver did. The Frenchman drove for nearly two hours. They covered every street and every boulevard within a five-kilometre radius of Donavan's apartment.

Eventually Donavan told the taxi driver to take him home and he cursed as he handed him the ninety-euro fare.

Elissa figured Donavan had to be looking for them and she quickly realised that the Paris streets in the hours of darkness weren't the safest place in the world to be. They'd climbed the railings into the park of Le Jardin de Cluny about half a kilometre from the apartment. She reckoned that someone must have been looking down on them as she spied a sheltered, old bandstand in the middle of the park. She was glad she had had the sense to put some extra clothes into the flight bag and they curled up in the corner cuddling each other like they'd never cuddled each other before. Cameron drifted off to sleep after about ten minutes and, shortly afterwards, Elissa lost the fight too.

It was six fifteen when Elissa checked her watch. She wasn't sure if the early morning traffic had woken her or the daylight. Perhaps a combination of both. She watched her little brother for another hour before his eyes flickered open. During that time, she'd figured everything out. They'd take a taxi to the airport as soon as the schoolchildren started making their way to school. That way they weren't likely to be picked up by the police. They'd be at the airport in plenty of time to change flights and get back to Newcastle, long before Donavan Smith turned up for the scheduled afternoon Teeside flight they'd been booked on. Yeah, she reckoned two hundred euros should be plenty for the taxi, the flights and even a little breakfast at the airport. It was a foolproof plan, nothing could go wrong as long as they got there a few hours before him. Anyway, Paris Airport is enormous, so, even if he did arrive sooner, he would never find them. At Newcastle, they'd take another taxi to Grandma's and she'd ring their dad. He'd come and collect them and they'd go and live with him in Spain forever.

"What time is it?"

"Nearly seven thirty. Are you ready to go?"

Cameron sat up on the hard wooden bench. "I'm aching and I need a poo."

Elissa pointed across the park. "Then you're in luck. There's some toilets over there."

"Will you come with me?"

Elissa stood up. "Sure, but don't expect me to wipe your bum."

They walked hand in hand over to the toilets and the little boy stepped inside. "It stinks."

"It'll stink even more in a minute," Elissa laughed.

He shouted loudly from inside the cubicle. "And I'm hungry too!"

This parenting lark is demanding, Elissa thought to herself.

They walked out of the park just before eight. The gate had been unchained and, although Elissa thought she hadn't slept, she figured she must have done as she hadn't heard the gate being opened.

She felt surprisingly good after the evening's adventures and their escape through the dark streets of Paris. She gave in to Cameron's whining and they ventured into a Parisian pâtisserie, adjacent to the River Seine. She looked over at Notre Dame while her brother stood in the queue, and she wished their captors had taken them to look inside. There was something mysterious about the eighteenth-century gothic structure. The cathedral had witnessed a lot of change over the years; it was steeped in history and Elissa thought the sneering gargoyles on the top must have seen more than their fair share of dramas, murders, hangings and, of course, the guillotinings during the French Revolution. Something was drawing her towards it, as if it had a tale to tell her. Never mind, they would see it another time with Dad.

Cameron munched on a huge apple pâtisserie as if he hadn't a care in the world. Elissa tried to eat hers, but gave up after the first bite. She offered it to Cameron and he devoured it within seconds.

"Can I have another one?" he asked.

Elissa shook her head. "We need to get to the airport because we need to change the tickets to Newcastle."

Cameron didn't argue. "Are we really going to see Dad today?"

Elissa paused, thought for a second, then said, "You bet we are, Cam. You bet."

CHAPTER THIRTY-FOUR

Bob Heggie pulled on a pair of old Levis, his favourite T-shirt, and a grey sweatshirt with a Newcastle United logo embroidered on the left breast. He laced up his battered old Nikes.

At exactly nine o'clock, he left Hannah in the New Kent Hotel. He picked up the dirty, old sports bag.

"Be careful," Hannah said, as he left the room.

He looked like any other member of the public, heading off to the gym on an unusually warm Friday morning. The only difference being that his sports bag didn't contain the usual items associated with a tough work-out. Bob Heggie's bag contained five hundred thousand pounds in counterfeit money.

The taxi was waiting as he walked out of the door of the hotel. Making the drop was easy. He followed Donavan Smith's instructions to the letter.

Afterwards, he boarded the 9.37 to King's Cross.

CHAPTER THIRTY-FIVE

Donavan's taxi arrived just before nine. He'd just about managed to snatch a couple of hours' sleep. The Parisian rush hour was at its height. Stay cool, he kept telling himself in the back of the taxi. The kids were headed for the airport; of that there was no doubt. Okay, Charles De Gaulle was a big place and there were two terminals, but Elissa was smart, quite grown-up for her age. Yeah, he was sure she'd make Terminal One sometime before the afternoon flight to Teeside.

The only thing that puzzled him was why they had fled the apartment. Surely, they didn't suspect anything. They were frightened. That was it. One of them had woken and found an empty apartment. God knows what they must have thought.

Then the doubts started creeping into Donavan's head. Maybe they'd overheard something? What if they went straight to the police?

The thoughts and ifs and buts built up during the fifty-five minutes it took to get to the airport. By the time the taxi pulled up outside Terminal One, Donavan had convinced himself he'd be met by a hundred armed gendarmes.

He climbed from the car and looked around. It was quiet. A lone French policeman stood at the entrance. He looked bored. He focused on nothing in particular. Donavan paid the taxi driver, then reached for his sunglasses, pulled on an old Adidas baseball cap and walked inside.

Elissa felt good when the huge control towers of the airport loomed into view. "The airport, Cameron, the airport."

The little boy's face lit up. "How long is the flight, Lis?"

"Oh, I don't know, an hour I think, maybe a bit longer."

He looked at his watch and traced his fingers along the numbers.

The taxi driver glanced over his shoulder. "Which terminal, Mademoiselle?"

Elissa looked at her brother. "Shit! There's more than one."

The driver smiled. "To where are you flying?"

"Newcastle," answered Cameron

"That's England," chipped in Elissa.

"That will be Terminal One," said the taxi driver.

After a few minutes, the taxi pulled up in front of the terminal building. The taxi driver smiled as Elissa counted the fare out in ten-euro notes. She handed him an extra five. "For you, Monsieur."

The Frenchman touched his cap and gave a little bow. "Why, thank you, Mademoiselle."

Elissa now felt very grown-up indeed. This was easy. She convinced herself that the difficult part was now behind them. They'd successfully escaped, slept rough, and now made their way right across Paris and into the airport. As long as they managed to change to earlier flights, they were home and dry.

She looked at the tickets: British Airways. She figured the British Airways desk would be a good place to start. "We're looking for a British Airways desk, Cameron. Can you see one?"

Cameron tugged at her sleeve. "There, Elissa, there. British Airways."

Elissa ruffled his hair. "Well done you."

He smiled, pleased to have contributed towards their daring escape from Paris.

Elissa bent down and took the little boy by the arm. "Right, Cameron, look sad and tired, and, if I give you a nudge, burst into tears."

"But why?" he asked.

"Just do as I say. I reckon there's some sort of rule about how old you have to be to travel on your own, but I'm sure it's allowed. I remember a little girl on her own once, on a flight to Malaga. The stewardess took care of her, gave her books and sweets and anything she wanted really."

"Cool. It sounds like fun."

The two waifs walked up to the girl on the British Airways desk. Elissa gave her best smile. "We'd like to change some tickets please."

The girl looked over Elissa's shoulder. "Certainly, Miss. Can I see your tickets and passports?"

This is going to be so easy, thought Elissa. Cameron tried his best to look sad.

"And what flight would you like them changed to?"

"Newcastle please. The next flight."

The attendant, Suzanne as her name tag read, looked around again. "There's a flight two minutes after twelve. You're lucky; we have availability. There are six seats left."

Elissa smiled. Cameron didn't look so sad anymore.

"Where are your travelling companions?"

"Sorry?" asked Elissa.

"Your parents. Where are your parents?"

Quick as a flash, Elissa replied, "We're travelling on our own. Our aunty dropped us off and Dad's meeting us at the other end."

Suzanne punched a few keys on the computer. "I'm sorry. Your parents need to have arranged that in advance. There's nothing registered on the computer."

Elissa shrugged her shoulders and gave Cameron a little nudge.

"Where's your aunty now?"

"She's gone."

"Gone? You mean she just left you here."

The tears started right on cue. "Waaahhh… I just want to see my dad."

"Louder," whispered Elissa through clenched teeth.

"My dad," he screamed, "I want to go home."

Suzanne came out from behind the desk, trying to comfort the little boy. She looked a little flustered and red in the face.

"Don't cry now, there, there."

Elissa grabbed the opportunity as Suzanne looked around. People were beginning to notice the commotion. "Daddy definitely telephoned you. I was with him when he did it."

"Okay, okay, young lady, I'm sure we'll have it somewhere. I'll check with the main office."

Another nudge and Cameron screamed even louder.

"So you'll change our flight?"

"Yes…yes… I'll change your tickets. Can't you tell him to be quiet?"

By this time, Cameron had attracted the attention of every passenger within fifty metres. Suzanne had returned to behind the desk, eager to get the youngsters off her hands. "It's gate number twenty-four, boarding at eleven thirty and there's a fifty euro admin fee."

Elissa peeled five ten-euro notes from the little bundle in her bag and handed them to the lady with a devilish, victorious smile. Now nothing could go wrong.

"The stewardess will meet you in the departure lounge and walk with you to gate number twenty-four. Then another stewardess will take you into the plane and you'll meet the flight crew and the captain, Thomas Purvis." She looked at the crew details on the computer. "I'll appoint Emily Douglas to look after you on the flight."

Suzanne smiled, pleased, but puzzled that the little boy had gained his composure so quickly. "She's nice."

The two children smiled back. Elissa thought it best not to speak anymore. Suzanne pointed them in the direction of gate twenty-four and Elissa couldn't resist a little wave before they disappeared around the corner.

"We've done it, Elissa. We've done it."

As they disappeared from view, Suzanne picked up the telephone and keyed in four digits.

Donavan Smith figured hanging around gate number twenty-four might not be a bad idea. He'd watch the passengers board the Newcastle flight and then, once it had taken off, he'd amble along a few gates to the departure gate for the Teeside flight. He doubted whether a ten-year-old and a six-year-old could make it safely across Paris. God knows what might have happened to them. It didn't bear thinking about. Even if the police had picked them up, the worst-case scenario for Donavan, it would take several hours for the police to match them up with their Dad. Donavan had tested them and he was confident that neither of them knew their father's telephone number, nor did they know his address in Spain. Elissa knew the street in which her grandmother lived but, again, not her telephone number. No, even if the French police had picked them up, it would be at least twelve hours before Bob Heggie took the call to say his children were safe and sound. By that time, Donavan Smith would have collected the ransom money and would most likely be back home in London.

He felt kind of smug.

And then, of course, there was the best-case scenario for Donavan Smith. The children may have been picked up by one of the Paris undesirables. God knows what would happen to them. The silly little bastards, it was their own fault. Why did they have to run? Yeah, it would serve them right if some pervert or paedophile had picked them up. The twelve-hour timescale wouldn't even come into it then.

Donavan took a sharp intake of breath. He couldn't quite believe what he had just seen. Walking towards gate number twenty-four, about a hundred metres away, were Elissa and Cameron Heggie. They were grinning and didn't seem to have a care in the world. He had to take his hat off to them. He stood up; he would cut them off at the gate; read them the riot act; scold them for running away; and tell them that Vicky was scouring Paris for them.

He removed his sunglasses and strode over towards them. Yeah… he'd give them a real dressing-down, frighten the shit out of them, - wouldn't their faces be a picture when they recognised him. He would enjoy the moment. And he breathed a further sigh of relief. They hadn't gone straight to the police.

They suspected nothing. They were frightened, that's all. Scared shitless, when they woke up to an empty apartment.

He'd take them for something to eat and they'd board the scheduled flight to Teeside. He'd book into a hotel for a couple of nights, make the pickup and send them up to Newcastle by train after he had counted the money and was absolutely sure Bob Heggie had carried out his instructions to the letter.

"There's gate twenty-four, Cameron. Another few hours and we'll see Dad."

The little boy held his sister's hand firmly. He'd placed his trust in her and she hadn't let him down. He vowed he'd never argue with her again and, whatever she wanted to play with, he'd let her... even his favourite wrestlers. Yeah... she could have anything she wanted.

Suddenly the two children recoiled in horror at the sight of the man standing in front of them, blocking their way to gate twenty-four.

"Please come this way," the French policeman said. "There is a problem."

"Shit! Shit! Shit!" cursed Donavan Smith as the uniformed officer intercepted the children. He quickly threw his sunglasses on and made a ninety-degree turn towards another gate. "Damn and blast."

Elissa and Cameron were taken to a police interview room and a friendly policewoman who spoke perfect English joined them. She handed them two chocolate bars and two cans of Coke. Although a little frightened, Cameron felt sort of important and Elissa relaxed, realising their great adventure had come to a happy end. She felt sure they would be reunited with their dad very soon.

The policewoman explained that the lady on the BA desk had checked and double-checked with the necessary departments and there was no trace of any phone calls from their father. In addition, under the strict rules for children flying unaccompanied, they would not be allowed to fly unless the airline had the written permission of a parent or guardian.

The flight from Newcastle took off without the Heggie children and, two hours later, Donavan Smith flew out of Charles de Gaulle on the Teeside flight.

The police had taken a very softly-softly approach and had asked Elissa about the adult due to fly out with them to Teeside. Elissa had refused to cooperate, fearing they would force the children to meet up with him again. It wasn't until the Teeside fight was halfway across the English Channel that Elissa acknowledged that she even knew him.

"We have his name, young lady," Policewoman Cirence explained. "He's called Donavan Smith. He is not your father. Who is he?"

"If I tell you, will you let me speak to my dad? My dad's name is Robert Heggie, he lives in Spain and my mum was killed in a motor accident in the south of France a few days ago. I want to speak to my dad."

The policewoman nodded. "If you tell me everything, I promise I'll let you speak to your father by the end of the day."

Elissa took a deep breath.

Madame Cirence was beginning to get a strange feeling about this one. It just didn't make sense. The little girl seemed to be protecting her little brother. She positively cringed each time Donavan Smith was mentioned. And who was this Vicky Mackenzie?

She'd asked her colleague to run a trace on Robert Heggie, Donavan Smith and Vicky Mackenzie. She'd also asked him to check out the story about the motor accident.

They broke for something to eat just about the time the Teeside flight touched down. Elissa and Cameron sat munching on French bread sandwiches when the male policeman came into the room. He whispered something into his colleague's ear. She stood up and walked around the table. Her face was deadly serious now, she'd lost the friendly look, and, all of a sudden, Elissa was a little worried. Madame Cirence's voice changed as she announced, "Okay, my friends, your story checks out. You were right about the road accident and…" She paused, as if struggling to get the next line out. "And… I'm sorry… but Vicky Mackenzie's body was found in the River Seine about two hours ago. She'd drowned."

Elissa's mouth gaped open and Cameron's eyes welled up with tears. He gripped his sister's hand, harder than he'd ever held it before.

"So you two had better tell me what's going on."

CHAPTER THIRTY-SIX

Donavan Smith hailed a taxi outside Teeside International Airport. "Newcastle Central Station, mate. And you can double the fare if you get me there within forty-five minutes."

The cabbie looked at his watch. "I'll try, buddy, but it depends on the traffic."

"Like I say, double the fare if you do."

Donavan sat in the back of the taxi, a nervous man. He'd tried to reassure himself that the French police wouldn't be able to piece the jigsaw together quickly enough and, as long as he could make the pickup and get back home to London, they'd never be able to prove anything. After all, it was hardly likely that Bob Heggie would ruffle any feathers. Besides, he'd only taken them on holiday.

He was biting his nails now, spitting half-chewed fingernail onto the floor. He realised that they had his name now. His name was on the tickets.

Think man! Think!

He smiled. The solution hit him like a sledgehammer. Of course, they were runaways.

He got out his mobile telephone, went into Vodafone live and searched for the telephone number of the Paris police. "Hello. I'd like to report some missing children."

He explained to the switchboard operator that he was due to meet his girlfriend, Vicky Mackenzie, and his friend's children at Charles de Gaulle Airport for a flight back to the UK. His girlfriend hadn't turned up with the children. He'd telephoned her mobile but it seemed to be switched off.

After several minutes' conversation, he pressed *end*. "Fuck me, Donavan Smith, you're a genius," he said out loud.

The taxi driver claimed the double fare by getting him to the station with two minutes to spare.

Donavan ran over to the left-luggage lockers, fully aware that he had no time to lose. It was now or never. He pulled the heavy sports bags from each locker and steadied himself before allowing himself a quick peek inside each bag. The sight within warmed the cockles of his heart as he realised he had carried it off.

A quick look around and he proceeded to walk along the narrow corridor of lockers and out into the bright sunshine of the station concourse.

At precisely 17.21, two hours after the flight had landed, he sat on the GNER King's Cross Express. He went straight to the restaurant car. Suddenly he felt hungry, a little bottle of champagne might not go amiss either.

An hour into the journey, the French police telephoned back. The young French policewoman was very sweet. She assured him that everything was okay and that the children were safe and well. They'd made their way to the airport after getting separated from Vicky Mackenzie. Unfortunately, they hadn't managed to find Madame Mackenzie yet, but she was sure she'd turn up soon. All that remained was to telephone their father and arrange to reunite them.

"Brilliant," replied Donavan. "I'm so pleased. Would you like his mobile number?"

Donavan pressed *end*. "A genius, you are. A fucking genius."

CHAPTER THIRTY-SEVEN

Charles de Gaulle Airport
"We've been kidnapped," said the little boy.

CHAPTER THIRTY-EIGHT

Bob Heggie took the most important phone call of his life just before nine thirty. He had been sitting in the hotel bedroom holding hands with Hannah for what seemed like hours. His tormentor had promised him a call on Friday lunchtime in order that Bob could confirm that the money had been deposited. In turn, the menace would give instructions on when and where he could pick up the children. That phone call would never be made. This phone call was far better.

"Hiya, Dad, it's Elissa."

The French policewoman shed a tear and her male colleague smiled at the little boy, who was patiently waiting his turn to speak to his father.

After Cameron had spoken to his daddy, Madame Cirence took charge and arranged for the children to fly out to Newcastle the next day. "They'll be fine," she explained. "We'll put them up in a hotel for the night. I'll stay with them."

Bob tried to protest, but the policewoman assured him that there were no flights to the north of England that night. "There's a nine thirty flight tomorrow, Mr Heggie. I assure you they will be placed on board. We'll send them first class and make a bit of a fuss over them. They've been through a big ordeal."

The British Airways flight took off at 9.41. Elissa and Cameron sat at the front of the plane, two rows from the front. Once the *fasten seatbelt* signs had been switched off, Zoe Betts, who had been assigned to them, fussed around like an old mother hen. Halfway through the flight they were taken through into the cockpit and Cameron sat in the co-pilot's seat, in awe of the mass of controls in front of him. Elissa stood behind him, hands on his shoulders, milking the doting parent role to the full.

Not long after, the aircraft began its descent into Newcastle International Airport. Two police officers were waiting at the bottom of the plane steps and they bypassed the immigration controls and security and were escorted into the VIP's arrivals lounge for an emotional reunion with their father and Hannah.

For the next week, Bob never let his children out of his sight and the final arrangements were made to relocate them to Spain. Bob figured they would settle better in an international school and had managed to secure places at Elian's School, a twenty-five minute bus ride away from Niebla.

London

It had taken Donavan Smith nearly two whole days to separate the money into bundles of hundreds. He had everything figured out and he felt it would be safe to begin to move the money by the end of the week. He would start by distributing fifty thousand between his UK-based bank and building society accounts. Anymore than that would likely trigger money laundering enquiries.

He'd flown out to Geneva the day before and opened a Swiss bank account. The six-digit pin number had been received by e-mail later the same day and it was now safe to start making deposits into the account. He planned to transfer £750,000 and the manager at the bank had agreed a time deposit bond guaranteeing seven per cent interest. Tax-free of course, good old Swiss authorities. That would give him an income of over fifty thousand a year. He had decided to sell the apartment in Paris and had arranged everything with an estate agent two hours ago. The agent said he already had a buyer; the area was much sought after. Somehow, he didn't think he'd be inspired to go there anymore.

The sale would net him around five hundred thousand euros

and, with that, he'd buy the boat he'd dreamed about owning for many years. A Sealine 420 Statesman would look right at home in the harbour at Cannes, just a few hundred metres from his villa. The money from the sale would just about cover the purchase price, together with a permanent mooring. It had six berths and an extended bathing platform. The 370 horsepower engine could comfortably cruise at around twenty-five knots.

Of course, he'd captain it himself; rent it out to exclusive parties: the Sloane Ranger set and the rich celebrity girls, partying the nights away on the French Riviera. But occasionally, he'd cruise the bars around the harbour looking for the vulnerables. The girls who maybe couldn't afford the asking price of the Sealine 420 for a night. But then again, he was sure they could come to some sort of arrangement. And if not, there were always his little packets of persuasion.

The telephone rang. Probably the Swiss bank manager; he said he'd call because he wanted to know when the deposits would be made.

"Hello."

"Donneee…hello it's Bobbeeeee…. How you doing?"

"Who's that?"

"Didn't you hear? It's Bobbeeeee."

"How did you get this number? I'm ex-directory. Nobody has this number."

"Oh yes they do, Donny, the Metropolitan Police have the number. Ex-directory doesn't apply to them. In fact, they know all about your little misdemeanours in the past and what you've been up to more recently."

"What are you talking about? I don't know what —"

"Just listen, Donny. Listen real well to what I'm about to say. In fact, I don't even want to hear you breathe. You listen. You listen real well. You see, Donny, you made some mistakes. The first one was getting photographed at Euro Disney. On Thunder Mountain, I think they call it. You didn't look like you were having much fun."

Donavan Smith's legs had turned to jelly. He wanted to speak but the words just wouldn't come.

"I managed to persuade those nice people at Disney to let me have the photo, and from there it was quite easy. I have a friend who has a mate in Northumbria Police. Well, not exactly a mate, but he does my friend the odd favour now and again, so to speak. And he found your mugshot in amongst the old computer files. We got your name, Donny, your address, and even who you worked for. So, I had your home watched for a few days. Only, you were in Paris, weren't you. So what did I do? I climbed on a train to London and marched into Bass and Richards. Deary me, Donny, I lost my temper a bit. You see, I thought they were covering for you, protecting you. I called you all the names under the sun and demanded to know when you were due back to work. I think I frightened your old boss a little, Donny, and, in the end, he admitted they'd sacked you some weeks back. I was escorted from the building."

Donavan Smith sought the comfort of a seat at this point, unable to stand up any longer.

"I thought I'd blown it, Donny. Thought I'd fucked up, running in there with all guns blazing, but no! Within a few hours, I received a phone call from Samantha Thompson. Remember her, Donavan? You raped her, you bastard. Drugged her and raped her."

Donavan eventually found his voice. "I did nothing of the sort. You can't prove anything."

Bob Heggie laughed. He laughed and then mimicked the laugh that Donavan Smith had used time and time again. "Oh, I think I can, Donny boy. Samantha had been alerted by one of your ex-colleagues in the office. Apparently, she'd been making discreet enquiries some weeks back, looking for the girls that had left Bass and Richards a little prematurely. Your ex-colleague figured that Samantha and I might have a similar axe to grind. So, we got together. I told her everything and she told me everything too. And do you know what we did, Donny?"

Donavan Smith's lack of reply spoke volumes.

"We tracked down four of the girls you raped and then made them sit and watch your sordid performances, and we persuaded them to testify against you in a court of law. Hayley Turnbull, Jackie Greenfield, Celina Fletcher, and Caroline Macbeth. Remember them, Donneee.... they've all been to the Met this week. And Jenny McArthur. Remember her, Donny? The police want to question you about her death too. They're fairly confident about a murder charge."

Bob Heggie laughed again. "In fact, Donny, they're on their way to see you right now. You'll be getting a knock on your door anytime soon, and they'll want to know what you're doing with a million quid in two sports bags. And get this, Donny, half of it's counterfeit."

"I don't know what you're —"

"Shit money, Don. Fake, hooky, dodgy. Half a million quid. You're in possession of counterfeit money. Wriggle and squirm your way out of that one. And there's more Don. Another little mistake. Didn't you know you could record conversations on mobile phones? Remember your little admission about tampering with some brakes on a certain VW Beetle that you own in the South of France?"

Donavan Smith was finding it hard to breathe.

"The tape is with the French police as we speak, and they've done a post-mortem on Vicky Mackenzie. Seems they found traces of a date rape drug in her. You're a killer, Don. A killer and a rapist. And my guess is that they'll find some of that drug in your beautiful penthouse within the next hour or two. I figure those crimes will just about put you away until you're an old man, Donny."

Donavan became aware of a blue glow radiating around his lounge. He pulled the curtains apart to see several police cars blocking the street, several storeys below. "You bastard, Heggie. You fucking bastard."

Bob laughed. "I haven't finished yet, Donavan. Oh no, I haven't finished yet. I have a friend, a man that fixes things."

Donavan's doorbell rang. Then there was a loud bang on the door. "Police. Open up!"

"Well, let's just say he moves in the wrong circles; born on the wrong side of the fence, so to speak. A little bit like me, I suppose, Don."

"Yeah… what about him?"

"He'll been in court when you get sentenced. I've paid him ten grand just to be there. And when you're sent down, he'll find out exactly where you're headed and then he'll call in a few favours. Get my drift, Don? Your life in jail will be absolute hell. In fact, I'd be surprised if you last a month. You see, we'll put the word out that you kidnapped two kids, tortured them and abused them. You'll be known as a nonce, Don. Got a little ring to it Don, hasn't it? Donny, the nonce."

"Open the door or we'll break it down."

Donavan let the receiver fall to the floor, walked over to the door and turned the key. Three policemen piled in and pushed him unceremoniously against the wall. He didn't resist.

"Well, I never." It was his old friend, God. "I knew you were a wrong 'un as soon as I set eyes on you."

God took the greatest of pleasure in cuffing him, - rather more roughly than was necessary, Donavan thought, given his total lack of resistance.

God whispered in his ear as they led him away. "My lads will be waiting for you in Brixton. The fixer's been on the phone. Seems you've been messing around with some little kids."

Epilogue

Donavan Smith was charged with four counts of rape, four counts of administering a noxious substance, and one count of murder: that of Jenny McArthur. In addition, he was charged with possession of counterfeit currency and several money laundering offences. He pleaded guilty to all charges when presented with the evidence.

He received a life sentence for the murder and periods of between eight and fifteen years for each of the other charges; the sentences to run concurrently. The French authorities had also requested permission to interview him in his cell in Brixton in connection with three other murders.

The fixer was as true as his word and Donavan Smith was battered and tortured and gang-raped for forty-five days. Gob and semen were to be found in each of his meals. On the forty-sixth day, he was found dead in his cell. It was strange as he'd been on twenty-four hour suicide watch. His own shoelaces had been confiscated but he'd managed to find some more. He'd crawled under the lone ceramic toilet in his cell and attached the laces in a loop around the raised wooden back supports. The authorities had surmised that he'd tightened the noose around his neck by twisting and rotating his body. As he'd blacked out, the natural weight of his head and body had completed the grisly task. The prison staff never did find out where he got the other laces from and the scratches and abrasions around his shoulders were assumed to have been from an earlier altercation.

Kevin Oxley delivered the news of Donavan's suicide to Bob Heggie, precisely thirty-five minutes after the unfortunate event.

Printed in the United Kingdom
by Lightning Source UK Ltd.
123078UK00001B/11/A